Elsa~

MUST LOVE MAGIC

MAGIC & MAYHEM #2

ERICA RIDLEY

So lovely to see you!!

♡ Erica Ridley

CHAPTER 1

Two troublesome occurrences jerked anthropologist Trevor Masterson from an exhaustion-induced slumber.

First, he'd fallen asleep face down on the folding specimen tray next to his sleeping bag, and now miscellaneous debris clung to his chin like a dirt goatee.

Second, the shapely blonde struggling to free herself from the tent's mosquito netting looked nothing like Katrina—the only female student on Trevor's team—and more like a bespectacled Victoria's Secret model.

He *had* woken up, right?

He rubbed the heel of one hand across his cheeks, dislodging assorted dirt and a skeleton's fossilized tooth. Brain foggy, he gave the intruder another look. Still there. And still one sexy silhouette. He had to be dreaming. How long had it been since he'd laid eyes on a woman who wasn't covered in mud? Three weeks? Four?

His heart began to race. A dusty tent on the edge of a Costa Rican rainforest was an unlikely place to encounter a moonlit silhouette like the one tangled in the mosquito net lining the tent flaps. Yet he was feeling more awake by the second.

"May I help you?" The words were scratchy against his dry throat.

He shoved the small folding tray to one side and tried to make sense of what was happening. No explanations sprang to mind.

"Shhh, Angus, *niñito*," came the soft reply. She broke free from the netting and half-fell, half-hopped into the tent. "*Duérmete.*"

Who the hell was Angus? He frowned as he tried to parse her words. Spanish made sense, but unfortunately he didn't speak much. *Duérmete... niñito...* Little boy?

"I'm not little." He swiped the debris from his chin. "Or Angus. Who are you?"

"I'm a tooth fairy, of course." The canvas flaps fluttered closed, enshrouding them in darkness. A faint vanilla musk spiced the humid air, masking the more familiar scents of fresh dirt and warm rain. "Go back to sleep or I won't leave any money under your pillow."

What was this chick smoking?

"I don't have a pillow." He squinted into the darkness. He struggled to his feet, then ducked when his head scraped the top of the tent. "And it'll cost you plenty if I have to replace my mosquito netting."

He groped for the fallen Maglite atop the folding tray and aimed the mega-watt beam at his curvy intruder. His lungs froze. The rest of him turned very, very hot.

Thin black cat-eye glasses framed wide hazel eyes. Chin-length silver-blonde hair fluttered above naked shoulders and a barely-there Tinkerbell-style dress shimmered from breasts to thighs. But even more bizarre was the pair of oversize glitter wings protruding from her back.

He choked back a bemused laugh. Either Halloween started in May this close to the equator or something was seriously wrong with this woman.

"Turn off the light!" She lunged at him.

Trevor ducked. His foot tangled in the open sleeping bag. He caught her as they fell, landing hard on his back with her sprawled on top of him and the beam of the flashlight glowing on the ceiling. The tip of her nose hovered against the side of his.

She stared at him without moving. He stared back, hyper-conscious of every warm inch of her body pressing against his. He didn't mean to suck in his breath and inhale her minty exhale, but once he did, he froze, her breath trapped inside his lungs and his thighs trapped beneath hers.

If he moved even a millimeter, her lips would be close enough to touch his. Matter of fact, their bodies were already perfectly aligned for some hot, sweaty, sleeping bag action. He willed his body not to react.

As if he'd spoken the thought aloud, she snatched the flashlight out of his hand, leapt across the tent and pointed the shaky beam in his direction.

Her stifled gasp and the wavering light indicated that his well-worn cargo pants did a poor job of hiding the effects of a good dream and a real woman. Maybe that would teach her not to flit around the rainforest in the middle of the night. Half-naked. Looking for Angus.

He crawled across his sleeping bag to turn on the battery-operated camping lantern by his tray. If she got to stare at him, then he should get a good look at her, too.

She poked at the flashlight until it went dark, and tensed when the warm light of the lantern still enveloped them. With a frustrated sigh, she lay the Maglite down.

"Who are you, really?" As he rose to his feet, he did a double-take at hers. "And where are your shoes?"

She glanced up at him quizzically, eyebrows arched high. Granted, his feet were also bare, but hey, this was his tent. He'd been sleeping. What was *her* excuse for being barefoot in a rainforest?

"I'm Daisy le Fey." Her fingers clenched. "And tooth fairies don't wear shoes."

He couldn't contain his disbelief. Daisy le Fey? *Tooth fairies?* Please. What kind of woman crept around the Costa Rican countryside in fake wings and painted toes? Trevor wasn't usually one for costumes of any sort, but cherry-red toenails on the other hand... cherry-red toenails were his kryptonite. He forced his gaze back to her face. If she wouldn't give him any straight answers, then there was no reason for her to stick around.

"Get out."

"I—I can't. I'm on assignment."

So was he. One that didn't involve crazy people invading his tent. He loomed closer in order to edge her toward the opening.

She scooted backward. Smart girl.

He prowled closer, hunching slightly as the canvas roof slid across his hair.

"Why wouldn't fairies wear shoes?" he asked, keeping his eyes focused on hers.

Her back hit the screened flaps. "Some do, just not tooth fairies," she stammered. "It's not part of the dress code. Now, where's Angus?"

He tried to assimilate her response for a moment, then gave up. "Who?"

"Angus!" Her eyebrows lifted as though pleading with him not to play dumb. "I must give him a boon in exchange for his tooth."

A boon? "Listen, lady." He paused. She was too articulate to be a strung-out drug addict, and too American-looking to be a local. Then again, red toenails or not, she was too crazy-sounding to be a rational person, so how could he get her out of his tent easily and safely?

Trevor crossed his arms over his chest. His *bare* chest. Great. He was without his shirt, and she was without her shoes. He clenched his jaw, forcing himself not to look back down at her toes. "Unfortunately, none of my students are named Angus, and you're trespassing. You need to leave." He risked another glance at her feet, then stabbed a finger toward the tent flaps. "Immediately."

"This will all be over in a minute." She ducked under Trevor's extended arm. She sank on all fours and began feeling around inside the bag, derrière aimed right at him. He swallowed. She groped around further into the tent. "Why don't you have a pillow?"

As her minuscule green dress rode further up her thighs, Trevor learned another new fact about tooth fairies: The dress code *did* include lacy lingerie. Cherry-red. Like her toes. He swayed. If someone had to invade his tent and interrupt his dig, at least she was an *attractive* someone. Nonetheless, he was a professor leading a student crew, not a frat boy looking for a hookup. He didn't know much about her career path, but his required him to keep things professional.

"Listen, lady," he began again, edging closer to his sleeping bag. "I have no idea what you're doing, but you have to stop. Now."

She peered at him over one bare shoulder. Her dispirited expression suggested she didn't mean to inconvenience him, but had no choice. "I can't. I'm working. And if you're not Angus... who are you?"

In lieu of an answer, he bent over, wrapped his arms around her waist, and hauled her to her feet.

Those bizarre wings crunched against his chest. Soft tendrils of hair fluttered against his chin. He could no longer see her lingerie—or her toes—because her derrière was now flush against his crotch. She made no attempt to move away. Mistake.

He lowered his mouth to her hair. "I think you'd better stay on your feet."

Her legs trembled as though she suddenly realized the tantalizing picture she'd made crawling across the floor of his tent. *Yes, sweetheart, it got bigger.* He smiled grimly. It would be best for both of them if she would take it upon herself to leave now and not come back.

Without unfolding his arms from around her flat stomach, he leaned his cheek against hers and breathed in her scent.

"I'm Trevor Masterson," he murmured into her ear. Her breath caught as the rough stubble along his jaw rubbed against the smooth skin on her cheek. "I'm an anthropologist. And you're trespassing on my dig."

He whirled her around until the tips of their noses touched. Her fingers clutched his biceps as her wide hazel eyes stared up into his.

"Oh." Her breath was soft against his chin. "I see." One of her bare toes rubbed across the top of his. "This is easily resolved. I'll be on my way as soon as you point me toward the tooth. Can I have—"

"No," he interrupted through clenched teeth, wishing he'd worn shoes or maybe installed a padlock on his tent. "You're not taking anything from my dig. Tell me the real reason you're sneaking around. And don't give me any of that tooth fairy crap."

Her breath mingled with his for a long moment, giving Trevor plenty of time to realize she hadn't yet pulled out of his arms. Her fingers still splayed around his biceps. He fought an inane urge to flex. Or to kiss her and be done. He contemplated releasing her—he really did—but somehow tightened his hold. Every inch of his flesh felt her shiver against him. His brain shut down as his breath caught in his throat. Why was kissing her a bad idea, again?

"Let me ask you something." She broke eye contact to briefly glance around the tent before locking gazes with him again. "How good are my chances of you handing over that tooth willingly?"

"Nobody"—he tightened his hold—"is walking off with anything."

She nodded slowly. With a sudden twist of her shoulders, she slipped from his grasp, turned, and parted the flaps of the tent as if afraid what might be outside. She jerked backward, then turned to glare at him.

"Sunrise? You've got to be kidding me." She slumped dejectedly. "I'm going to be in so much trouble for this. I wish I could spend the next hour searching your tent, but... Anyway, no time for this. On the clock, I can only travel under cover of night."

"Under cover of—" Trevor forgot all about her soft body and painted toes as he choked over the ridiculousness of her words. "Are you a tooth fairy or a vampire?"

"Technically, neither," she said with an irritated frown, and slipped through the brown canvas without a backward glance.

He followed right behind her in order to make sure she stayed safe and didn't invade any of the other tents. Except—

She was gone.

A few hours later, Trevor was up, dressed, and wrangling a gaggle of hyperactive undergrads from their tents to the dig. By the end of another grueling day, he could barely stay upright. Maybe that was why it took him a minute to notice a few of the kids off to one side, sneaking cigarettes.

He shielded his eyes from the last rays of the setting sun and stalked over to a red plastic cooler that doubled as a makeshift break table.

"You know the rules," he called out. "No smoking on the dig. Not even a vape pen." Everyone jumped. Everyone but his Teaching

Assistant, Katrina Demarco, of course. Nerves of steel. She hadn't even reacted when she'd pitched a no-hitter last year during the inter-departmental baseball league opening game. "Go on, put 'em out. If you want to start a wildfire, go somewhere else."

Katrina rolled her eyes, but stubbed out her Lucky Strike on the bottom of her boot. A pungent wisp of acrid smoke rose from the tread. "Thanks, Smokey the Bear. We aren't on the edge of any old forest—it's a *rain*forest." She ran a hand over her short black dread-locks. "How are we gonna burn down a rainforest in the middle of the rainy season?"

"I don't want to see you try. Besides, is it raining right now?" Trevor gestured toward the lush green landscape and a sky awash in pinks and purples. "I didn't think so. Break's over. Let's start loading up the trucks before it gets too dark."

"Why you always have to be bossing people around?" Despite her words, Katrina shoved her cigarettes into her canvas backpack and stood on cue.

"I'm bossy because I'm the boss." He made a shooing motion with his hand.

Since her gaze was focused elsewhere, he allowed himself a quick smile. Katrina liked to play tough and too-cool-for-school, but she was the first student ever to earn a perfect score on his infamously tricky Forensic Anthropology final exam—*and* she threw a mean curveball. He couldn't wait to coach this year's interdepartmental baseball league.

The other TA, Alberto Rodriguez, tossed Trevor an apologetic shrug before turning to Katrina. "Prof just wants a head start, Kat. How can we fly back home tomorrow night if our things aren't packed?"

"You call me 'Kat' again and I'll kill you." She trudged off toward the dig.

Alberto grinned at Katrina's retreating back. But before he took his second step after her, his cellphone rang.

"*Habla*," he answered cheerfully, without glancing at the screen.

Sadly, Alberto did not throw a mean curveball. Or ever turn off his cellphone.

Trevor quickly gave up on translating the rapid-fire conversation. For now. As soon as he made tenure, he'd finally have time to learn Spanish.

"¿*El jefe?*" Alberto darted a horrified glance at Trevor and lowered his voice to a murmur.

He needn't have bothered. Aside from the universally recognized term for "boss", he might as well have been talking Swahili.

Not that it mattered. Regardless of whatever Alberto was whispering about him, Trevor was confident he'd spill all once he hung up. Alberto'd never kept a secret in his life.

"*Gracias, 'manita,*" Alberto said at normal volume. "*Te quiero. Ciao.*" He stared at Trevor without blinking.

Trevor waited. A ripe mango rocketed down from where the howler monkeys nestled high above in the trees. Katrina's "Ouch!" and extended cursing rose amid raucous laughter around the dig. Alberto didn't move.

"Well?" Trevor prompted, when it looked like his student might just stand there staring for the rest of the evening.

Alberto sighed. "That was my sister."

"Yeah? Wait. Which sister?" Trevor tried to picture all the Rodriguez girls who'd played interdepartmental sports. "Maria José, with the winning hit in last summer's opening game? Or Rosa who works in accounting for the dean?"

"That's the one. Rosa. She says hi, by the way." Alberto tapped the phone against his cheek. "She also says the budget cuts are worse than projected and that most of the non-tenured professors won't be returning next year."

Trevor swallowed. Non-tenured professors. Like him.

"Well, no worries there." Trevor lifted a shoulder with more nonchalance than he felt. "I'm up for tenure right after finals. If the vote goes well, I'll be leading senior trips for the next two decades, which means I'll be eligible to keep coaching every summer. And you can tell Maria José I saved a spot for her on the upcoming team."

Alberto squinted somewhere over Trevor's shoulder. "Well, that's the thing."

"What's the thing?" Trevor shoved his hands into his pockets, partly to hide his suddenly white knuckles, and partly to keep himself from shaking answers out of Alberto. The kid wasn't being difficult on purpose. He might've been the first student in history to get fired from being batboy, but only because it took him an inordinate amount of time to do whatever it was he was doing. Although it took him an extra hour and a half, he aced every one of his exams.

Alberto fiddled with his smartphone. "Rosa was doing some snooping—she's had a crazy crush on you ever since she saw you in your baseball uniform and nobody can get her to shut up about it—and she found a board memo with the plans for next year. *Fatal*. Talk about slashing budgets... She says the Anthropology Department won't be able to offer everyone tenure because they'll have to let someone go."

"What? But the only other non-tenured professor is—Berrymellow." Trevor covered his face with his palms. This couldn't be happening. No way would he let Berrymellow wreck his career. If he found something publishable on this dig, there would be no problem. If he couldn't...

Refusing to continue that line of thought, he leaned over and plucked a misshapen stone from the moist soil. He turned and hurled the rock as hard as he could. A distant thwack and the squawking of displaced birds reminded him he was still in Costa Rica. All was not lost.

"Want me to find you more rocks, Prof?"

"No, I'm good." Trevor picked up another but didn't throw it. There weren't enough rocks in Costa Rica to make him feel better about this turn of events. "Well, which one of us is out here actively doing field research, putting the university's name on the map? Me."

He brushed the dirt from the rock as if proving his point.

Alberto grimaced. "But which professor has been back in Indiana for the past four weeks, treating the department heads to golf outings? Not you."

"Shit," Trevor muttered. His fingers tightened around the rock. Maybe he could blame his white knuckles on that.

Truth was, while Trevor was the better forensic anthropologist and paleo-anthropology professor, Joshua Berrymellow was by far the better schmoozer. Trevor sighed. It was a sad fact of life that many political decisions were made over eighteen holes and a case of Heineken. With or without an epic anthropological discovery, he needed to do some damage control as quickly as possible.

He glanced at his watch. The school had contracted a private jet company to make two trips to the U.S. the next day, one in the afternoon and one in the evening. Without having to deal with crowded terminals or boarding passes, hassle was kept to a minimum. And if Trevor took the first flight instead of the second, maybe he could arrange some face time with the dean before it was too late.

"Katrina!" he yelled toward the dig.

She jogged toward him as if she'd been hoping he'd call another break. "Yeah, Coach?" Her eyes tracked Trevor's hands as he nervously tossed the rock from one palm to the other. "Change your mind about taking a vape break?"

"No, I changed my mind about who goes home first tomorrow."

"What?" She gave him an aggravated glare. "You said me and Alberto head out on the afternoon flight with the equipment and the artifacts, and you were gonna take the evening flight with the kids."

"In the immortal words of Willy Wonka—scratch that, reverse it." Trevor considered the dozen tents lined behind a row of dusty Jeeps and made his decision. "Something has come up. I'm putting you in charge of the undergrads. I go back first with the skeleton and the artifacts."

Katrina scowled. "I don't want to be in charge of them anymore. Why do I always get stuck with people instead of pottery?"

"It's because I trust your ability to handle them." Trevor's stomach clenched. What if his early arrival wouldn't be enough to throw Berrymellow off his game?

"What about the laptop?" Alberto asked. "I downloaded all the pictures onto it this afternoon but Katrina hasn't had a chance to enter the metadata."

"Then let her finish." Trevor peered closer at the rock in his hand, then sighed. Too bad it was just a rock, and not something career-making like, say, a prehistoric baking tool, or maybe even proof of a previously undiscovered culture. *That'd* stop Berrymellow cold. "The second flight doesn't leave for several hours. Now that you'll have extra time, you can finish transcribing the written field notes while you're waiting for the plane."

With a long suffering sigh, Katrina crossed her arms and pouted. "Is it because—"

"It's because TA stands for Teacher's Assistant. I'm the teacher. Assist me." Trevor glanced at the waning sunlight. "And once you've got your stuff packed up, go ahead and get some rest. Early day tomorrow for all of us."

He glanced at his tent. The canvas flaps gapped at the bottom and a strip of mangled netting fluttered in the wind. Weird. Hadn't he zipped everything closed? He must be losing his mind. Hopefully no strange critters were inside eating all his power bars and peeing on his sleeping bag. And hopefully it wasn't—

As if conjured straight from the libidinous recesses of Trevor's mind, the tent flaps parted and a set of tiny, red-painted toenails poked through. He held his breath... and wished his students weren't watching right along with him. As luck would have it, the bare foot belonged to last night's pixie princess, as did the rest of the curvy body unfolding from his tent like a butterfly from a cocoon. How was he possibly going to explain this one?

"Damn, Coach." Katrina punched him in the shoulder. "Next year, can I bring a cabana boy?"

Before he could think of a professorial response to that one, the woman in the wilted wings and clingy green dress caught Trevor's helpless stare and started running.

Toward him.

"I don't know her," he said quickly, backing up a few feet just in case.

"Trevor!" Daisy waved wildly, a manic smile not quite hiding a certain desperation in her eyes. "It's me, from last night!"

Katrina let out a low whistle. "Don't know her, eh? Bet she could round the bases in twenty seconds. Look at those legs go!"

"I'm looking, I'm looking," Alberto breathed, clutching his phone to his chest. "I can't stop."

Trevor couldn't even reprimand him. He was doing the same thing.

Daisy sprinted toward them, still wearing the cat-eye glasses, the jagged-hemmed dress, and not much else. Bare shoulders, bare back, bare legs, bare feet...

She tripped on the rutted grass and ran smack into him.

He wrapped his arms around her shoulders to keep her from knocking them both down. Again. It was just for her safety, he told himself as his body responded to the welcome feel of soft curves against his hot skin. He meant to set her upright, but somehow his hands slid down her naked back to her waist, holding her steady against him. Vanilla-scented hair tickled his nose.

She hugged him tight, as if terrified he might have left camp without notice. "Oh, Trevor. You can't imagine how glad I am to see you."

If she kept clinging to him like that, she wouldn't need much imagination to know how he felt about having her pressed against him. He forced himself to untwine her arms from his neck and flashed a (hopefully) innocent smile at his students. "I have no idea who this woman is, I swear."

"Shyeah." Katrina quirked an eyebrow, not bothering to stifle her grin. "First name basis and on intimate terms with your tent? Clearly total strangers."

Ignoring the commentary, Daisy's face tilted upward, her wide hazel eyes blinking at Trevor in obvious frustration. "I looked through every inch of your sleeping bag, and I can't find it anywhere. What did you do with it?"

"If you're talking about what I think you're talking about," Katrina said with a smirk, "that's because it's out here with him. It goes wherever he goes. Unless he's got a detachable one."

Eyes fluttering heavenward, Daisy's jaw tightened. Maybe she wasn't as oblivious as he thought. She grabbed him by the shoulders and fixed him with an earnest stare. "*Do* you have it with you? I swear to Gaia I'll be out of your way faster than you can say 'pixie dust' if you just hand it over. Pretty please."

It wasn't until she twisted out of his arms in order to pat him down that Trevor realized he'd untwined her arms but hadn't quite managed to let go. Now that she was no longer plastered to the front of his body, maybe he really could get her out of his mind and off his dig.

"For the love of God, you're not allowed on—"

"I'm Alberto," said Alberto helpfully, stepping beside Trevor to shove his hand toward Daisy. "*Encantado.*"

Trevor knocked down the kid's arm. "We're not speed-dating. Nobody has to be introduced to anybody else. Miss... Miss..." Damn. What the hell was her last name? "Miss Daisy was just leaving."

Katrina's hands curled on her hips. "Like 'Driving Miss Daisy?'"

He cast her a quelling stare. She thrust her chin higher, but clamped her mouth shut.

"I'm not going anywhere." Daisy patted down his back pockets and then moved to the front. "I told you I would do whatever it takes. You can give it to me on your own, or... or... or I'll take it from you."

"*Dios mío,*" Alberto whispered, eyes huge. "What do I have to do to get women to talk to *me* like that? You're the professor. Teach me. Please."

"No hope for you, batboy," Katrina said with a smirk. "Get some muscles. Or a job."

"Okay, this is getting out of hand," Trevor began and then paused. Out of hand. Against all odds, he was still gripping the large stone. And important artifacts were often buried in rock.

"Here." Trevor thrust the stone into her hand.

Daisy cast a dubious stare at the dusty stone in her palm. "That's not a tooth. That's a rock."

"A tooth?" Katrina repeated, goggling at her. "What is she, a nympho dentist?"

"You're holding a very important artifact," Trevor explained to Daisy in his best "teacher" voice.

Alberto's starry-eyed gaze turned dubious, as if he no longer wanted to be taught whatever Trevor was up to.

"This is what I was working on last night. Paleo-anthropologists look for clues in the rocks, like archaeologists. Sometimes bones get fossilized." Trevor gave Daisy his most winning smile, blasting her with his rakish dimple. She was unmoved. "I was going to dig out the tooth for you, but I didn't realize you'd be back so soon. Go on. You can have it."

"Why?" Her eyes narrowed suspiciously. "This is a trick, isn't it? I won't get three feet away before you tackle me to the ground and wrestle it back."

Katrina snorted, but Alberto brightened and lurched forward. "Hey, Prof. If you don't, can I?"

"Nobody's wrestling anyone." Trevor stepped in front of Daisy to block Alberto's view. "Look. It's yours. I promise. You may leave freely."

Painted toes or not, he'd promise her anything to get her off his dig and away from the curious eyes of his students. The last thing he needed was to give Berrymellow ammunition against him. Just the thought turned Trevor's skin cold. If rumors of him and some tourist got back to the dean...

Daisy's shoulders relaxed and an expression of joyous relief smoothed the lines from her face. Instead of leaving, she threw her arms around his neck and hugged him.

"Thank you, thank you, thank you," she murmured in his ear, the plump fullness of her bottom lip scraping against his stubble. "And sorry about the tent. If I can, I'll conjure you new netting." Her breath steamed his earlobe and tightened his pants. "I owe you big time."

She tilted back her head and aimed a kiss toward his cheek. He leaned backward to keep his distance, but she didn't even pause. Her parted lips melded with his for the barest of seconds before he jerked away so quickly their noses clashed. From the heat crawling up his neck, he'd guess his cheeks burned as bright as hers. Shit. Definitely not what he needed. Nothing would screw up his chances of making tenure—or staying head coach of the most popular university employee baseball league in the Michiana area—like rumors of sex with strangers during a student trip. And from the twin expressions of avid interest on the faces of both his TAs, neither the accidental kiss nor the subsequent blushing had gone unnoticed. At least the trees had blocked the other students' view.

"Just… go wait over there for a second." Trevor's voice sounded raspy and strained even to his own ears. "Let me talk to my students."

Ignoring Katrina and Alberto's shameless stares, Daisy flashed him a grateful smile and turned toward his tent without further protest.

Trevor could still taste her kiss on his lips. Even though his rational mind knew she was at best a sexy psycho, he couldn't stop his eyes from tracking the sway of her hips as she headed across the grass toward the tent, hugging the rock to her chest.

"You ain't got to explain a single thing to me," Katrina informed him with a snicker. "You teach anthropology, not Sex Ed."

"Same," agreed Alberto without taking his gaze from Daisy. "But I'll loan you some condoms if you need them."

Katrina let out a bark of laughter. "Why the hell did you bring condoms to the middle of the rainforest?"

"Hey, always be prepared." Alberto shrugged off his backpack and unzipped the front pocket. "They can come in handy. Professor Masterson needs them, doesn't he?"

Katrina snorted. "You're no Professor Masterson."

"Enough, enough." Trevor waved them both back toward the dig. "I don't even know this woman. She's crazy. I'm just trying to make her leave. Go pack up equipment. I'll bring over the jeep in a minute."

"Better take more than a minute," Katrina called over her shoulder. "We'll time you."

Alberto grinned. "And then Facebook it."

"Christ." Trevor's jaw clenched. "I told you—I have no idea who that crazy lady is!"

He had to get her out of here. Stat. For the sake of his coaching career, his tenure, and his sanity. He strode to the tent, threw open the flap, and stumbled to his knees in shock.

Empty. *Empty.*

She was gone again.

CHAPTER 2

*D*aisy's homing ring deposited her back in her office, where she leaned her forehead against the closest wall and tried to dream up a plan that wouldn't get her fired. She *had* to earn her wings —real ones—if she was ever going to rise above being the laughing-stock of Nether-Netherland. But she was never going to ace her performance review if she couldn't get the tooth, which was already a day late, into the little glass vial sitting on her desk.

She plopped into her hot pink ergonomic swivel chair and stared despondently at the mandatory tooth transportation vial. If she were magical enough to separate the tooth from the stone, she wouldn't be in this bind. For the mission to count as a success, she had to follow regulation to the letter. But what could she do? There was no way to transport the tooth without bending more rules.

After making sure she was alone in the silent office, she lifted the assigned tooth vial from her desktop and peeled the "Angus, age 8" label from the glass.

The label refused to stick to the rock. She cleaned it with tissue and tried a fresh, new label. Still no luck. Crap. Well, what was one more bent rule?

She pulled a Pearly States delivery pouch out from her desk

drawer. Those were supposed to be for taxes, not teeth, but she was running out of options. She stuffed the stone, the empty vial, and both semi-crumpled labels inside the pouch and hesitated. A gnawing uncertainty rose from her stomach, but at this point, what choice did she have?

"Good enough for government work," she muttered, vowing to follow the letter of the law perfectly... starting with her next assignment.

With a whispered "Pearly States!" she pulled the pouch strings closed and the little red bag vanished with a pop. No going back—the fossilized tooth had already arrived at its destination. Finally. She hoped it wasn't a hassle to extract it from the stone. Maybe she should devise some sort of automatic tooth extractor for situations like this. Mechanical engineering was so much easier than collecting teeth. It just didn't get her any respect.

Not that she deserved any until she completed her tooth fairy apprenticeship. *If* she completed her apprenticeship.

Other tooth fairies got softly sleeping eight-year-olds every day of the week, but what did she get on her first night out? A giant hunk of man, that's what. Fully grown. Fully awake. And by the feel of his body pressed against hers, fully aroused.

Not that she'd been paying attention to that part of him. Much. Well, okay, she had, but come on. Even Nether-Netherland didn't have guys that hot. Who would have guessed how attractive a hint of stubble, tanned muscles, and unkempt hair could be?

Then again, she hadn't anticipated any part of the encounter. A tent instead of a bedroom was bizarre. An adult instead of a child was also bizarre. The tooth belonging to someone so old he had to be dug up from the ground was *beyond* bizarre. As for the sexy keeper of that tooth? Whatever impulse had led to their arms circling around each other and his mouth covering hers... She had to nip that in the bud. Forever.

Especially since the punishment for physical contact with a human was fierce.

She dropped her forehead to her desk. For the love of Venus, had she really kissed a human? What in the world had she been thinking?

She groaned. Clearly she hadn't been thinking. Wasn't that always her problem? Diving face-first into anything that caught her interest. Neurophysics, obsolete languages, toothfairying. Only this time, she'd jumped headlong into a warm, solid wall named Trevor Masterson. And kissed him.

Accidentally, but whatever. She'd wanted it, and so had he. He'd even invited her to stay. To meet him in his tent. Maybe his motives were innocent, but given they hadn't spent thirty seconds in each other's company without being spooned together or in a near lip-lock...

She lifted her head and shivered at the memory of his hard body against hers. Oh, who was she fooling? Tent, etchings, magic wand collection—the subtext was clear no matter what dimension a girl lived in. Subconsciously or not, Trevor's true invitation had been in the heat of his caramel skin, the half-lidded intensity of his dark eyes, the sensual promise of his touch.

And, oh, was he tempting. Mmm. If she hadn't needed to get that tooth back pronto, she might have considered joining him in his tent for an hour or three. Well, and if sexual human relationships weren't expressly forbidden to fairies under penalty of banishment. Daisy shoved away from her desk with a gasp. Cripes. *Banishment.* No human was worth that!

She leapt to her feet. Her chair banged against the filing cabinet, knocking a tiny lime green frog from his perch atop the Nether-Netherland Readers' Choice Condensed Encyclopedia of Human Slang and Culture.

"Sorry, Bubbles," she whispered, holding up a hand for her blinking where-frog. He hopped from the cabinet top to her outstretched palm and shot her a baleful look, as though he somehow knew she'd been out making a fool of herself. Again.

She grimaced. No harm done, right? Nobody had to know the mission hadn't gone according to plan. The humans wouldn't cause any trouble. Trevor didn't even believe she was a fairy. Because her mentor had the day off, Vivian would have no clue the tooth collecting had taken an extra day. And Daisy'd managed to turn in the odd-shaped tooth without anyone being the wiser. Nothing to worry about. Right?

Bubbles gave a loud ribbit of disapproval.

"Shh," Daisy whispered, covering him with her other hand. She was pretty sure Vivian never swung by the office on her free days, but there was no sense hanging around to find out. Daisy slipped the well-worn encyclopedia into her magically bottomless handbag and nodded to her where-frog. "Bubbles, take us home."

They materialized in the midst of pumpkin-strewn grass, each dusky orange gourd mocking her with its very existence. Normally she didn't mind the constant reminder that she and magic didn't play well together. Okay, she minded, but since it wasn't a new state of affairs, she didn't usually get that just-ate-raw-eggs feeling she'd been getting since sending off that tooth. At least she'd managed to complete a mission without turning anything into a pumpkin.

Ignoring the state of her accidental garden, Daisy headed across the lawn, taking time to enjoy the springy crunch of dewy grass beneath her bare feet.

Sunlight filtered through the thatch of trees flanking the property. Her best friend, a winged horse named Maeve, coasted down from the barn connected to Daisy's floating cottage and yawned, showing off an impressive set of teeth.

"How'd it go with Project Tooth?" Maeve asked in a sleep-thickened voice.

Daisy grimaced. So much for not dwelling on her mishap. "Not so good the first time," she admitted. "I had to leave without the tooth."

"You what?" Maeve stared at her in disbelief, velvety ears aquiver. "You can remember equations to integrate fractals, and yet on a *tooth fairy* assignment you forgot to pick up the tooth?"

"I didn't forget." Daisy crossed her arms defensively. She was a scientist, not stupid. Well, an ex-scientist. And it's not like tooth-fairying was easy. "He wouldn't hand it over."

"He… Oh, honey, no." Maeve twisted her neck in order to flick her thick violet tail across her face. The closest a winged horse could get to a facepalm. "They're not supposed to interact with you! Didn't you tell me that if the child woke up, all you're allowed to do is lull him back to sleep? If the Elders find out about this, buh-bye tooth fairy. You'll be lucky to return to your post at the Neurophysics Compound." Maeve's long, lavender head tilted to one side. "Let's think positive. Maybe if the little boy mentions you, his parents will just chalk it up to youthful imagination."

"About that." Daisy bit her lip and debated how much her best friend needed to know. Well, better she hear it from her first. "Truth is, I didn't see any parents. This particular boy had short black hair, long eyelashes, and a five o'clock shadow." She forced the mouthwatering image of Trevor's slow, bedimpled smile from her mind. The saying was, "Never trust a human." She probably ought to amend that to not trusting *herself* around humans. Particularly ones that looked good enough to eat. "Seeing as I'd never heard of an eight-year-old with a five o'clock shadow, that was my first indication something was wrong."

Maeve's tail flicked toward the lawn. "You're supposed to sneak in and grab the tooth, not stand around measuring whiskers and eyelashes."

"I got distracted by the anomalies." Daisy kicked at the wet grass, scattering tiny droplets across Maeve's purple hooves. "I knew the tooth collection system was glitchy, but wow. How could something as simple as collecting a baby tooth turn into such a disaster?"

"Beats me." Maeve's ears quirked. "What did Vivian say?"

"I didn't tell her," Daisy admitted. Vivian Valdemeer wasn't the sort of person you let down if you wanted to keep your job. And there wasn't anything Daisy wanted more than to make fairy and earn her wings. "Besides, it's all over now. I already turned in the tooth. Even if the Pearly States calls to say they received the package a day late, I can always pretend I got sidetracked and forgot to send it in. You know, play the nutty scientist." Daisy widened her eyes and blinked vacantly. "I may get in trouble, but at least I won't get anyone fired."

"I guess," Maeve said. "But I thought you said you came away empty-handed. How'd you get the tooth from Mr. Eyelashes?"

"I went back a couple hours ago." Daisy adjusted her glasses with the back of her hand. "And this time, Trevor handed it right over. Thank the seven gods of fortune."

Maeve tossed her violet mane. "Trevor?"

"Er... the human."

"And he was happy to cooperate the second time around?"

"Yep." Daisy set Bubbles onto a nearby pumpkin. He hopped down into the grass.

Maeve frowned. "Why?"

"What do you mean, why?" The fluttering of doubt curdled in Daisy's stomach. She'd been so desperate not to screw up her apprenticeship, she hadn't stopped to wonder why. Who lied to the Tooth Fairy? "Maybe I changed his mind when I accidentally kissed him?"

But wait... he gave up the goods *before* that oh-so-brief kiss... Which she probably shouldn't have mentioned.

"Zeus and Hera, Daisy, you kissed a human?" Maeve whistled through thick, square teeth. "What in Loki's name were you thinking?"

"I've been over this with myself already this morning," Daisy muttered irritably. She'd better not have mucked up her apprenticeship with her mouth's wanderlust. A single stolen moment with a human she'd never lay eyes on again was definitely not worth losing everything she'd worked for. "I was obviously *not* thinking. Can we let it go?"

Maeve whinnied nervously. "You better hope the Elders don't find out."

"I know, I know." Daisy located a wand and a pail of pixie dust behind one of the pumpkins. "I'm going to practice magic to take my mind off of my troubles. Want to help?"

"Depends," Maeve said suspiciously. "Is that a real wand or the pumpkin wand?"

"Neither. I call it Mechanical Wand 2.0." Daisy carefully lowered the wand and swirled the pink star tip in the glittering dust. "And it shouldn't do the pumpkin thing anymore. I upgraded the nano-transmutation firmware and adjusted the molecular infrastructure to correlate the transmogrification algorithm with internal switchback capacitors."

"Uh... whatever that means."

"It means, hopefully this time I can pull off something besides a boring old gourd." She took a deep breath and willed herself to be optimistic. Today would get better. It would. Despite the unnamed anxiety clawing at her gut. "I'd like to try a new spell."

"Hmm." Maeve's muzzle dipped into the pixie dust pail. "Where'd you get this stuff? It smells funny."

"I made that, too." Daisy straightened proudly. That pail represented *months* of lab time.

Maeve jerked her head from the bucket with a squeak of terror. "Like the previous pre-programmed wand?" She backed up a few feet, tail twitching double-time. "I'm not saying you're not a good scientist. You rock at neurophysics. But magic isn't science. Why don't you buy real pixie dust and a legit wand at the bimonthly bazaar like everyone else?"

"I'll buy a normal wand and normal dust when I can do magic like a normal person," Daisy bit out, tempted to upend the pail on her best friend's muzzle. "You know as well as I do that before I invented a custom-engineered wand, I couldn't magic my way out of a barn."

"And now you can fill one with pumpkins." Maeve backed out of harm's way. "Not sure science is pushing you in the right direction."

"At least it's *a* direction. I am so tired of staying stagnant. Of being nowhere. Pumpkins are stupid, but at least they're something. And Wand 2.0 has a faster processor for more spells." Daisy tapped excess powder from the hot pink wand, letting the surplus glitter rain back into the pail. "I have to progress somehow. How am I supposed to make fairy if I can't do magic?"

Maeve cocked her head to one side. "Maybe you're not fated to make fairy. Like I said, you're the best scientist Nether-Netherland has ever seen. Why kill yourself trying to be magical? Just because it's the one thing you're not good at?"

"Nobody but you cares if I'm good at science. There isn't a lowlier job in this dimension and you know it. Besides, half a decade of researching discrepancies in proto-apocalyptic patterns is more than enough lab work for one person. I could use some adventure." Daisy hesitated, wishing it didn't sting so much when the people she loved agreed how hopelessly unmagical she was. Just because something was true didn't mean it didn't hurt. "More than that, I want to be respected. Make a difference. And to do that, I have to be more than a mere scientist. I have to be magical."

Maeve nudged the pail with one hoof. "I can't deny any of that, but... I just wish there was an easier way. How will you ever get good at magic if you keep relying on science? Maybe artificial pixie dust isn't a wise choice, no matter how magically challenged you might be. Your mom's a fairy godmother. Can't she score some primo dust for you on the sly?"

"Maybe, if Dad weren't a guardian angel." Daisy straightened her glasses, hoping to hide her frustration from her eyes. "He doesn't believe in bending rules, and she doesn't believe in upsetting him. Mama would never traffic contraband dust. Even for me." Especially not for her. Mama wouldn't want her risking her father's wrath. "If I'm going to get anywhere in life, I'll have to do it on my own." She gestured with her wand. "Are you going to help me practice spells or not?"

"Okay." Maeve leaned backward to stretch her forelegs. "Let's do this." She glanced around the yard. "You see that barnacle tree over there? Aim at one of the branches without geese. We'd better start basic, with single-word spells." She slid a wary glance at Daisy's wand. "I still don't trust that thing. What's the simplest spell you can think of? Ooh, let's do a rainbow sequence on the leaves, one color at a time. Find a leaf. Visualize it turning the color of Santa's sleigh, speak the word 'red' very loudly and clearly, and aim carefully."

"All at once?" Daisy squinted at the barnacle tree, with its large brown trunk and oversize bud-shaped leaves filled with geese.

"Of course all at once. That's how spells work." Maeve took a few steps to the side as though worried about becoming collateral damage. "Go ahead."

Daisy sucked in a lungful of cool air and pointed the wand at the tree. Red, red, red. Santa's sleigh. Fire trucks. Gnome hats. Trevor's plastic cooler.

"Red!" Daisy shouted. A thick line of glittering light shot out from the tip of the wand and knocked a goose off its branch. The goose landed on the ground as a pumpkin.

A bright red pumpkin.

Daisy swore under her breath.

"Did you just—"

"Yes, yes, I did. I can see just as clearly as you can." Daisy's shoulders slumped. "I'm never going to get the algorithms right."

"I don't know," Maeve said slowly. "Maybe you will. It's red, isn't it? That's progress. Pick a different color and try again." She shot Daisy a warning glance. "This time aim for a leaf, not a bird. I don't want to have to turn a rainbow-colored pumpkin patch back into a flock of geese."

"I did aim!"

"Aim harder."

"Fine." Daisy dipped her wand back into the pixie dust and faced the tree again. Maybe green would be easier than red. Green, green, green. Troll skin. Dewy grass. Trevor's sleeping bag. "Green!"

A ray of sparkling light zapped another goose off the tree. This time, the odd-shaped pumpkin was a rugged, army green. Just like Trevor's sleeping bag.

"Daisy..."

"Trust me," she said with a sigh. "I know."

The remaining geese cast icy glares in her direction and took to the sky in a cacophony of flapping wings and indignant squawking.

Two familiar winged people dove in from the opposite direction and lighted on the ground in front of the colorful pumpkins. They strolled forward, hand in hand.

"Hi, Dad. Hi, Mama." Daisy dropped the wand and surreptitiously nudged the pixie dust pail behind a properly-colored pumpkin. No sense calling attention to her magical follies. "Out on a Sunday flight?"

"Oh, come here, sweetie." As usual, Daisy's mother looked gorgeous with her silvery upswept hair, delicate translucent wings, and flowing sky-blue gown. "I've missed you." She opened her arms and smiled.

Daisy dutifully walked over for cheek kisses.

Her father crossed his arms over his powerful chest, forcing his strong white wings to unfurl even further. He was more into guarding than hugging. "We wanted to know how your first assignment went. We expected you to drop by this morning and brief us."

"Yes, well..." Daisy tried for a casual expression. "I got sidetracked."

"Oh, sweetie." Mama held Daisy by the shoulders. "I knew it would be tough to acclimate at first. I hope you aren't too far out of your comfort zone." Her eyebrows lifted. "You didn't have an incident, did you?"

"No, no, nothing like that." Daisy gave her head a quick shake. "Everything went according to plan."

Maeve coughed. Daisy shot her a dirty look.

"How about you, young lady?" Dad boomed. "How's air traffic control these days?"

"Never better." Maeve tossed her purple mane from her eyes. "Got a second? I want to ask you a question about skyway traffic and flying monkey violations."

"Absolutely."

Maeve trotted off with Dad, leaving Daisy alone with her mother.

"Tell me the truth, now, sweetie." Mama patted Daisy's arm. "You aren't regretting giving up your career at the Neurophysics Compound, are you? Your research team and private laboratory and all those... uh... vials?"

"Not in the slightest." Well, not overly much. They hadn't hired anyone to replace her and she still had laboratory access and research privileges. They were trying to lure her back, but she couldn't give up her fairy apprenticeship without trying her hardest to succeed. "As soon as I earn my wings, you'll have reason to be proud."

Mama's forehead scrunched. "Neurophysics is... sort of... something to be proud of. Ish."

"Is it?" Daisy's fingers clenched at the obvious prevarication. Science was her life's work and meant nothing to her family.

She supposed a human mother would react much the same if her child's lifelong passion was for cleaning toilet bowls or mopping up vomit. There were no such menial jobs in Nether-Netherland, because everyone could perform magic on call. Science was not only the sole form of manual labor, but unlike cleaning toilet bowls or mopping up vomit, science was widely considered a useless endeavor. Why spend months or years researching and engineering and constructing something any child could conjure with a flick of the wrist? Daisy's own mother could perform successful spells with her very first words.

"Can you look me in the eye and tell me it doesn't bother you when people whisper to each other, wondering how a powerful fairy godmother could possibly have given birth to an ordinary, non-magical scientist?"

"I don't care what other people say." Mama's smile was a little too wide to be believed. "I'm your mother and I love you."

"Then you'll love me even more when I have real wings like you." Daisy turned away, unable to bear the gossamer perfection of real wings gently fluttering at her mother's back. "Can we talk about something else, please?"

"Certainly." Mama tapped a slender finger against her cheek. "I have just the topic. Maeve has a serious boyfriend. When are you going to find a man? You're not getting any younger, you know."

Jupiter's rings, any topic but that. Daisy massaged her suddenly aching temples and tried to think up an acceptable answer.

"I already did," she said with as much conviction as she could muster. After all, she wasn't technically lying. She did "find" a man, even if she couldn't keep him. The corner of her mouth quirked. Maybe she should've waited for Trevor in that tent after all, just to have something to tell her mother.

"Oh, sweetie, that's wonderful!" Mama's hands clasped to her chest and she beamed at Daisy, all thoughts of magic and science forgotten. "Well? Aren't you going to tell me all about him?"

Daisy swallowed. "Um, no." As in, *hell* no.

"Come on, sweetie, I'm your mother." Mama leaned forward. "I just want to see you settled and happy. I promise not to pry."

Daisy stopped massaging her temples long enough to lift an eyebrow.

Unabashed, Mama's tone turned pleading. "At least tell me his name."

"Fine. I found a cute guy named Trevor. Now can we discuss something else?"

"Trevor." Mama sucked on her lower lip as if tasting the word. "Trevor. Well, that's not a very magical name."

Daisy sucked in a deep breath. "Not everyone is born magical. Look at me, for example."

"Is he a scientist?"

Daisy paused. Was—what had he called it?—paleo-anthropology a science? In any case, it wasn't here in Nether-Netherland. It didn't *exist* in Nether-Netherland.

"Nope, not a scientist."

"Whew." Mama smiled in relief, then clutched her chest. "He's not... he's not a *troll*, is he?"

"Don't be prejudiced," Daisy scolded automatically, then tensed as the words sank in. "You think I'm so hopelessly unmagical that I can't do better than scientists and trolls?"

"I'm just saying, dating can be tough for some girls. I'm a fairy godmother, sweetie. I make the impossible possible all the time. If you would just let me do a bit of magic..."

Daisy's eyes stung. "*Never.*"

Blinking, she turned away before her mother could see how deeply her words had wounded.

"Arabella?" Wings aloft, Dad glided back over the hill with Maeve coasting alongside. "You about ready to go home? For some of us, Sunday is still the day of rest."

Before Mama could answer, a deafening thunderclap rattled the air. Daisy jumped back as scowling trolls in black Elders' Minions jackets tumbled out of nowhere onto the pumpkin-laden grass and swarmed the lawn.

She broke out in a cold sweat. Whatever the hired muscle wanted, she doubted they came bearing tidings of joy. Or requests for a date. Her heart began to race.

"DAISY LE FEY!" The loud, mechanical voice echoed through the countryside. "By order of the Elders Upon High, you are hereby brought under questioning for occupational misconduct."

Daisy fought down a sudden wave of nausea. What a fabulous way to top out the morning. Thick anti-magic netting whooshed down from the sky, trapping her in its sticky, spider-web-like threads. Overkill, given her lack of magical ability, but she was secretly pleased the Elders were taking no chances. At least *they* believed she had potential. Or maybe it was just protocol. The one thing keeping a magical world from total anarchy was the strict adherence to protocol.

Daisy wasn't any good at that, either. Her fingers scrabbled through the holes in the netting as she twisted to shout toward the trolls.

"All of this because the tooth wouldn't fit in a glass vial?" Unbelievable. It was hardly *her* fault she was summoned to an archeological dig instead of a nursery.

Daisy's father folded his arms over his chest and kept his feet on terra firma.

"Sweetie," came Mama's disappointed voice behind her. "You said the mission went well."

"Mostly well," Daisy amended, cursing fossilized teeth everywhere. "And then complications ensued."

"I knew you should've stayed a scientist." Mama stepped into Daisy's line of vision, right next to Daisy's stoic father. "You're so good at inventing machinery and dissecting brains. Even if it is embarrassing to the rest of us."

"And you shouldn't have kissed him," Maeve muttered. "Even if you're good at that, too."

Mama clapped a hand over her gaping mouth and fainted backward onto Daisy's father.

"Shut up, Maeve." Daisy glared at her big-mouthed friend. "That isn't what this is about. The Elders are just making a fuss because I didn't follow tooth containment protocol, that's all. Glass vials, labeling procedure, that sort of thing. This'll be cleared up in no time."

"DAISY LE FEY," the voice roared. "You are hereby summoned before the Elders' High Court. They will see you in one hour."

Trolls surrounded Daisy. They hoisted her over their sweaty shoulders in a tangle of scratchy netting.

"This is an outrage!" Kicking back, she twisted to face her father. "Dad, go get Vivian. She'll know what to do."

"Why is my daughter being arraigned for anything?" He propped up Mama's limp body with one arm and shook his fist at the melee. "I demand an explanation!"

A gnome stepped out from behind a row of Elders' Minions and unfolded an ivory scroll. "It has come to the attention of the Pearly States that Miss Daisy le Fey not only failed to collect the required tooth as is her duty, but also fraudulently and with malicious intent deposited a foul, misshapen rock in its place." He paused to take a breath, and then continued, "The charge is Defrauding and Deceiving a Government Body."

"Whaaat?" Daisy choked out. "Trevor said the tooth was buried *inside* the rock!"

The expression on the gnome's face confirmed what the clenching in Daisy's stomach had been hinting at all morning:

Never trust a human.

CHAPTER 3

*B*ack at his lab in Indiana, Trevor was unpacking the last of the crates when soft footsteps hesitated on the other side of the closed door. He frowned. There'd been less than a dozen cars in the entire parking lot. Who was sneaking around the Anthropology department on a Sunday evening? It had to be Berrymellow, spying on Trevor's research yet again.

He grabbed the first solid object on the lab counter and swung open the door.

"Gotcha!" he shouted and lunged forward. His momentum died mid-swing when he caught sight of the blue and white university jumpsuit. "Oh. Jeb." Trevor gave a sheepish smile. Finding a barefoot blonde in his tent had gone a long way toward fostering paranoia. "Hi."

The lanky janitor glanced up from the trash and shook his head. "What were you gonna do, son? Smack me with an arm bone?"

A what? Oh. Trevor lowered the impromptu weapon. "It's not an arm bone. It's a femur." At Jeb's dubious expression, Trevor bent one knee and brandished the bone like a light saber, hoping to play off his impulsive reaction as a joke. "See? Leg bone. Very masculine."

Jeb stared. "You catch jungle fever or somesuch down in Puerto Rico?"

"Costa Rica," Trevor corrected. He returned to the lab adjoining his classroom and placed the femur gently on the counter. "And I hope not." But maybe he was suffering from a mild case of insanity caused by annoyance and misplaced lust. Last night's dreams had been filled with images of a certain alleged tooth fairy, heating up his sleeping bag with good old-fashioned naked fun.

When Jeb bent to tie the trash bag, Trevor stepped forward and held the door open for the older man. "What's new?"

"Well, my grandkids got new pictures." Jeb dug a tattered leather wallet from his back pocket. He plucked a plastic photo-keeper from inside and handed it over. "That one there's the youngest, Cody."

Before Trevor could make any cute-baby comments, his cellphone vibrated against his belt. He held up a finger to Jeb before enabling the Bluetooth headset at his ear.

"Professor Masterson." Trevor pointed at the baby's face, smiled at Jeb, and then flipped to the next photo. Two little girls with messy braids and matching outfits grinned behind the worn plastic cover. A few more years, and they'd be old enough to play some baseball.

"Hey, Coach," came the loud, familiar voice in his ear. "It's Katrina. Three more hours until takeoff. The natives are getting restless. Can I kill them?"

Jeb pointed at the pictures open in Trevor's palm. "Them two are the twins."

"Cute." Trevor couldn't tell them apart. He smiled and turned to the next photo.

"Who's cute?" Katrina demanded. "Trust me, ain't nobody cute on this team. I might get wasted on Imperial *cerveza* so I can just pass out on the flight home."

Trevor grimaced. Maybe putting Katrina in charge of the second plane was a bad idea. Then again, he couldn't be on both flights, so she would've had to be in charge of one or the other. "What's wrong with them?"

"Not a damn thing wrong with them," Jeb snapped. He snatched the photos out of Trevor's hand and shoved his wallet back in his pocket. "Lots of kids have teeth what stick out like that."

Before Trevor could explain he hadn't meant any insult to Jeb's grandkids, Katrina's voice blasted in his ear again. "Can Alberto be in charge for a while so I can finish typing the field notes and adding metadata to all the dig photos?"

Trevor's eyelid twitched. If he ignored the question, would Katrina take initiative and exhibit some autonomy? He reached out toward Jeb. "No, come on. I didn't get to see the photos. Nobody's teeth were sticking out. Please hand it over."

"I have no idea what that means," Katrina said after a brief pause. "I can't hand the laptop through the phone. And what's your hang-up with teeth?"

Jeb turned and hefted a trash bag with each hand. "I'll come back when you're not so busy." He headed down the hall with a foul trail of god-knew-what leaking from the bottoms of the bags.

Trevor leaned his head back against the corner of the doorframe. "You're the TA. Remind them there's still an essay due, and they ought to concentrate on that. In the meantime, keep working on those files. Delegate what you want to Alberto." He checked his watch. "I just finished unpacking crates and now I'm headed to the office to start the prelim reports."

"Oooh, prelim reports," came a nasal voice from the other end of the hall. "So the great paleo-anthropologist returns from safari." Joshua Berrymellow strutted across the wet linoleum in his usual crisp white suit, goatee, and bolo tie. He always reminded Trevor of a redheaded Colonel Sanders.

"K, Coach," Katrina said with a sigh. "Catch ya in six hours."

Trevor disconnected the Bluetooth and turned to Berrymellow. "What sudden attack of industriousness brings *you* here on a Sunday evening?"

He smirked at Trevor. "I'm finalizing the acceptance speech I'll be giving at the tenure meeting."

Trevor raised an eyebrow, feigning disinterest. "Does anyone even give acceptance speeches at tenure meetings?"

"You'll never know." Berrymellow's lips curled into a pitying smile.

"So sorry about your job. What a shame you won't be joining us next year. I suppose it's all the more time to gad about being Indiana Masterson. If you could get paid for that, of course."

Trevor's jaw clenched. "Give me a break, Berrymellow. I'm up for tenure just like you."

"Doctor Berrymellow to you." He drummed manicured fingers on a black leather briefcase. "And you'll be getting a permanent break. Publish or perish, as they say. You don't have a chance."

"We're both doctors of anthropology. And I've got a massive chance." Trevor pushed away from the doorframe. Berrymellow flinched, and Trevor fought a smile. *Jackass.* "I managed to talk the Costa Rican government into letting me borrow a few artifacts for several months. I've got a partial skeleton in my lab *right now*. Once my TA gets here with the spreadsheets and photos, I'll have the foundation for one hell of an article." Trevor jabbed a finger at Berrymellow's bolo tie. "While you've been dicking around on the golf course with the dean, I've been doing actual fieldwork."

"Oh, yeah?" Berrymellow's chin jutted forward, bushy red goatee and all. "Well, while you were wasting time in the jungle, I was proofing an article that comes out this month, not next year. Guess who'll lead the next senior trip? Not you, cowboy."

"Please." Trevor folded his arms across his chest to keep from locking his fingers around Berrymellow's neck. "You haven't been on a single dig or alternate-culture expedition in the five years we've been at this university. What did you publish? Fried chicken recipes?"

"We can't all play in the mud like you." Berrymellow disguised a high-pitched snicker with a fake cough. "Being a leading socio-anthropologist, I concentrated my efforts on documenting local phenomena."

Tendrils of ice snaked through Trevor's gut. Behavioral sciences were always so... ambiguous. Berrymellow never seemed to need actual results or new findings. Just new theories. He arched a brow. "Such as?"

Berrymellow clicked open his briefcase. "A study of how the behavioral patterns of socially powerful men on golf outings differ from the passive-aggressive conduct of career-climbing individuals engaged in boardroom politics."

"*What?*" Trevor would have burst out laughing if it weren't his career on the line. "No self-respecting academic periodical would print that drivel."

"Read it and weep." With a flourish, Berrymellow thrust a copy of the magazine article at Trevor. "I took the liberty of stapling it for you."

"You've got to be kidding me." Trevor snatched the twenty-five-page monstrosity from Berrymellow's hands and flipped through so fast his fingers should have bled with paper cuts. "You actually dreamt up 3-D pie charts for this shit?"

"Ah, jealousy," Berrymellow chided, eyeing him delightedly. "Don't externalize your ill-managed aggression, or I'll write another paper on Destructive Behaviors Caused by Career Envy in the Workplace. I'm sure you won't go down in history as a *complete* failure."

Trevor's jaw ached from all the gnashing of teeth he was doing to keep himself from biting Berrymellow's head off. What happened to that leg bone? He'd be glad to go down in history as the lucky bastard who clubbed Joshua Berrymellow with a femur.

Berrymellow snapped his briefcase closed with a self-satisfied smirk. "If you think you can beat me at the tenure game, feel free to try. You've got until the end of the semester. And I just might get another important socio-anthropological treatise out of it."

He sauntered off down the hall with a sashay in his step.

Trevor's damp palm slapped angrily against the metal door frame. Unbelievable. Mere weeks to churn out a career-defining piece documenting the biggest find of his professional life—a partial skeleton unearthed from the bottom of a lake and a few mismatched artifacts— in time to save his reputation, his paycheck, and his academic future.

He glanced at his watch. His students would be boarding their jet within the next few hours. In the meantime, he needed a plan. There *must* be a way to beat Berrymellow at his own game.

Trevor just had to find it.

∾

"DAISY LE FEY," boomed the three-foot-tall court gnome from his perch next to the Elders' golden desk. His piercing blue eyes peered at Daisy from beneath bushy white eyebrows and a pointy red hat. "For the charges of Defrauding and Deceiving a Government Body, how do you plead?"

"Urgh," her attorney grunted confidently. "Urrrrrghhhh."

Daisy closed her eyes and concentrated on intonation and dissonance.

If it had been up to her, she might not have picked a yeti for a lawyer. Not that big feet meant small brains, mind you. Just that she couldn't quite comprehend his legal advice. It had been years since her grammar school language courses. She'd have to remedy her lack of fluency fast if she wanted to have any chance of following along at her own trial. If this went to trial. Note to self: Have Maeve conjure How to Speak Yeti in Just 10 Days.

She opened her eyes and nodded as though his guttural mutterings made sense. Since the Elders appointed every defense attorney for every defendant, you'd think they'd only hire multilingual representatives of the law. Then again, attorneys were only slightly more respectable than scientists, so perhaps she shouldn't judge. Daisy bit back a sigh.

"What's that?" squealed Judge Bedelia Banshee, who often presided over matters pertaining to the Pearly States. "Speak up, fairy."

"Er, not guilty." Daisy offered her most innocent smile.

"The people request remand, Your Honor." District Attorney Livinia Sangre, the most notoriously anti-fairy prosecutor in all of Nether-Netherland, tucked glossy black hair behind one pointed ear. "The defendant is a flight risk."

"I am not!" She shot a panicked glance at her attorney. Being several feet taller than Daisy, the shaggy white fur of his massive chest blocked her line of vision and clouded her nostrils with the stench of magical forests.

"Urgh," he gargled. "Urrrrrghhhh."

Frustrated at her complete lack of comprehension, Daisy sent a pleading look toward the fanged district attorney. Her fingers turned to ice as the D.A. remained stoic. Desperate, she tried to come up with legal jargon to defend herself. "On... on what grounds?"

"On the grounds that *fairies* are *flight risks*." D.A. Sangre bared her fangs. "By definition."

Daisy shivered.

"Urgh," the yeti lawyer groaned, and nudged her in the shoulder so hard that she stumbled against the hard-edged table. "Urrrrrghhhh."

She faced the golden desk and prayed for divine intervention. "Look, I'm not a fairy. Yet." She reached behind her back and carefully peeled her handmade wings from their Velcro base. "See?"

The courtroom gasped.

Daisy tried not to roll her eyes. Nobody in Nether-Netherland was shocked her wings weren't real. Many of them had watched her painstakingly carve them out on her parents' front porch, and whispered amongst themselves when Daisy drowned them in glitter glue and dried them stiff. No, the audience had to be gasping because she hadn't appeared in public without false wings in a good twenty years.

"Isn't the defendant appearing on charges of Defrauding and Deceiving a Government Body, Your Honor?" demanded D.A. Sangre, her claw-like nails skittering across the case files. "And when this defendant appears in a court of law for the Elders Upon High, her very clothing attempts to defraud and to deceive. Your Honor, you cannot intend to allow such an individual to walk out of this courtroom unchecked."

"D.A. Sangre," bellowed Judge Banshee, hopping on top of the golden desk in fury. "While I see your point, you do not tell a judge what she can and cannot do." She turned toward Daisy. "Miss le Fey. Have you any statement to countermand this argument?"

"Well," Daisy said and elbowed her furry lawyer for help. "I sure would like to be released on my own recognizance."

D.A. Sangre threw back her head and laughed. "And why would Judge Banshee do that?"

"Urgh." Daisy's attorney raked his gaze across the courtroom audience. "Urrrrrghhhh."

"What's that?" Judge Banshee frowned. "Her parents?"

"Your Honor," Daisy called, after meeting her father's concerned gaze. "My parents are valued and important members of this community. My mother is the High Chair of the Fairy Godmother Committee, and my father is the co-founder of the Heavenly Alliance of Guardian Angels." Daisy took a deep breath. "The daughter of these respected individuals would never shame them by running away from the consequences of her own actions."

"Urrrrrghhhh," murmured Daisy's lawyer reassuringly as he clapped her on the shoulder.

"Very well," Judge Banshee shrieked. "I hereby release you—"

"*What?*" D.A. Sangre demanded, her pallid complexion paling even further.

"—to your parents' custody." Her gavel crashed against the golden desk and exploded into a rainbow of glittering confetti. "Adjourned until Tuesday morning."

"*What?*" Daisy sucked in a horrified breath and swayed against the warm, wooly stomach of her defense attorney. "I have to live with my parents?"

Daisy caught sight of her mentor, Vivian Valdemeer, standing just inside the courtroom doors. Nervously, Daisy headed over to find out if this snafu would jeopardize her job.

"Hey," she managed, wincing when her voice cracked. "Thanks for coming out to support me."

"It's no problem." Vivian adjusted the strand of pearls at her neck. "Everything seems to be working itself out."

"Are you kidding?" Daisy gaped at her. "I'm on *house arrest.* Everything is going horribly wrong. Don't tooth fairies collect teeth from children? I went to that dig and there were no children in sight."

Vivian inspected her fuchsia fingernails. "That's a common misconception. Tooth fairies collect teeth—anyone's teeth—provided that they were placed underneath the head of a human before falling asleep."

"That was my original hypothesis after extrapolating based on context, given the parameters of the situation." Daisy bit her lower lip. "But I see flaws in such a system. For example, couldn't a bounty hunter of some kind purposefully sleep on a tooth in order to try and catch a tooth fairy?"

Her mentor gave an indulgent smile. "The automated system verifies the authenticity of every tooth summons in our grid."

Daisy shook her head. "But it sent me—"

"—to your mission," Vivian said firmly. "Yes, there have been a few bugs in the database. The details are occasionally wrong, but the tooth is always right. Don't worry about nefarious humans out to stir up trouble. I would never send you somewhere dangerous."

"I wasn't overly concerned about physical danger." She was mostly concerned with the danger of losing her job—and her last chance for respect. The one who should fear for his physical safety was that human Trevor. She'd like to throw that rock at his head. "It's just that the person sleeping on the tooth wasn't the person who'd owned the tooth. I'd never heard of such a situation."

"Once in a while, these things happen." Vivian patted Daisy's shoulder. "But rules are rules, darling. You can't change the system."

Daisy's brow furrowed. "But what if someone—"

"Do you want to be a tooth fairy or not?" Vivian interrupted, her tone tempered with annoyance. At Daisy's slow nod, Vivian bestowed a gentle, maternal smile. "Then chalk it up to yet another absurd facet of Nether-Netherland bureaucracy. I'm sure there's papers we could file somewhere, but who has the patience? We do what we have to, even when we don't want to. What if you were a genie and you were summoned by, say, a spider monkey? Would you rail and cry and say, 'Oh dear, I should only do the bidding of humans?'"

Daisy shook her head. "I like spider monkeys. They have double the relative brain size of howler monkeys. A good hundred and seven grams of gray matter on average."

"Well, there you go. We serve anyone with teeth, regardless of brain size." Vivian's smile faded. "But you shouldn't get into any more trouble, if you want to keep your apprenticeship. I expect perfection from here on out."

~

Daisy would never be able to achieve perfection, but she might be able to collect the correct tooth before her next court visit, and thus undo the damage she'd inadvertently wrought.

As soon as she managed to sneak out of her parents' sight, she corralled her where-frog and teleported back to Costa Rica. But when she materialized on rolling green grass underneath a brilliant blue sky, she wasn't sure Bubbles had his internal compass on straight.

The rugged brown peak of Volcano Arenal still rumbled with smoke and steamy lava above the horizon. Tiny islands with lonely trees and grazing cows still dotted the shimmering lake.

But where were the tents? Where was the dig? The tooth? Trevor?

The only human in sight was a skinny little boy with muddy feet and shaggy hair, sauntering along the edge of the rutted dirt road with two boisterous puppies at his heels.

"*Perdón*," Daisy called out and headed toward him.

The little boy glanced over with a cheerful grin. "*¿Sí?*"

"*Había un campamento aquí.*" She gestured toward the empty camp-site as she asked him what happened to the people. "*¿Sabe dónde está?*"

The dark-haired boy pointed off to the distance. "*El aeropuerto. En Liberia.*"

Ack! They went to the freaking airport? If they left Costa Rica before Daisy figured out where they were going, she'd lose her chance to find Trevor—and the tooth.

"*Gracias.*" She fished in her black leather B. Fendi handbag for local currency—was her purse considered a knockoff if her best friend conjured it for her?—and handed the little boy a fistful of *colones* for his time. As long as he didn't realize she was a tooth fairy, there was no harm in sharing some Pearly States-minted money.

Now what? There was only one way for her to get to the airport quickly. As soon as the boy was out of sight, she brought Bubbles to her lips and whispered, "Liberia Airport. Fast."

She materialized fifty yards from a jet being loaded with wooden boxes and young people in cargo pants. Two of the faces looked famil-iar. Thank Chronos there was still time.

"Katrina! Alberto!" Daisy waved to get their attention.

They jogged toward her surprisingly fast, considering the giant packs strapped to their backs and the other bags piled in their arms.

"Here," Katrina commanded, turning toward Alberto. "Take the laptop case."

"No way. Professor Masterson put you in charge, not me." Alberto turned to Daisy, wiping sweat from his forehead. "*¿Qué pasa, guapa?* I sure hoped to see you again."

Katrina whacked him in the arm with the leather case. "Get out of here, you horn-dog. I can handle Coach's bimbo much better without you drooling all over her."

Alberto slunk a hurt look toward Katrina, but trudged back toward the airplane.

She lit up a cigarette and blew smoke over her shoulder. "What do you want?"

"I want Trevor." Daisy scanned the unfamiliar faces boarding the plane. "Right now, if possible."

"I'm sure you do." Katrina smirked. "Too bad he's in Elkhart."

"Elkhart?" Daisy repeated. "What's that?"

"*Where's* that, you mean. Northern Indiana, honey. Six hours from Liberia International Airport by jet, if you don't have any layovers." Katrina jerked her head toward the runway. "He's long gone. Only way you can talk to him from here is if you got him on speed dial."

"Speed dial?" Daisy's fingers clenched. Crap. She'd aced English Slang at university... almost a decade ago. Heaven only knew how much had changed. She wondered if fishing out her current edition of Nether-Netherland Readers' Choice Condensed Encyclopedia of Human Slang and Culture would be too conspicuous a giveaway. "What's that?"

Katrina gaped at her. "Are you from the Stone Age or what? You sound like my grandmother. Look, I'll let you use my cellphone because I love to eavesdrop on the coach's conversations, but you can only talk for a minute." She gestured toward the diminishing queue with her lit cigarette. "If I'm not in my seat in fifteen, they'll leave without me." Katrina pulled out a rectangular phone, tapped on the screen, and then handed it to Daisy. "Here. It's ringing."

Daisy pressed the phone to her ear.

"Hello?" came a deep bass voice.

Her heart rate shot up. Mostly because she was ticked at him, she reminded herself, not because he sounded sexy. "Why are you in Indiana?"

"Katrina?"

"No, Daisy."

"Why do you have Katrina's cellphone?"

"She let me borrow it." Daisy shot her a grateful look.

"She—" he choked on his response. "Tell her I'll deal with her the very second she gets back."

Daisy nudged Katrina. "Trevor says he's going to deal with you the very second you get back."

She shrugged. "Knowing the sappy look on his face last time he saw you, that probably means I get an automatic A. Rock on."

"Katrina says 'rock on.'" Daisy's eyes narrowed. "Speaking of which, you didn't give me the tooth, you jerk. You gave me a dirty rock!"

"Hmm," he murmured noncommittally.

"That's all you have to say?" she demanded.

He chuckled. "How about: 'Hmm, yes, I gave you a rock.' I hope you didn't take it out of the country. I hear Costa Rica has stringent laws about such things."

"I cannot believe I trusted you." Daisy's entire body shook. Humans were despicable creatures. "I actually kissed you, you—you toad!" Her disgruntled where-frog glared at her from his perch on her shoulder. "Er... sorry, Bubbles."

"Did you just call Professor Masterson 'Bubbles'?" Katrina breathed, exhaling smoke. "I am *so* going to tweet this."

"That was no kiss." Trevor's tone thrummed with amusement. "If you were here, I could prove it to you. If I kissed lunatics."

She gasped in outrage. "If I were there, I'd brain you with that stupid rock, you jerk."

"I'll remember that." His voice turned hard, the deep timbre as dangerous and unpredictable as molten lava. "Stay in Costa Rica or go back to wherever you come from, but leave me, my students, and my anthropological discoveries alone."

"Leave *you* alone? If I don't get that tooth, you'll have single-handedly ruined—"

With a frantic glance at her watch, Katrina grabbed the phone from Daisy's hand and turned toward the aircraft. "Hey, Coach, I'm boarding the plane now. Takeoff in ten." She flicked the cigarette butt out of her path.

"Wait," Daisy shouted at Katrina's retreating form, frustration bunching her muscles. "Please!"

Even if she hadn't read the encyclopedia entry on the one-fingered gesture Katrina tossed up over her shoulder, Daisy would've had no problem extrapolating the meaning from context.

Desperate times called for desperate measures. Daisy plucked her latest wand from the bottom of her handbag. She took a deep breath, gripped the handle with both hands and pointed at Katrina's back. "Freeze!"

Daisy's shoulders jerked with the backlash as her wand-in-progress unleashed a current of light strong enough to bowl Katrina over. The phone clattered across the graveled tar. Katrina and her bags rolled a few feet and skidded to rest as one giant pumpkin.

A massive, *frozen* pumpkin.

CHAPTER 4

here the hell was Katrina, and the laptop with all his documentation? Trevor paced up and down the gray concrete hallway outside the Anthropology laboratory.

What time was it now? Ten? This was getting ridiculous.

Despite her smart mouth, Katrina was generally reliable. Sure, there was that one time after the away game in Indy when she'd disappeared with the opposing team's shortstop and hadn't shown back up for the rest of the weekend, but she'd sworn never to pull a stunt like that again. He could trust her. Couldn't he?

Trevor scrolled through his phone contacts and clicked Katrina's name for the seventh time in the past two hours. For once, he didn't get voice mail. However, the purr at the other end of the line was definitely not Katrina.

"Hello, cellphone?"

"Daisy?" he blurted incredulously. "Where's Katrina?"

"Uh…" Daisy cleared her throat. "She can't answer right now."

Oh, Lord. What the hell did that mean? Had Daisy snuck on the plane? Damn it. He knew they should've chosen an airline with flight attendants and boarding passes. "Please tell me you didn't follow her to Elkhart."

"No, I'm in Costa Rica. Where your tents used to be." Daisy sighed. "I wish I'd arrived when you were still here."

Worry and irritation quickened Trevor's pace as he stalked up and down the deserted hallway. "What are you doing with Katrina's cellphone?"

A moment of absolute silence came across the line and for a moment he thought the call had been dropped.

"She left it behind."

"Katrina forgot her phone?" He slumped against the wall in disbelief.

This was sounding more and more like the Indy escapade, when they'd dialed her phone dozens of times only to find it vibrating in her locker. Un-freaking-believable.

"Were you there when she left?" he demanded. "Did you see where she went?"

"I didn't see her actually go anywhere," Daisy said, her tone a little... sheepish? Even if Daisy was a bit unbalanced, it wasn't her fault if Katrina was off knocking boots with a local.

"You're sure she didn't say where she was going?" Trevor asked, trying to keep the irritability from his voice. He could teach anthropology, but he couldn't teach common sense.

"Nope," Daisy chirped. "Didn't say a thing about that."

Great. Katrina knew better than to not call. But if she'd gotten so distracted she'd left her phone behind, maybe she wasn't calling because she was afraid Trevor would expel her. Or maybe she was at the airport even now, scheduling a new flight. After all, tomorrow was a school day. She wouldn't miss that.

In the meantime, the main question was: why was the first person to inform him of his TA's disappearance a delusional, barefoot chick with cat-eye glasses and an identity complex?

"I've got to go," Daisy said, interrupting his train of thought. "Don't call me anymore."

"I didn't call you," Trevor pointed out. "I called Katrina."

"Don't call her either. Let's go home, Bubbles."

"Bubbles? Did you just call me Bubbles?"

No answer. The line was dead.

He shook his head. What a weird, weird woman. Pretty, yes, but also pretty wacky. Thank God she was half a world away. Alberto, on the other hand, should be back in town by now.

Trevor scrolled back through his contacts and dialed.

"*Habla*," came the cheery greeting amid a background of loud salsa music.

"This is Professor Masterson." Trevor raised his voice to be heard over the music. "Did you and Katrina see Daisy at the airport?"

"*Oh* yeah." Alberto whistled. "She looked really hot. Katrina made me get on the plane so I couldn't look at Daisy. But I ask you: Since when is looking a crime?"

"We'll discuss that another time." Trevor leaned against the cold concrete and dredged up a modicum of patience. "When did Katrina board?"

Alberto snorted. "She didn't."

Trevor smacked the back of his head against the rough concrete-block wall. "And when were you planning to inform me of this?"

"Well," Alberto said. "I didn't notice until we landed."

"How did you not notice?" Trevor thundered.

"I was mad at her. Still am. What's wrong with looking? *Por Dios*," Alberto asked indignantly. "I should be able to look at anybody I want to. I mean, even if Daisy's your girlfriend, I can't help but notice how hot she is, right?"

Trevor closed his eyes. "Daisy is not my girlfriend."

"Which means I can ogle her anytime I want, right? Anyway, I didn't want Katrina to give me a hard time, so I sat in the back of the jet with my music up full blast and stared out the window until we landed. There's no assigned seats or nothing, so I managed to avoid everybody."

"And when you noticed Katrina wasn't with you..." Trevor prompted.

"I was like, good." Alberto sniffed. "Serves her right."

"*What?*" Trevor choked out.

"Yeah, but then I thought, *puta*, I'm going back to cold, rainy Indiana and she gets to stay in Costa Rica with the hot chick! It just isn't fair." Alberto sighed. "Katrina really pisses me off sometimes, you know?"

"Alberto." Trevor pushed off from the wall and started pacing again. "Listen to yourself. Why would Katrina suddenly decide to stay in Costa Rica with Daisy?"

"I don't know." Alberto paused. "Hot girly action?"

Trevor's skin crawled with horror. Now *there* was an image of his star pitcher he really didn't need to have. "Please don't say that ever again."

"Hey, wait a minute." The blaring music cut off mid-song. "You don't think she hooked up with one of the locals, do you? I mean, she'll be on another flight, won't she?"

"To be honest," Trevor said, "I thought better of both of you. And now I don't know what to think."

Alberto sucked in his breath. "Am—am I in trouble?"

"I'm thinking it over. But ultimately, you're not responsible for the team." Trevor sighed. "I am."

"So, are *you* in trouble?"

Trevor banged his forehead against a row of cabinets. Universities tended not to hand out tenure to professors who misplaced graduate students in Central America. Even if the student was a legal adult who willfully misplaced herself.

"We don't know that yet," he hedged, so as not to alarm his student. But he bet he was about to find out.

Bubbles deposited Daisy and Katrina-the-ice-pumpkin underneath the floating cottage. He immediately hopped off into the bushes as if wanting nothing more to do with the rapidly deteriorating situation. Daisy set the freezing pumpkin down on the lawn and wished she could hop into oblivion with her where-frog.

Unfortunately, Maeve happened to be standing two feet away, with a classic "you've got to be kidding me" expression on her face.

"So." Maeve pawed at the ground with an idle hoof. "Whatcha got there?"

"Pumpkin," Daisy muttered, avoiding eye contact by calculating the total surface area of the non-icy pumpkins littering her lawn. "Duh."

"What's the white frosty stuff? Freezer burn?" Maeve craned her neck forward.

"Unfortunately." Daisy rubbed her pounding temples, kicking herself for digging an even bigger hole. "It's Trevor's assistant."

"*What?*" Maeve goggled at Daisy. "You brought a human to Nether-Netherland?"

"She's not human anymore. Besides, what was I supposed to do? Leave her in Costa Rica? Not without a ForgetMe orb." Daisy knelt next to the pumpkin and brushed a hand across the top. Yikes. Still freezing cold. Poor Katrina.

"I see your point." Maeve slunk an involuntary glance around the open countryside, as if checking for magical spies. "But she's at least got to be able to alert us if she needs help, right?" Maeve cocked her head to one side and considered the frozen pumpkin. "Let me just defrost her a bit and…" She chanted under her breath. "Voila!"

Daisy stared in dismay.

The good news? Katrina was no longer a frozen pumpkin. The bad news? Katrina was now a basketball-sized jack-o'-lantern.

A furious, if well-lit, bright orange jack-o'-lantern.

"What the hell is going on here?" demanded the flickering jack-o'-lantern, cutout teeth gnashing in fury. "Did I eat a rotten enchilada?"

"Neither." Daisy half-wished *she* were the vegetable. Or were pumpkins a fruit? "You used to be an ice pumpkin and now… you're not."

"You're a jack-o'-lantern," Maeve added with a flick of her violet mane. "And I'm Maeve. May I call you Katrina?"

Flames rose behind Katrina's triangular eyes. "You can call a cab to get me the eff out of crazy town, that's what you can do."

"First off," Maeve said, tossing her glossy mane down her back. "Don't be so ungrateful. I could have let you stay an ice pumpkin."

"Why was I an ice pumpkin in the first place?" Katrina spat at Daisy, voice rising. "I let you use my cellphone. That's international roaming!"

"Sorry," Daisy mouthed and backed up a few more feet. "I'm new at toothfairying. I used to be Head of Hard Sciences at the Neurophysics Compound." She crouched down to be eye-level with Katrina. "Look, I want to turn you back into a human, I really do."

"Then do it," Katrina shrilled, hysteria giving her voice a sharp, soprano edge.

"Trust me," Daisy said, sitting back on her heels. "If you de-pumpkin here in Nether-Netherland, we'll have more trouble than any of us want to deal with."

Worse, somebody had to erase Nether-Netherland from Katrina's memory when they took her back to Earth, and there was no way Daisy could do it on her own. Worse still, there was no way Maeve's hooves could fashion a useful ForgetMe orb. How were they going to get the jack-o'-lantern back to its home?

"Why should I trust you?" Katrina's swung from Daisy to Maeve the flying horse and back again.

"You can trust me because I want you gone just as much as you want to *be* gone. I just need to take care of a teensy-weensy tooth issue real fast, and then I'll get you back home as your normal self." Daisy affected her most confident expression, hoping her horror and desperation weren't broadcast on her face. "I promise."

"You better. I need my hands to smoke. Or strangle you. Which-ever." Katrina's cutout mouth frowned. "What am I supposed to do in the meantime? Hang out in this field with a bunch of other pumpkins? How many people have you done this to?"

"You're the first." Daisy forced a smile. "And yes, it would be lovely if you would stay here and stay quiet while I come up with a plan. Do you mind?"

"Hell yeah, I mind. I'm missing school, for one." Katrina blew seeds and pulp across Daisy's feet. "And for two, how boring is that?"

"I'll pumpkin-sit," Maeve offered with a sigh. She inclined her head toward the large barn floating on a magic cloud next to Daisy's cottage. "Since you're supposed to be on house arrest."

Daisy gave her best friend a grateful smile. "Thanks. I owe you."

"Don't you forget it."

After wiping the pumpkin pulp from her feet, Daisy crossed over to the hedgerow and knelt in front of the bushes to find Bubbles. Desperation ate at her belly.

She had to fix this situation, and she had to fix it fast. If she could just use a Mortal Locator, she could find Trevor's coordinates, get the tooth, have Maeve de-pumpkin Katrina and maybe then Daisy could finally get her life back together. Assuming she somehow got her hands on a ForgetMe orb. If only horse hooves could weave that sort of magic!

"Bubbles, would you come out already? Quit playing around. I've got to go to the office before anyone else gets there."

The tiny where-frog hopped from his perch on a yellow-tipped leaf onto Daisy's outstretched palm. He shot a pointed look over her shoulder toward the mouthy pumpkin talking Maeve's ear off, but he zapped Daisy into her darkened office without delay.

Out of habit, she sucked in her breath and listened for Vivian. It was before office hours, so with luck... She froze when a high-pitched voice filtered through the wall. Terrified, Daisy cocked her head to listen. Her mouth fell open when she realized the voice she heard yelling in the waiting room wasn't Vivian's after all.

What in Hades was her mother doing here?

"I *asked* you not to mentor my daughter," Mama was shouting. "She's a talented scientist with a promising neurophysics career. Or at least, she was until you put this tooth fairy notion in her head. Daisy's always dreamed of real wings and doesn't understand that you have to be magical in order to make fairy."

At those words, Daisy's lungs squished into cold, slushy goo. Now she knew where her mother's loyalties lay. Or didn't, to be precise.

Daisy crept past the Tooth Fairy Transporter on the other side of Vivian's office. The shiny Mortal Locator hung in its gilded frame, centered on the wall. Bubbles could take her anywhere she wanted to go, but only if she *knew* where she wanted to go. Too bad Trevor had left Costa Rica without a clear forwarding address.

Daisy stared at her reflection in the Mortal Locator's mirrored surface until a cloudy whirlwind twisted in the glass.

"Earth, Human Dimension," Daisy murmured, careful to keep her voice low. If Mama and Vivian caught wind of this unauthorized investigation, the trouble would only worsen.

The small planet's blues and greens swirled into focus. Humph. This was easy. Daisy'd have to beg Vivian for a turn at hunting up the assignments once in a while.

"Indiana."

A wide expanse of green plains and golden crops flooded the surface. Pretty.

"Elkhart," she requested softly.

Rather than farmland, roadways and rivers and precisely blocked neighborhoods swam in the aerial view. She had to be close.

She took a deep breath. "Trevor Masterson."

The image panned to a small white cottage with a two-car garage and an immaculate lawn. A shiny black car pulled into the driveway. The door opened. Trevor unfolded himself from behind the wheel. He strode up to the house, unlocked the front door, and disappeared inside.

"Perfect," Daisy breathed, suddenly aware the voices in the other room had ceased. She had to hurry. "Address, please."

"555 Briarwood Ct" flashed around the edges of the frame.

From the other end of the office, the Tooth Fairy Transporter's gears whirred. Daisy raced over to it in alarm, pressing everything she could see to turn it off. Nothing worked. It must start automatically after a successful address retrieval. Which would be great if she didn't have a where-frog of her own. And if she knew how to work the thing. Dials lit and flashed, lighting up an assortment of standard-issue tooth fairy homing rings. Tufts of pixie dust plumed out from the access panel.

An ear-piercing screech blared through the office. "Illegal Teleportation Attempt! Illegal Teleportation Attempt! Illegal Teleportation Attempt!"

"Aargh," Daisy choked, nearly apoplectic with panic. She punched in her access code, banged every button and flipped every lever in a frantic, futile attempt to shut off the brain-melting clamor. Nothing.

Note to self: Reprogram the Mortal Locator's automatic configuration.

The big golden door flew open and bounced against the office wall. Mama and Vivian bounded into the room. As they ran, their faces twisted into twin incredulous expressions.

"Bubbles," Daisy gurgled desperately as both her mentor and her mother sprinted toward the shrieking Transporter at full speed. "Briarwood Court. Now. *Please.*"

With a beleaguered sigh, Bubbles snuggled into Daisy's trembling palm and complied.

CHAPTER 5

*T*revor sat on the edge of his recliner, but did not lean back against the soft leather. Instead, he was hunched over, elbows over knees, poring through a worn Spanish-English dictionary.

The private jet company's twenty-four-hour hotline had turned out to be both expensive and an utter waste of time. He hoped like hell he could locate Katrina before the other students realized she hadn't returned, and rumors of a terrorist kidnapping, prison stint, or alien abduction flew around the school. None of which boded well for tenure… or Katrina.

He lifted his face from the dictionary and stared broodily into the unlit fireplace. She had *sworn* never to repeat her Indianapolis stunt. If she broke her promise and decided to take an extended fiesta with the locals, then she deserved academic punishment for her actions.

But if she *didn't* take an impromptu vacation… If she *hadn't* broken her promise and was actually stranded in Central America…

A tiny pop echoed from inside Trevor's bedroom, as though someone muffled the sound of a champagne bottle uncorking. He leapt to his feet, eyes narrowing at the empty hallway.

Before placing his brief international phone call, Trevor had gone into in his bedroom to toss his button-down shirt into the laundry basket and trade his chinos for jeans. As far as he could recall, no champagne bottles lurked inside his bedroom. And even if he'd filled his closet with liquor, champagne tended not to go about opening itself.

Tense, he kept still and waited, listening for further sounds.

Nothing.

Maybe the noise was just the central air kicking on, knocking one of his signed baseball cards from its little plastic stand. After all, sometimes a noise was just a noise. Probably he was overreacting.

He slid a Louisville Slugger out from behind the couch just in case.

Holding the grip with his right hand so the bat hovered above his head, the fingertips of Trevor's left hand made contact with the door. He slammed the door open with his hip and swung into the room with a loud, "Hiiyah!"

"Oh, hi, Trevor." Daisy knelt on all fours beneath his sheets —*beneath his sheets*—and rummaged below his pillow. "I wondered if you were still home."

"You what?" Trevor choked, dropping the bat and staggering backward. The slugger fell to the floor with a thunk before rolling beneath the bed. "You hear that? That could've been your skull. What were you thinking?"

"That you wouldn't hit me?" She fluffed his pillow with both hands, her derrière, once again, aimed right at him.

Of course he wouldn't hit her. He hadn't been in a fight since high school, and he'd never hit a female in his life. All the same, having a "tooth fairy" pop up uninvited in his bedroom didn't exactly inspire warm fuzzy feelings. She'd have to be stupid to think he—Wait a second.

No way could a stupid person track him from his dig in Arenal, Costa Rica to his home in Elkhart, Indiana that fast.

Either she was a psychic psycho with limitless time and money on her hands, or she was working undercover for someone with an agenda. And there was exactly one person who not only hated Trevor enough to sic a pseudo-fairy femme fatale on him, but who also might have just enough analytical socio-anthropological skills to determine exactly what kind of woman he'd find irresistible.

Berrymellow.

Well, screw him. Trevor wasn't falling for the sexy tooth fairy routine. He couldn't believe he hadn't realized the truth sooner. It explained everything. Why else would an English-speaking blonde randomly appear on a dig in Central America? Alone, barefoot, and trying to confiscate his find? Sure, she'd thrown him off with her painted toes and fairy talk, but now he was onto her.

Or rather, now she was on his bed. No doubt intending to seduce him into confessing everything he'd discovered in Costa Rica, so Berrymellow could undermine Trevor's progress or steal his research outright.

"How did you get in here?" he demanded as Daisy fluffed another pillow. "And what in the world are you doing?"

"Me? What about you?" She rolled to her back and propped herself up on her elbows, her tanned skin in perfect contrast with the snowy white of his sheets. Her breasts pointed skyward and her head lolled just enough to expose the smooth curve of an eminently kissable neck.

Definitely his taste. And definitely trying to seduce him.

"I live here," Trevor reminded her, and then reminded himself not to be affected by wide eyes and enticing curves. His body ignored the order. "What's your excuse?"

"I looked for you in Arenal. You weren't there." She nibbled on pouty pink lips and glared at him through lowered lashes.

Fine. She wanted to play it like that, did she? Well, she could try to seduce him all she liked, but she wouldn't get any answers. In fact, two could play at this game. Let her see how she liked being on the receiving end of some ulterior-motive charm.

"No, I'm not there," Trevor agreed, letting his voice go low and rough. "I'm right here."

He kicked the door shut behind him. She jumped, the movement jiggling her in all the right places. But instead of giving him that wide-eyed ingénue stare, she now watched him warily, as though realizing the balance of control had just shifted from her to him.

Good.

Maybe having Daisy cavorting around in his bedroom wasn't a bad thing. Maybe this was his chance to figure out who she really was, what secrets she was after, and how to stop her dead in her tracks. Hey, maybe they could even have wild hot monkey sex before he turned her over to the police.

Trevor smiled. Daisy looked doubtful.

He stepped forward until his jean-covered knees brushed against the blue comforter. "When you saw Katrina at the airport, you're sure she didn't mention where she was going?"

"Nope." Daisy's eyes widened as though startled by the question. "She was rather… cold."

Cold was Katrina's middle name. Or maybe "smart ass". Either way, if Katrina didn't mention Elkhart before she took a late Spring Break, the only way Daisy could wind up in his bedroom was if she had another informant. Say, for example, a disgruntled professor armed with a staff directory.

"How did you find me?" Trevor asked, careful to keep his voice calm and modulated as he ran the tips of his fingers along the corner of the bed.

Her hazel eyes tracked his every movement. "I'm not supposed to tell, and you wouldn't believe me if I did."

"Try me."

Trevor leaned sideways, resting one hip against the mattress. What if she was Berrymellow's sister or girlfriend? Trevor had always assumed the putz lived with his mother and spent his Friday nights at home frying chicken, but he wouldn't put anything past him. Berrymellow was full of sleaze.

Daisy shifted her elbows, pushing her chest up even higher. "I said I can't."

Trevor forced an encouraging lift of the eyebrows.

She arched one of hers and stayed mute.

He tried a suave, you-can-trust-me stare.

Her eyebrow remained arched.

Fine. As she was apparently immune to his raised eyebrows and lingering glances, he'd have to try harder if he planned to throw her off balance enough to get to the truth. He prowled around the perimeter of the bed. He paused next to the pillows, looming over her, his zipper at eye level with her upturned face. She swallowed, but didn't blink.

"So," Trevor said, trying not to wonder what color lingerie she was wearing today. He was supposed to be seducing her, not seducing himself. "You're on a secret mission that involves invading wherever I sleep?"

"No," Daisy stammered, her head jerking to watch when he ran one finger along the edge of her pillow. "Well, yes, I guess. I'm a tooth fairy. Tooth fairies invade bedrooms."

Trevor propped his palm against the wall above the slatted headboard. He allowed himself a slow, predatory smile when Daisy's elbows slackened and the back of her head whooshed down onto the pillow, blonde hair fanning outward like an angel's halo. Her vanilla-cream scent spiced the air between them, sending the blood rushing faster through his veins.

"What I'd like to hear," he said, "is why you think I'll believe this drivel about you being the Tooth Fairy."

"Not *the* Tooth Fairy, *a* tooth fairy. It's a unionized conglomerate." Her chest rose and fell with each breath. "And you're right. I haven't been completely honest with you."

He inclined his head. "You think?"

"I'll tell you this much, since you already know I need that tooth." She stared at him for a second, gnawing at her lower lip as if about to give away the secrets of the universe. "I'm just an apprentice. I won't earn my wings until I make fairy. And I can't make fairy until I complete my apprenticeship successfully." She expelled a long breath. "Now do you see why it's so important I collect that tooth?"

"I do see why it's important you return to your home planet," he muttered, ready to give up on his whole seduce-the-sexy-spy plan.

Why did Berrymellow think he was this gullible? Tooth Fairy apprenticeship? Please.

Trevor stared down at the gorgeous woman in his bed and wished he knew the real reason she was there. What was her deal?

Maybe he should go with it. Act as though he believed her to get this over with. And as soon as he caught her contradicting herself, he'd point out the flaws in her story and force her to tell the truth.

"So," he said, trying for a casual tone. "You're an intern."

Man did he hope that was another lie. Having young, sexy interns in his bed looked shady during the professorial review process. Even if she'd been sent there by a colleague out to discredit him any way possible.

"If you're thinking I'm too old to be apprenticing, stop right now." Daisy's arms quivered at her sides, and Trevor realized he was still angled over her, one hand on the headboard and the other hooked on his belt loop. "There's nothing wrong with changing careers," she murmured, gazing up at him with cautious eyes. "Besides, it's not like twenty-seven-year-olds can't learn new tricks."

Twenty-seven. Thank God. His thirty-three no longer seemed ancient. Trevor leaned his thighs against the edge of the bed, expecting Daisy to jump up in alarm.

She didn't.

He smiled, making no attempt to hide his perusal as he swept his gaze down the length of her body.

The navy comforter lay bunched around her knees. The white cotton sheet came up past her waist. Her fingers clutched at the hem, but didn't tug it up higher. The little ivy-green dress stretched tight across her breasts. Her neck was bare, the pulse point there beating only slightly more rapidly than the shallow breaths escaping her parted lips. The pillows tilted against the headboard, her hair still fanned across them in seductive disarray.

Daisy lay in the center of his king-size bed, no longer propped up on her elbows. Her eyes were heavy-lidded and cautious, as if it were he invading her space and not the other way around.

In a flash, he ached to cover her mouth with his, as he'd sarcastically threatened to do when they'd spoken on the phone scant hours earlier. What had he said? That he'd show her what a real kiss was? The idea had never been so tempting.

Trevor eased down on top of the sheets. Her subtle vanilla musk rose to greet him. He inhaled deeply. From now on, he would forever associate the sweet scent with the soft heat of her skin. If only he could make her feel half the pull that he did...

"No wings tonight?" he asked softly, gliding the tips of his fingers across the curve of one bare shoulder, arrogantly pleased when a subtle trail of goose bumps marked his path. She was not immune to him either. "Weren't you wearing some glittery things the last time I saw you?"

Her neck flushed, although whether from the question or his touch, he didn't know. "Yes." A slight defensive tone tinged her voice. "I made them myself. Don't want the little tykes waking up and screaming, 'Hey, you're not a tooth fairy! You don't have any wings! Help, help, some lady's stealing my teeth!' and so on. That sort of scene could look bad to my supervisor during my post-apprenticeship review."

His eyebrows lifted in agreement. That particular concern echoed his professional life a bit too closely. He wasn't doing very well at keeping her off-balance if she was still thinking about work.

"So, explain this unionized conglomerate." He stretched out next to her, careful to stay above the sheets as he aligned the front of his body with the side of hers. He was inexplicably desperate to tangle limbs with her, but he wouldn't pursue that impulse until he trapped her in her lies and got to the bottom of this charade. "Until today, I thought there was only one tooth fairy."

She struggled for breath as if she, too, felt the searing heat wherever his flesh touched hers. Trevor struggled to tamp down a rush of desire.

"You'd be right in the sense that there's only one to a grid." She bit her lip again... and then licked it, watching him as her tongue left a trail of moist heat. "Kind of like Santa. He can't be everywhere at once, so he's got minions to help him."

"Santa has minions?" Trevor fought a smile, and allowed himself to rub his thumb against the warm flesh of her arm. His plan was working. Her story was ridiculous. He'd have her drowning in her own illogic any moment now. "What kind?"

"Elves or whatever." She stared up at him, not moving closer but also not moving further away. "If you want to be a tooth fairy, you've got to apprentice with an established one. The more prestige, the more clout, the better. Vivian is bad-ass, as far as tooth fairies go."

"Tooth fairies are bad-ass?" Trevor repeated doubtfully. "Can any gender be one?"

"Some are bad-ass," Daisy amended, shivering with every stroke of his thumb. "But no, they're all women. Can you picture a man in this outfit?"

Um, no, and Trevor sure didn't want to. He was too busy trying not to picture Daisy *out* of hers. Somehow he had to stay on track.

"How do you get to and from the people world?" That ought to trip her up.

"On the clock? We use Tooth Fairy Transporters for departure and homing rings for return travel." Daisy lifted her hands to show off a small silver ring. "I can use my where-frog, if I'm on my own time."

Werefrog? Like a werewolf, but... ribbitier? Trevor wasn't even going to ask. The woman had an answer for everything. But how far was she willing to go to sabotage his career?

He took hold of her raised hands. Sliding them above her head, he trapped her slender wrists against the soft pillow. With a slow, sensual, now-I've-got-you smile, he rolled on top, so that his body was flush against hers, thigh to thigh and chest to breasts.

Her body tensed. Her lips parted. Unchecked desire flickered in her eyes.

"What are you doing?" she whispered.

"Kissing you." He lowered his face to a breath above hers. "As promised."

He trapped her mouth under his, softly, gently. When she responded in kind, the urgency of their kiss increased in intensity. He gave up on gentlemanly restraint and slid his tongue between those delectably plump lips to taste her. Her teeth grazed against his tongue. His body tightened as he imagined her mouth elsewhere. His grip tightened on her wrists. She arched her back, pressing her breasts against his chest. He swept his tongue across hers.

She moaned into his mouth, and Trevor was lost.

He released her wrists to slide one hand beneath the small of her back and the other into the softness of her hair. She tasted like peppermint and springtime. He growled as she suckled his tongue, her mouth hot and sweet, her body warm and supple. The kiss lengthened as she arched deeper into his touch, her thighs trapped beneath his, his arousal straining between them. And then somehow, he ended up flat on his back with Daisy straddling his thighs, and *his* hands were the ones pinned above his head. When he opened his mouth to complain, she licked the edge of his jaw. He decided right then he didn't much care who was on top as long as she kept kissing him like this.

"Where's the tooth?" she murmured against his mouth between hot, wet kisses.

"Hmm?" He tugged his hands from her grip in order to glide them down the swells and hollows of her sides. He wanted to rip the devastating Tinkerbell costume from her body and slide his tongue along—

"The tooth," she repeated, pressing a hot trail of kisses along the line of his jaw to his earlobe. Her mint-laced breath steamed against his neck and tickled his stubble. "The one you slept on."

The one he'd slept—Ha! Trevor's mouth curved. He'd known Berrymellow wanted to sabotage the dig. Trevor just hadn't realized how far he'd go.

"It's not here," he answered with a chuckle. "Who keeps skeletons lying around the house?" He reached around her hips, eager to feel the warm curve of her ass against his palms.

Daisy splayed her fingers on his chest. Within a heartbeat, she pushed herself into a sitting position, muscles tensed, all traces of passion gone from her eyes. "Then what did you do with the tooth?"

"Put it somewhere you won't find it." He tried to stifle the frustrated desire still thrumming through his veins. He couldn't believe she'd been faking attraction throughout the entire makeout session—or that he'd forgotten he was supposed to be the seducer. "Do you really think I'd hand it over?"

"You *jerk!*" She punctuated the word with a fist to his solar plexus.

"Oof," he grunted, and grappled for her hands.

With a huff, she jerked from his grasp. She slid off the bed, stormed out of the room, and slammed the door behind her.

"Damn it." He leapt from the bed and stormed across the room. "Daisy!"

He threw open the door and gaped at the hallway.

Empty.

Trevor sprinted through every room of his house.

Living room? Empty.

Bathroom? Empty.

Kitchen? Empty.

He double-checked the alarm system. Still armed. *Still armed?* That meant nobody could come or go from any door or window without an ear-splitting screech blasting through the night and a round-the-clock operator calling to make sure he wasn't being robbed or murdered. As in, she wouldn't have been able to enter his bedroom undetected in the first place. Had he been sleepwalking? Sleep-sexing?

Trevor ran back into his bedroom and sniffed the rumpled sheets. Vanilla musk still spiced the air. Definitely not his scent. He was more an Axe body spray kind of guy. But then what had just happened?

Trevor slumped against the wooden doorframe and dropped his head in his hands.

Maybe *he* was the crazy one.

With her blood still pounding from Trevor's mind-melting kisses, Daisy belatedly materialized in her parents' spare bedroom, hoping they weren't waiting around to lecture her about disobeying the judge's custody declaration.

No such luck.

Mama sat on the corner of the mattress, polishing the silver star at the tip of her wand. Dad stood before the closed oak door, arms crossed, fingers drumming against his biceps. The warm sunlight filtering in through the window failed to brighten the atmosphere.

"Dad. Mama." Daisy forced her most innocent smile, hoping her wild hair, swollen lips and trembling body didn't scream just-been-kissed-senseless-by-a-human. "How are you?"

Mama aimed an absent smile at the incoming shaft of sunlight and went back to polishing her wand. Daisy's father, on the other hand, looked like he was prepared to flay her alive.

"Where have you been, young lady?" he thundered.

Several possible responses presented themselves as Daisy dropped her handbag next to her feet. Mentioning anything at all having to do with Trevor's scent and taste and touch, however, was quite out of the question. Everything, really, was out of the question.

Her father was Mr. Follow-the-Instructions. And the instructions had been "remanded into your parents' custody." Daisy could *try* saying she'd been there all along, out of sight trimming the hedges or something, but she knew better than to lie to an angry guardian angel.

"Uh, Earth actually." Daisy placed Bubbles on her shoulder and tried to arrange her posture in some semblance of nonchalance. "Just got back."

"Earth!" her father roared. "When you were placed into my custody, under my care, and commanded to go straight to my home?"

Yep, pretty much the reaction she'd expected.

"Figured we all needed some space." Daisy pulled at her dress to straighten the wrinkles. "I know I did."

Except there hadn't been much space between her and Trevor. Her skin still tingled from the remembered heat of his flesh against hers. Even as a memory, he still managed to steal her breath. Jerk.

"You intentionally disobeyed Judge Banshee's direct order." Her father kicked off from the doorframe and stalked toward her. "What do you have to say for yourself?"

Hmm. That she was incompetent, foolish, and horny for a human?

Daisy backed away from his livid expression until her bare shoulders hit the wall. "I just wanted to put things right."

"No excuse." Dad pounded a fist onto his palm. "Judge Banshee expected you to comply with her directives. So did I. Rules are rules, and they're meant to be followed."

Mama held her wand up to the window, as though checking for smudges in the sunlight. "But... did it work?"

Daisy slid down the wall, wincing as her shoulders hit the wainscoting. "I tried, but no."

Her father aimed a furious glance at her mother before focusing his scowl on Daisy. "You tried? Well, you can *try* to get yourself over to the Elders' High Court, because your attorney is presenting your case in ten minutes."

"What?" Daisy shot upright. "They said not until Tuesday morning… Crap, it is Tuesday morning." She reached for her shoulder, making sure Bubbles hadn't tumbled off in her inelegant scramble to her feet. "And I'm stuck with a yeti. Is there any way I can trade up for a vampire or maybe a nice basilisk?"

Dad's ivory wings unfurled even wider, casting the room in shadow. "Defense attorneys are assigned randomly in order to ensure complete fairness. If you don't want a yeti for an attorney, stop getting into trouble."

Since there was a rapidly diminishing probability of *that* happening, Daisy double-checked her handbag to make sure she had the LinguaLearner she'd had Maeve conjure for her. Thank Hermes it was still there, stocked with yeti language vocabulary builders.

Before her parents had a chance to impart any other words of wisdom, Daisy and Bubbles transported to just outside the open courtroom doors.

"NEXT CASE," bellowed the court gnome. "Pearly States v Daisy le Fey."

Crap. No time to confer with her lawyer. Not that she was fluent quite yet. Her stomach clenched. With luck, she'd be able to translate maybe half of what he said.

Sucking in a deep, calming breath, Daisy squeezed next to the big hairy attorney behind the defendant's table and prepared to listen carefully.

"D.A. Sangre," Judge Banshee shrieked. "Are you prepared to present the prosecution's case?"

"I am." D.A. Sangre's blood-red lips parted in a stomach-curdling display of teeth and fangs. Daisy imagined she was supposed to interpret the expression as a good-morning smile. Or not. "I call Jeremiah Lagobovid to the stand."

Daisy's shoulders tensed. Who in the world was Jeremiah Lagobovid?

"Urgh," her lawyer whispered in hushed tones. "Urrrrghhhh."

Crap. Daisy's limited vocabulary meant all she got out of that explanation was "he is an urrrghh." Note to self: invest in a conversation course.

She tensed as the soft slap of furred feet hopped down the aisle toward the witness stand.

Tall beige antlers jutted from the top of short, spiky hairs. Two long, flat ears, covered in the same white-dotted brown fur as the rest of his back, flopped at either side of the antlers. Downy, pure-white fur covered his face, belly, and forepaws. A tiny wet nose twitched below lidless black eyes as he leapt from the floor to the witness stand. Wiry whiskers sprang forth from both plump cheeks and a hint of strong white teeth flashed below the notch of his upper lip.

In this context, "urrrghh" apparently meant "jackalope". Which meant he was a representative of the Pearly States. Which meant his testimony was bound to be ugly.

D.A. Sangre nodded at the court gnome and a hologram of the infamous rock hovered before the jury. The two crumpled sticky-labels accompanied the display. "Mr. Lagobovid, do you recognize these items?"

His fleshy lip curled, revealing even more of his large front teeth. "You're looking at the 'tooth' Miss le Fey sent to the Pearly States via magic pouch."

"Exactly. I present the People's Exhibit A." D.A. Sangre's fangs glistened behind her triumphant smile.

Murmurs rippled through the courtroom.

"Jackalopes have been running the Pearly States since the dawn of time," Mr. Lagobovid said with a sniff of his little pink nose. "Miss le Fey is arrogant beyond the pale to believe us too foolish to recognize the difference between a rock and an incisor."

Daisy leapt to her feet. "I can explain—"

"Mr. Squatch, control your client." Judge Banshee banged her golden gavel. "The defense will have a chance for rebuttal once the prosecution is finished."

"Urgh!" The shaggy white yeti shoved Daisy back into her chair. "Urrrrrghhhh."

"Fine." The back of Daisy's head slumped against her chair. "Go on."

"Oh, I will." D.A. Sangre pointed a talon at the flickering image. "In no way does this abomination resemble a tooth. Miss le Fey presented an ordinary, fist-sized rock from the human world knowingly and maliciously, with intent to deceive and defraud the Pearly States, a highly-respected government body staffed by dentition experts like Jeremiah Lagobovid. Thank you for your testimony, Mr. Lagobovid. And thank you for bringing such shameless disrespect of Nether-Netherland authority to our attention."

"That's not true," Daisy whispered to Mr. Squatch, who held a furry finger to his lips and rose to his feet.

"Urgh," her lawyer began as he approached the witness stand. "Urrrrrghhhh."

Mr. Lagobovid jerked a floppy ear toward Judge Banshee. "Which means?"

The judge climbed atop her golden table to peer down at the witness. "Can you prove the defendant's act was planned?" she translated shrilly.

Daisy's spine straightened. Good question, Mr. Squatch.

"Planned?" the jackalope repeated to Mr. Squatch in a mocking lilt. "You expect anyone in this courtroom to believe she labeled and delivered an Earth-rock inside a Pearly States delivery pouch by *accident?*"

Mr. Squatch glanced over one hairy shoulder at Daisy, who motioned him back to his seat. Absolutely nothing Mr. Lagobovid said could help her. Even if he knew the truth behind the odd package, she'd get worse sentencing in the court of public opinion for believing the lies of a sexy anthropologist.

D.A. Sangre tore through her files. "I now call Vivian Valdemeer to the stand."

Oh, no. Daisy covered her face with her hands as Vivian was sworn in. Nothing said "goodbye, job" quite like your supervisor appearing in High Court to testify against you.

"Ms. Valdemeer." D.A. Sangre checked her notes. "You are one of the top-ranking tooth fairies in all of Nether-Netherland, is that right?"

"I am the highest-ranking, yes."

"And you recently took on the defendant as an apprentice, is that also correct?"

"Yes, it is." Vivian's eyes scanned the audience as though searching for something or someone. "Daisy is a joy and a pleasure to have in the office. She is naïve and ignorant of the rules and rigors of tooth-fairying. Under my tutelage, she can achieve great things. Daisy is both an eager apprentice and—"

"Ms. Valdemeer," D.A. Sangre interrupted with a snarl. "Miss le Fey is on trial for defrauding and deceiving a government body, not running for governor of Nether-Netherland."

"Urgh." Daisy's attorney patted her hand and grinned. "Urrrrrghhhh."

"Oh, dear, was I going on about Daisy again?" Vivian's eyelashes fluttered toward the crowd. "I just love her so much. She's highly competent in many ways, if not fairying. Bless her heart. She tries so hard."

From the furious expression on D.A. Sangre's face, Vivian might single-handedly save Daisy from this mess.

"She may be new," D.A. Sangre snarled, "but she's not untutored. Is Daisy aware of the Two Rules of Toothfairying?"

Her mentor smoothed flyaway hair from her face. "Of course. They're posted on placards throughout the office and marqueed on the bottom of all our training materials."

"Very well." D.A. Sangre gestured to the jury. "Please state those rules for the record."

"Rule Number One: Deposit a boon in place of the tooth. Rule Number Two..." Vivian cast an apologetic moue toward Daisy. "Keep human interaction to a minimum."

"Urgh," Daisy's lawyer whispered urgently. "Urrrrrghhhh."

"I don't know what you're saying," Daisy whispered back, "but this sucks."

"Keep human interaction to a minimum," D.A. Sangre repeated

smugly. "I submit exhibit B. Alarm records for Vivian Valdemeer's private office in Tooth Fairy grid 418."

Holy Hera, this was bad. Daisy slouched into her seat.

"An unauthorized teleportation attempt on the Tooth Fairy Transporter triggered the alarm on Monday evening. That's yesterday, Your Honor, *after* you'd delivered the defendant's injunction to remain with her parents." D.A. Sangre smirked at Daisy. "I'd like the jury to notice the destination shown on the logs. This is the residence of one Trevor Masterson, well outside the Central American grid Apprentice le Fey was to be servicing."

Mr. Squatch vaulted over the defense table. "Urgh! Urrrrrghhhh!"

"Sustained," shrieked Judge Banshee. "Mr. Squatch, return to your seat. D.A. Sangre, you will not present evidence of misconduct taking place subsequent to the initial charges. Jury, please disregard counsel's previous statements."

Daisy sank even lower in her seat. Sure. The jury would forget everything the D.A. just said. And a sphinx might fly out of her sphincter. Curse that D.A. Sangre! Well, if vampires weren't already damned.

Judge Banshee fixed her wild gaze on Mr. Squatch. "Care to cross-examine?"

Mr. Squatch shook his furry head with a defeated "urgh".

The D.A. swiveled toward the crowd, the slash of a victorious grin splitting her face. "Then I'd like to call Miss Helicon to the stand."

Daisy strangled on a cry of protest. Maeve? Maeve was a witness for the prosecution? Why hadn't she told her? Daisy's outrage sickened into defeat as she realized Maeve had no doubt wanted to discuss it at length. Unfortunately, Daisy hadn't exactly been hanging out at her parents' house as instructed.

Maeve trudged up to the stand, wings and muzzle drooping. Her pleading eyes met Daisy's in abject misery.

"Miss Helicon." D.A. Sangre strode forward. "Were you aware of Miss le Fey's attempt to defraud and deceive the Pearly States with a common Earth stone?"

"No."

Daisy's spine straightened in sudden hope.

D.A. Sangre scowled. "No, you were not aware of Miss le Fey's deception? I thought the two of you were best of friends."

"Yes, we're best friends." Maeve's lavender nostrils flared. "No, Daisy wasn't trying to defraud anyone."

"Is that right? Then can you tell us whether Miss le Fey made an unauthorized visit to earthling Trevor Masterson?"

Maeve tossed her head, violet mane flying. "No."

Daisy leaned forward, elbows propped on the table before her.

The D.A. bared her long, pointed teeth. "No, you refuse to disclose this information?"

"No, I can't say she did a single thing you're accusing her of. I don't follow her around on Tooth Fairy expeditions. I've got a job and a life of my own."

D.A. Sangre's skeletal fingers clenched her sheaf of papers. "Can you say with certainty that she did *not* visit human Masterson?"

Maeve snorted. "I can't say with certainty that she didn't jaunt to the North Pole to whittle toy trains with Santa's elves. Like I said, I wasn't with her."

"Urgh." Daisy's lawyer grinned at Maeve. "Urrrrrghhhh."

"Fine." D.A. Sangre threw her file folders back into her briefcase. "Did Miss le Fey say or do anything to give the impression that she interacted with one or more humans, while out on assignment or unauthorized visit?"

"Objection," Daisy called out.

D.A. Sangre whirled to face her. "On what grounds?"

"Uh…" Daisy faltered, sliding a desperate glance toward her lawyer, who just shook his head. "That I don't want her to answer?"

"Overruled!" shrieked Judge Banshee. "Answer the question, witness."

Maeve gave a low, whinnying sigh. "Maybe."

"Your Honor." D.A. Sangre stomped up to the golden desk, the heels of her thigh-high black vinyl boots clicking against the silver tiles. "If the witness refuses to comply with questioning, I will have no choice but to request a Truth Spell be employed."

Yikes! Daisy shot straight to her feet. A Truth Spell would cause far more damage than just proving a human glimpsed her. She made mad "go ahead" motions to Maeve.

"Okay, yes," Maeve announced. "Daisy was, er, seen by a human while on her mission."

A Cheshire smile curved across D.A. Sangre's narrow face. "And what was this human's name?"

"Um..." Maeve slunk a beseeching grimace toward Daisy. "Trevor?"

"Aha," D.A. Sangre crowed. "The very individual whose domicile triggered the alarm on the Tooth Fairy Transporter."

The crowd gasped in titillated satisfaction.

"Urgh," Daisy's lawyer gurgled. "Urrrrrghhhh!"

"Livinia Sangre," shrilled the judge. "The next time you mention an unrelated incident in this courtroom, you will be held in contempt of court!"

"My apologies, Your Honor," the D.A. purred, looking anything but apologetic. "I'm done with this witness. Counsel?"

Mr. Squatch moved to rise, but Daisy tugged on his matted pelt. She couldn't believe Maeve had managed to deflect the D.A.'s questions as well as she had. There was no point in pushing her luck.

"In that case..." D.A. Sangre stalked to the jury. "Today you have seen evidence that the defendant, Daisy le Fey, knowingly attempted to defraud and deceive a government body. Did she know she was supposed to collect a tooth? Yes, but she did not comply. Did she know she was not to interact with humans? Yes, and she went so far as to ascertain his name. That means *conversation with an adult human*, which is expressly forbidden to tooth fairies. Did Miss le Fey deliver the assigned tooth to the Pearly States? No. She delivered a rock. An ugly, grimy, misshapen rock. You have no choice but to find the defendant guilty of—"

"Wait!" Daisy cried. "This speech sounds suspiciously like... like closing arguments. Don't I get a chance to defend myself?"

Judge Banshee peered over the golden desk at Daisy. "Is there someone you can to call to the stand to refute these charges?"

Was there? Daisy racked her brain. She hadn't initiated contact with Trevor on purpose. He was supposed to be a child. And asleep.

When he wouldn't hand over the tooth, she'd been forced into trying to persuade him. But if she dared to press the point, D.A. Sangre's line of questioning might uncover the kissing—or worse, Katrina the ice pumpkin—and Daisy's hot water would get a whole lot hotter.

"No," she admitted quietly.

"Do you have concrete evidence to present that will mitigate the prosecution's claims?"

Daisy shifted in her seat. "Er, no."

Judge Banshee harrumphed. "Then Mr. Squatch will present his arguments once D.A. Sangre finishes hers. Carry on, Livinia."

Her yeti lawyer had to sway the jury? Great.

"There's no choice," D.A. Sangre snarled, pointing a long, white finger at Daisy while addressing the jury, "other than to find the defendant guilty as charged."

A shocked hush settled over the courtroom.

Mr. Squatch rose to his feet. "Urgh," he gurgled, casting a sweeping gesture around the courtroom, his voice deep and impassioned. "Urrrrghhhh." He patted the top of Daisy's head. "Urrrrrrrrr—"

Heavens and Hades! At least half the jury didn't speak Yeti and were frowning in confusion. The other half just smirked.

Daisy sprang to her feet.

"Look," she began. "Yes, I knew I was supposed to collect the tooth. That's what I was doing in that tent in the first place." She straightened her shoulders. "It's not my fault Trevor was awake when I arrived. It's not my fault he's an adult. And it's not my fault he wouldn't hand over the tooth. There's no provision demanding tooth fairies manhandle the humans or force them to relinquish requested specimens. So, I decided to return at another time in the hopes of greater success and minimal human interaction."

She gazed around the courtroom at all the wide-eyed faces. "When I did so, he claimed the tooth was fossilized within the rock. Seeing as I'd been transported to an archaeological dig, it seemed reasonable enough. In retrospect, I obviously should not have believed him. But nowhere in the training videos do *any* of the children lie about the location of their teeth to the tooth fairy!" Daisy turned to the jury. "I was wrong. I admit my gullibility. But I'm wiser now. I've learned not to trust humans. I can fix this. I *will* fix this." Daisy faced Judge Banshee. "If you give me a chance."

"A chance to what?" blurted D.A. Sangre incredulously. "Fetch the tooth and erase the human's memory?"

"Excellent suggestion." Judge Banshee slammed her gavel on the golden desk. "If we can eradicate these charges, there'll be less paperwork for everyone. Miss le Fey, you have your chance. Report here tomorrow morning with the results of your mission. If, at that time, the Pearly States are in possession of the exact tooth you were sent to retrieve, *and* the human has no recollection of any magical happenings, I will instruct the jury to devise a punishment less than or equal to six months' probation. But." Judge Banshee scrabbled on top of the desk until her shadow loomed across Daisy's face. "If you fail to achieve either of those objectives, I will recommend the jury to consider the full five-year sentence. And you will never make fairy."

CHAPTER 6

"What do you mean you don't have the laptop?"

Trevor had to remind himself that throttling grad students was expressly forbidden under the Anthropology Department's professorial guidelines. Even if Katrina had eloped with freaking Enrique Iglesias, the least she could've done was hand over the laptop to Alberto before heading on her honeymoon. "Every photo, every chart, every spreadsheet, every *everything* is on that hard drive."

"Not everything." Alberto tapped his cellphone against his chin. "What about the backups?"

"What backups?" Trevor asked sourly. "We never had cloud connectivity because there was no internet service at the dig, and the version on my flash drive is from just before my flight took off."

Alberto's face fell. "Oh, right. From before we transferred the photos. And before all of Katrina's data entry."

"Exactly. Without that laptop, we've got nothing."

"We've got our memories." Alberto offered a hopeful smile. "Does that count?"

"Count for what? Publishing? Sure, sure. I'll explain it just like that." Trevor leaned back in his swivel chair and propped his booted feet on his desk. "'Dear Editor, this article is only three paragraphs long and minus all supporting documentation because the details of the dig reside in the collective memories of my TAs and me.' They'll understand. No sweat."

Alberto fiddled with his backpack. "Prof, are you mad at me?"

"No, no, not at all." Trevor chucked his pencil across the room in frustration. The sharp graphite tip sank into the drywall partition separating his office from Joshua Berrymellow's. Good thing he hadn't had a baseball in hand—it might've gone straight through. "I'm angry with myself. I entrusted last-minute data entry to the one person who didn't make the flight home."

"Maybe she got side-tracked when she ran off with the hot chick."

"She didn't run off with the hot chick. The hot chick is here in Elkhart. If Katrina was home, she'd be in class today. Katrina is not in class."

"The hot chick is *here*?" Alberto glanced around with delight.

"*Concentrate.* Where might Katrina go?"

"Gotta be partying," Alberto said with a nod. "You know, live it up a little before the summer baseball team starts and all that."

Trevor's lungs filled with air and he let out a long, slow breath.

The situation could be far worse than a party-hearty grad student. And not just the ever-increasing likelihood that his job security was a thing of the past. After all, the only person that particular misfortune affected was Trevor himself.

But if Katrina wasn't running around the lush rainforest drinking Centenario rum and indulging in an off-season Spring Break with a hot-blooded *tico*—Trevor's feet slid off the desk and slammed to the floor. He'd never forgive himself if something happened to one of his students. Ever. As soon as Alberto left the office, Trevor was calling the Costa Rican authorities, just in case.

"Why, it's Dr. Masterson," came the ingratiating voice of the self-proclaimed master of applied socio-anthropology. "Fancy seeing you here."

"This is my office, you schmuck. Where else would I be?" If Trevor hadn't already speared his pencil into the wall, Berrymellow's stringy bolo tie would've served as a far more satisfying target.

The red-goateed professor slipped into the doorway, clicking his tongue. "I'm shocked you talk like that in front of your students. Dear me, what would the dean think?"

"Alberto, go. I'll see you in class." Trevor raised an upturned palm toward the door. "Don't want to warp your young mind with any more mean words like 'schmuck'."

"I've heard worse," Alberto said cheerfully. "That's why my *abuela* hates *reggaetón*. Daddy Yankee is always like, 'We peeps don't give a fu—'"

"Okay, that's great," Trevor interrupted, ushering him out the door. He swiveled to face Berrymellow, who edged a few inches backward as though he just realized he'd cornered a tiger in its lair. "What do you want?"

"The same thing you want, of course. Tenure. Security. Job satisfaction. A future." Berrymellow's wobbly chin lifted as he adjusted the strings of his tie. "Only one of us will achieve those goals, and unfortunately for you, that someone is me. I dropped in as a favor. A professional courtesy, if you will."

"Since when are you courteous?" Trevor leaned one shoulder against the doorframe. "Or professional?"

Berrymellow shrugged. "I wouldn't want to be you right now." He slithered into the hallway and tossed Trevor a self-satisfied smirk. "Don't be surprised if certain individuals take your 'situation' the wrong way."

"Whatever." Trevor slammed the door and headed back to his desk. "Wait, what situation?" Trevor pivoted on one heel. He stalked to the doorway, jerked the pencil from the wall, and threw open the door.

No Berrymellow.

What was it with people disappearing every time Trevor shut a freaking door?

At least this time there was a logical explanation. Muffled voices from Berrymellow's office indicated he'd crawled back under his rock. Wondering who he'd managed to lure into his dungeon for a chat, Trevor crossed his arms and decided to wait him out. He turned his mind to the other disappearing act in his life.

Last night defied logical explanation. Unless Trevor wanted to admit he might be a raving lunatic—and he did *not* want to consider this possibility—the only explanation he could come up with was that Daisy really was some sort of super spy. Why Berrymellow would've sent some kind of Black Widow / Splinter Cell against him, Trevor couldn't say, but how else could she have gotten past his motion-sensitive house alarm?

She could be here. Now. Watching him.

He peered down the hallway just in case. Ever since Daisy's disappearance, he'd been glancing over his shoulder, waiting for the other shoe to drop. Well, not literally. She didn't wear shoes.

Berrymellow's door swung open and the Anthropology department head strode into the hall.

"Ah, Dr. Masterson." Dr. Celine Papadopoulos tucked her briefcase under one arm and held out her hand. "Just the man I hoped to see."

As he shook her hand, Trevor's insides churned like saltwater taffy on a stretching machine. Dr. Papadopoulos was his boss twice over, being not only the head of the Anthropology department but also in charge of granting summer camp coach positions to staff members. "Why do I get the feeling this isn't a pleasant social call?"

If Dr. Papadopoulos had tried for a reassuring smile, she'd failed. "May I come in?"

"Sure. Of course." Trevor motioned her into the office and closed the door in case Berrymellow lurked in the hall. "What would you like to talk about?"

"First, let me say that I don't believe any of the rumors circulating around campus." Dr. Papadopoulos's manicured fingers slid through her short black hair as she sank into Trevor's black leather swivel chair. "The university's official policy has always been 'innocent until proven guilty,' just like a court of law."

"Until proven guilty," Trevor repeated blankly. He stood, facing his own desk, feeling very much like an eighth-grader called in front of the principal for unknown reasons.

"With budget cuts and limited faculty positions being what they are, we simply cannot keep individuals who reflect badly on the university. Founded or unfounded, public opinion drives our attendance, our standing, and our funding." Dr. Papadopoulos propped her elbows on Trevor's desk and laced her fingers. "I'm sure you understand."

Trevor crossed his arms and promptly uncrossed them, not wanting to appear defensive. Was this Berrymellow's barely-veiled threat? If so, the jerk could've included a bit more information with his warning.

"The semester is almost over," Dr. Papadopoulos continued, "and we will be casting our tenure votes the first Monday after end of semester. That is to say, two weeks from yesterday. As you are well aware, there is only an opportunity for one of our respected faculty members to achieve tenure at this time. As you may not be aware, budget constraints require me to limit next year's contract renewals. Due to the nature of the concern surrounding your recent student trip, I feel it only fair to warn you, the odds do not bode well in your favor."

No odds. No coaching. No tenure. No job. Trevor swallowed a thick lump of anxiety. "What, precisely, causes the department concern?"

Was it his casual repartee with his students? The informal collaborative methodology used in his classrooms? The unforgettable almost-kiss he shared with a certain unbalanced tooth fairy in the middle of a student anthropological dig? Thank God there'd been no hidden cameras during Daisy's in-home follow up visit.

Dr. Papadopoulos tilted her head to observe him. "As I said, I cannot believe that you would fabricate the results of your recent expedition in a misguided attempt to publish a sham 'discovery,' despite any professional jealousy you may feel toward Dr. Berrymellow."

"What?" Trevor choked out. The audacity of that sanctimonious bastard—

"Nor do I imagine for one second that you would resort to violence against any of your students simply for refusing to go along with any ill-advised plans you may have had for falsifying the nature, field notes and photography of the dig's alleged discoveries."

"Of course not!" He couldn't even believe his ears.

Had Berrymellow told the department heads that Trevor lied about the success of the dig and *killed* Katrina to cover it up?

Christ, that guy was a complete asshole.

All Trevor had to do was show Dr. Papadopoulos all the corroborating evidence, and—

Christ, that guy was an evil genius.

No Katrina, no laptop. No laptop, no proof. No proof, no job.

"I assume you are taking this matter as seriously as we are." Dr. Papadopoulos rose to her feet with a glance at Trevor's Wrigley Field wall calendar. "If you cannot present both your proof and your student before grades are due, I'm afraid we'll be unable to renew your contract. You understand."

She held out her hand.

Forcing a brittle smile, Trevor shook her hand and followed her out of his office. She strode down the hall, black pumps clicking on the smooth tile.

Trevor glared at Berrymellow's closed door. He should've stabbed the little bastard with his pencil when he had the chance.

Finally free of her hopelessly unmagical apprentice, head tooth fairy Vivian Valdemeer stirred the big black cauldron perched in the middle of her backyard and sniffed the steam rolling off the bubbling liquid.

Perfect.

She knelt at the pyre beneath the wide iron pot and conjured a small, ripe peach. Her ex-boyfriend might think he could resist renewing their one-time intimate acquaintance, but no man, woman, fairy or angel was immune to the galvanizing effects of the Himalayan Lust Charm.

He'd told her he wouldn't settle for less than the best. Guess what? Vivian *was* the best. Two months ago, she'd finally won Fairy of the Year—and A.J. *still* hadn't come crawling back as promised. Even when she'd taken his worthless daughter as her apprentice! But it was no problem. Vivian could fix that. After all, she was Fairy of the Year.

She lifted the peach to her nose and smiled. Was it selfish to steal A.J. back by magical means? Perhaps. But all was fair in love and war. As this situation was both love *and* war, she'd cast a new spell every week if that's what it took to win her ex-boyfriend back.

The words of the incantation flowed from her lips to surround the dewy peach with a shimmering glow. She dipped the fruit in a bowl of sparkling pixie dust, covered the soft skin with both of her hands, and concentrated.

Within moments, a thin layer of molten gold hardened around the peach.

Once the metal cooled against the warmth of her hands, Vivian opened her palms and peeked at her reflection in the gold-plated peach. A mouth-watering shiver of sexual arousal hardened her nipples and heated her skin. The charm worked even faster, even *better*, than she'd dared to hope.

With a flick of her wrist, Vivian conjured a black velvet pouch. She dropped the peach inside the narrow opening, pulled the silver strings closed, and clutched the pouch to her chest.

A.J. didn't have a chance.

She rose to her feet, still clutching the soft velvet pouch with both hands. The second Arabella disappeared to play fairy godmother, Vivian would be right there by A.J.'s side, ready to unveil the Himalayan Lust Charm and—

"Ribbit."

Ribbit? Vivian whipped around, her back to the steamy cauldron.

"Daisy." Great. Exactly who she needed to throw a big fat wet blanket over her favorite fantasy, just when A.J.'s surrender was finally within her grasp. "What are you doing in my backyard?"

"I'm concerned about the impact this latest turn of events may have on my career," the ex-neurophysicist replied, her rosy lips even poutier than usual. She carried her pixie dust pail on one arm, her oversize handbag on the other, and her where-frog atop one shoulder. "What are you doing?"

Preparing to jump your daddy's bones until he forgets about your mama seemed like the wrong reply. Vivian shrugged. "Just casting a spell."

"And making..." Daisy's button nose wrinkled. "Potato soup?"

"I'm multi-tasking," Vivian snapped, and whirled to stir the cauldron. Blast. She'd forgotten the damn soup while she was working on the lust charm.

"You're just so good at everything, magical or not," Daisy said with a little sigh. She was always so—so—*complimentary*. Disgusting. "Wish some of that talent could rub off on me. I've got to do the impossible. If I don't find that tooth tonight, I'm toast."

Vivian suppressed a smirk. "Oh, and make him forget he ever saw you. Don't forget."

That ought to be good. Indiana's pumpkin population would increase by one disgruntled professor, and Daisy would be in an even bigger mess than before. Arabella would run off to help her magic-challenged daughter, and Vivian would have A.J. all to herself.

"I—I don't think I can. That's why I'm here." Daisy nibbled her lower lip. "Do you think you could help me make a ForgetMe orb?"

A Grinch-worthy smile stole across Vivian's face as she choked with the force of her good fortune. ForgetMe orb, Himalayan Lust Charm... a science-nerd like Daisy would never know the difference until it was too late.

"I already thought of that, darling. I'm so glad you stopped by." Vivian held the black velvet pouch out to the clueless scientist, the golden peach warm and heavy through the thin fabric. A bit disappointing to hand over the charm to someone else, but she could make one for A.J. another time. The moment was too perfect. "I went ahead and whipped one up for you already."

"Really?" Daisy cradled the pouch in both hands. "How does it work? What do I do? I've never used a ForgetMe orb before."

Vivian gave her cheek a light pinch. "When the moment is right, pull the charm from the pouch and hold it out so both of you can see it. That's all."

Daisy frowned, no doubt racking her encyclopedic brain for footnotes on ForgetMe orbs. "I thought it was a spell. Don't I have to say 'Forget' or something?"

"Er, yes," Vivian agreed quickly. "Just make sure you're both looking right at the charm while you say it. That's the important part."

"Okay." Daisy's lips trembled into a brave smile. "Thank you so much. I appreciate all your help." She took a deep breath as though preparing to take a high dive into the ocean. "And I sure hope this works."

"Oh, it will." Vivian turned back to the cauldron to hide her mirth. "I promise."

CHAPTER 7

*D*aisy had never been in a room with so many human bones before. That is, unless the bones were inside living people. But these scattered bits and pieces that *used* to be people thinned the air and covered her flesh with goose bumps. The good thing about being the only breathing creature in Trevor's laboratory—well, except for Bubbles, of course—was that Trevor wasn't here to get in her way.

The bad news? None of the skeletons wore helpful name badges—not that she'd expected one to read "Little Angus", but come on. Was labeling a crime?—and she couldn't tell at a glance which teeth belonged to whom. Fabulous. In the interest of time, she'd have to collect them all and then return whichever ones the Pearly States didn't need. She gazed around, daunted.

And pray she didn't get in even more trouble for over-collecting.

If she'd known Trevor had a freaking tooth *fetish*, she'd've brought her Genetic Teradata Carbon Dentition Spectrometer with her instead of her mechanical wand and pixie dust pail. She'd never admit it in front of a Nether-Netherlandian, but science was often more useful than magic in situations like these. Especially when you found yourself scurrying around a strange laboratory, hoping the owner didn't drop in to distract you with his bone-melting kisses.

Bone-melting. Gross. She *so* did not want to go there.

With tiny, ginger steps, Daisy picked her way around the chilly laboratory and gathered up all visible teeth, stuffing them in the bright red Pearly States specimen pouch.

Three of the laboratory walls were made of grey concrete blocks, lined with a long, continuous work area. Miscellany crowded the countertops in layered chaos. How did Trevor find anything in all this mess? It would probably be weeks before he noticed any of the teeth missing. If ever.

Along one wall, floor to ceiling windows faced an empty classroom. All of the brown plastic chairs had cute little folding desks attached, and each row was up a little higher than the one before. A tall metal door stood offset to one side. Perhaps this was the way to Trevor's office. She'd better make him forget fast, before she started thinking dangerous thoughts.

Thoughts like: Trevor was a professor. He enjoyed an intellectual career like the one Daisy used to have. He taught people. He enriched lives. He enjoyed baseball. He seemed, when not lying about the location of baby teeth, like a good guy.

Thoughts like: Despite his stubborn antagonism regarding the tooth issue, there was no denying she turned him on. When he'd trapped her in his bed and pinned her wrists above her head, his body had presented her with hard evidence of his arousal. And much as she wanted to hate him for thwarting her at every turn—in her entire career as a neurophysicist, nobody had ever, *ever* thwarted her!—she couldn't deny the attraction was just as strong for her.

Thoughts like: Trevor was a human whose memories she planned to erase without permission using the ForgetMe orb nestled in her handbag. He would never forgive her if he knew. She wasn't sure she'd ever forgive herself. But nobody said she had to alter his brain the very second she saw him. Trevor was a man. Daisy was a woman. She could erase his memory *after*wards…

No. No, no, no. Bad Daisy.

She cut across the classroom, opened the door, and stepped out into the hall. More cold gray concrete block. Disgusting. This place could really use someone who knew her way around a magic wand.

"May I help you?" came a nasal voice from right behind her.

Daisy jumped, and turned to face the speaker. "Oh. Hi."

A medium-sized man with a medium-sized belly stood scowling before her. He rubbed a red mustache with his thumb and forefinger as he gave her the once-over. His lip curled.

He jerked his thumb over his shoulder. "Theater building's that way."

"I'm looking for Trevor Masterson." She did her best to ignore the redheaded man's continued smirk. "Do you know where I could find him?"

"Of course." He turned and started down the corridor. "My office is right next to his. We share a common wall."

Daisy frowned. A common wall? As opposed to an uncommon wall? She hurried after him, eager to see where Trevor worked when he wasn't in his laboratory or off in a tent somewhere. "Slow down, please. I'm... new here."

"Humph." Sneering Man rapped several times on the closed door. "Professor! Someone here to see you."

After a moment, the door opened.

Trevor stood before her, looking just as surprised and delicious as when she'd left him gasping on his rumpled bed sheets.

Dark stubble coated his angled cheeks. Taut muscles filled out the lines of his khaki pants and half-buttoned dress shirt. Intelligent brown eyes and curly black hair. Confusion gave way to suspicion as his gaze focused on her.

"You." The single syllable erupted from Trevor's lips with the venom of Medusa's snakes. "Both of you, conspiring together. I knew it."

Daisy stepped closer. His eyelashes were just as long and beautiful as she remembered. "Hi, Trevor."

Sneering Man frowned. "You let your students call you by your first name?"

"Oh, it's okay," she assured him. "I'm not a student."

"Berrymellow." Trevor reached past him and gripped her by the upper arm. "Go away. I'll deal with you when I'm done dealing with *this* imposter."

"Imposter?" Sneering Man's hard green eyes turned calculating. "If you're not a student, what are you?"

"Daisy," Trevor commanded, his fingers tightening on her bicep, his hand as warm and strong as when he'd captured her by the wrists the night before. "Do not even attempt to hide the truth. He knows quite well what you are."

"Ohhh." The man tossed Trevor a knowing smirk. "It's like that, is it? And on school grounds, too. Very naughty."

"It's not like anything," she muttered as Trevor tugged her forward, scowling at both of them. She wondered if the still-smirking man was Trevor's boss.

"Right." Sneering Man extended one hand. "Interesting to meet you, Miss... Daisy."

Trevor jerked her into his office before she could take the proffered hand.

Not wanting to get Trevor in worse trouble with any rudeness on her part, Daisy poked her head out the doorway and waved. "You too, Barry Manilow."

The man gagged against his skinny little tie. "What?"

"*Out*," Trevor roared and slammed the door in his face. He dragged Daisy to a wing-backed chair facing the desk and shoved her onto the seat cushion without letting go of her arms. "You may be surprised to learn," he bit out, "that I have bigger fish to fry than dealing with my coworker and his accomplice. At the moment, I'm more concerned about Katrina than whatever plot you and Berrymellow cooked up to sabotage me."

"Katrina?" The word squeaked from Daisy's mouth and she winced.

Oh, crap. While she was over at Vivian's asking about the ForgetMe orb, she should totally have come clean about Katrina the ice pumpkin. Vivian would've known what to do. She might've even turned her back into a human and whipped up another orb.

Trevor's jaw fell open. He released Daisy's arms and knelt at eye-level in front of her chair, face twisted in suspicion.

"I was wrong," he said. "Either Berrymellow is more ruthless than I ever imagined, or you are far too devious to be a garden variety spy.

I'm only going to ask this once." His jaw clenched and then unclenched. "Did that schmuck send you to kidnap Katrina?"

Daisy gave her head another shake. Definitely not. She'd never met Sneering Man before in her life, and would never have kidnapped anyone. Unless, you know, they morphed into an ice pumpkin on a Central American runway.

Trevor was silent for a moment, as though weighing the likelihood of Daisy's honesty. His dark eyes narrowed. "Do you have any idea where Katrina is? Any idea at all?"

Daisy couldn't stop herself. She blushed.

"I knew it!" He sprang to his feet and jabbed a finger in her face. "You did something to her. You talked her into going somewhere. You —you're keeping her someplace. Somehow. For some reason." He paused. "Okay, none of my theories are very well thought out. Regardless of interdepartmental rivalry, I can't believe Berrymellow would go so far as to—never mind. None of that matters right now. Just tell me the truth. Where's Katrina?"

Daisy chewed her lip. She hated lying, but she couldn't tell him the truth because humans weren't supposed to know about—wait. Sure she could. She was going to erase his memory in a few minutes anyway, wasn't she?

"In Nether-Netherland." She closed her eyes and waited for the backlash.

Nothing. The ticking of a distant clock was the only response.

She opened her eyes. Trevor wasn't there. He was lounging against his closed door, one ankle atop the other, arms crossed, brows raised in disgust.

"Oh, really?" he asked, his tone harsh and sarcastic. "Are we back to that again?"

"It's true." She rose to her feet. "I'm not supposed to talk about Nether-Netherland with humans, but I don't see the harm at this point. Here, I'll prove it." She opened her handbag and tilted it toward Trevor's desk. "Come on out, Bubbles. I want you to meet Trevor."

Bubbles tumbled from the bag and landed on a sheaf of papers. With a soft ribbit, he leapt from the desk to the windowpane and nestled against the glass.

"What is that?" he demanded. "A toad?"

"Frog," she corrected. "Where-frog."

"What's that supposed to prove? That you're friendly to animals?"

"That I'm a fairy! Er... but off-duty," she added quickly. "Earlier, I got caught up in the moment."

"You're no more a fairy than I am. But don't worry. I wouldn't kiss you again if you paid me."

"I—I wouldn't pay you," she snapped and then grimaced. *I wouldn't pay you?* Was that the best comeback she had? Criminy. At least she hadn't added, *I'd kiss you for free.* She leapt up from the metal chair and scowled at him. How come she could only think of incisive, clever retorts when it was far too late to use them?

"Fine." He retrieved the cellphone at his side, sliding his finger across the screen to conjure a number pad. "If you're not going to tell me where Katrina is, I'm calling the police. They'll get it out of you."

Police? She stumbled backward. Oh, no. She only had one ForgetMe orb in her handbag, not a whole squadron of them. But if she could use it on Trevor in time, one might be enough.

"Wait," she choked out, scrambling for her bag. "I've—I've got something else to show you."

His finger paused over the numbers. He glanced up, eyes hard and cold. "This better be good."

She fished inside her bag until her hand closed around the soft velvet pouch. Her trembling fingers tugged at the scratchy ribbons until they loosened. She slipped one hand into the pouch and scooped up the ForgetMe orb. The hard round ball was big and heavy and cold against her damp skin.

With a deep breath, she thrust it in front of her chest with both palms, holding her hands flat so the charm rested halfway between them, directly within both their lines of sight.

"What *is* that?" He leaned forward and squinted. "A golden peach?"

Daisy frowned and looked closer. Weird. It really did look like a golden peach. The sight of which, for some reason, kind of turned her on. Nonetheless. She could analyze her fits of random horniness some other time.

"Forget," she commanded, lifting the charm higher. "Forget. Forget. Forget."

Like magic, Trevor's eyes unfocused and glazed over. Wait. It *was* magic. God bless Vivian for helping her out of this jam.

"Forget what?" he asked, low and husky. The very timbre sent a warm shiver of impending wickedness skittering down her spine.

"F-forget... me," she stammered. Her arms, oddly weak and languid, seemed unable to keep the charm aloft. "Forget you ever saw me."

Trevor lifted his hands to his chest and slowly, painstakingly, unfastened the topmost button on his deep blue shirt. "Why would I want to do that?" he asked. Another button came free.

And another.

"Uhhh," she faltered. She hobbled backward. Not to put distance between them, but because her leg muscles had gone inexplicably limp, trembling with the mere task of keeping her body upright. "Because I asked you to?"

Even as the words tumbled from her mouth in a strange, smoky whisper, she knew she didn't mean them. She didn't want him to forget. She wanted to give him something to remember. A part of herself. Or rather, all of herself.

Something was seriously wrong with the ForgetMe orb.

She brought the golden peach under her nose and gave a little sniff. Peach blossoms and sunshine. The subtle scent sent her blood rushing to the surface of her skin, flushing her cheeks and neck, and sending sharp pangs of need into her belly. Why was she getting turned on by metal fruit?

While coherent thought was still at least somewhat possible, she rubbed the golden peach against the side of her dress as though polishing an apple, and then peered again at its reflective surface.

An even stronger wave of white-hot desire coated her belly like lava bursting from a volcano. She clutched her trembling thighs together. The peach fell from her hands and rolled beneath the desk, taking the last of her self-control with it. She risked a glance at Trevor.

Mistake.

His button-down shirt lay at his feet in a forgotten heap. He yanked off the white cotton t-shirt in one quick movement, whipping the soft fabric over his tousled head and flinging it against the far wall.

Without taking his molten gaze from hers, he set to work ever so slowly removing his belt, sliding the strip of smooth brown leather from his khakis loop by loop. His attention was complete, the deep brown of his eyes intense and unwavering. If he'd forgotten anything, it was the bit about him wanting her to go away. In fact, she couldn't quite recall any of the reasons she'd had for not acting on her own attraction to *him*.

"I can't explain it," he said now, his voice low and urgent, "but if you don't touch me, right this second, I might die."

Daisy gulped. Was it positive or negative that she felt the same way?

The ForgetMe orb seemed to be malfunctioning. Without its magic to rein in their runaway libidos, there was nothing to stop them from acting on their desire. Except Daisy's professionalism, of course. No sleeping with humans. She could follow that simple rule, couldn't she? Maybe?

But with naked desire blazing through her veins and Trevor kicking off the last of his stubborn pant legs on the other side of the office, it was really hard to work up any desire for chastity. And speaking of really hard...

Completely bare and fully aroused, and with every inch of his mind-melting body exposed to her starving eyes, a slow, sexy smile spread across Trevor's chiseled features. Her limbs twitched in response, as though aching for her to toss herself into his waiting arms and beg him to slake the desire thrumming deep in her—

"Come." He prowled closer, arms outstretched. "I want you."

Daisy nodded weakly. She could certainly see that. And Venus above, she wanted him, too. She wanted his mouth on her shoulder and on the base of her throat. She wanted his tongue along the side of her neck and down the curve of her back. She wanted his hands grabbing her to him and forcing her close while he slid their bodies together.

As if reading the capitulation in her eyes, he was right in front of her, his breath on her cheek, his hands fisted in her hair, and his hard arousal against her belly.

She dug her fingers into his waist, sucking in a shaky, Trevor-scented breath.

Tilting up her face, she dragged her parted lips across the scratchy line of his jaw, reveling in the harsh, helpless sensation of stubble against sensitive skin. She could *feel* her lips reddening, swelling gloriously against his rough heat. She imagined the same reaction throughout the rest of her body, her skin flushing and heating in blatant arousal.

From the erratic beating of her heart and the throbbing dampness between her thighs, she wasn't sure how much longer she could fight the effects of the spell—or if she even wanted to. Every nerve in her body screamed at her to give in, to submit, and to seize.

She coasted the tip of her tongue along the hard, masculine path from beneath his ear down along his jaw. He was coarse and salty and delicious. She licked him again, darting her tongue across the prickly surface. She couldn't imagine why she hadn't tasted him sooner.

The scratchy hair on his legs rubbed her thighs as she rotated her hips against him. He let out a ragged groan. Her muscles quivered and clenched in anticipation and she pressed herself tighter against his hard length.

His body shook in response, muscles trembling, as if only the force of his will kept him from turning the temptation into reality. She told herself that he was smart to hold back, to prolong the exploration time before acting on desire, but the tightening of her skin betrayed the truth. She wanted him badly. And she wanted him now.

"I've been thinking about you all day," she breathed against his skin, her mouth traveling from his jaw line to his cheekbone.

"I've been thinking about you since I met you," he purred, his voice a bass rumble as he nibbled along the circumference of her ear.

She sank against him in surrender. The answering pressure of his body flattened her spine against the wall. The scent of arousal clouded the air. If they didn't make love soon, the flimsy material of her dress might spontaneously combust, forcing their naked limbs together at last.

If the almost painful hardening of her nipples was any indication, she couldn't wait to feel the wiry hairs on his chest against their aching peaks, the scratchy stubble of his face between her breasts, every hot inch of him between her thighs.

Even so, she couldn't make love to him as anyone except who she truly was.

"I—I really am a tooth fairy," she confessed, as soon as she remembered to breathe. He continued to nip at her ear. "Well, apprentice tooth fairy. And not a very good one. Quite bad, actually." His tongue licked against the corner of her mouth and she could feel her explanation fading into incoherency. "I'm competent at analyzing brain patterns and multiplying matrices and easy stuff like that, but I'm hopeless at magic," she managed to add, despite the fact that his fingertips had just found her straining nipples. "I didn't make this spell, I want you to know. I thought it was something completely different."

"Mmm." His murmur came from between steamy, open-mouth kisses, his breath caressing the side of her neck. "I do like good girls." He mouth rubbed against her shoulder, nibbling and licking her exposed skin until she moaned with pleasure. "But I love bad girls."

He reached behind her and tugged at her form-fitting dress. His hands skimmed her sides and back as if searching for buttons or zippers. Tiny lines creased between his eyebrows and his gaze turned beseeching.

"How does this come off?" He stole another searing kiss before she could reply. "Show me."

"It's magic," she admitted. Suddenly desperate to be as naked and vulnerable as he, she stretched her arm toward the handbag on the desk and grappled for a pinch of sparkly clothes powder. She may not be able to work a proper wand, but she could at least get in and out of her uniform. "Watch," she commanded, startled that the smoky, teasing voice she heard was her own.

With a slow, seductive smile, she sprinkled the magic glitter over her torso. The little green dress vanished in a shimmery poof. She stood before him, naked and wanting.

"Wow." He closed the distance between them, his smooth, hard flesh unbearably hot against hers. "I need some of that."

"I need some more of *this*." She gripped his hair with her fingers and ran her tongue along the top edge of his lower teeth. He captured her mouth with a growl.

His hands framed her face, trapping her lips beneath his as their tongues touched and licked and mated. She sagged against the wall, her legs incapable of holding her weight. He caught her to him. Somehow he made her feel sexy and desirable and protected all at the same time. She wrapped her arms around his neck and kissed him. Her nipples hardened even further as her breasts rubbed against the hairs on his chest. He nudged his knee between her thighs, entwining their legs.

She gripped his taut biceps, drowning in the illicit pleasure of his kiss. She had wanted him from the beginning. Wanted him more and more with every stolen glance. She had dreamt of this moment. The golden peach might have sparked their lust into action, but this feeling of contentedness and rightness was all him. All *them*. Together.

Without breaking the kiss, he lifted his knee, slightly, now a little more, until the edge of his leg rubbed the responsive wetness between her thighs. She rode against his leg and nearly doubled over from the intoxicating pleasure brought on by his touch.

His smile was infectious. She collapsed against his shoulder, then arched in pleasure as he dipped his head to suckle one of her nipples. One of his strong hands curved to cradle the back of her head, his thumb gently caressing her cheek. Still suckling her nipple, he lifted the other breast, bringing it flush with his cheek. As if her every secret desire was written on her face for him to see, Trevor rubbed the sensitive skin against the rough planes of his jaw, suckling one nipple while teasing the other.

"If you would've been a good boy and given me the tooth when I first asked for it," she whispered against his tousled hair, "I might've done this sooner." She slid her palms down the warm muscles of his back, then forward along his waist until her knuckles nudged against the throbbing erection burning between them. She closed her fingers around the shaft, squeezing and stroking, matching the rhythm of his mouth on her breast.

He shuddered, gasping against her flesh and grazing her nipple with his teeth.

"Oh, yeah?" He noticeably reined in his passion. "Well, if you would've stayed a few minutes longer in my bedroom, I would've done this." He leaned sideways and swept an arm along the cluttered desktop, knocking everything to the carpeted floor in a jumble of colored pens and textbooks. His blinking telephone fragmented on impact.

He kicked the mess out of the way. With an expression alarmingly close to mischievousness, he hoisted her up and sat her on the edge of the desk.

His eyes met hers. "I've been dreaming of this moment since I met you."

Rough palms widened her quivering thighs. Still holding her legs, he leaned forward until her breasts flattened against the warm wall of his chest. His shaft rubbed against her curls, first lower, now higher, wetting them both.

He peppered a trail of kisses along the line of her brow, around the rim of her ear, down the curve of her neck, along the edge of her shoulder. Daisy's body had no choice but to arch into his touch.

"Just in case you don't forget this... this interlude after I go, remember that you took off your clothes first," she managed, gasping as his hands closed around her breasts, his tongue laving between them. "This was all your idea."

He grinned up at her from the direction of her nipple. "Believe me," he said, coasting skilled fingers between her legs and along the slippery perimeter of her heat. "This is the only idea I've had since I met you."

"Same here." Her eyes fluttered with pleasure. At least she wasn't the only one struggling to fight an impossible attraction.

At her words, he swelled against her, hardening even more.

She reached one hand down to stroke him and he responded in kind. Her muscles clenched around his slick finger, his thumb teasing exactly the right spot. Thanks to an unexpected Himalayan Lust

Charm—and Trevor's talented, wicked fingers—she was close to coming with or without him. She guided him closer, lifting him so their bodies aligned, the scent of sweat and arousal spicing the air.

"You'd better hurry up if you want to do this with me," she said, her voice uneven and her tone pleading.

"Mmm," he murmured again. "I was just waiting for you to ask."

In the space of a breath, he buried himself inside of her. She gasped with the sudden, heady fullness of him and locked her legs around his rocking hips. His sweat mingled with hers as the wet sounds of lovemaking grew faster and more urgent.

He tilted her backward, propping her against his arms and supporting her head with his hands. His mouth moved from her forehead to her lips. He varied his long and short strokes with the rhythm of their kisses, as though willing himself to take it slow, and tilted his head back to watch her expression. When their gazes met, he smiled, knowledge of her reciprocated lust for him glittering in his eyes.

The pace increased with the pounding of their hearts, their bodies slipping, rubbing, stretching.

"I don't care if you *are* a tooth fairy." His voice was husky with desire. "Right now, you're mine."

At those words, she came, contracting helplessly around him. With his gaze locked on hers, he thrust deeper, faster. And with a delicious shudder, he climaxed with her.

He held her for a moment, his lips to her hair, their muscles still throbbing gently.

She tightened her hold around his neck. Had that really just happened? She rested her cheek against his chest. His heartbeat thrummed beneath her ear. She tried to calm her own racing heart. He felt so good in her arms. As if he belonged there. As if they belonged together.

With a smile, he collapsed onto the desk, his chest to her side. He rolled her into his arms, one leg slung possessively over her thighs. His heart now pulsed against her breast, their skin slick and warm and their bodies wholly satisfied. She sighed contentedly. Even without a lust charm, she couldn't imagine ever getting enough of being in his arms.

At that moment he mumbled something incoherent, but she was far too sated to bother asking what he'd said. She stroked her fingers through his hair. Right now she didn't care about conversation. She just cared about being here, in his arms.

Happy.

CHAPTER 8

$\mathcal{T}$revor wasn't sure which roused him from his stupor—a crick in his back from balancing on the hard desk, or the stiff nipple poking his ear.

Maybe the nipple.

With a satisfied smile, he slowly breathed in. Vanilla, peaches, and the thick musk of sex. Mmm. Raising his head, he rested his chin on a soft, flat belly and gazed across the office. His favorite wrinkle-free dress shirt was balled and forgotten in the corner. A ruined telephone lay jumbled against the wall. His khakis were nowhere to be seen. He tilted his head toward the window.

A shiny little frog gazed back. A *were*-frog, if he remembered correctly.

Dawning horror chipped away at his fleeting contentment. Slowly, carefully, Trevor peeled his face from the warmth of naked skin and stared at the curvy woman stretched across his desk, her fingers twined with his. He jerked his hand free. Did he really just have mind-blowing office sex with Daisy the undercover spy? With his parking-lot-view window blinds wide open?

"What did you dope me with?" He scooted his naked ass to the other side of the desk and glared at her. She crossed slender arms over bare breasts and declined to answer. His voice shook in anger. "Ecstasy? Acid-laced Viagra? Some fast-acting street drug I don't even know about?"

"I didn't give you anything! All I wanted to do was..." Her eyes widened in horror and she clapped a hand to her chest. "Maybe it didn't malfunction. Maybe I brought the wrong *charm*. Maybe it was a..."

Charm? She *had* drugged him. With some sort of pharmaceutical love potion. Er, *lust* potion.

Trevor vaulted from the desk. All the honest attraction he'd felt for her before she'd pulled this stunt disappeared with his rage at being *forced* to act on his baser instincts. His fantasies were meant to be just that—fantasies. He should get to decide whether they became reality. Not her. And definitely not like this. He stalked over to the window and jerked the blinds closed. The tiny frog hopped off the ledge in surprise.

By now, Berrymellow would have live video feed of Trevor's latest professorial indiscretion streaming straight to YouTube. Maybe that'd been his plan all along. Clever bastard.

"Now that I'm myself again..." He leaned against the window frame and willed his brain to catch up to the rest of him. "Why don't you tell me what's really going on here?" Arms crossed, he speared her with his most cutting glare. Probably he should throw her out.

And then probably he should find his pants.

"Uh..." Still sitting on his desk, she blushed—everywhere, damn her—and then covered her face with her hands.

Please. His arms locked tighter across his chest. He wasn't buying the innocent-little-me act. Not while she was still naked, her breasts and belly still sheened with his sweat, the scent of their lovemaking still spicing the air. Christ, that had been amazing. But what kind of spy seduced people for a freaking *living*? He shook his head. Unbelievable. Well, at this point, quite believable. "Well?"

With a soft sigh, her hands fell from her face to her lap. "What do you want to know?"

"What do I want to know? Everything!" He gaped at her. "Who *are* you? Why are you following me? How did we end up naked in my office in the middle of a workday? What the hell did you do with Katrina?"

Daisy gave a weak smile, but the expression didn't reach her eyes. Her shoulders slumped forward. "All very good questions."

"Wonderful." His fingers clenched in exasperation. "What are the answers?"

"Answers a human could understand? The thing is..." Her voice trailed off. She rolled forward, tumbled to the floor in a gust of papers and crumpled post-its, and army-crawled beneath his desk.

Trevor shook his head. This was one weird chick, even for a spy.

She backed out from under the desk on all fours, giving him a view guaranteed to haunt his dreams for the next thousand years. Damn it. How could he be so pissed off and turned on at the same time? She *played* him. She *used* him. She was not to be trusted.

"The thing is, I don't have any answers. At least, not any good ones." She looped the strap of a large handbag over one shoulder and sighed. "I'm just thankful the effects are starting to wear off or I'd never make it back in time."

"You admit drugging me? And refuse to explain why?" He eyed her bag suspiciously. "What else do you have in there, Tasers and tranquilizers?"

Lower lip trembling, Daisy looked the perfect picture of misery. Trevor didn't buy it for a second. Nobody *accidentally* infiltrated your dig, broke into your armed home, and had sex with you in your office. Nothing about her made sense.

"I'm so sorry," she said, forehead scrunched, eyes downcast. "About everything. I don't have any drugs or—or Tasers. I'm not even sure what that is. I don't even have a ForgetMe orb, which is the one charm I actually meant to bring." Her eyes hardened. "The only thing I apparently do have is what I now suspect to be a wickedly potent Himalayan Lust Charm. See?" She pulled a fist-sized gold-plated peach from her handbag.

He reared back. Of course he could see. Just the sight of the damn thing sent blood rushing through his veins. He jerked his gaze away. He wasn't horny anymore. He was livid.

As an anthropologist, he should be analyzing which aspects of the classic symbolic peach triggered his animal instinct to mate with such urgency. As a professor drugged by a pseudo-fairy, he should be furious she kept sidestepping his questions. As a man who just had sex with a near stranger on top of a desk, he should at the least be concerned about wild, unprotected sex in the workplace. Although part of him wasn't sorry at all that it had happened, this was not something he could just let go. He reached for her.

She backed against the desk. Wariness and desire clashed in her eyes, as if she wanted him but was afraid he might throttle her at any moment.

Good. She should be. He might throttle her yet. But first...

His hands trapped her wrists high above her head. This time, he didn't bother being gentle, and his fingers dug into her skin until she whimpered. The peach fell free, plopped down on top of the scattered telephone and rolled across the floor. If she wanted physical contact, he'd give her physical contact. He leaned in to punish her with a bruising kiss. Or maybe he was punishing himself.

With every ounce of self-control he possessed, he forced himself to freeze when his face was mere millimeters from hers, when their breath filled each other's nostrils, when their mouths were almost touching. Now what? Even without the effects of the peach clouding his judgment, his body and his brain still had different opinions on what course of action he should pursue next.

Once was enough, he told himself desperately. *You don't want to kiss her anymore. You want to kill her. Walk away while you still can.*

But how could he toss her aside when her every glance, her every shiver, her every touch started an inferno of lust raging through his veins? That infernal peach hadn't made him do anything he hadn't already been fantasizing about. Even without it, he still wanted her.

"Um, Trevor?" She twisted her wrists against his grip.

"What?" he rasped, his mind fighting a losing battle with his body. He tilted her over the desk, aching with renewed desire

"I—I can't do this. Can't let you do this. Er, again." Her breath came quick and ragged, her arms limp. "Much as I'd like to stay, I—I— Goodbye." She jerked her fingers to her face, touched her lips to a small silver band, and disappeared with a tiny pop and a shower of sparkling glitter.

Literally freaking *disappeared*. What the hell?!

Surprise and gravity united to destroy Trevor's balance. His arms swiped at thin air just before he crumpled face-first into the corner of his desk and thumped to the floor in a boneless heap. When his head —and heart—stopped pounding, he opened his eyes.

The ceiling looked the same. It was probably the only part of his office left intact. The only part of his entire life still intact. Groaning, he mentally checked himself for cuts or broken bones. If he'd cracked a rib when he landed on the broken phone, he was going to be pissed. And if a disappearing fairy meant his *mind* was cracked, he had even bigger problems than he did an hour ago. His left eye was rapidly swelling due to its unforeseen encounter with the corner of a desk, but it had been perfectly fine at the moment when the girl he was kissing vanished without a trace.

Either the woman was as magical as she claimed, or he ought to consider seeking some serious therapy. Maybe both.

He rolled into a sitting position and gingerly touched the base of his eye. Enormous. Great. Now he could either swing by a pharmacy for an eye patch or he could walk around campus with Berrymellow spreading rumors that a hundred-pound fairy managed to clock the big, bad baseball coach in the face.

Trevor paused with one hand cupping his eye. Berrymellow might be the more practiced socio-anthropologist, but a paleo-anthropologist Trevor was no stranger to hypothesizing from evidential clues.

If Daisy could disappear in a shimmering burst of fairy dust... if her clothes popped on and off with a magical flick of her wrist... if she'd been just as helplessly horny as he, thanks to something called a Himalayan Lust Charm... then maybe, *maybe*, she wasn't a Splinter Cell after all. Maybe Berrymellow had nothing to do with her arrival or subsequent actions. Maybe Daisy really was a tooth fairy.

Trevor sighed. Or maybe he was going quietly insane.

But then, he wasn't the only one who saw fairy people. Alberto and Katrina both interacted with Daisy in Costa Rica, albeit briefly. Even that prick Berrymellow spoke to her, saw her here, in his office. If

Trevor was going crazy, there had to be a hefty helping of group hypnosis floating around. What he needed was—

A soft *ribbit* interrupted his racing thoughts.

One hand still cupping his throbbing eye, he poked his head up over the desk ever so slowly, hoping against hope he'd heard incorrectly.

No such luck.

From his seated position on the glittery base of what had to be a hot pink magic wand, Bubbles the lime-green were-frog looked Trevor in the eye. And belched.

When Daisy materialized on her best friend's front lawn wearing nothing but a knockoff handbag, she'd sort of hoped Maeve wouldn't be standing right in front of her.

"You know what?" Maeve said with a swish of her tail. "Just in case I'm forced to testify again, I'm not even going to ask."

"Good call." Daisy reached into her purse for a handful of shimmering clothes powder so she could at least not stand around naked. It was one thing for a winged horse to be au natural, but an apprentice tooth fairy? Not so much.

Dress back on and sack of teeth in hand, she reached to her shoulder for her where-frog.

No Bubbles.

"Ah, crap." She closed her eyes. Today couldn't get any worse. "I forgot Bubbles."

Maeve nickered in disbelief. "You've had Bubbles since you were four years old. How could you possibly misplace him?"

"It wasn't a matter of me forgetting Bubbles so much as nobody forgetting anything." Daisy's fingernails curled into her palms. She couldn't wait to hear Vivian explain that one. "I needed the orb in order to have Trevor forget, but he got naked and remembered everything, and since Bubbles was on the other side of the room when Trevor put me on top of his desk so we could—"

"Like I said." Maeve sidestepped backward. "Not even going to ask. Too busy grazing. La, la, la. Goodbye."

"Hopefully Bubbles can hang tight until I can go fetch him." Daisy rifled through her bag. No magic wand, either. Cripes. Guess she really did show up with just the skin on her back. Well, and with a bagful of random teeth nestled in her handbag. "Will you give me a ride to the office, please?"

"No. I'm grazing." Maeve gnawed at some grass as if to prove her point. "Why don't you use your Tooth Fairy ring? Isn't that how you got here without Bubbles?"

"I can't. It's a homing ring, not a universal teleporter. It just brings me back to Nether-Netherland if I get stuck somewhere else. I chose here instead of the office for obvious reasons."

Daisy pasted on her most winning smile, even though the word "office" would conjure completely new images in her brain forevermore. Images involving intense brown eyes, hot sticky sex, and a warm stubbled cheek resting against her chest. Too bad none of it had been of his own free will.

A rancid what-have-I-done feeling curdled in her belly. "How am I going to earn my wings if the Elders find out I just had wild, sweaty office sex with a human?"

"I can't heeeeeaaar you..." Maeve sang out. She backed up a few more steps, turned and ambled off, presumably to entertain Katrina. Or escape Daisy.

She sighed. Just as well. Unlike the unfortunate Himalayan Lust Charm incident, Katrina was one hundred percent Daisy's fault. Maeve was helping. Like a good friend. The least Daisy could do was not drag Maeve down with her.

Resolute, Daisy kicked at the springy grass with her bare toes and made her way toward town. Every step reminded her more and more acutely of her missing where-frog.

Poor Bubbles. Too bad he didn't have a homing ring of his own. He might be afraid for his life, surrounded by all those bones and books and safety goggles. Daisy grimaced. Once she got him back, he'd be in a mood for weeks. Probably pop her to the wrong places on purpose. She'd have to think of a really good way to make it up to him.

And she'd have to think of a great way to make it up to Trevor.

Her stomach clenched in self-recrimination. He was an innocent human. He hadn't understood what was happening, hadn't known who or what she was, hadn't wanted to make love. She'd meant to erase his memory—and likely he wouldn't have been thrilled with that either—but she *hadn't* meant to spring a Himalayan Lust Charm on him.

That he'd admitted already possessing an attraction toward her was gratifying and all, particularly when she'd found him sexy (if infuriating) right from the start. But outside of the sexually charged tussle in his bedroom, he hadn't acted on his feelings. Thanks to the ForgetMe spell that wasn't, he'd been forced to. Before she wiped his memories, she had a lot of explaining to do. Even if he wouldn't remember it, she wanted him to know she never meant to cause him any harm.

The person who she needed to confront first, however, was Vivian Valdemeer.

~

"What's going on in there?" Relentless banging accompanied Berrymellow's words. "Open up! I heard a crash!"

Galvanized, Trevor yanked on his t-shirt and dug his crumpled khakis out of the trash, cursing when his feet got tangled in the pant legs. Could the situation possibly be any worse? When Daisy'd set out to screw him six ways to Sunday, she'd done it in every sense of the word. His dig was screwed. His career was screwed. The safety of his students was screwed. His professional reputation was screwed. *He'd* been screwed. Or, at least, magically encouraged to do the screw*ing*. And he couldn't forgive her for any of it.

"If you don't open the door right this second," Berrymellow shouted, "I will march straight to Dr. Papadopoulos and tell her you're perpetrating violence on the student body or, worse, engaging in hanky panky at work."

Trevor fumbled with his zipper. Hanky panky was worse than

violence? Nice. Glad to see Berrymellow had his priorities straight. Why couldn't *he* have been the one plagued by tooth fairies?

Giving up on his shoes, Trevor ran his fingers through his messy hair and failed to smooth any of it down. Screw it. He twisted the lock and cracked open the door. "What?"

Berrymellow stumbled backward. "Your eye!"

Shit. In his hurry to clothe himself, Trevor had completely forgotten his charming new shiner. Yet another lovely gift from the friendly neighborhood fairy. "I, uh... walked into a wall."

With a snort of derision, Berrymellow recovered his poise. For a moment. He shoved open the door and immediately went slack-jawed at the state of the office.

Trevor rolled back his shoulders and tried to see his workspace through Berrymellow's eyes. It wasn't pretty.

Phone, broken. Desk, cockeyed. File folders, red pens, safety glasses, student papers, scattered willy nilly. Shiny gold glitter still shimmering in musk-scented air. Royal blue dress shirt, pooled in the corner. Left loafer, lying against a potted plant. Right loafer, nowhere to be seen. Mysterious female "student," likewise absent. Professor Trevor Masterson, bruised, sock-footed and decidedly rumpled. Poking from the professor's back pocket, some sort of hot pink magic wand. North-facing windowsill, garnished with a tiny green were-frog.

The plus side was that even a renowned socio-anthropologist like Berrymellow couldn't possibly guess the events that transpired on this side of their common wall.

"Where's the student?" he managed to choke out, still gawking at the room. "The little blonde?"

"What student?" Trevor kept his manner indolent and his voice curious. "I don't see a student."

"Don't play games with me, Masterson. Did she hit you? Why did she hit you? Were you exhibiting inappropriate behavior?"

Trevor almost laughed. If he ever laid eyes on Daisy again, he'd exhibit inappropriate behavior aplenty. First thing he planned to do was inappropriately wring her little neck. But he couldn't exactly share those plans with Berrymellow.

Instead, he waved a hand at the windowsill. "I turned her into a frog. You caught me."

Berrymellow loosened his bolo tie and squinted toward the window. "Bullshit."

"Huh." Trevor lifted a shoulder. "Guess there's no getting anything past you."

"This isn't over, Masterson." With a huff, Berrymellow turned on his heel and pranced out of the room, no doubt jetting off to type up a socio-anthropological special report for the Weekly World News.

Trevor placed the pink wand on top of his desk and rooted underneath for his other shoe. Bingo. Sitting right next to that weird golden peach. He pulled both out from under the desk. He slid his foot into the shoe.

The sight of the peach no longer sent him into a hormone frenzy. The intoxicating garden-of-aphrodisiacs scent no longer pulsed from its smooth surface. Weird. Maybe the effects only worked when Daisy was around? Just in case, he couldn't leave it here for his boss or Jeb to stumble across.

He pulled himself to his feet. Maybe Daisy the sexy siren had disappeared from his life for good this time. Limping a bit from his hard landing, he headed to his lab. He might be able to regain a morsel of equanimity if he made progress on his research. The one and only safe zone left in his unraveling life.

Or it was, anyway. The big steel door to his laboratory stood several inches ajar. And he always closed the door.

He rushed inside to inspect the lab's treasured contents. The teeth from every single one of his recent expeditions were conspicuously AWOL. Berrymellow wasn't above sabotage, but a stunt like this could only have been perpetuated by one relentless, scheming blonde. Trevor slumped against the steel counter. The least she could've done was leave money behind.

Enough to compensate for the job she'd just helped him lose.

~

Daisy pushed open the front door to the Tooth Fairy Regional Headquarters and wheezed. Her mentor's flowery perfume swirled in the air like dust motes in a windstorm. She couldn't control an impromptu coughing fit. Perhaps excess eau de toilette was Vivian's low-tech version of an intruder alarm.

Before Daisy could catch her breath, Vivian swept into the lobby with raised brows and pursed lips.

"Finally," she said, with a brief close-mouthed smile. "How did it go?"

"Fabulous," Daisy said guardedly. "Until the end."

She stared at Vivian, hyper-conscious of the fact that her mentor was the one soul capable of granting her deepest desire… provided Daisy did nothing to jeopardize that relationship. The last thing she wanted to do was antagonize the one person who could help her, but if Daisy didn't stick up for herself, who would? With a deep breath, she rolled back her shoulders and stared her mentor in the eye.

"Why did you give me a Himalayan Lust Charm?"

"Did I?" Vivian's features smoothed into the perfect appearance of confused innocence. "I must've handed you the wrong pouch. What a silly mistake. I do hope it wasn't a bother. Did you bring it back?"

"Did I bring it—" Daisy choked in disbelief. Her voice rose until it cracked. "No, I didn't bring it back! And of course it was a bother." Not that Daisy could perform a competent spell of any kind herself, mind you, but she certainly recognized the difference between Trevor losing his memory versus Trevor losing his mind. "What were you doing with a Himalayan Lust Charm in the first place?"

Vivian's smile froze. Her gaze narrowed and hardened. "My love life is none of your damn business."

Daisy's lips parted but no sound escaped. Of all the responses she'd expected—reproach, accusation, outright lies—a casual admission of having created the charm and unflinching admission of planning to use it herself were the last things she'd imagined coming out of Vivian's mouth.

Maybe Daisy had misjudged her. Maybe even someone as talented as Vivian Valdemeer made mistakes once in a while.

After all, her apprentices' success or failure impacted Vivian's reputation as a mentor, too. She would have no reason to intentionally sabotage Daisy's would-be career. And she hadn't tried to lie about possessing the lust charm. Daisy appreciated honesty. And dearly hoped she wasn't the only one who occasionally made extremely big mistakes.

Besides, hadn't Vivian been the one to champion Daisy when her mother had barged in and tried to get her fired? And defended her in the courtroom? Now that she paused to think it through, Vivian had stood by her side through a whole lot of hassle. It would be the biggest mistake of Daisy's life to destroy her own career for refusing to forgive someone else's goof up.

"Okay," she said slowly, once it became clear no further commentary was forthcoming from her mentor. "Fair enough. Your private life is your business. But I'll go elsewhere for another ForgetMe orb."

"Agreed. See that you do." Vivian disappeared in a glittery burst.

Daisy trudged into her office, her guilt and frustration doubling in size. She may not have lost her job (yet) but she'd certainly lost the easy working relationship she'd once shared with her mentor.

Now who would make spells for her?

Maeve could conjure non-magical things like handbags and LinguaLearners, but her hooves prevented her from creating charms, like love spells and ForgetMe orbs. And Trevor and Katrina both still needed one. ForgetMe orbs, that was. But without Bubbles, how was Daisy going to get Katrina back to Earth anyway, with or without her memory?

As Daisy threw herself into her chair, her handbag thumped into her lap.

One thing at a time. At least she finally had the teeth. She jerked open a drawer to grab a Pearly States delivery pouch. Empty. Freaking empty. She'd used the last one to deliver that stupid rock and hadn't had time to order more. She'd have to *walk* the damn teeth to Headquarters. What was one more humiliation after a day like today?

When she stalked from her office into the next room, the gilded frame of the wall-mounted Mortal Locator caught her eye. Stupid thing. She still couldn't believe it had complicated her life twice—once by tripping the illegal transportation alarm and later by giving D.A. Sangre more fodder against her in court.

Daisy paused. How had the D.A. known, anyway? Did the Mortal Locator keep usage records?

She changed course and strode closer to its swirling surface. She'd only ever seen the Mortal Locator utilized to, well, locate mortals. What command would let her access its internal settings?

"Uh... Settings," she guessed. Nothing happened. "Preferences." Still nothing. "Menu. Options. Configuration. Choices." More nothing. Her forehead banged against the cool surface. "Help me out here," she muttered.

And the glass sparkled to life.

She jerked her face from the mirror just as "Help Menu" marqueed across the top, followed by "Would you like to: Reset into original condition? Locate a mortal? Access activity logs?"

Daisy breathed at her good fortune. "Activity logs."

The heading flashed to "Location Request Logs" and the submenu became "View Request History" and "Request Processing Rules".

She bounced on the balls of her feet. "Request Processing Rules."

"Current Settings," the mirror proclaimed. "Auto-send all location requests to the Tooth Fairy Transporter. Copy all log files to Vivian Valdemeer."

To Vivian, not D.A. Sangre? Well, Daisy supposed that made sense. The D.A. no doubt subpoenaed the logs for evidence. Just like she'd subpoenaed Maeve.

Before the choices faded from the mirror, Daisy altered the configuration settings so activity history was only stored locally and the alarms were deactivated. There. Now she could use it without being spied upon.

Time to visit the Pearly States.

CHAPTER 9

a tall, gangly jackalope with big teeth and even bigger antlers loomed from behind the Pearly States' customer service counter. "May I help you?"

"Yes, please. I'm a tooth fairy and I'd like to turn in some teeth." Daisy upended her bag and coughed as enamel dust plumed into the air like smoke from the Arenal volcano.

The tip of one long furry ear curled downward. "Why are they in your purse and not an official vial?"

"They wouldn't fit."

"Then why didn't you transport them via Pearly States standard issue magic pouch?"

"I ran out." She fought the urge to kick the counter. "Are you going to take them or not?"

His ears twitched as he thought it over. "Whose are they?"

Daisy's neck tightened. Ugh. The question she'd been dreading since the moment she realized she couldn't find the Angus tooth and she'd have to take them all.

"It's hard to say with absolute certainty," she hedged. "Empirically speaking."

He gaped at her, horrified. "You don't *know?*"

"Well, at least one belongs to my assignment. 'Angus, age 8.' Human archaeologists regularly steal teeth. I don't know which is which, so... Here they are."

The jackalope's whiskers trembled in bureaucratic dismay. "Miss le Fey, this is highly irregular!"

"I know, I know. But look." She flattened her palms on the counter and leaned forward. "Doesn't the Pearly States utilize skeletal thermo-enamel dental imaging in conjunction with human history micro-holograms to verify the chronology and source of all incoming specimens?"

His tiny pink eyes blinked in confusion. "Well, yes. We've got a station for that in the back office."

"Then you'll figure it out." Daisy looped her purse back over her shoulder. "Just tell me where to sign and I'll get out of your hair."

"Hare?" He frowned, pink eyes narrowing. "Is that some kind of joke?"

"No, I didn't mean hare-hare, I meant hair-hair." Biting back a curse, she held up both palms in surrender. "Never mind."

He glared at the pile of teeth and then at Daisy. "What's your badge number, fairy?"

"Four eight six three two."

His paws flew over the keyboard. "Says here you're in a spot of trouble regarding a tooth you claimed to collect, but didn't."

"It's right in front of you." She gestured at the pile. "Think they'll drop the charges?"

"Maybe. If you return the right tooth."

Daisy cast a nervous glance at the miniature tooth mountain she'd dumped from her purse. "I'm positive it's there. Can you check for me real quick? Please?"

"No." He scooped the teeth into a series of pouches. "I'm a customer service representative, not a Dental Chronology Diagnostician." He punched a few keys and the pouches disappeared. "Go home, fairy. We'll send the Elders' Minions if there's a problem."

And wouldn't that be a delight.

Daisy pivoted and headed for the exit. Fabulous customer service. No wonder tooth fairies dealt with these jokers through disappearing delivery pouches. Somebody ought to write a letter to upper management.

The doorway was within another stride or two when Daisy caught a glimpse of a long marble table piled high with forms.

Maybe she *could* file a complaint. It was practically her civic duty.

Daisy inspected each meticulously labeled stack until she came upon the General Complaint packets. Twenty-seven pages. Lovely. They were probably hoping if they made it hard enough, nobody would bother complaining. Well, too bad. Scientists persevered.

She grabbed a feather pen from the floating repository and settled into a plastic seat. Using her Encyclopedia of Human Slang and Culture as a makeshift desktop, she attacked the first page.

Name, Daisy le Fey. Occupation, apprentice tooth fairy. Superior, Vivian Valdemeer. Beat, Central America Grid 418. Height, five foot three. Weight, one hundred and—weight? Daisy scratched out her response. What in Hades did body dimensions have to do with anything? All they really needed was contact information and customer comments. Annoyed, she flipped through the stapled stack until she got to the actual complaint box on the last page. Figured.

Suggestion for improvement? Quit making such stupid forms.

Daisy poised her pen over the comment block and contemplated her words.

"Dear esteemed members of the Pearly States advisory board," she began. "I have recently become embroiled in a legal situation due to difficulties inherent in the collection of an assigned tooth. My supervisor provided the name and pertinent details of the owner (Angus, age 8) and personally adjusted the Tooth Fairy Transporter for the appropriate address. Although the location was correct, I arrived in a tent, not a bedroom."

She shifted in her seat. Considering the heat level of recent nights, perhaps it was just as well she hadn't first met Trevor in a bedroom.

"As it turns out, the person asleep on the tooth was not the tooth's owner. Furthermore, said owner was not present at the scene, as he happens to be dead." Daisy went to nibble the end of the pen and choked when the feather coated her tongue.

Gagging, she pulled a long quill hair from her mouth. Gross.

"I propose that checks and balances be put into place to prevent other apprentice tooth fairies from running into troublesome situations similar to mine. I further suggest the Pearly States stop collecting teeth from dead people."

Daisy signed her name and returned to the customer service counter.

"I have a complaint." She pushed the papers across the counter to the same churlish jackalope.

"Well, we're experiencing a delay." He tossed the stapled pile over one shoulder onto a teeming bin of other forgotten stapled piles. "As you can see, there's a bit of a backlog."

Several forms teetered on the edge of the bin before tumbling to the floor in a flutter of crumpled papers. Daisy gritted her teeth. "When do you suppose mine might be attended to?"

The jackalope shrugged. "Twenty-four to forty-eight."

"Hours?"

"Months."

"Right." Daisy gave up and headed for the door. Enough time-wasting.

She had to tell the court the tooth-retrieving mission was successful—whilst praying to the gods that they never learned about the shenanigans with the naked human—and then hurry back home to figure out what to do with an ice pumpkin named Katrina.

Good thing Daisy disappeared when she did, or Trevor would have to add murder to his ever-growing list of professorial misconduct.

His fists clenched at his sides, he stalked back to his ruined office. Fuming.

He couldn't believe she'd stolen his teeth. He couldn't believe she'd put him under some crazy lust spell. But most of all, he couldn't believe he'd just gotten naked with an actual freaking tooth fairy. Who could disappear into thin air.

Trevor snatched the wand from the desk and the frog from the windowsill and glowered at both.

"I wish I knew where the hell that woman was right this second." He scowled at the stupid wand and the tiny blinking frog. "I really would turn her into a toad." He closed his eyes to savor the image. "But first, I'd drop in on *her* house, make a mess of *her* job, screw up *her* life. I wish she was right in front of me so I—"

With a soft pop, Trevor's cramped office was replaced by a massive, rolling meadow of bright orange pumpkins. A large red-and-white barn floated overhead, flanked by ivy-laden cottages. Also floating.

"Holy shit," he breathed.

"Let me guess," came a dry female voice from behind him. "This isn't Angus."

Trevor whirled to see an open-mouthed Daisy standing next to a lavender horse. A lavender, winged horse. Make that a lavender, winged, *talking* horse. Had reality merged with Disney?

"He's kind of cute for a human," the horse stage-whispered. "I can see how you might get sidetracked into illegal office sex."

He blinked.

Cheeks infusing with color, Daisy studiously avoided eye contact. "Shut up, Maeve. Stay out of this."

Maeve. Wow. The horse had a name. And attitude.

Trevor shook his head, trying to control his tumbling thoughts. Forget about being angry over missing teeth. Think like an anthropologist. This was the most incredible—and incredibly bizarre—opportunity to observe a wholly foreign culture. He could publish an entire set of Trevor Masterson encyclopedias. If he had proof. And material.

Start with the talking horse. Of course it had a name. Even Mr. Ed had a name. The world over, most high-functioning, socially communicating creatures identified themselves in some manner, names included. Why wouldn't that phenomenon be true in—in—wherever he was?

He cleared his throat. "Uh, where am I?"

"Nether-Netherland," supplied Maeve with a horsy snicker. "How'd you get here if you didn't know where you were going?"

"Look who he's carrying." Daisy pointed to the tiny green frog sunning himself on Trevor's hand. "Bubbles brought him, the traitor."

"Nether-Netherland. Okay." Trevor frowned as the implications multiplied in his brain. "Is this where you're keeping Katrina?"

Maeve whinnied. "Is *that* why you're here?"

Daisy's gaze finally lifted from Bubbles to Trevor. She gasped. "How'd you get the black eye?"

"Lost my balance when you pulled your disappearing act. And you didn't answer my question." He glared at Daisy. The horse—Maeve—sidestepped out of the way as though he might be able to shoot lasers with his eyes. "Is Katrina here or not?"

"Well... yes," Daisy answered, cheeks flushing anew. "I'm so sorry. She—I—we ran into difficulties in Costa Rica and I brought her here until I could figure out what to do. I still don't have an action plan. I'm no good at spells and I—"

He nearly choked. "You seemed plenty good at them back in my office."

Maeve's snort sounded suspiciously amused.

"I didn't *make* that one." Daisy's eyes glistened. "I didn't even know I had it. I thought it was something else, and I... Oh, Trevor. I'm sorry about that, too." Her gaze dropped. "I really am. If I could make it up to you, I would."

"By what, stealing from me?" His lip curled. "I saw the lab. Thanks for dropping by." He shifted his weight, wishing there was some way to cross his arms without snapping the wand or crushing the where-frog. "You're unbelievable. You tampered with my discoveries. You abducted one of my students. You drugged me for sex. I think you're sorry, all right. A sorry excuse of a person. You're a thief, a kidnapper, and a—a—seductress."

A strangled cry of outrage burst from Daisy's throat as her gaze snapped back to his. Before he had a chance to rephrase his comeback a bit less provocatively, Daisy snatched the black handbag off her shoulder and whirled it at him full strength.

Screw being nice to her.

Before the bag could bean him in the face, Trevor aimed the bright pink wand at the incoming missile and called out "bippity boppity boo" in his smarmiest, most condescending tone.

With a flash of light, the bag morphed into a large leather pumpkin and thudded to a stop at his feet.

Trevor staggered backward. "What just happened?"

"You turned a purse into a pumpkin." Maeve tapped at it with one hoof. "Well done, human. Your magic skills are on par with Daisy's."

His frustration mounted. He shoved the wand in his back pocket so he wouldn't be tempted to turn the smirking horse into a pumpkin, too. As if sensing Trevor's volatility, Bubbles the where-frog leapt from Trevor's palm and disappeared into the grass.

Maeve cocked her head toward Daisy, who stared at the ground for a long moment before speaking.

"Look." Her voice was scratchy and defeated. "I said I was sorry, and I meant it. I know that's hard to believe right now. I imagine it's equally as tough as finding yourself in Nether-Netherland unexpectedly. But, honestly? The only thing I can do is take you home."

"Take me home?" Trevor repeated in disbelief. "And leave you free to flit about ruining lives? Not hardly." He gestured overhead. "Sure, if you hadn't disappeared from my office in a puff of smoke—"

"Glitter, most likely," interrupted Maeve.

"—glitter, I would have a hard time wrapping my brain around this... unanticipated turn of events." He shifted his gaze from the floating barn to Maeve the talking horse. "Okay, I give. I'm still having a hard time. Why is that building floating? What are you planning to do with all those teeth? Do the snozzberries taste like snozzberries?"

Daisy crouched next to a cluster of pumpkins. "What are snozzberries?"

Ill-advised attempt at sarcasm. He shook his head. "Let's go back to basics. Why do you keep stalking me? What happened to Katrina? And why is that horse talking?"

Maeve sputtered. "I'm no ordinary horse. I have wings. Just like—"

"Like Pegasus, whose hoof created the fountain of muses after he sprang forth from the still-warm body of Medusa," he intoned in his lecture-hall voice. "I get it."

"Holy Hippocrene," Maeve gasped. "He knows the history of my ancestors. He's my love match!"

Ignoring them both, Daisy continued sorting through the pumpkins.

His jaw tightened. "I know the history of everybody's ancestors. I have a PhD in paleo-anthropology and fifteen years of field experience." He paused in shock as the meaning of her words sank in. "Are you telling me the ancient legends that shaped the culture of man from the hominids to the Romans are all based on actual fact?"

"This is Nether-Netherland," Maeve explained. "All religions are valid here."

"Prof," called out a suspiciously familiar voice. "Is that you?"

"Katrina?" He shielded his eyes from the bright yellow sun and glanced around the vast field of green grass and orange pumpkins. Daisy stepped forward with one of the larger gourds cradled in her arms. Carefully, she set it on the lawn before him. He stepped away. "Katrina, where are you?"

"Down here." The voice came from within the large, candlelit jack-o'-lantern in the grass at his feet. "Hiya, Prof."

Trevor fell to his knees in front of her and gaped.

Her square-cut teeth twisted into a grimace. "I'm the one dressed like a talking pumpkin. Oh, wait. I *am* a talking pumpkin. Are you here to save me?"

CHAPTER 10

*A*lthough she enjoyed a man on his knees as much as the next woman, Daisy had the sneaking suspicion that if she didn't get Trevor out of her front lawn on the double, her professional life was about to take an even bigger dive.

She hadn't counted on her personal life blowing up at the same time.

The moment "Bubbles, get your shiny green butt over here!" shot from her mouth, two familiar silhouettes soared in from the sky. An impromptu parental visit. Daisy tried to force a smile. Yay.

"Hi, sweetie," Mama called out with a cheery wave.

Her father, however, took one look at the motley tableau and rolled his eyes heavenward.

Daisy happened to feel about the same. She took a deep breath. "Dad. Mama." She gestured at the kneeling man deep in conversation with a jack-o'-lantern. "You might as well meet Trevor."

"*The* Trevor?" With a squeal of delight, Mama rushed over, grabbed him by the collar, and hauled him to his feet. "Oh, he's cuuute. Well, except for the black eye. At least he's not a troll."

"He's not cute." Dad's wings twitched. "He's human. A troll would be an improvement."

Daisy gritted her teeth. At least they hadn't questioned the talking pumpkin.

Twisting, Trevor extricated himself from Mama's grasp and angled his head at her parents. "Interesting. It seems everyone in Nether-Netherland has wings." He slanted a pointed glance toward Daisy. "Well, except you."

"You don't say." She glared at him. Jerk.

He tilted his head back toward her parents. "Are you both tooth fairies, as well?"

Mama gasped. Dad scowled. Maeve laughed so hard she farted.

"Just little ol' me," Daisy interrupted before anyone could fly off the handle. "And I'm still an apprentice. Mama heads the Fairy Godmother Committee. Dad's a bigwig in the Heavenly Alliance of Guardian Angels. Maeve is in air traffic control."

Attempting to exude nonchalance, she herded everyone further from the pumpkin patch before Katrina could pipe up.

Trevor's gaze darted from Dad's thick, white-feathered wings to Daisy's wingless back. He speared her with a doubtful glance. "You're half angel?"

Maeve snorted. "You believe in fairies but not angels? Get with the program, buddy."

"I believe in angels," he protested. "I just didn't think they interacted much with, say, members of the Fairy Godmother Committee." He cocked an eyebrow at Daisy. "And I doubt real angels act like you."

Daisy's face burned, but her mouth was retort-less. He was right. Most angels weren't thieves and kidnappers and seductresses. Accidentally or otherwise.

"Believe me." Mama rubbed a palm over Dad's bare chest. "We interact often."

"Too much info." Daisy made time-out signs with her hands and wished she were invisible. Or adopted. Could the situation get any more awkward? "Let's pretend we're normal people meeting under normal circumstances. Mama, meet Trevor. Trevor, meet Arabella le Fey. Dad, meet Trevor. Trevor, meet Abram Junior, known more casually as A.J."

Tiny lines formed above Trevor's eyebrows. "Abram Junior? As in, 'son of Abraham'?"

"Father Abraham," her dad intoned with pride, "had many sons. The real question is, what in God's name is a human doing on my daughter's front lawn?"

"Bubbles brought him," Maeve put in with a swish of her tail. "The little scamp."

"See?" Daisy lifted her arms. "I had nothing to do with it."

Her father's eyebrows disappeared into his hairline. "So, Bubbles just decided to have a bit of a walkabout down on Earth, did he? Blow off some where-frog steam? Bring back a souvenir for his flat-mate?"

Daisy's bravado faltered under her father's pointed gaze. "Okay, maybe I had a little to do with it."

"A little?" Trevor choked out, his jaw dropping in outrage. "You knowingly and blatantly used my body and my paleo-anthropological discoveries to further your stupid tooth fairy career."

She glared back at him. "Trust me, none of this is helping my career."

Her fingers clenched. It wasn't fair to dismiss her professional goals out of hand. Although from Trevor's perspective, she probably hadn't come off as particularly fair herself. Feeling worse than ever, she gazed at the dark-haired, black-and-blue-eyed man before her.

If only he'd been an eight-year-old child. If only he'd handed over the right tooth, right away. If only she'd been good enough at magic to make her own supply of ForgetMe orbs. If only they'd met under better circumstances, as equals instead of fairy and human...

"You took my teeth and I want them back." Trevor's voice was low and cold as he bit out each word.

Mama squinted at him curiously. "Looks to me like you've still got them all. How many did you start with?"

Trevor's voice rose. "Hundreds!"

Looking as though he'd rather be in purgatory than visiting his daughter, Dad rolled back his shoulders and took a step forward. "Those are some wild accusations, young man."

"Wild? Wild?" Trevor spun toward Daisy and jabbed a finger in her face to punctuate his words. "You trespassed on my dig, into my house, and in my lab." His breath steamed against her eyelashes and she blinked involuntarily. "You *slept* with me and then you *stole* from me."

"What?" Dad's wings unfurled as he roared.

Just as predictably, Mama fell against his chest as if in a dead faint. Her father's wings twitched. If things didn't turn around soon, he was going to start smiting people. Somehow, Daisy had to get the situation under control.

"I told you I didn't mean to," she enunciated as clearly as she could. "And, technically, it was the other way around."

"Tell me you didn't sleep with a human," came her father's hoarse voice. "Lie if you have to. You can repent later."

Maeve let out a low whistle through her large teeth. "You had already swiped his teeth before you, er, 'interacted' with him? Business before pleasure, then. Good job."

Trevor froze to stare at Daisy. "If you already had what you came for, why did we end up sprawled across my office desk?"

"That does it," her father growled. He lunged toward Trevor, whose posture immediately went defensive. "I'll destroy him."

Mama serendipitously unfainted and locked her arms around her husband's waist in restraint. "What are you going to do, A.J.? Smite him with righteous glaring? You're a guardian angel. Guard your self-control."

Trevor's stance relaxed and his eyebrows rose. "I guess nobody in your family has any self-control."

"Leave my parents out of it. They're in shock." Daisy met his eyes. "As was I, when I realized the ForgetMe orb was a lust charm. It was an accident."

"Is that what kids say these days?" With a droll expression, Maeve pitched her voice falsetto. "Oops, how did a Himalayan Lust Charm get in there?"

"I said shut *up*, Maeve."

Dad's face was so red and his muscles so tense, he looked like his head might explode at any moment.

"What's a ForgetMe orb?" Trevor asked, suspicion lacing his voice.

"Just what it sounds like," Maeve said. "One glance at that thing and your office desk 'interaction' with Little Miss Tooth Fairy will disappear from your memory bank forever."

Outraged, Trevor whirled toward Daisy. "You were going to make me forget *sex?*"

She tried to keep her focus on what the court demanded she do—make him forget her completely—and somehow ignore the ice twisting in her gut. Him preferring to remember made her feel simultaneously better and worse. She couldn't forget making love with him if she tried. Each stolen moment was carved into her brain for the rest of her life.

"It's for the best." Her heart twisted. "And also court-ordered."

"I don't have a say in any of this?"

Daisy flinched. "You weren't supposed to see me in the first place."

A muscle pulsed in his bruised temple for a moment before he spoke again. "Fine. Bring it. A real ForgetMe orb this time, and none of your tricks. I want one for me and for Katrina. And I want her in human form, stat." He reached up to run a hand through his hair and winced when his palm brushed the growing bruise around his eye. "Do you hear me? I want to go home, I want to forget I ever saw you, and I want my teeth back. Now."

Mama's arms tightened around Daisy's father. "Who's Katrina?"

Daisy froze.

"A pumpkin." Blades of grass protruded from Maeve's teeth as she spoke. "A mouthy one."

Traitor.

"A what? Where?" Mama glanced around in dawning horror. "Not the jack-o'-lantern Trevor was chatting with in the field…"

"Yup." Maeve yanked up another chunk of grass. "That's the one."

Daisy wished the earth would swallow her whole.

"These are our demands." Trevor held up a hand and ticked points off his fingers. "Home. Human. Teeth. Forget. Goodbye."

"I'm afraid it's not as simple as that," Daisy said with a wince. "Especially the part about the teeth."

"Why not?" Her father's wings unfurled once more. "Sounds like an excellent plan to me."

"Because I already surrendered the teeth to the Pearly States."

Daisy gave Trevor an apologetic half-shrug. "Our government is a black hole of red tape. Once teeth go in, they never come out."

～

A full hour into his visit to Nether-Netherland, Trevor felt no more at home than when he'd arrived. Everything was surreal and unexpected. Take, for example, the clear plastic carpet runner tacked to the white shag covering Daisy's parents' spiral staircase. He couldn't tear his eyes away.

It was just so normal. So *ab*normal. He hadn't seen a clear plastic carpet runner—or, let's face it, shag carpet—since the long-ago afternoons spent playing Matchbox cars in the dusty sunlight of his great-grandparents' house. Of course, their carpet runner had been rigid and straight, not a magically molded spiral, but still. Carpet runner. Couldn't they just magic the dirt away?

"Won't you have a seat?" Daisy's mother's smile was brittle but her tone polite.

Trevor shook his head. No, he wouldn't have a seat. He stood tall and carefully took in the situation.

After Daisy's father had stormed out of the house and up into the clouds in a classic display of rage, relaxing on the sofa seemed a pale response in comparison. Even though he wasn't sure of the anthropological connotations behind gestures and emoting here in Nether-Netherland, Trevor didn't want to start off looking like the weaker male.

Second, he just didn't trust floating couches.

Why, with the instant gratification of magic at their fingertips, wouldn't Daisy's parents conjure up some nice wooden legs for their furniture? Hell, even metal ones or little plastic rollers would do.

Trevor thunked the back of his head against the wall and waited for the next disaster.

Daisy was off in the kitchen. Again, why bother? Why didn't she just conjure up some Kool-Aid, if that's what she wanted? If he didn't feel like such an interloper, he'd love to ask a thousand questions. Wait. He wouldn't be here at all if it weren't for these people's daughter. And since he *was* stuck here, an anthropologist in a strange land, why not take advantage of an opportunity to learn more about their culture?

"Mrs. le Fey," he began, but stopped short when Daisy's mom burst into laughter. "What?"

"You can call me Arabella like everyone else. I'm not Mrs. anything. Government-defined unions are a distinctly human construct." She nestled against a pile of plump red pillows on the beige microsuede couch. "There's no marriage in Nether-Netherland. We simply do what our hearts desire."

Wow. He blinked at her in silence. Maybe he would take a seat after all.

He crossed over to the matching recliner and eased onto the soft leather. Much to his delight, the chair stayed afloat.

"How long have you and A.J. been together?"

"Thirty wonderful years." She smoothed the long blue skirt of her gown and grinned. "Best of my life."

He reached for his back pocket. Dammit, no notebook. Just the stupid wand. "If there's no marriage, what's to stop either one of you from seeing someone else?"

"Trust. Respect. Love," she answered simply. "Same as on Earth."

Trevor nodded slowly. Interesting point. *Man*, he wished he had his notebook.

"Any other questions?"

"Well, I was wondering why anyone in Nether-Netherland would bother with carpet runners."

Before Arabella could answer, Daisy strode into the room with a tray bearing two lemonades and a salt-rimmed margarita on the rocks.

She set the lemonades on the square glass coffee table and kept the margarita.

"You two are awful chatty." She settled onto a couch near Trevor, at the opposite end of her mother, and licked the edge of her margarita glass. Chunky salt crystals coated her tongue, then disappeared behind moist lips. "What are you talking about?"

Arabella smiled. "Marriage, for one."

"Venus and Aphrodite, Mama, he's a human!" Daisy jerked upright, sloshing ice, salt, and wet liquid to the floor.

"And that should answer your second question." Arabella patted her daughter on the knee. "Marriage regarding your father and me, not you and this charming human."

"Oh. Right. Carpet runners." Daisy grimaced at the mess spreading across the floor. "Would you...?"

"Of course." Arabella plucked a wand from a basket beside the couch and zapped the floor. Spotless. She pointed at Daisy's glass. Instant refill. She aimed at Trevor.

He recoiled in alarm.

Arabella laughed. "I'm just teasing you. " She dropped the silver wand back into the basket. "Settle down."

Trevor tried to settle down, but not until after he double-checked to make sure the pink wand still protruded from his back pocket. In case of emergency, he hoped it could make more than pumpkins. Speaking of which...

Worry tensed his muscles. "Where's Katrina?"

"Kitchen counter." Daisy gestured toward the swinging doors. "She wanted a margarita but I thought it'd be a bad idea, what with her flaming candle and all."

Good call. Trevor started to say so, and then frowned. "Why don't you just make her human again?"

The front door opened and A.J. burst inside, the breadth of his wings barely squeezing through the wide double doorway. Trevor imagined large wings on a guardian angel were like large antlers on a stag—more for intimidation than aggression. But just in case the wings meant trouble, he eased the wand from his back pocket.

"I can't." Daisy toyed with her margarita. "I'm no good at spells."

"Not true. My daughter makes a damn fine pumpkin," A.J. corrected gruffly. His eyes narrowed at Trevor. "Much like you. Where did you get that wand?"

"My desk."

Arabella gasped in recognition. "That's Daisy's!"

No kidding. Did Trevor look like the sort of guy who shopped for hot pink fairy accessories? "Finders keepers."

"Hand it over," A.J. demanded. "Now."

"No." Trevor gripped the handle with both hands, pointed star aiming toward the ceiling. He was disadvantaged enough without giving up his single source of power, girly as it may be. "I want to go home."

A.J. took a step closer. "Not with that wand, you're not."

Arabella's voice rose in indignation. "It's Daisy's."

Daisy gazed at Trevor over the rim of her margarita. "It's sparkly."

"It's against the rules." A.J. held out an oversized hand like a parent waiting for a recalcitrant child to give up a stolen cookie.

"I want to go home," Trevor repeated calmly. "And I want Katrina with me. In human form."

"Son—"

Daisy finished off the second half of her margarita in one long draught and clinked the empty glass onto the coffee table. "I want that, too."

What? A tic twitched in Trevor's left eyelid, stretching his bruise. It was one thing for *him* to want to go back home to safety and sanity, but why was Daisy so eager to get rid of him? Wait a second. She had the teeth long before they were tangled and naked. If she carried around a Himalayan Lust Charm, it wasn't on accident. It was because she wanted him!

He smiled. "You 'liked' me just fine back at the office."

A growl rumbled deep in A.J.'s throat.

Arabella turned to her husband with a nervous smile. "Honey, let me take care of this. I'll pop him and his assistant back to his office and do up a quick ForgetMe orb. Things will be back to normal in no time." Her tone turned contemplative. "Well, as long as the Elders don't find out." She brightened. "But other than being completely against the rules, I don't see a problem."

Trevor glanced at Daisy. She slumped in her seat, gazing at her empty glass as though yearning for more tequila.

"The problem," A.J. bit out and took another step toward Trevor, "is that this—this *human*—slept with my daughter."

Trevor tightened his grip on the wand. Apparently, bending a sexy siren over an office desk incited reams of fatherly rage, no matter what dimension you happened to be in. But if there were no shotgun wedding to drag him to, what kind of retribution was A.J. planning?

"Sit, honey." Arabella patted the empty space on the couch between her and Daisy. "Let's talk about this."

Daisy closed her eyes and crumpled against the arm of the chair. "Let's not. Please."

"What's done is done," Trevor said, keeping his gaze focused on A.J. The angel hadn't made a single move to follow his wife's...or whatever's...advice. Damn. Trevor *knew* sitting would be seen as a sign of weakness. "If it makes you feel better, I didn't want to sleep with her." At A.J.'s renewed scowl, Trevor added, "I mean, of course I did, but I wasn't going to do anything about it other than... Anyway."

Daisy's gaze tilted heavenward, a strangled expression on her face.

A.J. was far from appeased.

"Look, I couldn't *unsleep* with her, even if I wanted to." Trevor frowned to realize he *wouldn't* want to. Accidental or not, forgetting their lovemaking was the major downside to the current plan. Now that some of the shock had worn off, he could admit to himself that he hadn't exactly hated it. He'd been dreaming of doing just that ever since he met her. "But the one thing I can do is go back to Earth with my T.A. and act like none of this ever happened. Right?"

At three silent nods, relief coursed through his body. It was almost over. He relaxed his stranglehold on the wand and pictured what his next steps would be back on Earth.

He could pop back into his disheveled office at the very moment he'd left it, no longer worried about Katrina's safety, never remembering the heat of Daisy's body against his, the taste and texture of her hardened nipple against his tongue. Er, not that that was a primary concern.

But how did he feel about her remembering him? He shifted in his seat. Turned on, apparently. It was kind of erotic to think about a woman in another dimension, thinking about him, reliving his kisses, his touch, his cock.

Daisy's next words shattered the fantasy.

"Do ForgetMe orbs work on non-humans?" She bolted upright and stared at her mother. "I want one too, Mama."

Arabella nodded thoughtfully. "I can grant all the wishes of your heart. But first, let me fetch Katrina so we can take care of everything at once." She rose from the couch and glided into the kitchen.

"What?" Trevor finally found words, and twisted to confront Daisy. "Why would you want to forget having sex with me? I *know* you enjoyed—"

A.J. stormed forward. "Why, you unrepentant little—"

"Stay back or I'll shoot!" Leaping to his feet, Trevor pointed the wand straight ahead, arms flush and parallel. "I turned a purse into a leather pumpkin and I'll do the same to you."

"You'd turn a guardian angel into a leather pumpkin?" The horror in Daisy's tone rankled. He preferred her looking guilty and miserable to outraged and disappointed. She raised a brow. "That'll look fabulous on your entrance interview for Heaven."

True. He lowered the wand to concede the point. A.J. chose that moment to leap into the air, spearing across the room.

Trevor instinctively swept the wand back upward, blurted his sole magic phrase, and let fly with the magic.

He missed.

The blast of glittery light from his wand streamed over A.J.'s shoulder and covered the wall just as the two-hundred-pound angel collided with Trevor. The floating glass coffee table shattered beneath them.

The walls moistened and colored, suddenly dripping with strands of light-orange goo. The shards of glass beneath Trevor's back hardened into greasy off-white seeds. A.J. knocked the wand from his fingers and reached for Trevor's neck. Slime saturated their clothing. Stringy pulp tickled their faces like heavy cobwebs as the walls curved inward.

The room closed in around them until the porous orange walls squeezed against their skin and exploded with a Thanksgiving-scented blast of splattered vegetable innards.

"Congratulations. You turned my parents' house into a pumpkin." Daisy pulled a slimy glop from her hair. "You're the second person in Nether-Netherland to earn that dubious honor."

"Daisy was the first," Arabella added helpfully, her arms clutched around Katrina the jack-o'-lantern.

A.J. shoved Trevor aside and struggled to his feet, goggling at the bright orange mess that used to be his home.

Trevor sat up, wiping pungent sludge from his forehead. "Well, I guess I oughtta be heading back to Earth. Will someone please hand me Katrina?"

A.J. whirled to face him, but before the livid angel had a chance to try any more of his heavenly jujitsu, a large black net dropped from the sky and tightened around Trevor's body, binding him to the slippery grass like a gnat in a web.

"TREVOR MASTERSON," a mechanical voice thundered. "By order of the Elders Upon High, you are hereby arrested for one count of Destruction of Property Belonging to a Government Official and two counts of Unsanctioned Use of Magic."

Trevor's head collapsed against the rope netting. He had no idea what kind of punishment went with charges like that, but when a horde of army-green creatures hoisted him over their shoulders, he knew it couldn't be good.

CHAPTER 11

*D*aisy ripped her arms free of her parents' grip and burst into the gigantic metallic sphere labeled Elders' Minions: Nether-Netherland Regional Headquarters. She didn't stop running until she faced the hawk-faced, lion-tailed receptionist.

"Where is he?"

"Who?" was the griffin's bored response. He leaned back in his chair with a dramatic sigh as though Daisy had interrupted an important navel-gazing session. "Did you fill out the proper form?"

"Did I fill out a *form?*" Before she could tear the feathered wings from his furry back at the thought of completing any more paperwork, a stout green troll with an Elders' Minions ID badge stomped around the corner.

"You're inquiring about Trevor Masterson, I presume?" He gestured down a long, round hallway. "He's in the Human Containment Compound."

"The what?" Daisy blinked. Good Ganesh, hadn't she ruined Trevor's life enough? "I didn't even know we *had* a Human Containment Compound."

"We didn't." His eyes glared at her from both sides of his bulbous nose. "Until today, nobody's been stupid enough to bring one here."

Daisy bit back a retort. Technically, Bubbles was the one to bring Trevor to Nether-Netherland, but under the circumstances that wasn't much of a comeback.

"I think you're in enough trouble for one day, young lady." Dad's piercing gaze pinned her to the gravel floor. "Why don't you let the Elders handle this? Besides, it's dusk. Shouldn't you be heading to work?"

"Work? If it weren't for Vivian Valdemeer," Mama said, "Daisy would never have met any humans in the first place."

"If it weren't for Vivian Valdemeer," Daisy began through clenched teeth, then stopped.

If it weren't for Vivian, Daisy would never have met Trevor. Never have licked his lips with her tongue, never have rubbed her naked body against his, never have indulged an impromptu romance, never have broken her mortifying four-year streak of celibacy.

"If it weren't for Viv," Dad said, shattering her salacious thoughts, "Daisy would still be working at the Neurophysics Compound."

"And what's wrong with that?" Mama planted her fists on her hips. "Neurophysicists may not make fairy, but they're... special people in their own way. All scientists are special."

"Shhh." Daisy's cheeks heated as she slunk a look over her shoulder at the smirking receptionist. "Please stop calling me 'special' in public."

"Daisy just wants an opportunity to earn her wings and be a respected fairy," her father boomed. "Vivian's giving her that chance. Vivian earned her wings through hard work and perseverance. Daisy'd do well to mirror her example."

"She was doing well enough on her own." Mama patted Daisy on the shoulder. "With or without real wings, I'll always be proud of you, honey."

With or without real wings, Daisy wanted to melt through the floor.

"As I'm sure you're well aware from Section V, Paragraph 14 of the Nether-Netherland Regional Headquarters code of conduct," interrupted the troll with the ID badge, "the lobby of a government facility is not the appropriate place to air family issues."

"Right." Daisy inched toward the cylindrical metal hallway. "I'll just pop in to see Trevor, then."

Mama shot Dad a venomous look and grappled for Daisy's arm. "I'll come with you."

The troll intercepted Mama's reaching fingers. "I'm sorry, ma'am. One visitor at a time. And Miss le Fey visits no prisoners unless accompanied by a cell guard. Elders' law."

"Fine." Mama swiveled to confront Daisy's father. "I'll meet you back home—once I finish re-conjuring it."

With a flash of sparkling glitter, she was gone.

Dad's wings twitched. "She thinks it's sooo funny that some of us have to fly home manually." He faced the empty space where Mama had stood and sighed. "I'd better hurry unless I want the silent treatment for the next month." He twisted and jabbed his index finger in Daisy's direction. "Don't do anything stupid."

Heat stung the backs of her eyes and she glanced away. Sure, her apprenticeship had been a cluster from day one. But she wasn't on duty right now. She was at the Nether-Netherland Regional Head-quarters. "What trouble could I possibly get into here? Trevor's in lockdown."

"And he better stay that way." With that, her father turned and strode out the door.

Dad thought she was here to set Trevor free? Daisy nearly laughed. She could get in huge trouble for a stunt like that. Well, if they caught her doing it. Which they probably would if she was crazy enough to try. But if not, and she somehow managed to smuggle him and Katrina back home... well, then the Elders' case would completely fall apart. No humans, no physical evidence, just hearsay. It's not like *they'd* jet off to Earth to fetch evidentiary material for trial. That would be breaking the rules.

Hmm. Interesting idea.

She flashed her most innocent smile at the denizens of the semi-crowded waiting area and edged toward the curved tunnel leading to the newly minted Human Containment Compound.

Nobody stopped her.

She inched closer. Where was the alleged cell guard? She took a few slow steps down the hallway, wondering whether humming aloud would make her appear less suspicious or less innocent. She opted not to hum and concentrated on rounding the corner as surreptitiously as possible.

The second she was out of sight and earshot, she took off at a dead run until she arrived, breathless, at the burnished silver bars lining the single oblong compartment.

A yellow-eyed troll stared back at her from a few feet down the hall. Crap. They hadn't been exaggerating the cell guard factor. She fluttered her eyelashes at him. He remained impassive. When Daisy made no move to speak or to come closer, he returned his focus to a crinkled copy of the Trans-Dimensional Times.

Sagging in relief, she turned to the view beyond the bars and let out a low whistle. As far as detention cells went, it wasn't half bad.

A small, private bathroom hovered in one corner. A massive, four-poster canopy bed rested along the far wall. A calming waterfall hologram burbled and glistened on the facing partition.

Trevor stood in the center, soft tousled hair hanging in his dark, hooded eyes, arms crossed and jaw set, fuming. But even with the fuming and the arm crossing and the bruise purpling one eye, he looked absolutely delicious. Rumpled, dangerous, sexy.

Bad train of thought.

"Um, hi," she ventured, not entirely ungrateful for the bars between them. "How's it going?"

He gave a humorless laugh, his normally even tone now tinged with panic. "How did this happen? Why did this happen?" He stalked forward until both fists gripped the thick silver bars and his subtle, masculine scent wafted closer.

She backed up a step, away from his anger and away from his familiar scent. "I didn't mean to cause you trouble."

His eyes hardened mercilessly. "So says the *thief*."

"Well… you got me there." Daisy nibbled her lip. She tried to think of an ameliorative response and came up blank. "Would you be less mad if I dropped off silver dollars for each of the teeth I took?"

Veins protruding from his neck, Trevor rattled the bars. "No!"

"All right, all right." She glanced from the still-reading guard back to Trevor. "I won't."

His knuckles whitened and his expression grew grim. "Where's Katrina?"

"With my mother. Safe."

"Good." His dark lashes lowered, as did his voice. "What's going to happen to me?"

"Nothing." Daisy hoped to Hades that was true. "They might make you testify and whatnot before they send you back to Earth, but it'll be me that gets into trouble, not you."

"Good." He pushed away from the bars with his palms and turned his back to her. She loved his back. And his shoulders. But she wished more than ever he'd stayed in Elkhart where he belonged. He stalked away from her. "You deserve trouble."

"That's not very nice," she muttered, although she could hardly discredit his point of view. "I said I was sorry."

With a derisive snort, he climbed onto the wide bed and leaned back against the pile of plush pillows.

Several moments passed. In silence.

The cell guard turned a page.

Another moment passed with only the rustling of a newspaper to break the silence. Daisy couldn't stand it anymore.

"Trevor?"

He didn't respond. Instead, he laced his fingers underneath his head and bent his legs so that both his knees and his gaze pointed toward the crimson canopy.

She frowned. "Don't ignore me. I'm trying to help."

He reached out one hand and slid the bed curtains closed.

Daisy shook her head. "Humans." With another quick glance at the still-reading guard, she held her hand to her shoulder. When her where-frog hopped onto her palm, she whispered, "In."

When she materialized on the other side of the bars, she knelt to let Bubbles roam the cold marble floor. She tiptoed over to the bed and threw back the curtains. "Boo."

"Aargh!" Trevor jumped so high she feared he'd crack his head. "What the hell are you doing in here?"

She climbed on top of the bed and re-closed the curtains, so as not to broadcast her presence should the troll in the hall put down his newspaper long enough to glance inside the containment cell. "Considering whether or not it's worth the risk to rescue you."

"What?" Shadows hid his expression, but his doubtful tone spoke volumes. "Really?"

She sat on her heels between his open legs, her knees brushing the bare feet poking from the ankles of Trevor's khakis on either side of her. She tried not to think about the two of them sharing a mattress. Or at least not to give away the direction her mind had taken. "Of course. Didn't you hear me say I'd be in big trouble if you testified against me?"

"Oh, right." His words slid down her spine like ice. "For a moment there, I thought you might have an altruistic bone in your body."

Stung, her fingers gripped the edge of her dress like claws. "Do you want to go back home or not? You may not realize it, but I'll be in heaps of trouble either way."

He sighed, his arms and legs flopping limp to the mattress. "I do realize it. And yet I'm asking you to do what it takes to get me out of here." His voice crackled with defeat. "Please."

Her breath caught. Did that mean he'd forgiven her?

She didn't realize how much his forgiveness mattered to her until she finally received it. Her fingers lightened their death grip on her hem, as if they suddenly remembered how to relax.

If only it could last.

As she weighed the wisdom of a Great Escape, she tried to ignore the feel of her body nestled between Trevor's outstretched legs. He felt so warm... And looked so good... And smelled so enticing... Good Gitche Manitou, she'd definitely need a ForgetMe orb of her own if she didn't want to become the first tooth fairy stalker.

Staging a breakout was unquestionably stupid, but... the sooner she got out of his life, the sooner she could move on with hers. Right?

"Okay, here's the plan." The hope in his face came into focus as her eyes adjusted to the limited light. She tore her gaze from the curve of his mouth and forced her features into their most businesslike demeanor. "Step one, we try to get the entire case thrown out. At least for you, anyway."

"And if step one doesn't work?"

"Then I'll be back. Step two, Bubbles will take us to my parents' house, where—"

Trevor let out a humorless laugh. "We were just there, and look how well that worked out." Both his legs brushed against hers, warming her calves and her belly. "Besides, I turned their place into a pumpkin and it shattered."

"Welcome to Nether-Netherland." She kept her palms immobile atop her thighs so she wouldn't be tempted to touch him. Or at least not act on it. One of his legs continued to rub idly against hers, stoking embers they'd both be better off not igniting. "Mama's re-conjured everything by now, no worries. Besides, it's where Katrina is. And I'm going to need Mama's help with the ForgetMe orb." His legs stilled, no doubt recalling the same images imprinted in her own brain. Her voice trembled. "The last thing we need is another mix-up."

"Speaking of which..." Trevor's hand slipped into his cargo pocket. "You forgot this."

Before Daisy could blink, the Himalayan Lust Charm rested inno-cently in his palm, as though he expected her to reach out and grab it. Adam offering Eve the apple. Her wide-eyed expression reflected back at her from its shiny, golden surface.

Lust charms blessedly being single-use objects, she and Trevor were in no danger of an involuntary repeat. Any lovemaking from this point forward—not that she expected any more lovemaking, mind—would be of their mutual desire. And risky as all Hades, considering the troll just down the hall. Although, if she were honest, the idea of fooling around behind a closed curtain with the guard none the wiser was more than a little sexy. She wasn't reckless enough to *start* any shenanigans... But if Trevor so much as hinted he'd like to get naked, she wouldn't be able to stop herself from launching into his arms and begging for Round Two. May Artemis save her soul. Daisy closed her eyes and tried to think of formulas and matrices—anything but the sexy man whose warm limbs flanked her own.

His husky voice lured her ever closer. "I can't stop thinking about your body beneath mine."

Her eyes snapped open. Had he read her mind? Or was the Himalayan Lust Charm somehow still active? She snatched the peach from his open hand and stared a hole through it, waiting for the lust bomb to hit. No flowery scent, no clenching of the loins, no total loss of her judgment. Nothing dangerous at all, except the normal lust bomb Trevor incited just by existing. But the peach in her palm? Ordinary, run-of-the-mill golden fruit. Completely harmless.

Trevor, on the other hand... not so harmless. His eyes stayed locked with hers, but his upturned hands lowered centimeter by centimeter until they nestled at the dip between her thighs. The barest scrap of fabric separated her skin from his knuckles. Her thighs heated beneath the backs of his hands. His breathing quickened. So did hers. He didn't pull away.

Why was he doing this? Daisy gave the peach another nervous sniff. Everybody in Nether-Netherland knew lust charms had a shorter lifespan than twinkle flies. But the heat of his skin and the expression on his face suggested an entirely different scenario. One requiring a few less clothes.

Wait. Trevor wasn't from Nether-Netherland. He was from Indiana. Which meant he *thought* he was under the renewed influence of a Himalayan Lust Charm, but in reality, he was suffering from one hundred percent natural male desire.

She smiled. Nothing was hotter than that.

"I want you to know," she said urgently, "you're not under the influence of magic."

He paused. "I'm not?"

The peach dropped from her hand and rolled off the mattress, tinkling like a child's toy when it hit the floor. Neither of them reached for it.

She shook her head. "This is you. And me."

"In that case..." A slow, sexy grin spread across his face. "What should we do about this?"

Now wasn't the time to analyze. Now was the time for action. No, no, now was the time to hold strong. To resist indulging his passion. Even if she shared it. This was the absolute worst time to act on their desire. Yet her legs quivered beneath the soft weight of his hands. Or maybe they quivered for other reasons.

Daisy shook her head. She was going to put a stop to this nonsense very, very soon.

"You're even beautiful when you think too hard." He caressed her cheek with his thumb.

Her insides melted into molten mush.

Instead, Trevor's legs tightened against her shins. His warm fingers closed around her arms and hauled her on top of him lengthwise.

He smiled again, keeping his teasing gaze on hers until she couldn't help but smile back.

After all, her ankles crossed his ankles. Her thighs covered his thighs. His arousal pulsed against her belly. What more could she want? She swallowed. *Lots* more.

Her sensitized breasts pressed against his chest and she surrendered, as he'd known she would. He was irresistible. Without breaking eye-contact, she fumbled in her handbag. She tossed a pinch of clothes powder over her shoulder and divested herself of her dress. And while she was at it, a little more sparkling powder and... there.

Naked Trevor.

"Nice," he murmured, his palms skating a feathery touch up the backs of her thighs, the curve of her bottom, the small of her back, the sides of her ribcage, the edges of her breasts. His fingers closed around her upper arms and with a sudden whoosh of breath from her lungs, he was on top.

She sucked in air, saturating her pores with his masculine scent. The truth was undeniable. Trevor wanted her. With or without a potent lust charm, *he wanted her.*

His lips smoothed into a delicious, lascivious smile. Daisy arched her brows.

"You sure do a lot of smiling," she grumbled, but she curved her hand around the base of his neck and pulled him to her.

His tongue flicked into her open mouth, trapping her somewhere between the pillow and heaven. He nipped at her lower lip, pulling it into his mouth and suckling.

Daisy's hungry fingers splayed across his skin, memorizing every angle and line of his tight, hot flesh. Inch by inch, her legs lifted. Her ankles crossed behind his thighs. She wanted him as much as he wanted her. Oh, Venus, did she ever. Her wanton body wriggled against him, rubbing moist heat against his hard length.

Trevor grinned again, the jerk, and slammed his palms against the headboard to balance his weight. He captured her mouth in another searing kiss. Slowly, he lifted his hips so that the tip of his erection coasted down the aching heat between her thighs and nudged inside her—

"Miss le Fey," came a sharp, gravelly voice from the containment center corridor. "You are not allowed in the captive's cell. Desist at once or we will be forced to detain you as well."

"Crap," Daisy gasped, hurling herself out from under Trevor as though his body had suddenly caught fire.

Hers very nearly had.

"Coming," she called and blushed at the unrestrained passion shadowing Trevor's eyes.

"You could be," he murmured, still reaching for her.

Ignoring him, Daisy tossed frantic handfuls of clothes powder around the mattress to clothe them both. She slid out the crack between the curtains so the impatient troll wouldn't have a chance to see Trevor's fully aroused state and form an even better picture of what the erstwhile tooth fairy was doing inside his captive's cell.

She scooped the golden peach into her purse before meeting the troll's gaze. Thank Bacchus it no longer worked. The last thing she needed was an interlude like *that*.

"Hurry up." He raised thick black eyebrows and tapped a clipboard against the bars. "The hearing is at ten tomorrow morning. You can see the human in court when he testifies."

"Fabulous," she muttered, crossing to the other side of the bars without checking to see whether Trevor watched her. She could *feel* his gaze burning the back of her neck.

As Daisy knelt to motion for Bubbles, she tried not to think about the complications she and Trevor had been just about to make. He'd sure have plenty to testify about now.

~

The next morning, Trevor hurled himself against the unyielding metal bars keeping him trapped within a resort-style jail cell.

As before, nothing bent. Nothing moved. Nothing changed.

What had he thought? Muscle would triumph over magic in a fortuitous burst of cosmic irony, thereby allowing him to break free of his concierge-class confinement and, what?—*Walk* back to Earth?

With a muttered curse, he kicked at the ridiculous waterfall hologram lining one wall and lost his balance when the burbling fall of icy water drenched his leg.

Hologram waterfalls were actually wet? *Damn* it.

"Mr. Masterson?" growled the guard's deep voice from the hallway. "You have a visitor."

Trevor spun around on his dry heel, his raised foot sending a scattered spray across the marble floor. Great. Now he'd probably break his neck walking across the room and go down in infamy as the first human in Nether-Netherland felled by a hologram.

Fighting for composure, he step-sploshed, step-sploshed back to the metal bars. Yep, he had a visitor, all right.

And the tall, big-haired woman dwarfing the troll guard sure wasn't Daisy.

First of all, the lacy, translucent wings fluttering between her shoulder blades were anything but cellophane and glitter glue.

Spare appendages aside, this woman was watchband-thin where Daisy was hourglass curved, drenched in floral perfume instead of shower-fresh, and buried under a metric ton of makeup instead of glowing with natural beauty.

He hoped like hell she wasn't bearing Himalayan Lust Charms.

"Who are you?" he asked suspiciously.

"My name is Vivian Valdemeer," she purred in a practiced, throaty voice. She motioned for the troll to give them a few meters of privacy before turning back to Trevor. Her crimson-painted lips stretched into an over-large smile, revealing matching rows of too-small ivory teeth. "I'm a very powerful tooth fairy."

Trevor's arms locked across his chest. Even if he weren't an anthropologist, he doubted he'd trust someone who paid social calls to jail cells while dressed for a night at the Oscars. Surely morning was an odd time for floor-length ball gowns, even in Nether-Netherland.

"So you're a tooth fairy," he repeated with his most disinterested expression. "Is that supposed to impress me?"

"Trust me, darling." Her lips contorted into a knowing smile. "It will."

She brought her fist from behind her back, unfurled long, manicured fingers and blew a stream of glittery dust into the room.

He jumped backward, sliding on the slick marble with his slippery shoe. He grabbed one of the bedposts to break his fall. "What was that?" he demanded, checking to make sure he was still clothed. You never knew with fairies.

"*Veritas vos liberabit,*" Ms. Valdemeer intoned before brushing her palms on the sides of her shimmering emerald dress.

"Latin? You speak Latin in Nether-Netherland?" Trevor glared at her until the translation of the familiar quote registered in his mind. "The truth will set me free? What kind of bullshit is that?"

"So, tell me," she said with a smirk. "What's the one thing you love more than any other?"

Although Trevor wanted to tell the crazy witch to mind her own damn business, he opened his mouth to say "baseball." After all, wasn't that his number one passion? But the message got lost between brain and mouth, and what tumbled over his teeth was, "My job." He frowned, blinking in confusion. "My job?"

Her eyes gleamed in the magical light. "By the classic expression now gracing your face, I can only assume the truth has been set free."

Trevor leaned forward, his sodden sock squishing in his shoe.

"What are you talking about?" he demanded. But he was pretty sure he knew.

"Daisy, of course." Ms. Valdemeer inspected her long ruby fingernails. "Would you say you know Miss le Fey... intimately?"

"I wouldn't say one way or the other," Trevor bit out, struggling against the unbidden words, "if I could help it. But yes. Quite intimately. The first time, I thought she slipped me some kind of drug. Not that I didn't enjoy myself. The second time, I was the one stupid enough to flash around that golden peach."

At the word "peach," Ms. Valdemeer's eyes glittered with amusement. "Twice with the same peach," she mused softly, casting a pointed, volatile glance toward his crotch. "How fascinating."

His left hand contorted into the most universal of American gestures.

"Look, bitch. I—" He stopped speaking when his fingers slid around the frosty bars. "Wait. How am I saying what I want?"

"You can say anything you want," she said with a toying little smile, "as long as it's true."

Trevor lifted an eyebrow. "So, you're saying... it's true you're a bitch?"

"No," she snarled, eyes flashing. Within seconds, her twisted features calmed. "It's simply true you *think* I am."

Before Trevor could verbalize his outrage toward her unsolicited Latin spell-casting, she fluttered a hand toward the waiting troll, pivoted on one black vinyl stiletto, and stalked off without a backward glance.

"It's true she's a bitch," Trevor muttered to the guard as the cell clicked ajar. "What was that about?"

One pocked green shoulder shrugged in apathy. "Witnesses and defendants alike are occasionally given Truth Spells to ensure accurate testimony and expedited sentencing." He motioned toward the open door. "Come. I will take you to the courtroom."

"Trevor Masterson." D.A. Sangre leaned one elbow on the witness stand and bared her teeth in a ferocious smile. "Do you swear to tell the truth, the whole truth, and nothing but the truth, all blessings to Apollo?"

That was a whole lot of truth. Especially since Daisy was now the one under the microscope. Mr. Squatch had managed to get the case against Trevor dismissed, but there was no chance of similar reprieve for Daisy. The D.A. was practically salivating at the opportunity to grill Trevor for salacious tidbits to use against her.

Daisy shifted on the hard wooden bench. At least the Elders hadn't ordered a Truth Spell. A maneuver like that could've ruined everything. Truth Spells were rarely granted—and their moderated use had to be announced before the jury instead of a swearing-in like Trevor was undergoing—but she had sure worried.

Swearing to Apollo was another bonus. Most humans had moved on to newer gods.

"Yeah," he mumbled, his dark eyes uncharacteristically sullen. Daisy couldn't help but feel sorry for him.

"Speak up," Judge Banshee shrieked, leaping onto her chair. "I can't hear you!"

Trevor's palms slapped against the burnished edge of the witness box. "Yes, I'll tell the truth. What else can I—"

"Are you aware," D.A. Sangre cut in, her saccharine tones permeating the room like sugar in rat poison, "of Miss le Fey's profession?"

"Tooth fairy." Trevor shot an unreadable glance toward Daisy. "I didn't believe it at first, but by the time I got trussed up in the troll net, the situation was obvious."

The D.A. whirled toward the jury.

"He *knew* she was a *fairy*," she reiterated, pointing first to the witness then to the defendant for emphasis. "The first broken rule."

"Objection," Daisy called out. "Children know we're fairies, or why would they put their teeth under their pillows? And we're allowed to lull them back to sleep. I tried."

"Did you?" D.A. Sangre bared her teeth. "Is the witness a child? No? Is he the owner of the tooth? Also no? Then the *rules* were *broken*." She turned back to Trevor. "Were you brought in for questioning yesterday, following illegal use of magic?"

Tiny lines creased his forehead as Trevor glared at her. "Yes. But if you're taking me to trial for that, you better extradite me right back to Indiana because this crowd doesn't begin to resemble a jury of my peers."

The D.A. waved away his comment. "What wand did you use to wreak your havoc, human?"

Trevor looked at Daisy, his expression once again unreadable. She arched her eyebrows and kept her gaze focused on his. He rolled his eyes toward the audience. She turned to scan the crowd, but didn't see anything out of place. Her family, her best friend, her boss, her ex-coworkers, and a few random gossipmongers. The usual. She lifted a shoulder. His eyes widened as if annoyed she wasn't getting his bizarro body language. She raised her palms and stared at him in question.

With a snarl, D.A. Sangre leapt between them.

"Human," she purred, one red-lacquered fingernail trailing across the smooth wood of the witness stand. "Allow me to repeat myself. Whose *wand* did you *use* to wreak *havoc*?"

Trevor slumped back in his chair, arms crossed. "Daisy's?"

D.A. Sangre cast a knowing smirk toward the jury. "And how did you happen across Miss le Fey's magic wand? Did you, perhaps, steal it from her without her knowledge?"

Daisy gulped. Let's hope Trevor retained a sense of poetic license.

"Sort of." He stared at his lap. "She left it in my office."

"She *left* a *wand* in his *office*," D.A. Sangre repeated for the jury, utilizing her infamous stabbing finger motions for emphasis. "Another broken rule. And how did you get the magic wand from your office on Earth all the way to the residential subdivision on Cloud Nine?"

Trevor touched the outer edge of his black eye. "Bubbles brought me. Daisy's, uh, where-frog."

"*Bubbles* the *where*-frog," D.A. Sangre crowed.

Daisy wanted to smack her. The jury was paying plenty of attention without the extra theatrics. They sat bug-eyed and slack-jawed, peering over the banisters so far she wouldn't be surprised if they started tumbling over the edge like lemmings.

"And why do you suppose Miss le Fey left such obviously proprietary magical items behind in your office?"

"Urgh!" Daisy's lawyer leapt to his feet. "Urrrrrghhhh!"

"Overruled," Judge Banshee snapped, twisting to face Trevor. "The witness will answer the question."

"She was in a hurry." Trevor tossed an apologetic grimace in Daisy's direction. "I'm sure it was an accident."

"Oh? And what could possibly discombobulate a *scientist* like Miss le Fey?" D.A. Sangre's tone implied that even the rising and setting of the sun could discombobulate the ever-unmagical Miss le Fey. If she wasn't already on trial, Daisy really would stomp up there and smack her.

"We…" Trevor's teeth clenched together, as if he didn't want to speak his next words any more than Daisy wanted to hear them. "We had just made—uh, sex—and I was sort of trying for more. Sex. So, she disappeared without all her stuff because I had her… somewhat… trapped on the edge of my desk."

The courtroom gasped.

"Aha!" D.A. Sangre beamed at the jury before jabbing at Daisy with her blood-red talon. "The *defendant* had *sex* with a *human*."

Daisy closed her eyes and pretended she was invisible. Matter of fact, if she'd known an invisibility spell, she'd chant it right now, even if she ended up turning herself into a pumpkin in the process. At least she'd be an invisible pumpkin.

When she pried open one tentative eye, the jury was still staring at her in scandalized glee. They probably expected a fiasco like this from an ex-neurophysicist.

"In her defense," Trevor ventured, straightening his shoulders. "I—"

"You are not her attorney," D.A. Sangre interrupted. She jerked her thumb toward Mr. Squatch. "*That* is. And he'll have his opportunity to cross-examine in a moment." With a self-satisfied nod to the jury, she crossed over to the prosecution's table and slid into her seat.

"Urgh?" the big yeti whispered to Daisy. He tilted his furry white head toward Trevor. "Urrrrrghhhh?"

CHAPTER 12

*T*he last thing Daisy needed was for the judge to deem her a menace to society and instate the maximum five-year sentence after all.

"Don't bother cross-examining," she said to Mr. Squatch, and rubbed the tips of her fingers against her pounding temples. "Trust me, nothing Trevor could say would help the case."

"Urrrrrghhhh," Mr. Squatch muttered in reply.

Daisy's sentiments exactly.

She dropped her head face-first onto the hard table. Even if Vivian *had* attempted to claim responsibility for the charm debacle, who would the jury blame for the resulting trouble? The popular, glamorous fairy with the magical powers and the gorgeous wings? Or the ordinary, wingless wannabe, with her pathetic where-frog and unenviable non-magical track record?

"Human," Judge Banshee screeched. "Would you like to return home now?"

"Yes." Trevor fell back into his seat as though relieved the D.A.'s interrogation had ended at last. "Please."

"With a proper ForgetMe orb," D.A. Sangre interjected, jerking her head in Daisy's direction. "And this time, performed by a competent fairy. Sound about right, human?"

Trevor tensed, as though offended on Daisy's behalf. "To be honest, I'm not looking forward to losing memories of Daisy. She's smart and funny and sexy. If she were, say, an earthbound human, things might be... possible between us."

She couldn't help the rush of warmth that flooded her cheeks. Hadn't she wished the very same thing, but in reverse?

"But she's not," Trevor said, the muscles flexing around his jaw. "And I need to straighten my life out. Fast." He turned his gaze to the judge. "It's time for me to leave this world behind."

Although she knew he had to return to his own world sometime, she couldn't quiet the icy thorns pricking her stomach at his words. He couldn't wait to forget, to return to a life without magic, without her. She tried not to be hurt. She wanted the same things, didn't she?

"Any more witnesses?" Judge Banshee scrambled to the center of her desk. "No?" Her sharp eyes pivoted toward Mr. Squatch and D.A. Sangre before refocusing on Trevor. "Is there anything else you'd like to add, human?"

"Well, there's something else I'd like to *have*. Even if you do erase my memory, my career will be ruined if I don't go back with my teeth."

"Objections?" Judge Banshee asked D.A. Sangre, whose skeletal palm lifted in a why-would-I-care expression. "Very well. I hereby order the Pearly States to produce the confiscated teeth—"

"Urgh," Daisy's lawyer interrupted, leaping to his furry feet. "Urrrrrghhhh."

"All right, good point." Judge Banshee nibbled on the edge of the gavel. "So that Miss le Fey is not docked any apprenticeship points, since she did in fact collect the tooth she'd been sent to retrieve, I hereby order the Pearly States to produce all the teeth but that one—"

"What?" Trevor's mouth fell open. "I want them all!"

"You'll get what you get, and like it!" Judge Banshee shrieked.

"Pretend you hadn't found one," put in D.A. Sangre with a flash of pointy incisors.

"That's stupid. Nobody even knew whose it was!" Trevor's voice rose in outrage. The D.A.'s face whitened, but he was too busy glaring at the judge to notice. "I need them more than any of you. What do you guys even *do* with them?"

Judge Banshee shook her gavel at him. "None of your business, human!"

D.A. Sangre's face stretched into a sudden feline smile. "Can you even tell which teeth go where, human? Would you even know how to replace them?"

"Not by sight alone," Trevor hedged. "But my database has notations that might help indicate which set belongs to—"

"Then there's little impetus for Nether-Netherland to return anything at all." D.A. Sangre turned her back to him. "Judge Banshee, the human cannot use the specimens if he can't tell one from the other. There's no sense allowing him to—"

"I could," Daisy ventured, earning a furry nudge from her lawyer and general confusion from everyone else.

D.A. Sangre found her voice first.

"You could what?" she asked, speaking slowly and carefully as if to a frightened, feebleminded reindeer lost in the snow.

Daisy's face heated under the sudden scrutiny. "I could put them back."

"How?" the D.A. demanded. "Did you minor in dentistry at Nether-Netherland University?"

"No," Daisy admitted. "I double-majored in engineering and neurophysics. But I did make a Genetic Teradata Carbon Dentition Spectrometer for one of my electives."

D.A. Sangre's pointed teeth clicked together. "A what?"

Even Trevor gaped at her in surprise. His unblinking eyes locked on her face, as though replaying her words in his mind and still only hearing Sasquatchian.

"Layman's terms, Miss le Fey," Judge Banshee warned. "Don't try my patience."

"Well, it's a... a machine that does automatic microanalyses. Of teeth. I invented it for class, but didn't get credit since it's not magical." She tried not to remember how frustrating those days had been. She'd sorted teeth ten times faster than fairies and jackalopes alike, but had only scored half credit for having used mundane resources. And the laughter... She shivered and straightened her spine. "In a nutshell, the GTCDS is a diagnostic device in which the foreign key relational data infrastructure trips the light emitting diodes, or LEDs, as soon as the internal mechanism calculating the density and molecular origin of the specimen sends an ambit of nucleic tissue to the collimator prism, thereby initiating a—"

"Fine," Judge Banshee screamed, hopping onto the edge of the table. "Miss le Fey will accompany the human and return his teeth to the proper location, with the exception of the tooth kept by the Pearly States. Non-negotiable. Afterward, she will utilize a ForgetMe orb and return to Nether-Netherland posthaste." She lifted the gavel above her head.

"Please," scoffed the D.A. "Miss le Fey is the worst spell-caster in the entire tri-dimensional area. She couldn't turn a pea into a pumpkin."

"Yes she could." Trevor's eyes narrowed. "She could turn a pea into a *talking* pumpkin if that's what she wanted to do. With a candle inside!"

"Silence!" shrieked the judge. "Whom do you suggest perform the spell-casting, Livinia?"

D.A. Sangre's gaze flitted from Daisy to Vivian and back again. But when she answered the judge, what she said was, "Why not... Arabella?"

Daisy started. Mama? Seriously?

"Hmm," Judge Banshee murmured. "Objections, Mr. Squatch?"

After a quick glance at Daisy, her lawyer shrugged and made a shooing, go-ahead motion with one white-furred paw.

"Fine," screeched the judge. "I hereby charge Arabella le Fey with preparing any appropriate ForgetMe orbs in advance to ensure no further 'mistakes' on the part of the defendant." The judge hopped from one side of the table to the other. "Daisy le Fey, you are ordered by the court to return this human to Earth, replace all but one of the confiscated teeth, erase all memories of yourself from his mind, and leave him behind forever. Understand?"

Oh, she understood all right. Daisy wasn't sure what stung worse

—the shuddering in her bones at the cold word "forever" or Trevor's obvious relief at hearing the same news.

"You are a collector of teeth, Miss le Fey, not a disruptor of human lives." The judge gave Trevor a sharp nod before refocusing on Daisy. "Do not return until you've put things back to rights. Everything. Hear me?"

Daisy gritted her teeth and nodded. Everything. Got it.

"Due to political picketing by a coalition of scientists from the Neurophysics Compound," Judge Banshee continued, "you have certain ties to this community that make me hesitate to impose the maximum punishment allowed by law."

Daisy slid a grateful half-smile at the clusters of ex-coworkers present in the audience. They nodded supportively. The judge kept shrieking.

"You are hereby sentenced to a six-month probationary period. Once you return, you will report daily to your current mentor, Vivian Valdemeer. Should anything—and I mean *anything*—bring you back to this courtroom before those six months are up, I will recommend the jury consider nothing less than Purgatory."

⁓

Maeve was waiting just outside the front steps when Daisy exited the court building. Daisy gave her long neck a quick hug and then collapsed onto the steps.

"That couldn't have gone much worse." She dropped her head to her knees, then turned her face toward the last withering tendrils of sunlight.

Maeve tossed her forelock from her eyes. "Why wasn't Vivian in the stand explaining how you ended up with a lust charm? That woman's a two-faced liar."

"She didn't lie. When I confronted her, she never once denied having one," Daisy said. "Wouldn't she have been less forthcoming if she were hiding something? As it was, I showed up uninvited to beg for favors, and if she handed me the wrong pouch..." Her voice trailed off. She was still ticked. Maeve was right. "The point is, Vivian's got her own reputation to protect. And now she's got the power to make or break *mine*. She's my court-appointed hall monitor, for Hermes' sake. Now is not the time for me to cop an attitude with her."

"Should've let me." Maeve bared her teeth. "I'd've bit her."

"Negatory." Daisy gave a light kick at one of her best friend's hooves and swore when she stubbed her toe. "How am I ever going to earn wings if you run amok biting my superiors?"

"Ah, your precious wings." Nickering softly, Maeve shook her head. "I knew they were the root of all evil."

"Wings aren't evil!" Daisy jumped up and gave her a shove. "They're—they're glorious."

Maeve chuffed. "They're killing you, sunshine. They're your monkey's paw of bad karma."

"You were born with magic." Daisy couldn't quite keep the resentment from her voice. "You can't possibly understand."

"I understand you were making gooey eyes at the sexy human."

"Whatever. Gooey or not, his return is court-mandated."

"Oh, so you would like another desktop tryst or two?"

"Stop twisting my words. I don't care about him." Well, not exactly. She already missed him. He was an excellent lover and she was sorry she had to take his teeth, but business was business, right? "Besides, what would it matter? He said he couldn't wait to go home."

Maeve snorted. "Men lie."

"Well, he didn't lie about anything else, did he?" But boy would it have been better if he had. Daisy rubbed her forehead. Of all the men in the universe, she had to tangle with an honest one. "He had the opportunity to deny everything, but chose to sit there blabbing to the jury about my sex life."

"That is pretty weird. He seemed so into you." Maeve frowned. "Maybe he was under a Truth Spell."

"Be serious." Daisy propped one elbow atop Maeve's back. "You know those have to be authorized by the Elders and announced on record before any testimony. Judge Banshee didn't say a word. Maybe Trevor doesn't give a Mayura Feather whether I get into trouble or not. After all, I did steal his teeth."

"Maybe he didn't realize you would get into trouble." Maeve

dislodged Daisy's elbow with a flick of her tail. "It's not like he's familiar with the Nether-Netherland penal system."

"Why are you sticking up for him?" Daisy's shoulders tightened. "I'm your best friend. Shouldn't you be on my side?"

"I'm always on your side. I'm just not sure whose side *you're* on."

"What's that supposed to mean?"

"Forget it." Maeve jerked her head in the direction of the darkening horizon. "Better hurry to your parents' house if you want to pick up the mouthy pumpkin and ForgetMe orbs before you drop Prince Charming back in his office."

"I know what to do." Daisy held her palm up for Bubbles before Maeve could offer any more unsolicited advice.

In a blink, she and her where-frog materialized in her parents' kitchen. Mama and Dad were seated in the breakfast nook, Dad with a glass of white wine and Mama with a shot glass and a bottle of tequila. Both flashed lopsided smiles.

Probably Daisy shouldn't hang around any longer than necessary.

"So," she ventured as casually as she could. "I'm off to Earth to set 'everything' to rights and all that. I just swung by to—"

"Kitchen counter." Mama poured another shot, slopping most of it onto the table. "Light blue pouch will de-pumpkin Katrina. Pink pouch contains ForgetMe orbs. There's two so you can use one on Katrina. Don't forget the ten-second window."

Daisy's father set down his wine glass in order to give her a hug. "Good luck, honey," he said gruffly.

"Pop back by if you need anything," Mama said, gripping the sides of the bar stool as though she might topple off any moment.

With a sigh, Daisy skirted the granite-topped island and slid the heavy pouches into her purse. Pouches that contained true ForgetMe orbs. Yay. She was off to erase a human's memory for real this time. Why didn't the thought make her happy?

"You know..." Mama's words slurred into each other. "You never got arraigned in front of the Elders' High Court when you worked at the Neurophysics Compound. The only things *they* hauled you into were awards banquets."

"Huh," Daisy said through gritted teeth. Hefting the sleeping jack-o'-lantern to her belly, she bent down to whisper to Bubbles. "Quick, before the science-is-special lecture starts. Human Containment Center. Trevor's cell."

The popping in her ears had never been sweeter.

When they materialized in front of the waterfall hologram, Trevor's eyes lit up.

An answering warmth spread out from her belly until he breathed, "Katrina!" and snatched the lightly-snoring pumpkin from her arms.

"Um, yeah." Daisy wished she was as excited to permanently part ways as he was. Forcing a smile, she gestured at the pumpkin. "Figured she should head home with you."

His eyes narrowed. "Sure you know how to put her back to normal?"

"Of course I know how," Daisy snapped, and double-checked her purse for the Genetic Teradata Carbon Dentition Spectrometer and the two small pouches her mother had fixed for her. "I've got the spells right here. Are you ready to go?"

"Am I ever. Wait—you're bringing spells with you? Hold on." He took a deep breath. "The ocean is dry. The moon is made of green cheese. The Cubs just won the World Series."

Daisy touched the back of her hand to his forehead. "What in Quetzalcoatl's name are you talking about?"

"Just testing lies. I'll never take them for granted again." He tilted his head away, and cradled the sleeping jack-o'-lantern to his chest. "Let's go. Do I have to do anything special?"

"Just hold Katrina." Daisy threaded her hand between Trevor's thick bicep and the warmth of his side. She gritted her teeth when he tried to jerk out of her grasp as if she were a carrier for Yersinia Pestis. "Hold still, Mr. Fidget. I'm not going to bite you. Bubbles can only transport multiple beings if we're all touching."

"Oh. Okay." He cast a sidelong glance toward her as if he wasn't sure whether or not she was making up rules on the fly.

Ignoring him as best she could with their bodies pressed together, Daisy held out her other hand for Bubbles and whispered, "Trevor's lab. Now."

CHAPTER 13

*R*ather than relief, Trevor's first reaction to the shadowy sight of his anthropology lab was irritation. Why hadn't Daisy taken them to his office, so he could pick up his life in the exact place and time he'd left? With Berrymellow eavesdropping outside Trevor's door, wouldn't it look weird for Trevor to just saunter down the hallway, *outside* of his office?

Disengaging her slender fingers from his bicep, Daisy stepped forward to face him. She held out her hands. When he raised his brows in confusion, she plucked the pumpkin from his arms, knelt to sit on her heels, and gently placed it on the ground.

Oh, right. Katrina.

He hadn't forgotten her—he just hadn't considered that it would look even worse to Berrymellow if Trevor's office door opened, and out walked a completely different student. Materializing in the lab was a much better choice than materializing in Trevor's office.

He headed toward the door. "Should I hit the lights?"

"To further illuminate our talking pumpkin?"

"A simple 'no' would suffice," he muttered. "What's first then?"

"Well…" She pulled a drawstring bag from her purse. "First, we get this party started." She stuck her fingers inside the cloth pouch and frowned.

"What?" Trevor demanded. "What's wrong now?"

"It doesn't feel like a charm," she mused. "It feels like... cornflakes. But real heavy. Like steel. Or iron."

He gaped at her. "You brought a bag of iron cornflakes?"

"My mother made it for me."

"Your mother packed you breakfast? It's after dark! The only thing you should be carrying around is something to de-pumpkin Katrina."

"She did. It is. I did." Balancing on her knees, Daisy brushed some invisible dust off the top of the pumpkin. "She just neglected to include directions."

Lord help them now. "You will not feed Katrina iron cornflakes. Excess iron is poisonous to humans."

She slanted an irritated look up at him from behind her cat-eye glasses. "Oh, no, really? I don't suppose ingestion of an iron overdose irritates the stomach, causing ulceration of the lining followed by abdominal pain, nausea, vomiting, and a severe blood chemistry imbalance leading to profound shock while the poison destroys the lungs, liver, kidneys and brain?" At his sudden lack of response, she returned her attention to the contents of the pouch. "Why would something that debilitating be used as pabulum to restore someone to the human condition? Think logically."

"Well, what are they for, then?" he muttered defensively, irked at himself for voicing his objection aloud. How would he know what the damn things were for? And how did she know so much about the chemistry of humans?

Daisy rose to her bare feet. "Since there's a bagful, we're dealing with a spell, not a charm. And since Mama didn't mention an incantation, I have to assume there isn't one." She tugged open the pouch and tilted the mouth downward. "Here goes nothing..."

A jumble of—well, iron cornflakes—tumbled out like jagged black hail, streaming over the pumpkin. Bouncing at odd angles, they clattered to the concrete floor and exploded into tiny bursts of glitter, disintegrating on impact. As the last piece bounced off the stubby stem, a tremor shook the lab.

The pumpkin imploded in a flash of light.

"Katrina!" Trevor staggered forward, arms outstretched.

Before his eyes had adjusted back to the sudden darkness, an uncertain voice rang out.

"Coach?" Katrina's words echoed against the solid walls. "What the hell just happened?"

Oh, thank God. "Don't worry." Trevor sprinted to the doorway. "You're okay now. I'm okay now. Everything's okay."

And now that Katrina was no longer a jack-o'-lantern, he could switch on the lights.

He turned around, relieved to see her standing there in the middle of the lab wearing the same muddy camouflage pants she'd had on the last day of the dig, her backpack still slung on one shoulder and his laptop case in her arms.

His laptop case!

"Here." He strode toward her. "Let me take that. Thanks. Do you want to take off your backpack? What about your boots? Do you want to sit down? Do you want—"

"Like I said, I want to know what the hell happened." Katrina slid a wary look toward Daisy. "Please tell me that whole Nether-Nether-land experience was the result of a bad enchilada."

Trevor spun to face Daisy. "She still remembers!"

"Of course she remembers. That was a de-gourding spell, not a ForgetMe orb." Daisy pulled a cotton-candy pink pouch from her purse. She reached inside and pulled something out, careful to cradle it between her palms to hide it from view. "What's the story you want her to remember? She was getting ready to board the airplane and then... what?"

"I don't know." Trevor drummed his fingers on his biceps and considered Katrina. "Something believable, but not likely to have negative repercussions. No kidnappings, no illegal activities, no alien abductions."

Katrina snorted. "Trust me, if I was going to miss that plane on purpose, I'd've been too busy drinking in the tavern with the locals to be jacking around getting abducted by aliens."

Trevor gripped the laptop case to his chest. "What, like last time?"

"The shortstop was a mistake, I admit. I'm just saying, drinking with *ticos* is better than—"

"Good enough." Daisy opened her palm toward Katrina like an oyster bearing a pearl. Whatever was between her fingers held Katrina transfixed. "You remember nothing after arriving at the airport to leave Costa Rica. You do remember spending several fabulous days and fun nights, drinking in the taverns with the locals, before catching a flight back to Indiana. Trevor—"

"Professor Masterson," he corrected.

"—Professor Masterson picked you up at the airport and brought you back to the school so you could return the laptop you'd forgotten you still had." Daisy glanced over her shoulder at him and whispered, "Good?" At his nod, she turned back to Katrina. "You will not question your memories, nor will you take seriously anyone who might. Oh, and... you quit smoking. It was bad for your human lungs. Awake."

Daisy slapped her hands back together and dropped the ForgetMe orb, whatever that was, back into the pink pouch.

Katrina stood motionless, mouth agape and eyes zombie-vacant.

"She doesn't *look* awake," he ventured, hesitant to snap her out of it. How cool would it be if Daisy'd managed to hypnotize Katrina out of smoking?

"Shhh," Daisy hissed. "There's only a ten second window." She dug a handful of sparkling powder from her purse and began tossing it at herself.

The sexy jungle-princess dress morphed into a skinny black skirt. The long hem grazed ankles now covered by a pair of low-heeled suede boots. Her previously bare back and shoulders hid underneath a collared white blouse, buttoned down the front and at the wrists, and tucked loosely into the waist of the skirt. Several bronze pins clipped her shoulder-length blonde hair behind her head in a neat bun. A thin gold watch circled her left wrist.

In fact, the only remaining Daisy-like accessory was the omnipresent cat-eye glasses, now folded over the parted neck of her shirt.

She no longer looked like some fly-by-night would-be Tinkerbell. She looked like—she looked like—Trevor swallowed. He didn't know what she looked like, but she looked good. Respectable. Approachable. Human.

Her wide hazel eyes met his. Their sparkle briefly hid behind a slow blink, as though something in his expression surprised her as much as his reaction to her new appearance surprised *him*.

He smiled. He couldn't help it.

Her brows arched. Not with condescension or arrogance, but with question, as if she hadn't been confident she'd chosen the right look... until she'd seen his face.

If she had any clue about the sudden war raging between his brain and his body, she'd know exactly how "right" she looked. How was it possible high heels and a button-down shirt tripped his trigger even more than her painted toenails did?

His lips parted, but before his traitorous mouth could say something stupid to embarrass them both, Katrina popped out of her trance.

"Coach!" She took a halting step forward and then caught sight of the laptop in his arms. "Oh. I already gave it to you." She glanced at Daisy. "Who is...?"

"She's—"

"I'm Professor Fey," Daisy interrupted, her voice authoritative and steady. "I'm a professional scholar and scientist, on loan from... Greece."

If Trevor hadn't known better, he would've believed every word.

"Greece is awesome! But what are you doing here?"

Daisy held out her hand. "I'm an old friend of Professor Masterson's and on holiday. Did you have a good time on your trip?"

Katrina grinned and gave Daisy's hand a quick shake. "Man, did I! Costa Rica rocks. *Pura vida* all the way, baby. I gotta get back there soon."

Daisy's lips curved into an indulgent teacher smile. "I certainly hope you do. Well, I believe we're done with the lab for the night. Do you need a ride home?"

"Nah." Katrina shook her head. "I'm parked in the student lot." She jogged to the exit and called, "See ya Monday for finals," to Trevor before disappearing out the door.

With a ragged sigh, Daisy slumped against the nearest counter. "Thank Ganesha it worked."

He stared back at her. "You doubted it would?"

She gazed at him for a moment, looking beautiful, vulnerable, and exhausted. "Every second of the way." When he stepped forward, she pushed away from the steel surface and straightened. "Well, I guess I better get those teeth put back so I can leave you in peace."

"Wait."

Her eyes widened, but she didn't move.

Wait? Why *should* she wait? Trevor forced a quick smile. Didn't he now have everything he wanted? Shouldn't he send her on her way? He wasn't stalling just to spend a few more moments with the erstwhile fairy, was he? "I, ah… I want to make sure nothing's wrong with the laptop."

Well, that was true. He did want to make sure nothing was wrong with the laptop. The hard drive contained all the notes, all the photography, all the spreadsheets—all the research he needed to craft his dissertation on the dig.

Daisy gestured toward the computer case. "Go ahead."

"Not here. All the metal interferes with the Wi-Fi. We'll have to go to my office. I want to transfer a copy of the files to my network directory before anything else happens."

She shrugged, slung her purse over one graceful shoulder, and strode out into the hallway.

Trevor cursed himself. He had plenty of detailed notes for each of the previous digs. Now that he had the laptop, he could put the teeth away himself if he really wanted to. There was no legitimate reason for her to stick around.

Unless you counted "because I don't want her to go" as a legitimate reason.

He snuck a sidelong glance. She'd stolen from him, yes, but as it turned out, she was just trying to do her job. Just like he'd been trying to do his. And then there was the way the stretchy skirt clung to the lines of her legs, reminding him with blood-pounding force of the welcome heat of her thighs against his.

Life had been so much easier when he could hate her.

He followed her out of the lab, unable to divert his gaze. He should be peering into a ForgetMe orb, not staring at the way her derrière moved under the thin black skirt. He should be sending her straight to Nether-Netherland, not inviting her back to his office. She wasn't his coworker and they weren't actually dating. He wasn't even sure it was possible. Although, part of him would certainly *like* it to be possible…

At the sound of Daisy's gasp, Trevor tore his gaze from the curve of her ass and goggled at his once upright office door, now off its hinges and slanting against the doorframe like an impromptu wilderness lean-to.

She gazed at him in shock. "What in the world happened?"

"No idea." He ducked beneath the tilted wooden door and slipped into his office. "Probably a senior prank."

Other than the bizarrely remodeled entranceway, everything else looked just how he'd left it. Floor, strewn with office miscellany and bits of shattered phone. Desk, askew and free of all its pens and papers. Just looking at the smooth surface heated his flesh with the memory of Daisy, pinned beneath him as he—

"Sorry about all this," she said, interrupting his train of thought. Thank God. "I'll clean up while you check your files."

Half expecting her to break out some sort of purple clean-up pouch, he wasn't sure how to react when she dropped to her knees and started collecting post-its and red-capped pens. He willed himself to concentrate on the dig instead of the excellent view down the front of her shirt.

Trevor stepped gingerly around the scattered file folders and paperclips. He dropped into his swivel chair, tugged the laptop free from its case, and hit the power button. While the machine whirred to life, he watched Daisy surreptitiously through lowered lashes.

What had she called herself? Professor Fey. She did look the part. A young, sexy professor, fit for screen time in a remake of Van Halen's "Hot for Teacher" video. Her legs, long and firm… her breasts, molding the thin white fabric into classic Barbie-doll perfection…

As if he'd telegraphed his thoughts through the searing, charged air, she glanced up at him, cheeks tinged a dusky rose. "What are you thinking about?"

He shifted in his swivel chair. Nothing he wanted to share, that was for sure.

"Katrina," he fibbed. "I'm glad she's back, safe and sound."

An indecipherable shadow flickered over Daisy's eyes and she returned her focus to the floor. His writing implements were back inside his Greg Maddux collector's cup. His file folders were back in their metal desktop divider. His papers were back in a neat pile on top of his desk. His phone was still broken, but the pieces had been relegated to his blue plastic trash can.

Everything was back to normal.

Except Daisy. She was normal for the first time. He couldn't tear his eyes away.

But it wasn't just her looks. He understood her better now. She might be a would-be tooth fairy from another dimension, but she went through the same 9-to-5 nightmare as any office monkey on Earth.

Between her bitch of a supervisor, her nutcase of a father, and her trouble with the law, she had plenty on her mind. A mind that was nowhere near as diabolical—or ditzy—as he'd once thought. Dentition spectrometer? Mechanical wand? Double major in engineering and neurophysics?

"How'd you know so much about iron poisoning?" he asked, then kicked himself at the incongruity of the blurted question.

She shrugged and righted his fake potted ficus.

"Undergrad requirements." She turned, hands on hips, and surveyed the room. "Good as new. How're your notes coming?"

Notes. Shit.

Trevor logged onto the computer and paged through the files. Photos with descriptive labels, tagged and organized. Spreadsheets, with charts and calculations crammed onto each tab. Field notes, dutifully transcribed and saved under the last name of each participant.

He pulled up the one marked "Masterson."

Day One, hobnobbing with the locals. Day Two, breaking ground. Scroll, scroll. Day Seventeen, finding the first bones. Day Eighteen, finding the broken pieces of pottery. Scroll, scroll. Day Twenty-One, taking the rock-encrusted skull back to his tent. Day Twenty-Two, Little Angus, followed by three question marks. Little Angus?

He clicked to read Katrina's comment. *Don't know what this means, but it was in the margin of your notes.* He'd thought the incongruous name was part of a grifter con. But what if it wasn't?

"Did you mean what you said?" Daisy asked suddenly. His gaze jerked to hers and she blushed at the sudden eye contact. "About wanting to forget me. Wishing we'd never met."

His jaw clenched. That damned Truth Spell.

"I didn't mean to hurt you," he said, his voice sounding scratchy and strange even to his own ears. "And I don't wish we never met. I just want my life to get back to normal."

"You didn't hurt me," she said quickly, her hand fluttering in an "it was nothing" gesture.

"Daisy, I…" He paused. He'd been around enough women to know wounded pride when he saw it, but how much of himself was he willing to give away in order to assuage her hurt feelings? "If it makes you feel better," he said, and then cringed at the unholy badness of that opening, "it's not about wanting to forget you. I did and do find you attractive even without the Himalayan Lust Charm. But you're a fairy. From another dimension. And, apparently, some kind of tooth felon. Which means we could never be anything—not even friends."

CHAPTER 14

The top of Berrymellow's red head poked out from under the slanted door. He stared at them for a second and then slithered into the room with wide, blinking eyes.

"Masterson!" he shouted, knocking the door even more off-kilter in his haste to greet Trevor. The unbalanced wood slid down the wall and clattered to the floor.

"*Doctor* Masterson," Daisy corrected haughtily.

Trevor could've hugged her.

"You." Berrymellow's shaking forefinger pointed at Daisy's face. He scowled at Trevor. "Thought you said you turned her into a frog."

Daisy shot Trevor an annoyed glare. He shrugged. "I got better."

"Oh yeah?" Berrymellow clutched his omnipresent briefcase to his chest. He'd probably published thirty more pointless papers in the past ten minutes. "Then how'd you leave this office? I was waiting right outside the door."

Trevor's fists clenched. He *knew* that sanctimonious bastard spied on him.

Daisy inched closer to Trevor. "Maybe he left through the window?"

Berrymellow tugged at his goatee. "Thus disappearing from an obvious crime scene? Hey. Wait." He gaped around the office. "What happened to the crime scene?"

"There is no crime scene." Trevor leaned back in his swivel chair and propped his feet atop his desk. "What are you talking about?"

"This!" Berrymellow's arms widened, encompassing the tidy office. "I saw you come in here with her. There were noises. Crashes. Screams. And when I came knocking, there was only you standing in the midst of a mess. I knew you'd killed her, just like you killed Katrina."

"I'm right here," Daisy offered.

"I see that now," Berrymellow snapped. "But Katrina—"

"Is probably home in bed," Trevor interrupted in his best professional-negotiator-talking-with-an-imbalanced-psycho voice. "We ran into her leaving campus an hour ago."

"You—" Berrymellow clutched at his bolo tie as if choking on his own reply. "Really?"

"Really." Trevor closed his laptop and slid it into his case. "What were you doing hanging around outside my office? Perhaps you're not respecting professional boundaries."

"I was worried about you." Berrymellow whirled to face Daisy. "Miss le Fey, why are you dressed up like a professor instead of a student?"

"I am a professor." She flashed him a brilliant smile. "Trevor—that is, Professor Masterson—and I are old college friends. I, too, am an anthropologist, but at another university."

He gazed at her appreciatively. Good one. She had to know at least as much about humans as Berrymellow did. Probably more.

Trevor crossed his arms and froze his coworker with a glare. "Why were you worried about me?"

"Well, first I was worried about Miss le Fey." Berrymellow dipped in a sycophantic bow. "Or is it Professor le Fey?"

"I prefer Professor Fey." Daisy leaned against the edge of the desk and idly flipped through a binder. "It's easier to remember."

Berrymellow shrugged and returned his focus to Trevor. "So anyway, I heard you come back—noises, anyway—and I knocked on the door again, but that time you didn't answer. So I waited. And when the minutes turned into hours and the hours turned into days, how could I *not* worry?" He turned to Daisy again, eyes narrowed. "If you're a professor at some other university, then what are you doing here?"

"An anthropological study, of course," Daisy said smoothly. She removed her cat-eye glasses from the front of her blouse and slipped them on her face. "While many of my colleagues have tried to infiltrate the lives of high school kids to document the trials of troubled teens in today's society, I decided to pose as a college student and focus my energy on deciphering the interconnectedness between hazing rituals and post-baccalaureate dropout rates."

Berrymellow gaped at her in wonder. "That's brilliant!"

Trevor wasn't so sure. The minutes had turned into hours and— what? His tongue finally found words to express his incredulity at the alleged time-lapse. "What exactly do you mean, 'days'?" he demanded, his voice deteriorating into a dangerous growl.

"Well, you disappeared Wednesday night, didn't you?" Berrymellow gestured at Trevor's Wrigley Field wall calendar. "And now it's Thursday night. I guess that's just one day, but still."

"Thursday," Trevor seethed through clenched teeth, searing Daisy with a scowl guaranteed to melt lead. He swung his feet to the floor and stood, hooking the strap of his laptop case over one shoulder. "You have got to be kidding me."

"What?" She jumped off his desk, knocking over the plastic trashcan in the process. "You knew you stayed the night."

Berrymellow's eyes widened with fascination. "You stayed the night with a visiting professor? What kind of college 'friends' were you?"

"I thought," Trevor bit out, "that you were taking me back to where I left off."

Daisy's glossy mouth stretched into a nervous smile.

"Where, yes," she mumbled, pushing up her glasses with the back of her hand. "When, no."

"I missed all of today's classes?" he roared, advancing toward her with icy fire racing underneath his skin. "I missed my appointment with the dean?"

"And I humbly thank you for that," Berrymellow said with a smirk. "Way to cement my tenure for me." He bent down to right the toppled trashcan and gasped. "Ha!" His hand flew inside and pulled up a handful of broken phone. "I knew it!" he crowed. "I told you!"

"Get out," Trevor warned him softly, "before I cement your teeth into our connecting wall."

Berrymellow dropped the bits of phone and held up shiny palms. With an unrepentant shrug, he bolted from the room.

Rather than meet his eyes, Daisy suddenly appeared fascinated by the ceiling tiles.

"Fix this," Trevor commanded, jabbing his index finger at her, then at the calendar. "I will not have that imbecile supplanting me in this university simply because I got embroiled in some inter-fairy courtroom drama. Fix this *now*."

"I'm sorry," she stammered, her pretty face contorting into a pale, miserable expression. "But I can't."

Daisy tried not to notice the expression on Trevor's face go from horror to rage.

She closed her eyes and slid her hands down over her hips. How could her palms be so sweaty and her fingertips so cold? And what was with this slippery non-absorbent material? She opened her eyes and glared at her dress.

No comfy dress. Performance polyester.

"I'm sorry," she said, for what felt like the hundredth time. When would her messed-up life stop messing up his? "There's really nothing I can do."

"Oh?" The hint of forgiveness she'd glimpsed before Berrymellow's arrival had vanished from Trevor's eyes. "As a matter of fact, there is."

With one quick stride, he was at her side. He snatched Bubbles from her shoulder and strode from the office.

Choking on a lungful of outrage, Daisy sprinted after him. "Give him back! Trevor! Wait!" She raced down the cold gray hall, chasing him past closed doors and around twisting corners. She stumbled twice, thanks to the unfamiliar pitch of heeled shoes beneath her feet, and almost lost him.

At last, she followed him into a small white-tiled room and found him opening and closing cupboard door after cupboard door. She sagged against the doorjamb and debated going barefoot.

"Where are we?"

"Break room."

"Why are we here?"

"I'm looking for something."

"What are you doing with Bubbles?"

With one hand, he pulled a dented Harry Caray lunch box down from a shelf, flipped open the metal tab, and dumped its contents into the trash.

He placed her where-frog inside.

Daisy lurched forward to make a grab for Bubbles, but Trevor turned his back to her and lifted the refastened lunchbox high above his head.

He stalked to the refrigerator and slammed open the door without making eye-contact. "What do where-frogs eat?"

"Uh, meat," she stammered. "He used to be a where-wolf."

"He used to be a were-what?"

"Wolf. Not the lycanthropic kind, the teleportation sort. W-H-E-R-E. I accidentally transmogrified him into a frog while testing a first batch of scientifically engineered pixie dust. I haven't been able to fix him yet."

"You screwed up some poor creature's life? Imagine." Trevor snapped open the lunchbox lid. He rummaged through the fridge and tossed a slice of bologna and a few saucy meatballs in with Bubbles. "Why not ask someone competent for help?"

Daisy turned an automatic retort into a tight-lipped grimace. She deserved that.

"They've tried," she admitted. "Apparently, straight magic can't always counteract scientific magic. Something to do with unnatural hybrid energy endangering the molecular balance between—"

"Katrina," Trevor interrupted, gaze narrow. "The talking pumpkin. Straight magic or scientific magic?"

"Uhhh…" Crap. She stared at her shoes. "Scientific magic?"

"You risked her *life?* And didn't tell me?" He snapped the lunchbox closed, brushed past Daisy, and stormed out of the break room.

"Wait," she called, taking off after him, her heels skidding on the slick tile. "Don't suffocate Bubbles!"

He cracked open the lid without breaking stride. "He's not immortal?"

"Nobody's immortal."

His steps faltered as he twisted his neck to meet her gaze. "You're not immortal?"

"No, of course not." Daisy reached Trevor's side. She wanted him to realize she was a bad fairy, not a bad person, but wasn't sure there was much of a difference in his eyes. And she wanted to make a grab for the lunch box, but if she did, she was pretty sure he'd club her with it. "Where are you going?"

"Home."

"Now?" She struggled to keep pace. "Why?"

"It's late," he answered, without turning to face her again. "I'm too tired to deal with this crap."

"What are you doing with Bubbles?"

"Keeping him away from you until my life is back the way I like it." He sped up. "I've got to get some sleep and I don't trust you not to poof back to Nether-Netherland in the middle of the night and leave me stranded."

Daisy was forced to jog to keep at his side. "Where are you going to put him?"

"In an old aquarium."

"What about me?"

"You're a bigger fish."

Trevor ended up housing Daisy in his bedroom and taking the living room couch so he could keep an eye on the where-frog. He'd finally fallen into a fitful sleep after padlocking the aquarium closed, but he couldn't stay asleep for more than an hour at a time.

He'd never kidnapped a where-anything before—or an apprentice tooth fairy—but he knew better than to trust either one. "You're Fired!"kept haunting Trevor's dreams. When Trevor's alarm blasted from his cellphone atop the rack of Blu-Rays next to his couch, he didn't feel the slightest bit rested.

Nonetheless, Trevor shut off the alarm and stumbled into the bathroom, only to discover his impromptu houseguest already in the shower.

That woke him up.

If he'd made better architectural choices, his shower door would be made of massive, floor to ceiling, see-through glass. His senses would be overcome with Daisy's wet, naked silhouette through the steamy, beveled door. And they'd be three seconds away from getting it on.

Well, if she weren't an unbalanced scientist whose magically-challenged wand destroyed everything it touched.

In any case, he hadn't had the presence of mind to install clear glass shower doors. Instead, a blue vinyl shower liner flanked the inside of the tub and a white cloth curtain covered in Cubs baseball helmets hung on the outside. Both were pulled tight.

"I need to take a shower," he shouted toward the curtain. He parked himself right next to the sink to wait. She had to come out of the tub sometime.

"So do I," she hollered back, without so much as poking her head from the curtains.

The spicy scent of his Irish Spring bar soap filled the air. Definitely not her usual. He should keep some sort of flowery, girly stuff on hand just in case hot fairies stayed over without packing an overnight bag. "Don't you have some kind of... of magic shower?"

"I left it at home," she called back from the other side of the curtain.

Then again, her running around smelling like *him* was kind of erotic, in an unsettling sort of way. He hated her again, Trevor reminded himself. She should try to smell like someone else. "Can't you wave your wand and conjure one up?"

"I left that at home, too."

"What?" He frowned. How was she going to fix things? "No wand? Seriously?"

"Well, I didn't know you were going to kidnap Bubbles," came the defensive reply above the slippery sounds of water running over wet skin. "I thought this would be easy. Fast. In and out."

Easy. Fast. In and out. Trevor shifted his boxers as the memories flooded back. "But... I saw you poof out of your fairy outfit."

"Not with my wand, you didn't." The tips of her elbows appeared above the curtain, as though she were sudsing up her hair just beyond his line of sight. "I used my clothes powder."

"Clothes powder?" he repeated, barely following the conversation.

"I carry it in my handbag. Makes it much easier to dress for work. And undress."

Dress. And undress. Right. Trevor stared at the open black purse flopped on top of the toilet seat. Without the clothes-powder, she'd have to stay as naked as the day she was born. Did half-angel tooth fairies even *get* born?

Damn it.

Trevor pushed out of the bathroom and slammed the door behind him. For a libidinous minute, he'd forgotten who she was and why she was there. He wouldn't make that mistake again.

He strode into the kitchen, plucked his red, white and blue Chicago Cubs coffee cup from the dish drainer, and beelined to the coffee machine. Thank God for automatic timers. Caffeine might not be as good a wake-up call as, say, hot sex, but it would help unmuddle his mind.

Before he'd finished his second cup, Daisy sauntered around the corner. Not naked and glistening, as a lesser man might have hoped, or even clad in nothing but a fluffy white towel. Nonetheless, he had to admit she looked good.

Once again, her hair was tucked into its tiny, nape of the neck bun and her cat-eye glasses nestled between her breasts. Today's blouse was crimson silk, peeking between the open lapels of a form-fitting black business jacket. He glimpsed a mouth-watering triangle of tanned flesh between the top two unfastened blouse buttons. Just a couple more and he'd have a great cleavage view. Not that he was interested in her chest.

If it weren't for the bare feet poking out from the tapered cuffs of the tailored black pants, he'd've thought she was, well, normal.

"Shoes?" he prompted hoarsely, gesturing at her painted toes with his empty mug.

She glanced at her toes. "Right." With a flick of her wrist, she rose a few inches taller as her slender feet angled into strappy, high-heeled shoes. "I thought you were in a hurry. Don't you want to shower?"

Well, yes, that was somewhere on his unexpectedly reordered wish list of things to do this morning.

He set his empty coffee mug in the sink and eased past her into the hallway. His knuckles accidentally-on-purpose grazed against the side of her thigh as he passed. How could he hate someone and want to screw her senseless at the same time?

Catching sight of the hall clock, Trevor decided a nice, subzero shower temperature was probably best. He was running late enough as it was. No sense taking up even more time masturbating in steamy water while fantasizing about the magical disrobing power of clothes-powder.

After drying and dressing the normal human way, he stopped by the pantry to leave the where-frog a snack before heading for work.

"How does Bubbles feel about Slim Jims?"

Daisy closed whatever massive tome she'd been reading and shoved it in her handbag. "Who's that?"

Trevor grabbed one from the shelf and whipped it toward her. "It's a long... salty... meat thing."

She caught the package between her palms. "Sounds delicious. Do you mind?"

Why, not at all. He'd love to give her a—Trevor tore his gaze away. No matter what else he managed to accomplish today, he had to get his mind out of the gutter.

"Will he stay here if I let him out of his cage while we're gone? He won't pop off to Bali or anything?"

"Bubbles is a good boy. He doesn't go anywhere unless requested. And what do you mean, 'we'? Am I going to school with you now?"

"Of course."

After leaving Bubbles some water and some snacks, Trevor led Daisy out the door by her elbow and helped her into the car.

"You didn't seriously think I'd let you stay home alone, did you? For one, you've still got all my teeth. For two, I heard the judge tell you not to come back until you'd put everything to rights. Everything is still wrong. And for three..." He leaned over, hyperconscious of every curve of her body as he stretched her seatbelt across her breasts to buckle her in. "I don't trust you."

Her nose lifted, but she didn't respond. Fine. He didn't want to talk anyway. She stared out the passenger window for most of the trip before blurting, "I said I would put back the teeth. Won't that help?"

"Not enough." He slanted her a dark look before pulling off the bypass onto University Blvd. "The first item of business is to figure out how my office door got off its hinges. If that's some magical shrapnel side-effect from blasting into another dimension, I expect you to put it back to normal before anyone else starts asking questions."

Daisy followed Trevor down the gray hallway to the Anthropology lab, careful to stay at least two feet behind him so he wouldn't singe her eyelashes with his perpetual glowering.

"Fairies first." He swept open the heavy metal door and ushered her inside with a big show of icy chivalry.

She strode into the lab and took a surreptitious glance around. Windowed walls faced the empty classroom and shiny stainless steel covered the continuous counter, artifacts and skeletons strewn on top. Everything looked how she'd left it.

Well, except for the infamous missing teeth.

"Go do your thing with the Super Cool Tooth Tool or whatever it's called." He eased onto a stool, crossed his arms, and glared at her. "I'll be right here."

With a quick nod, she turned toward the countertops. At least he wasn't breathing down her neck. Not that she minded his breath on her skin, but those days were obviously long gone. She rolled her shoulders in a futile attempt to release tension. Right now, she needed to concentrate on matching the teeth with their owners.

She withdrew the first pouch of teeth from her handbag and peeked inside. This one contained the bicuspids. With a guilty sigh, she lined the small dry teeth on the cold metal counter with the rest of the pouches. Sixteen bicuspids. She frowned. Shouldn't there only be fifteen? Why hadn't the Pearly States confiscated the one belonging to Angus, age 8? Disconcerted, she pulled the Genetic Teradata Carbon Dentition Spectrometer from her handbag. With a quick flick of the power toggle, the handheld device hummed softly in her hands.

She snuck an over-the-shoulder glance at Trevor. He watched in silence, his expression unreadable.

Hopefully this would impress him. She'd never forget how nonplused he'd been when he learned she'd invented something useful. Granted, before she took a soldering iron to the motherboard, the dentition spectrometer had begun its life as an intraoperative magnetic resonance portable imaging system from a primary school Magic Fair project, but hey. Minor detail.

What she needed to focus on was finding Angus's tooth. The sooner she had the right tooth, the sooner everyone's lives would be back on track.

Doing her best to tamp down the ick factor, she approached the closest skeleton. She slid a bicuspid into the spring-loaded dentition spectrometer receptacle and waited. Within seconds, the display panel read: "Adult male. Japanese ancestry. Twentieth century. More? Yes/No."

Not the right set of teeth. Crap. She perused the specimens displayed throughout the lab. The eye ridges and wide hip bones indicated two of the skeletons were female. One was smaller than average, but might be a child and not an Asian woman. Or not. Daisy frowned and double-checked her pouch. If this were a child, she would have milk teeth, not adult teeth. Yet all the teeth she'd collected were of a uniform size. She'd not only put her trust in her mentor and the Pearly States automated assignment system, she'd also been so focused on confiscating the teeth to keep out of jail, she hadn't even considered the possibility that the tooth didn't belong to a child. There would be hell to pay if she'd managed to deliver the wrong tooth all over again. She gulped.

"Hey." Trevor slid from the metal stool, curiosity erasing the surliness from his tone. "What's the magic tooth-box say?"

"It says, 'hold your flying horses.' Also, I hope this thing is broken." Gripping the dentition spectrometer with shaking fingers, Daisy gestured across the lab. "Does that skeleton belong to an Asian woman?"

Jaw dropping, he flew off the stool like a flaming chariot.

He made a grab for the dentition spectrometer. She pivoted, jerking the portable machine to her chest. He plastered the front of his body along the back of hers, grabbing the tops of her arms with both warm hands, and forcing her spine flush against him.

His breath steamed lightly against her neck. Then ever so slowly, she peered at the display panel. Her skin tingled beneath the unfamiliar clothes at the heat and hardness of his solid, masculine body. The edge of his jaw brushed against her cheek, inciting a familiar pelvic fire at the feel of his stubble against her face.

"It says… uh…" After a moment of wordlessly sucking in the scent of his aftershave, Daisy gave up and handed him the device.

He let go of her arms but did not step away. Instead, he tilted the display panel toward the light. "Awesome," he breathed, his voice low with admiration. "You invented this?"

She hesitated. Now would probably be the time to admit she'd merely tweaked the circuitry of the primary processor after coding a new graphical user interface to access her re-designed ontogenetic relational database, but all she could do at the moment was nod her head and try really hard not to kiss him.

"Can I try it?" Without waiting for a response, he rushed to the nearest counter, leaving Daisy's cheek and arms and back and thighs chilly with his absence.

When she turned to face him, he already had the first tooth out of the spectrometer and new one sliding into place.

"Sure," she mumbled, since it clear he wasn't listening for a response. "Go ahead."

Preoccupied, she familiarized herself with Trevor's lab while he analyzed the first few teeth and seemed to commit every word of the resulting data to memory. He clearly had every intention of taking his time. Too bad she hadn't brought her wand along for tinkering with. She might've been able to work some of the kinks out during her stay on Earth. Judge Banshee had said not to come back until everything was put to rights, but surely someone would notice if Trevor trapped her here *forever*.

Trevor. Forever. Two words that didn't belong in the same sentence.

Maybe if he hadn't been human. Maybe if they'd met under better circumstances. Maybe if he miraculously forgave her for forking up his career, discovered he couldn't live without her after all, and decided to move to Nether-Netherland to woo her undying love.

"Sweet," he crowed from across the room. "I'll have everything put to rights in no time. That is, if it's not already too late."

"Yeah." The ridiculous fantasy disintegrated. It was an illogical hope. He would've forgiven her by now if he were ever going to. He would've come to her last night if he still wanted her body. And he would've let the poor where-frog out of its cage overnight if he trusted either one of them an iota. Daisy leaned back against the counter, elbows propped against the stainless steel. "You can keep the spectrometer, if you like."

"Aren't you afraid I'll be the Edison to your Tesla and exploit your ingenuity to increase my own fortune and fame?"

"I have no need for money, and humans shouldn't even know I exist. The fame can be yours. Go for it."

"Nah." He exchanged the current spectrometer tooth for another. "I was just kidding. You can have it back when I'm done. I'd never steal anyone's anything."

"Except my where-frog."

"No, he's temporarily detained. Believe me, I'll be giving him back. I don't want to have anything to do with Nether-Netherland ever again in my life."

"Uh… thanks. I guess." Although an understandable stance, it was hard not to be hurt. Particularly since every molecule of her being was directly tied to home. She had just really, really wanted to be the exception. In a good way, for once. Wanted. She fiddled with her glasses. Maybe she should go back to the Neurophysics Compound. But only after she made fairy. Once people saw she was as accomplished as any of them, she could focus her passion wherever she wanted, without fear of judgment. "All righty then. I'll be out of your hair just as soon as you're done with the spectrometer and I pop you with a ForgetMe orb." When he didn't respond right away, she couldn't stop herself from adding, "Right?"

Stupid, stupid, stupid. She shouldn't expect him to say no. She shouldn't want him to say no. She shouldn't *hope*—

"No."

A choked laugh-sob tangled in her throat. Holy crap. He'd said no! Maybe he dreaded her leaving just as much as she did. Maybe she'd read him all wrong.

"No," he repeated even more firmly, without glancing up from the spectrometer. "Absolutely not. You've still got to fix this time-lapse thing."

She jerked her head toward the far wall so he wouldn't see her cheeks heat with self-derision. The last thing she wanted was for him to realize she cared. "I can't. I told you."

When he finally glanced up, his eyes were hard. "Why not?"

She lifted her chin, determined to act as calm as a scientist instead of as a would-be fairy with a crush on a human. "Just think of all the chaos and paradoxes that would ensue if time travel were possible."

"Well, you have to do something. You can't just jet back off to Fairyland like you didn't screw up my entire life. Hey, wait." He squinted at the non-reflective spectrometer screen. "What did you call me when you first came to the tent? Angus?"

"Yeah, but I didn't know you'd be sleeping on someone else's tooth," she shot back defensively. "That was not in the manual."

"Trust me, it wasn't on purpose. But look here—this must be one of his teeth." Eyes shining, he hovered over a skull in the corner. "This is the skeleton from the dig. Male, check. Scotland, who knows, but makes sense based on the name if not location. Have to dig into that.

Remind me. Twelfth century... Hmm. I'm not sure I can believe that one. Are you sure this is accurate?"

Twelfth century? She sighed. "Fool-proof. It's a modified copy of the teradata triple-index system currently in use at the Pearly States, which warehouses and analyzes dentition data from multiple dimensions. Don't worry, I already filed a complaint for having to fetch the tooth of a dead child."

"Child?" He tilted the glowing display panel in her direction. "There are no child skeletons anywhere in my lab. Look—even your toy says 'adult'. Besides, only one of these specimens is even from the Costa Rica dig. All the rest are other projects."

"What?" The sick feeling returned to her stomach. She rushed across the room and grabbed the dentition spectrometer from him. "Please tell me that's not right."

"You just said it was fool-proof." He grinned to himself, his excitement apparently making him forget his anger. "Are the people who run the Pearly States fools?"

"Utterly." She stared at the digital readout with a mix of horror and confusion. "But Vivian isn't. The assignment dossier she gave me clearly stated that the collection subject was eight years old."

He shrugged and tugged the machine from her. "Maybe she made a mistake."

A mistake? Slimy fingers of doubt slithered inside Daisy's stomach. Yeah. A silly mistake. Just another bug in the system. Kind of like forgetting which pouch held a ForgetMe orb and which one would unleash a Himalayan Lust Charm. Whoops-a-daisy.

Trevor strode back and forth through the lab, dentition spectrometer in one hand and various pouches of teeth in the other. "Lemme tell you, this thing rocks." He was down to the last pouch before he glanced over at her again. "What's the matter? You're not mad about collecting an adult tooth, are you? You're a tooth fairy. I would figure you'd collect anybody's teeth. Does it matter if the... the previous hosts are children?"

"I don't know." She narrowed her eyes at the teeth resting innocently on his palm. She had never heard of tooth fairies collecting adult teeth... but his point was well made. Whose jurisdiction would adult teeth fall under, if not tooth fairies? "A mentor could at least warn her protégé of such things. Old and *dead* make for a bit of a surprise."

Note to self: Go back to the Pearly States and file a whole stack of formal complaints.

Trevor's gaze turned contemplative. "If you're so worried about whether or not she lied to you, why don't you just give her a truth spell? You know, like the one I got at the jail."

"Like the what?" she choked out, her stomach full-on nauseous. If that were true, she hadn't been given a fair trial and Trevor hadn't been as callous as she'd thought. At least, not on purpose. "Who gave you a truth spell?"

"Vivian. That's who we're talking about, right?" He popped another tooth in the dentition spectrometer. "Vivian Valdemeer. Big hair, bigger ego, tiny teeth?"

"*Vivian* administered a truth spell?" Her stomach roiled. She swallowed with difficulty as the bitter taste of betrayal coated the back of her tongue. "At the Human Containment Center?"

"Right before the trial." His upper lip curled in remembrance. "What a bitch."

Normally, a comment like that would provoke Daisy's automatic "defend the mentor" speech. Not today. As much as she hated to believe anything uncomplimentary about the one person who'd given her a chance to be magical when the rest of the world accepted her relentless mundanity as a foregone conclusion, she couldn't deny the ever-increasing probability that her glamorous mentor had an agenda of her own.

One that didn't include Daisy succeeding.

CHAPTER 15

*B*ack in his office after his round of morning classes finished, Trevor scowled over the top of his laptop at the long-legged pseudo-anthropologist idly browsing his bookcase. How was he supposed to get work done with her standing around looking sexy? The dean had been pleased to hear him report Katrina was back safe and sound, but he was still a far cry from having job security.

Berrymellow thought he had the tenure position in the bag, and from where Trevor was sitting, the little worm actually might. And God help the university when Berrymellow ran the program and Trevor was nowhere to be found. The school's anthropology ratings would be in the toilet in no time, and Trevor would be fresh out of luck.

Daisy *had* to be able to help him. His life, his students' education, and the future of the anthropology department depended on it. But how?

He tried to brainstorm in the back of his mind while organizing dig data with the front of his mind, but he caught himself staring at Daisy instead.

With an odd-shaped iPod clipped to her belt, she removed another anthropological tome from the shelf. Cat-eye glasses perched at the tip of her nose. Wispy blonde tendrils escaped a schoolmarm-like bun adorned with one of his pens. She rifled through the each reference archive, flipping through every single page in less than thirty seconds before returning it to the shelf and reaching for another. Every now and then, her lips pursed and she gurgled something that sounded like, "Urrrrrgh." Much like her furry lawyer.

She licked her lips and mumbled. Probably thinking about something mindbogglingly esoteric. Why did he find that so appealing? Maybe because Daisy was just as incredible as the place she was born. That fascinating mind of hers had a unique way of interpreting the world around them. No one else was quite like her. Perhaps that was why he always wanted to be in her presence. Well, that and her kisses.

He dragged his attention back to the glowing flat screen. *Concentrate.*

Carefully, he scrolled through the dig photos, double-clicking a thumbnail now and then to pop open a larger image and update its metadata.

Before long, the warm, prickly sensation of someone else hovering around his office while he tried to work began to grate on his nerves. Not just because he remembered in vivid detail the last time they shared a room with a desk, but because if he hated one thing in this world, it was not having his life under his control.

Anthropology was about scientific process. Baseball was based on a strict set of predefined rules. Tenure was the culmination of a systematic series of accomplishments. He *liked* having set boundaries and a clear path. He *liked* that everything adhered to the playbook. And he loved the freedom it gave him to guide his own destiny. He well knew that no one else was going to step in and pinch hit. That wasn't how the game was played. People like Daisy threw curveballs. And people like Berrymellow should get benched.

Trevor opened the next set of photos. He hadn't gotten this far in life by relying on other people. He'd gotten where he was by relying on the one person he could count on—himself. No way was he letting all that hard work foul out without a fight. But what could he do?

He hit the icon for Slideshow View and watched the dig photos display in slow motion. The excavation jerked forward through time, blossoming like the stop-animation footage of an orchid in bloom. He smiled at the memory. God, he loved every senior trip even more than the last.

There was the team, excavating bits of pottery from the earth. And there, bones poked up through the dirt and rock. Excitement shone in the face of every single student. Excitement and the thrill of victory. They'd played by the rules and were rewarded with a find. A satisfying end to weeks of hard work. Pottery and skeletons were logical artifacts any self-respecting paleo-anthropologist would expect to discover when digging near the site of a known underwater city in the heart of Central America.

Women wearing glitter wings, on the other hand, tended to not crop up on archaeological digs. And that was the moment his rational, ordered life began its inexorable descent into absurdity. Pausing the slideshow, he cast another sidelong glance toward the mysterious fairy paging through his research books. His growing conviction that a sexy, stubborn tooth fairy had invented a Genetic Teradata Carbon Dentition Spectrometer, and was speaking yeti under her breath, blew his freaking mind.

But that didn't mean he could trust her—or the magical data provided through pseudo-science. He would earn his continued employment by hard work, not by trickery. First he'd fact check every single detail, and personally research a thousand more. He would be an expert on every grain of dirt, every sliver of pottery, every shard of bone.

Speaking of which... He alt-tabbed to Chrome and clicked his Google bookmark. This was probably a fool's errand, but anthropologists were nothing if not thorough. He would begin with the obvious. Tilting back in his swivel chair so his laptop screen faced away from Daisy, he tapped out A-N-G-U-S S-C-O-T-L-A-N-D C-O-S-T-A R-I-C-A and pressed enter.

205,000 matches. A soft puff of disbelief came out unbidden. He'd have to hire an intern just to page through all the crap in search of something useful. He scrolled through the first page of results.

Apparently, Angus was the name of a town in Scotland. Angus was the name of a hotel in La Fortuna, Costa Rica. Angus was the name of the fabled Scottish explorer who'd set sail in the late 1100s with his faithful crew and a boatload of stoneware to barter, never to be heard from again.

Wait. What?

He clicked the Wikipedia link and got a highlighted disclaimer in a giant blue square at the top of the screen.

"This article needs additional references or sources for verification."

Great. A crowd-sourced article with no legitimate sources would be a fabulous component to a well-received academic treatise.

He paged through the article anyway, beginning with the inauspicious qualifier, "According to Scottish lore," continuing past, "Since no substantiation has ever been found, such a tale can never be proven," and ending with, "Although the legend is no doubt an apocryphal myth to reimagine Leif Ericsson for Scotland, the tale of Angus the Explorer has entertained children and adults alike over the centuries for both its sense of adventure as well as its Amelia Earhart-like ending."

Despite his misgivings, Trevor's breath scraped against his throat. What if it was true, at least partially? Was it too much to hope? Was it even *possible*? His shoulders sagged. Even if the cosmos were aligned in his favor, how would he prove it?

He needed to get to a university library computer as soon as possible in order to scour every academic article in every database system. He needed to know, unequivocally, if he might be the first person to prove the legend as fact.

If so, it wouldn't be easy. He followed link after link with a mixture of cautious excitement and full-blown misgiving.

Angus the Explorer, if he truly existed, disappeared a millennium ago—long before dental records and handy Interpol databases. Even if Angus kept a conveniently detailed diary of his travels, the pages would have rotted away centuries ago, in the moist soil and humid environment.

But... if it *was* true... and he could somehow prove it... Trevor caught himself wriggling with excitement. *Man* would that be something to publish! Eat that, Berrymellow.

He tore his gaze from the web browser long enough to see Daisy pluck yet another encyclopedic volume from the shelves and carefully flip through the pages, bobbing her head to whatever played on that weird-looking iPod. He couldn't stand it anymore.

"What are you doing?" When she didn't respond, he teased, "Looking for pictures?"

She shook her head without taking her eyes from the falling pages. "Reading."

Trevor chuckled. But before he could call her bluff, a knock rapped against his doorframe. He snapped his laptop closed and buried it beneath a sheaf of student papers. Just in case there was something to this Angus stuff, no sense giving Berrymellow any inkling of potential excitement on the horizon. "Come in."

The door swung open.

"Professor Masterson." Dr. Papadopoulos stepped into the office and caught sight of Daisy, who was tugging headphones from her ears. "Oh. You do have a… guest."

He jumped to his feet. "Dr. Papadopoulos, meet Professor Fey, an old college friend of mine here on sabbatical while she researches a new theory. Professor Fey, meet Dr. Papadopoulos, the head of the Anthropology department." He hoped he conveyed enough emphasis that those last words translated to Daisy as "keeper of my job."

Daisy re-shelved the book she'd been browsing and turned to Dr. Papadopoulos. "Pleased to make your acquaintance." She smiled warmly and shook the other woman's hand. "I've heard such good things about you."

He held his breath, inwardly pleading the Lord above for Dr. Papadopoulos not to ask what, specifically, she'd heard, since he'd never once mentioned his boss to Daisy.

Dr. Papadopoulos thanked her without pressing for details and turned to face him. "Perhaps needless to say, I was quite—Trevor. What happened to your eye?"

"My eye?" His fingers touched his still-tender bruise. "Oh, my eye. Side-effect from sliding into home. I'm fine, I promise. You were saying?"

His boss stared at him as if she'd much rather discuss the unlikeliness of this tale than whatever she'd dropped by to announce. But after a tense moment, she nodded and picked back up where she'd left off.

"Yes. I was quite disappointed yesterday when I learned you missed all your classes as well as your appointment with the dean. Without so much as a phone call. And I'm particularly disappointed to learn you were not beset by an emergency, but rather the urge to play baseball."

Yikes. Maybe he should've told her he got the shiner falling onto his desk after all.

Daisy cringed at his strangled expression and stepped a little closer. "I'm afraid his absence was my fault. He was... helping me. An out-of-town personal matter cropped up quite suddenly, something neither of us could have possibly prepared for. Once the emergency had passed, I would've offered Trevor the use of a telephone, but cell service is sparse in remote locations. I do apologize."

"Hmm." Dr. Papadopoulos didn't break eye contact with Trevor, even during Daisy's impromptu alibi. "I see. In any case, certain things came to light that might have positively affected faculty opinion in your favor for the upcoming tenure vote. It's too bad that you were not here to take advantage of them. The board was displeased."

Fantastic. The great and wonderful "almost" strikes again. He fought the urge to bang his head against the wall.

"Words cannot convey how sorry I am to hear that." He swallowed. "I won't miss another meeting."

"You may not be invited to another." With her trademark blank expression, Dr. Papadopoulos inclined her head and strode out of the room, quite possibly taking Trevor's last chance for tenure with her.

Shortly after Trevor's mentor left the room, he made a beeline toward the university library. Intrigued, Daisy followed close behind, marveling at the sea of overflowing bookshelves. How strange and wonderful to have so many books just waiting to be read!

Libraries didn't exist in Nether-Netherland. The inhabitants conjured whatever book they desired, or obtained knowledge by some other means, such as the handheld interdimensional digital fact-sharing database of charms and magic.

But libraries like this... Oh! She could stay here for hours, days, weeks. Not just because she couldn't conjure a book to save her life, but because of the freedom to browse. How could she know what book to summon if she didn't even know it existed? This was wonderful. And if she'd thought Trevor's bookshelves were cramped with a plethora of eclectic volumes, this seven-floor building knocked her speechless.

Unfortunately, the sexy, stubborn anthropologist wouldn't let her wander the aisles and take it all in. Instead, he dragged her to a large, multi-windowed room filled with students and computer screens.

"Where are we?"

Trevor pointed a finger toward a wall-mounted sign. "IT lab."

"Why?" She tugged her elbow free from his grasp.

"Periodical databases. Lexis-Nexis. Electronic journals. High-speed Internet. Starbucks."

He yanked a wheeled chair over to an empty monitor and gestured her to sit. She sat. Although she couldn't claim to understand the exact terms he'd used, she imagined he referred to a network along the same lines as the interdimensional digital fact-sharing database system.

She peered at the screen while he searched in vain for another empty chair. "Your laptop doesn't have these things?"

A muscle at his temple twitched. "If it did, would we be here?"

She shrugged. So he was back to surly again. Fine.

After failing to find a free chair, he returned to her side.

She scooted sideways to give him room. "Now. What do I type?"

His jaw tightened as if it pained him to have her help. It was the same expression fairies wore when they were forced to include her during magic practice. But this time, her spine was tall. Those who can't conjure essays learned to type very, very quickly. And if he didn't want her assistance, he could feel free to send her home. Until then, she intended to do her best to fix the mess she'd caused. Maybe then he'd truly forgive her.

"Well?" she prompted, fingers poised over the keys. "Now what?"

He tugged a little notebook from his back pocket and knelt down beside her. "Type, 'Angus the Explorer.' 'Scotland.' 'Legend.' Boolean 'and'. No, don't type 'boolean', just click on the little box." A tiny burst of static leapt from the monitor when her fingernail touched the screen. "No, with the mouse. This thing." He slid a device toward her. "Now hit 'enter.'"

"What?" Heat tingled from her neck to her cheeks as he gestured to one of the keys. "Oh. There." Maybe she should've let him type after all. She might be the best typist in Nether-Netherland, but she was mortifyingly incompetent on Earth. There were no "browsers" at home because there wasn't any "Internet". Everything operated on magic.

Except her. She couldn't even operate a human-grade computer.

Faced with a choice between giving up and bursting into tears of humiliation, she chose to back away from the table. He stopped her progress with his shoe.

"It's okay." His smile was sincere and spine-melting. "You'll get it."

"Maybe," she muttered under her breath, but she let him ease her chair back in front of the screen. Probably Trevor was just being nice. Probably he wished she'd never stepped foot outside Nether-Netherland and into his university. But it sure felt nice not to be ridiculed for not being able to do what everyone else could do. He seemed so confident she'd catch on quickly that she couldn't help but regain a little optimism. She peeked at him over her shoulder. He smiled encouragingly.

He *cared* about empowering people to learn and grow, she realized suddenly. Not "cared" like just trying to earn a paycheck, but *cared-cared*. As passionately as she felt about earning wings. He must be the best coach and best teacher of the entire university. No wonder his students loved him. And no wonder her heart melted a little more every time he—

She froze when he leaned over her to squint at the screen, his hard, muscular torso scorching the thin layers of fabric between them. His warm, calloused palm slid over the back of her hand, covering her trembling fingers.

With his index finger atop hers, he clicked the little mouse and scrolled through pages of text. If he was absorbing anything from the paragraphs that raced by, he could speed-read almost as fast as her. If he wasn't... Then maybe his every nerve, every sense, every pore was hyper-attuned to their entwined fingers curling over the mouse. Maybe he could barely breathe with the searing sensation of physical closeness. Just like her.

"You're partially right." The heat of his breath steamed against the back of her ear.

She started, and fought a wave of panic. Could he read her mind? Bless Venus, she hoped not. But then, partially right about what? The part where she wanted him to clear the row of flat, rectangular monitors off the table so they could—

"*Thirty*-eight." He grinned at her, triumphant.

She stared back blankly. Every time she tried to breathe, her lungs sucked in the spicy scent of his aftershave and muddled her brain with his nearness. "Thirty-eight what?"

"Years old. He's Angus, age thirty-eight. Not Angus, age eight."

Her brain crystallized. With a gasp, she snapped her attention to the flickering screen. Dear Sophrosyne, the man was right.

"Typo?" she intoned darkly, blood pressure rising. "Or sabotage?"

"What are you talking about?" His brow furrowed, then cleared. "Vivian?"

She pointed at the screen. "The evidence is undeniable. But what would Vivian possibly gain from sending me out to repo old, dead teeth?"

"Who knows. I don't try to force logic on crazy people." He clicked a few articles and scanned their contents. "What does she usually send you for?"

She lifted a shoulder. "This was my first assignment."

"Maybe she thought not having the owner around would be easier. Do kids ever fight for possession of their teeth or sometimes haggle for more money? Dead guys can't do that. Typically." His voice lowered to a theatrical whisper. "Do you see dead people?"

She thought it over. "Not usually. I'm only allowed in Heaven on Family Appreciation Day, and I've never had a reason to visit Purgatory. Or worse." Daisy rapped her knuckles on the gray plastic folding table, hoping it counted for wood in a pinch. "And I doubt Vivian thought the Angus tooth was easier."

He paged through more search results. "So, what's your theory?"

She sighed in frustration. "I don't have one yet."

"I sent all the articles to the printer." He rose to his feet. "C'mon, you can help me staple while you think."

Casting longing glances over her shoulder at the rooms full of books, she trailed after him to learn the art of stapling.

Once they had the entire stack organized, they headed back across campus to the Anthropology building.

Before they reached his office, Trevor paused at a door marked "Men."

"Stay here." He handed Daisy the heavy stack of papers. "I'll be right out."

Daisy leaned her shoulders back against the cold cement block wall and balanced the pile of printed articles in her arms.

The door opened. Instead of Trevor, the nosy redheaded man stepped out.

"Professor Fey," he said, overemphasizing each syllable. One hand stroked the metal disc hanging from his string tie. "What have we here?"

"Obviously we have Professor Fey." She gave him a sunny smile. "And Barry Manilow."

"*Berrymellow,*" he bit out between clenched teeth. "Dr. Joshua Berrymellow."

"Ah." She flattened her back against the wall.

"Take my advice—you don't want to align yourself with Masterson. He's a wily devil. And trouble."

Daisy shivered as Trevor's image formed in her mind. He was definitely hot as Hades.

"We have a stress-free professional relationship," she managed to say without choking. "You, however, have an astounding capacity for slander and rumormongering. Professor Masterson has never hurt me, or killed me, or turned me into a frog."

"I never believed you were a frog!" Cheeks pink, he drew himself taller. "It looked nothing like you."

Daisy raised an eyebrow. "I see."

Face empurpled, Dr. Berrymellow spun away and stalked down the long hallway without another word.

Before he'd disappeared from eyesight, the air crackled and a flurry of pixie dust flooded the corridor. Followed shortly by a worry-lined fairy godmother.

"Mama. Joy."

Daisy didn't even realize she'd spoken the words aloud until Dr. Berrymellow halted, one penny-loafered foot mere inches from the ground. His voice sliced through the drafty air like a kraken on the attack.

"My dear Professor Fey," he drawled. "Did you just call me a mama's boy?" One leg still hovering above the cracked tile, he pivoted toward the bathroom hall.

"Mama!" Daisy hissed, gesturing madly. "Wings! Wings!"

With a tiny huff, Mama tapped her wand behind her back and transformed her wing-highlighting ball gown into a conservative button-down ensemble mirroring Daisy's own.

"Who is that?" Dr. Berrymellow demanded, tugging his string tie away from his neck as though choking on his words. "Where did she come from?"

"This is... Professor Bella." Daisy shot a pointed glare at her mother. "She walked around the corner when your back was turned."

"She did not!"

"Since your back was turned, how would you know?"

Dr. Berrymellow's voice rose several octaves. "Because there is no corner! Where did she really come from?"

"The bathroom, obviously."

He planted his hands on his sides. "The women's bathroom is at the other end of the hall. Unless—you don't mean—"

The bathroom door swung open, saving Daisy from having to dream up an appropriate response.

Trevor stepped out into the hallway and stumbled when he saw the unexpected visitor. "Arabella?" He seized the pile of papers from

Daisy's hands as if worried she and her mother might fly off with them. "What are you doing here?"

"Aargh." Dr. Berrymellow edged toward them. "You know this mystery woman, too? No way is her name Arabella Bella. What's the meaning of all this, Masterson?"

"Mama," Daisy muttered, frantic. "Do something."

In a flash, Mama's magic wand shot a ray of light down the almost-empty hallway and encased Dr. Berrymellow in a thin layer of stone.

"Shit!" Trevor snatched the wand out of her hand. He let go as though the silver staff burned his fingers, and the dainty rod clattered to the floor. "You can't go around turning people into stone!"

"It's not stone." With a graceful dip, Mama retrieved her wand. "It's Remember Rock."

"Remember Rock?" Trevor repeated. "Like, he's going to remember you materialized out of thin air and turned him into a rock?"

"No," Daisy corrected. "As in, he won't remember turning into a rock and he's not aware of what's going on around him."

He squinted at her suspiciously. "Will he remember what happened *before* he turned into a rock?"

"I don't know." She cocked her head toward her mother. "Will he?"

Mama shrugged. "Maybe. But that's not why I'm here. I needed to make sure my baby was all right. I know the judge didn't give you a specific deadline, but when you didn't come by for dinner, I got worried."

"She's fine." Trevor gestured down the hall. "But my colleague looks like he lost a battle with Medusa."

Mama patted him on the shoulder. "It'll wear off." She turned to Daisy. "When will you be done helping the human? Are you coming home tonight? If you like, I'll conjure spinach lasagna."

Trevor stepped in front of Daisy to face down her mother. "When? When will the spell wear off?"

Mama cast him a disapproving frown. "Five or six minutes from now, so shush for a second."

With a growl of frustration, he stalked past her toward the statue at the end of the hall.

Daisy cleared her throat. "To answer your questions, Mama, I have no idea. I thought it would be easy, but complications ensued. Again. No—don't make that face. I'm fine and I'll be home... I'll be home..." She swallowed and chanced a sidelong glance at Trevor, who was now nose to nose with the rock-encrusted Dr. Berrymellow. "I'll be home as soon as I can," she finished. "But listen, you can't just teleport in where you're not expected. Stay home with Dad. And promise me you won't come again unless I call for you."

"Sweetie, I'm your mother. I can't help but worry. What kind of daughter tells her mother not to come visit? I need to check up on you from time to time. Make sure you're okay."

"Trust me for once. No more magical visits. I'm serious. You could make things worse." She jerked her head in the direction of the impromptu Berrymellow statue. "Trevor's life is messy enough without extra fairies popping up. Not to mention the possibility of you getting yourself in trouble on top of everything else. Okay? *Promise* me, Mama."

"Okay, okay. I promise." Mama stepped forward and hugged her before disappearing in a burst of sparkling pixie dust, leaving Daisy's open arms around nothing but glitter.

The following morning, after yet another sleepless night guarding a frog-inhabited aquarium, Trevor remembered to knock before barging into the bathroom.

Unfortunately, no wet and naked Daisy lounged inside the tub. The bathroom was clean and empty. He could brush his teeth in peace.

Damn it.

Not that he aspired to be romantically involved with a tooth fairy, apprentice or otherwise. He liked his uncomplicated, unmagical life just the way it was. At least, just the way it used to be before Nether-Netherland's unwelcome imposition.

Which only went to prove a basic cosmic truth: Nothing good came of magic.

People were better off doing things themselves. The old-fashioned way. Elbow grease, self-reliance, and unwavering determination. Then again, if he hated the taint of magic so much, why was he spending the night on his couch in order to let a tooth fairy sleep in the bedroom?

It was probably past time for him to send her packing. If she couldn't turn back time, what mystic future was he still holding out for? She'd returned him home, as promised. She'd returned Katrina to normal. And she'd returned the teeth he could've put away himself. She'd even helped him in the library with a can-do attitude, despite the fact that he'd hijacked her only means of returning to her home dimension. She had to have been resentful.

He set down his toothbrush. Maybe he'd been the tiniest bit unfair after all. Unable to make eye contact with his reflection, he rinsed his newly brushed teeth with tap water from a Chicago Cubs Dixie cup and spit suds into the sink. He wasn't holding her hostage for revenge, was he? No way was he that petty. Despite the destruction she left in her wake, that surreal farce of a trial proved her an innocent party who had never been out to get him.

Maybe he was keeping her close at hand just to make sure she didn't inadvertently screw anything else up. Maybe he was hoping she would dream up a way to dig him out of the mess his missing day had created.

Or maybe he didn't want to examine his motives too closely.

He headed to the kitchen to check the status of the automatic coffeemaker. Daisy was already there, pouring dark, aromatic coffee into two matching 1921 Wrigley Field "opening day" collector's mugs. He opened his mouth to say, "Those cups aren't for drinking! I keep them behind glass for a reason!" but what came out of his mouth was a simple, "Thanks."

He couldn't say for sure, but his lack of rancor might have something to do with the fact that she'd thought of him. Was trying to be nice. Had been trying to be nice from the moment she'd brought him back to Earth, despite everything. He couldn't help but respect that.

"Hi," she said shyly, the lower half of her face obscured by the coffee cup and her eyes hidden behind steam-misted glasses. She held the oversize mug with both hands, her full lips pursing in tiny, tentative sips. "How did you sleep?"

Like crap, of course. With her lying in his bed without him, how could he possibly sleep?

Instead of answering her question, he eyed her as he sipped his coffee. "Nice robe. Why are you in a robe? Are you naked underneath? Don't answer that. Why aren't you dressed? I can see your bare legs. I can see your collarbone. I can see—is it that cold in here? Where did you get bunny slippers?"

"Clothes powder," she answered simply, choosing to ignore the majority of his questions. "And I thought it might be nice to start the morning in pajamas. Don't you?"

Pajamas? He didn't own any pajamas. He owned worn, holey baseball t-shirts and soft cotton boxer shorts. Oh God. Boxer shorts. Without a robe of his own, he couldn't disguise how much he liked her taste in pajamas.

He pivoted away from her, sloshing coffee on his hand in the process. Shit. Holding his burnt fingers to his lips, he strode into the living room, set the no-longer-mint-condition mug on a helmet-shaped coaster, flopped onto the couch, and covered his crotch with his laptop.

CHAPTER 16

$\mathcal{T}$revor stared blankly at the laptop screen, trying not to think about the delectable body underneath his houseguest's soft robe. Just because it was Saturday didn't mean he couldn't concentrate on work. If concentration were possible, with the tousle-haired fairy just a few yards away.

"Break time over already?" Daisy asked, wandering into the room and joining him on the couch.

He ground his teeth. Why didn't she sit in the recliner? The proximity of her thigh to his wasn't helping matters one bit. It's like she *wanted* to torture him.

"Why aren't you talking to me?" She nibbled her lower lip.

Totally trying to torture him.

"I am talking," he muttered. Okay, he wasn't. He was too busy trying not to say something stupid, like, "Hey. Wanna get it on?"

Stupid because, what if she said yes? If she said yes, then he probably *would*. And enticing as that sounded, he didn't need the complication. And neither did she. He wasn't sure when the tides had turned, but he'd begun to build a grudging respect toward her. Fine, he liked her. And he didn't want to mess that up.

Instead, he fired up his email program, determined to concentrate on saving his career. Back at the library, he'd emailed himself articles from the university database system, just in case something happened to the hard copies. He scanned his inbox to make sure all of them came through.

The plump softness of a ripe breast grazed his bicep. Daisy craned her neck to see the screen. "Can I help?"

"No."

His jaw clenched. Lord save him. He leaned further away, hanging sideways over the edge of the armrest. So help him, if she scooted any closer, he'd be forced to push her down onto the couch cushions, throw himself on top of her, and make love until the couch caught fire.

"What would you like me to do?"

Since he could only come up with X-rated answers to that question, Trevor unplugged his cellphone from its charger and dialed the number on his computer screen.

"Museum of Scotland," came a deep, guttural voice with an accent so thick Trevor had to pause to decipher the words.

"Yes, hello. This is Dr. Trevor Masterson, from Michiana University in the United States."

"Good morning, Dr. Masterson. How can I help you?"

Trevor took a deep breath. "Are you familiar with the legend of Angus the Explorer?"

"Who isn't?"

"Um, okay." He grabbed his notebook from the coffee table. "I read an article published by your archiving division about an extant text from that time period, referencing the legend. Can you verify this? I'm looking for any legitimate data indicating evidence of his existence."

The voice paused. "Here?"

Trevor frowned. What kind of question was that? "Anywhere."

"There is a—well, it's largely unsubstantiated as far as the legend goes, but carbon dating has proven the time frame matches, and— legitimate, you say? Yes. Well, maybe. Then again... no, probably not. My apologies."

"What?" Trevor choked out. "What were you going to say?"

"I'm sure it's nothing. It's part of a traveling exhibition of many others of its kind. To be honest, I wouldn't bother calling the exposition if I were you, because it's no doubt a dead end the size of—"

"Give me a contact. Any contact. Please."

"Okay. But don't say I didn't warn you. Country code—"

"One sec." Trevor uncapped his pen. He scribbled the number on a blank sheet in his notebook, repeating each digit back to verify. "Thanks."

"What happened?" Daisy asked when he hung up the phone. "Is it Angus?"

"I don't know yet. Gotta call some traveling exhibition." He punched in the numbers and tried to ignore the proximity of Daisy's pink-painted toes. "Hold on, it's ringing."

The person on the other end of the line said something so completely unintelligible, he almost chucked the phone through the nearest window. Instead, he clapped the receiver to his chest and grimaced.

"What?" Her big hazel eyes widened. "What did they say?"

"I don't know. Sounded like 'mushy, mushy'."

To his surprise, Daisy laughed so hard she fell off the couch. "Do you mean *moshi moshi*? Give it here."

She reached for the phone. Trevor batted her hand away. He'd made his way this far in life on his own. Surely he could place a simple phone call without her help. Then again, *moshi moshi* meant something to her and absolutely nothing to him. No sense spiting himself.

He helped her back onto the couch and handed her the phone.

She spoke into the receiver, her voice both amused and sexy, biting out staccato syllables Trevor could never reproduce.

He couldn't believe Daisy spoke—whatever she was speaking. Japanese? Chinese? Korean? What were the freaking chances?

She covered the mouthpiece with one hand and whispered, "Do you have a pencil and paper?" before resuming her incomprehensible conversation.

Trevor handed her his pen and notebook, and tried not to look too impatient. Or too impressed.

While she chattered into the phone, her hand flew across the paper, jotting down row after row of neatly printed letters. He hung onto every stroke of the pen.

"Angus definitely existed," read the first line. "Museum has papers detailing partial inventory of ship prior to sailing, donated centuries ago by the merchant who provided the pottery for barter. Only recently did the Museum of Scotland archival team realize the connection between the itemized list of stoneware and the contents on the legendary voyage. Hence the article you read." A plethora of bulleted dates and items followed. "Everything's in Tokyo for an exhibition on twelfth century bookkeeping. They're not interested in Angus, specifically, but they've only got one collection on display from Scotland, so that's got to be it."

She covered the mouthpiece again. "You can't borrow the actual papers, of course. But thanks to a worldwide trend in digitizing museum archives, Tanakasan says he can email you a copy of the manifest and a list of found objects."

Trevor scratched his email address on the notepaper so fast he ripped a tear through the top two sheets. Before she even hung up the phone, he popped open his email and clicked Receive thirty times.

"Settle down." She nudged his shoulder. "Give him a chance to look for it first."

He glowered at his flickering inbox. No career-making emails appeared. All that flooded in was spam from email marketers concerned about his erectile functioning. Certainly no problem there. Too bad they weren't sending him free trials of whatever invention could reverse time before his life got all off-track. Then again... if Daisy hadn't been here, how would he have made it through that phone call by himself? Would his "big discovery" have stalled out before he even knew he'd discovered something?

He glanced at her askance. "I didn't know you spoke Japanese."

Her eyes widened. "Of course. I'm an aspiring tooth fairy."

"Isn't your beat Central America? Shouldn't you have learned Spanish?"

"It is. I did. But I didn't know ahead of time what my grid would be, so I felt it best to be prepared for anything. Everything. Plus, it's fun to shake things up. That museum official could probably speak

English just as well as me, but how often do I get to practice Japanese? Thanks for letting me talk to him." She grinned happily, as though he'd just surprised her with a dozen red roses and a lifetime supply of chocolate. "I love languages. They're my favorite hobby."

"Prepared for everything." The memory of her speaking yeti to his bookcase flooded back to mind. "Hobby. What the hell does that mean? You learned every language spoken on the face of the Earth?"

She shrugged as if learning another language was as easy as memorizing baseball stats. "And a few no longer spoken, which is too bad. Anyone else you want me to call?"

Before Trevor's head could explode, he turned his attention back to his email. He was making progress. Some would say he was leaping and bounding.

And he couldn't have done it without her.

∾

"So," Daisy said later that afternoon as she peered through Trevor's windshield. She shifted against the unfamiliar pressure of the seatbelt as she gazed at the rows of neat houses and trim yards. "Where are we going?"

"There's something I want to show you that I think you'll really like." He drummed his fingers on the steering wheel and glared at the third train in a row to inch across the tracks in front of them.

She stared out the window and tried not to think about how she wasn't in a rush to go home, how she hadn't thrown much of a fit over her alleged "capture", how she had enjoyed curling next to Trevor on the couch and helping him place telephone calls.

After a while, the red-and-white striped wooden arms lifted and Trevor bumped across rickety rails. He refused to tell her where they were going until they pulled up in front of an adorable ranch-style house on a little hill, with bright green perfectly trimmed grass and a big chalice-shaped stone fountain in the middle of the front yard.

"Where are we?" Daisy bounded out of the car when Trevor opened the passenger door. "Do you know these people?"

"No." He pulled her out of the car and laced her fingers through his. She shivered. "But it doesn't matter."

"Why doesn't it matter?" She tried not to notice how warm and soft and couple-y their hands felt together. If Trevor had been a guardian angel or a sandman or a genie or even one of the Elders' attorneys instead of a paleo-anthropologist, maybe she could believe their hand-holding meant their relationship was possible.

But he wasn't, and it didn't. He was human. She was not. And she had better not hope for things that could never be.

"You'll see." He tugged her up the shoulder-high incline and led her to the water-filled basin.

"Aua and Eros." Daisy ran the tips of her fingers along the bumpy rim in wonder. "It's covered in teeth!"

Trevor squeezed her hand and grinned.

"Who lives here?" She stared up at him. "Retired tooth fairies?"

He laughed. "A local dentist. He's been pulling out troublesome baby teeth for decades. He built this fountain for the birds to come drink from, and covered it with all the teeth he'd collected over the years. Most residents think it's creepy."

"I love it." She ran her fingertip along the edge. "I'm going to drop a note in the Suggestion Box at the Pearly States the second I get back."

With those words, the last remaining vestiges of sunlight dipped behind the single-story house, obscuring the detail of the fountain and casting them in shadow.

He tugged her into his arms, his face unreadable but his skin scalding to the touch. She knew she should break free from his embrace if she wanted to return to Nether-Netherland with her heart intact. And yet her body pressed against his and her arms looped around his neck.

She rose up on her toes and pulled him closer.

As soon as his lips touched hers, she was lost. From the moment his tongue swept inside her mouth, from the moment his palms glided up over her hips, from the moment his arms hugged her to him as if he never wanted to let go, she knew he just had to say the word and she'd make love to him right there at the base of a baby tooth fountain. She kind of hoped he would.

But he didn't.

He loosened his hold around her waist. He lifted his mouth from hers. He pressed his lips to her forehead and then turned back toward the car.

She tried to slow her runaway heart.

Becoming attached to a human was not a smart thing to do. Fantasizing about the rough stubble of his jaw line against her cheek, the passionate heat in his eyes first thing in the morning, the way he wanted to do something nice for her even though she'd swooped in and ruined his life, were all Very Bad Things to think about. Letting him into her heart even the tiniest bit was the worst thing she could let herself do.

But it had never felt more right.

When night fell, Trevor laced his hand with hers and drove home in silence. In the driveway, however, he couldn't bring himself to lug his briefcase back inside and refocus on work. Once Daisy translated the last of the documents, she'd be that much closer to disappearing for good. Not that he didn't want them translated—he did, desperately—but maybe he could wait to write his life-changing article for just a few more minutes.

A few more minutes with Daisy.

He circled the car to open the passenger door, and helped her out. "Let's go this way."

Hand in hand, they followed the narrow path leading from his backyard into the adjoining woods. He tried not to analyze how companionable an early evening walk seemed, how surreal and relationship-y the moment was with the rustling of the leaves and the dappled sunlight and the twittering birds and the scent of recent rain. He tried not to think too much about how he'd stopped thinking of her like a necessary evil and more like... a girlfriend.

He didn't want strings attached. Did he? No. Of course not. He had too much responsibility and far too busy a schedule to fritter time away being anyone's boyfriend.

If there was room in his life for relationships, he'd already be married with two kids and a dog. He had so little free time he couldn't even have goldfish anymore. This was hardly the time to strike up an inter-dimensional romance with, say, an apprentice tooth fairy. No matter how comfortable her hand felt in his. Or how he yearned for her kisses.

They were far too different for such a thing to work. She'd pointed that out herself. He was human. She was not.

He was used to doing things the hard way, controlling his own future, forging through life on his own steam. She was used to jetting from here to there with a where-frog, getting dressed with a handful of clothes powder, sharing a floating farm with a winged horse. He liked his life meaningful and uncomplicated. He *liked* driving from Point A to Point B in the car he'd had to give up golfing to afford. Even more, he liked following the laws of physics and knowing everyone around him was doing the same.

Textbook irreconcilable differences.

No matter what ridiculous fantasies his idiot heart might be wishing, his brain knew without a doubt that when she left, it would be for the best. On the other hand, his body seemed to think that if he was already on borrowed time, he might as well make the most of it. His backyard was nice and private. What was holding him back?

Before he could ruin a good idea with logic, his arms were around her waist, pinning her against a tree. Eagerly, his mouth devoured hers.

He hadn't meant to kiss her. Mostly. But once he started, he couldn't find the will to stop. Didn't want to find the will to stop. Especially since she wasn't stopping him.

Her arms wrapped around his neck, pulling him closer. He deepened the kiss, his right hand in her hair, cradling the back of her head. The sharp, scratchy bark busted up the backs of his hands, but at least he was protecting her from getting hurt. Her tongue licked against his, slowly, temptingly. He loved the feel of her body against his. He could kiss her forever.

He slid one hand over the curve of her hip and beneath her mint-colored sweater. She didn't break the kiss. Neither did he. He wasn't sure what was softer, the cashmere against the back of his hand or the smooth skin beneath his palm. Her flesh was definitely hotter, searing him with shared desire.

His pulse pounded. Unlike him, she'd never bothered to hide the reluctant attraction brewing between them. He could appreciate that. More fool him for not wising up sooner.

He moved his hand a little higher, grazing the underside of one breast with his fingertips. God, he ached to touch her, to feel her, to have her. Needed this. Needed her. He edged his hand along the left side, knuckles grazing the plump curve.

It had been pure torture to keep away from her as long as he had, but it had been the right thing to do. Reluctantly, he forced himself to stop, to pull away and break the kiss.

Sensing his withdrawal, Daisy's arms unwound from his neck. She covered his hand with hers, just like he'd done in the computer lab. He'd wanted her then, and he wanted her now. Her hand still guiding his, Daisy slid his palm up over her silken bra until his trembling fingers closed around her breast.

She was his dream woman.

He cupped the soft weight in his hand and tried to breathe. She arched into his touch. He rubbed the pad of his thumb over her nipple. She moaned into his mouth, chocolate-y and sweet. He nudged her legs apart with his knee, wishing he had a free hand to explore between her thighs.

Her right hand still covered his, as though afraid he might stop touching her if she let go. No worries there. He'd rather die.

Her left hand skimmed down his back, around his waist, to the front of his jeans. With only minor fumbling, she managed to figure out both the button and the zipper and slide her warm palm beneath the elastic of his boxer shorts.

His cock leapt into her hand. With agonizing slowness, her fingers closed around its hot length and squeezed. He gasped into her mouth, more desperate for her than ever. His hips bucked forward as she stroked him, but his mouth never left hers.

What was he going to do when she left? God, he couldn't think about that. The thought of having his memory erased created an ache deep in his soul. He held her even closer, kissed her even harder. He might not have any say about forgetting her, but he wanted her to remember *him*.

He hauled her up so her legs straddled his waist and then flipped around so it was his shoulders and back leaning against the trunk of the tree. With his hands cupping her tight derrière, he rubbed her pelvis against his throbbing cock and wished like hell she wasn't wearing pants so he could make the simulation a reality.

He tore his mouth from hers long enough to ask, "Where's the clothes powder?"

"Passenger seat." She nudged her mouth under his for another kiss.

He rubbed his stubbled cheek across her lips and grinned when she licked him. "Too far. Luckily, I know how jeans work." Then he stilled, holding her body close. "But I don't know how the fairy reproductive system works. I've got condoms in the house. Do we need them? Do fairies even have to worry about becoming impregnated by humans?" Something they definitely should have discussed the first time, if they hadn't been under the influence of a lust charm.

She bit her lower lip. "I don't know. Maybe? Since I'm half fairy, half angel myself, I'd have to guess that cross-fertilization could be quite possible."

"As far as I'm concerned, you're all angel." He let her slide onto the ground. "But since neither of us wants the complication of a colicky quarter-angel just yet, maybe we'd better head back inside."

The passionate heat of frustrated desire glinting in her eyes almost made him reconsider, but then she nodded, re-buttoned his jeans, and reached for his hand.

The powerwalk back to the house held a much different charge than the stroll into his backyard.

He squeezed her hand and they shared a conspiratorial grin. The only magic between the trees back there was the magic they'd created themselves. There was no coercion, no spells, no Himalayan Lust Charm. They hadn't been about to rut like animals in some drunken pixie dust haze.

They'd been about to make love—and that was much, much scarier.

CHAPTER 17

$\mathcal{O}$n their way to the front door, Trevor retrieved his briefcase from the back seat. Daisy scooped up her handbag and slung the strap over her shoulder. She wasn't sure what was crazier—that she'd almost had sex up against a tree, or that her aching body wished they hadn't stopped.

She followed Trevor to the front steps and watched him from the corner of her eye while he slid his key in the lock. He hadn't spoken since they'd disentangled in front of the tree. Despite the breath-stealing heat in his eyes, maybe he'd decided a romantic interlude with her was one complication he still had time to stop.

She cleared her throat when they entered the house. "Should we get started on that Angus paperwork?"

"Daisy." He shot her his professorial "I'm in charge" look. Probably it shouldn't have turned her on. "You have your purse. You have your clothes powder. You have exactly ten seconds to get naked or I'm going to tackle you to the floor and rip your clothing right off of you, Incredible Hulk-style."

Well. She gulped. That was straightforward. Except for the bit about the Incredible Hulk.

He stood motionless, his dark eyes never straying from her face, as though waiting to see her comply with his order.

She could hardly wait. She started to slip a hand into her bag for the clothes powder, then stilled. Would Trevor really rip the clothes from her body? What if she said please?

He gazed at her as though her silence and immobility were an arrow through his heart.

"What?" he demanded, his voice hoarse and raw. "If you're having second thoughts, I totally understand. I might crumple and die, but I'll understand. Or, I might masturbate and *then* die. Yeah, probably that."

She shook her head and nibbled on her lip. "It's not that. It's... well, I've never *had* anybody undress me. To be honest, I didn't even consider it a possibility until you mentioned it just now." Crap. She could *feel* the blush burning her skin. "And I wondered if it'd be nice."

As the last word left her mouth, he scooped her off the ground and into his arms. She gasped. He cradled her close, one arm around her shoulders and the other beneath her knees. She craned upward, trying to gauge his expression. He lowered his head until his breath misted against her earlobe, steaming her skin and expanding her heart.

"I'm going to take off every single thing you're wearing, one piece at a time," he murmured, the words hot and moist against her cheek. "And I'm going to make you love every minute of it."

His words lit her blood with a blaze to rival Beltane.

A delicious shiver raced across her skin, her body already responding to the promise of an undreamed of seduction. Her arms twined around his neck. He strode down the hallway, holding her tight to his chest. She pressed a thousand and one kisses to his neck.

He went for the bed and settled her onto the covers. Eyes dark with passion and something much, much stronger, he stood at the edge of the bed and gazed down at her. "Would you like your sneakers off?"

She nodded, breathless.

A wicked grin tweaked the corners of his lips. "Say please."

She'd say anything he wanted, as long as it got them both naked. "Take off my shoes. Please."

With a graceful incline of his head, he knelt at the foot of the bed.

He tugged off first one shoe and then the other, taking the socks with them. His hands closed over her left foot. His strong thumbs massaged the arch, the pad, each toe. She could have swooned. He repeated the process with the other foot, smoothing out the tension with slow, purposeful swirls of pressure.

As much as she enjoyed the heavenly massage, she couldn't help but imagine those warm fingers working other parts of her body. She gave her hips a wiggle, just to make sure he knew that the rest of her was eager for his touch, too.

"Don't worry, I haven't forgotten." He sat on the edge of the bed to slide off his shoes and socks. He started to lie down next to her and then paused. "Fair's fair. I took off something of yours. Now you can take off something of mine."

She bolted upright, pulse racing. She hadn't thought of that. The idea was thrilling. Decadent. She couldn't wait.

"What should I take off first?"

One strong shoulder lifted. "Anything you want. But no clothes powder allowed. You have to do everything with your hands."

Mmm. She would *love* to do everything with her hands. Lifting tentative fingers to his throat, she undid the topmost button of his collared shirt. Without breaking eye contact, he tilted a little closer. She unfastened the next button ever so slowly and peeked up at him through her eyelashes.

His unwavering gaze filled with fire and passion and naked desire.

Emboldened, she took her time with the next few buttons, scratching her nails against the white cotton t-shirt underneath. His muscles twitched each time she touched him, as though he wished he'd ripped their clothes off just like he'd threatened to do.

Maybe she could ask for that next time.

When the last button slid from its hole, he jerked his arms free from the sleeves and flung the shirt across the room.

"Cheater!"

"You took too long," he growled, sliding his palms up over her hips. "My turn."

She raised her arms above her head obediently, expecting him to whip off her sweater with the same impatient ferocity he'd shown his own shirt. *Hoping* he would.

Instead, his hands inched upward, bringing the first folds of fabric with them. Although the heat from his skin sent waves of delicious shivers skating up her spine, his fingers barely grazed the swell of her hips, the curve of her waist, the arc of her ribs.

He stopped, his fingers splayed close to her sides, his thumbs resting just below her breasts. They swelled and tightened in anticipation of his touch. *Everything* swelled and tightened in anticipation of his touch. She held her breath, dying to feel his palms scrape across her nipples and wishing like crazy she hadn't conjured a bra.

He dipped his head forward, capturing her mouth with a series of kisses. Every time his tongue flicked across her lips, teasing her, tasting her, his fingers edged closer and closer to her puckered nipples.

Arms still crossed high above her head, she arched toward him, sucking his lower lip into her mouth.

Without lifting his mouth from hers, he finally, *finally*, held her breasts in his hands. He rolled her nipples between his fingers. A whimper escaped her lips. He smiled. Breaking the kiss only long enough to fling off her sweater at last, he held her to his chest and reached behind her back for the bra strap.

"Wait. It's my turn."

Grinning, he raised his arms.

She shook her head. She planted both hands on his chest and pushed him backward onto the covers. His legs hung over the mattress. She slid from the bed to kneel before him. Trembling with desire, she undid the round button at the top of his jeans. The dark blue cotton strained beneath her touch. She ran the tips of her fingers along the outline of the zipper, teasing him as he had teased her. Bit by bit, she tugged the little metal tab downward.

His breath caught with each click of the zippered teeth. She thrilled with the knowledge she affected him every bit as much as he affected her.

With the zipper unfastened at last, she curled her fingers around the waistband and tugged. He lifted his hips from the edge of the mattress, making the pants slide off that much easier. She trailed a palm along his heated skin, up his calf, around the back of his knee, the side of his thigh, beneath the front edge of his boxer shorts.

Just as the tips of her fingers skated alongside his hot, hard length, he slid his hands underneath her arms and hauled her onto the bed.

Without bothering with more than a growled, "My turn," he had her jeans unbuttoned, unzipped and disappearing down her legs.

She nestled back against the pillows and grinned. She loved his turn.

With a final tug, her jeans flew against the far wall next to the other discarded clothes. He climbed on top of her, his fingers buried in her hair, his mouth covering hers.

She looped her hands around his back and rolled them both over until she was on top. Heart racing, she pushed herself up, so that her knees were on either side of his chest and his erection rubbed against her damp panties. He groaned and reached for her.

She tucked her hands beneath the bottom edge of his t-shirt and pulled upward.

"Off," she commanded.

As though he'd been waiting to hear that exact word, he jerked off his shirt with a speed that rivaled top-grade clothes powder.

His hands gripped her hips, forcing her body to rub against his with a slow, agonizing friction. Her legs were jelly. She could barely even pant. This exquisite torture only made her want him even more.

She fell forward, her fingers grasping fistfuls of pillow to either side of Trevor's head. Maybe people in Nether-Netherland used clothes powder so they wouldn't spontaneously combust.

Trevor's face nuzzled between her breasts. He tugged on the bra with his teeth and began to suckle her through the thin fabric. She wasn't sure she could take much more. His hips rocked beneath her thighs, pressing his rigid length right where she wanted it.

"Your turn," she managed to gasp, her belly aching with frustrated desire. "For the love of Venus, take off my bra so we can get rid of your boxer shorts."

Without lifting his mouth from her nipple, his hands glided up over the tense, warm skin covering her spine, leaving shivers of gooseflesh in their wake. She gasped and tried to hold on. With one hand, he unhooked the back of the bra. The straps slid down her shoulders. He nudged the now-damp fabric upward. At last, he captured her naked breast with his mouth and tongue. She could barely breathe with the pleasure of it.

Her fingers threaded into his soft dark hair as she squirmed against the barrier of his boxers. Her body was so *alive* with him. After last night's kisses had led nowhere, she'd been so afraid he hadn't felt the same sense of—of—what? "Attraction" was too weak of a word to describe how she felt. The utter devastation in every dimpled smile, the shivers from every brush of stubble against naked skin, the helplessness to do anything but pull him to her for more...

He rolled over, pinning her beneath him. With his lips locked with hers and one hand against the mattress for support, he reached down with his other hand to tug off his boxers.

She sucked in a breath to comment and then realized she didn't really care who took them off so long as he was naked. She was dying to feel every inch of him.

He started a trail of slow steamy kisses from the sensitive skin behind her earlobe, down the side of her neck, around the curve of her breast, along the center of her belly, over the silk of her panties. He licked the thin, wet material, his tongue probing in tantalizing circles.

"Take. Them. Off." She wiggled against him, her thighs trapping his face even closer. "Please." She moaned when he slid a finger beneath the silk, then joined it with his tongue. "Or not," she breathed, arching against him.

After a long, delicious moment of tempting and teasing, his face shifted away. The stubble on his cheek grazed the inside of her thigh as he peppered her skin with little kisses. She lifted her head to look at him and rolled her eyes when she caught him grinning.

"Hurry up," she grumbled.

He had her panties off and was back on top of her in no time, pausing only for a condom. In seconds, his mouth was on hers and his arousal was between her thighs. She tilted her hips. With a searing kiss, he drove home inside of her.

Her breath caught. Her muscles contracted around him. He felt wonderful. He *was* wonderful. His teeth nipped at her lower lip. She nipped him back. His hands slid under her shoulders. He turned, rolling onto his back, still buried inside her.

"Straddle me," he said, "like you were before." The corner of his eyes crinkled as he smiled up at her. "Please."

"My pleasure." She began to ride him. His hands circled her waist, pulling himself upward. She pressed her breast to his lips. Her muscles tightened as she watched him suckle her.

Every moment she spent with him was better than the last. She loved her fingers in his tangled hair, his mouth on her swollen nipple, the feel of him thrusting inside her. He was everything she'd ever dreamed of. She breathed in his scent and moved in rhythm with him, her thighs flexing around his waist, her hips rising and falling with his.

She felt the warmth and closeness of his body through every pore of hers. His heat mingled with her heat, his breath with her breath. He even tasted like he belonged to her. Like she belonged to him.

"You're amazing." His eyes locked with hers, his gaze passionate. "And I can't hold back much longer."

Neither could she. Not when someone this incredible thought *she* was amazing.

He slid one of his hands between her thighs to touch where his body joined with hers. Her eyes fluttered shut as his touch focused on bringing her to a frenzy. He rubbed the pad of his thumb against the slick heat, matching her rhythm until she convulsed around him, gasping.

"Thank God," he muttered and seized her mouth with a soul-quenching kiss. He thrust inside her, urgent, desperate. She rode him, kissed him, until he shuddered and came. They collapsed against the pillows. He pressed his lips to her forehead, then snuggled her to his chest.

Possessively. Not that she minded.

She closed her eyes, her sated body relaxing into a pool of bliss. She loved being in his arms. He cuddled her even closer, wrapping her in his arms and nuzzling the top of her head. She smiled contentedly, her cheek resting against the warm, steady thump of his heartbeat.

For once, she felt like she belonged.

Sunday disappeared in an all-too-comfortable mix of research and lovemaking, and then it was Monday and Trevor should've left for work fifteen minutes earlier. After all, he had his papers translated and his job on the line, right? But here he was, standing before a locked aquarium, staring through the glass at a lime green where-frog.

The smiling, bespectacled owner of the where-frog was on her knees, tapping at the glass and murmuring her usual litany of reassuring I'll-miss-yous and We'll-be-right-backs.

"Do you want Bubbles back?" he found himself asking.

"What?" Her blonde head jerked away from the glass. She stared up at him, long thick lashes blinking in confusion. "I thought you didn't want me to leave until I helped you."

"I am. I was. You did." He kicked at the briefcase leaning against one leg of the corner table. The briefcase fell over with a thump, startling Bubbles into hopping back from the glass. "In all fairness, I can't keep the little guy trapped forever."

"What do you mean?" She sucked her lower lip between her teeth and nibbled, her gaze suddenly wary.

He wasn't sure he knew. He hadn't even meant to start this conversation at all.

"I mean, thanks to you I now know that the partial skeleton we uncovered may be much more than a long-buried local." He nudged the fallen briefcase with the toe of his boot. "You've given me an incredible head start toward publishing the paper of my career."

"I see," she said, as though she wished she didn't. "Are you saying I've now 'put things to rights'?"

Why did he feel that was a trick question?

"Well," he said. "You've more than upheld your half of the bargain."

Lips pursed, she glanced away.

Okay. He stepped next to her and spun the dial on the combination lock. "How can I continue to hold you hostage?"

She let out a soft sigh. "You never were."

He stopped twirling the dial. "What do you mean?"

"The lock's a nice touch and all, but come on." She rose to her feet and gestured at the old aquarium. "I don't need magic to break glass. Bubbles and I could've headed back to Nether-Netherland long ago."

He paused, fingers still frozen on the lock. She was right. Duh. His chin touched his chest. No wonder he'd never published anything. He was a freaking moron.

"If you could go at any time," he said slowly, "why didn't you?"

Her lips quirked into an uncertain half-smile. "Because I'd have to buy you a replacement?"

His fingers fell from the lock. "You *chose* to stay?"

Her smile faltered. She inspected her fingernail polish.

His heart beat faster. She *did* choose to stay. That was the only explanation. She could've left any time she wanted to, and didn't. Because she wanted to be with him. A strange emotion laced Trevor's lungs with hope and then slithered down his spine like ice.

Stupidly believing she wanted to leave, he'd thanked her for a job well done and told her she could get packing. Brilliant.

"Daisy," he said. "I didn't mean—"

"You were right," she interrupted with a wave of her hand. "I did owe you. I knew it, you knew it, everybody in Nether-Netherland knew it. I screwed up your life. You said so yourself. The least I could do was help to put things back to normal, like you wanted."

Like he wanted? He fought the urge to grab her by the shoulders... and kiss her senseless. Good lord. Did he even know what he wanted?

He thought she'd screwed up his life. But had she? He'd alternately thought she was a spy, a ditz, a saboteur out to get him, and none of those things had turned out to be true. For an anthropologist, he'd sure let his suspicions and assumptions get in the way of objective observation.

Maybe he should publish a dissertation entitled "Boys Are Stupid After All."

He lifted the now-unlatched lock from the metal hook. Without meeting Daisy's gaze, he reached in one arm and laid the back of his hand flush on the cold pebbles.

Bubbles shot him a wary "Don't even think about running off with me" expression before hopping onto Trevor's outstretched fingers.

Trevor glanced back up at her in triumph and his heart stopped. While he'd been futzing around with Bubbles, she'd apparently been futzing around with clothes powder. Instead of the besuited, professional-looking Daisy he'd come to expect, she was once again barefoot Daisy, standing before him in a somber expression and a moss green dress.

"So..." was all he said to the woman that he'd curled his body around all last night. So, what? What could he possibly say to her? Hey, stick around awhile? Let's go for another walk in the forest? Have our where-frog escort us to a candlelit dinner in Paris? What could he possibly ever give her that would be better than the magic of Nether-Netherland?

He stared down at Bubbles, who stared right back up at him as though reading his mind and judging him a colossal fool.

Daisy stepped forward until the tips of her painted toes brushed his black leather shoes. Her small, slender hands slid beneath his, as though helping him support Bubbles' negligible weight. He was probably supposed to tilt his hands, drop the where-frog into her open palms, step away from them both.

But he didn't.

His gaze focused on her shoulders, her neck, her mouth, everywhere but her eyes. If she was happy to go, he didn't want to see it. And if she wasn't... he wasn't sure he wanted to see that, either. "Do you have to leave right this second?"

"Maybe." The word trembled from her lips, as though there was something important he was supposed to say at this point, something that could change both their lives forever.

His temple began to throb. He was a reasonably intelligent anthropologist. Well, most of the time. And he could guess what that something was that she hoped he would say.

But he couldn't say *that*.

She couldn't truly expect romantic words of any kind. From

everything he'd seen and heard during his twenty-four-hour adventure through the looking glass, delaying the moment between now and goodbye would screw up her life even worse than his. He had to deal with Berrymellow, sure, but at least Trevor didn't have any court charges just for having spoken to a stranger. Who certainly wasn't a stranger any longer.

He cared about what happened to her. If he was a stand-up guy who wasn't ruled by his own selfish wants, he wouldn't force her to make that choice. He would let her go. But was it better or worse for her to realize he didn't want to?

And which was better for him?

CHAPTER 18

*T*revor handed Bubbles over, and then crossed his arms to keep himself from reaching for Daisy. She stared at the where-frog in her hands without speaking or moving.

As the silence stretched into self-conscious stiffness, he knew his next few words would make the difference between whether she stayed another night or disappeared in a puff of smoke. If he had to let her go, he wanted a lot more than just one more night. But that was hardly fair to her. He'd have his memory wiped, but she'd have to live with whatever final words were said between them. The least he could do was make her think it was for the best.

He swallowed, his tongue scraping against the scratchy roof of his dry mouth.

"I like you," he said softly. "If you were the girl next door, I would've asked you out the day we met. But with the... *differences*... between us, we'd be foolish to keep prolonging the inevitable. It's time for—"

"The inevitable," she repeated dully. "By 'the inevitable', do you mean getting booted out the door the morning after having sex?" Her eyes were empty. "I can't believe I didn't see that coming."

Frustration raced through his veins. Was it possible to screw up a conversation worse than he was destroying this one?

"It has nothing to do with that," he said, steel reinforcing his words. Christ, couldn't the woman see this was killing him? "A few more days of a doomed romance isn't worth life in a magical jail cell. For either of us. From the moment that crazy judge shrieked 'ForgetMe orb' we both knew... *this*... couldn't go anywhere."

Speaking of, where the hell was that thing? At least he wouldn't remember making a colossal ass of himself.

She stared down at her toes. "So that's it?"

"That's it. What else can we do?" he asked, unable to keep the strain from his voice. "Even if you put the tooth fairy thing on hold to explore what's developing between us, your life back in—"

"Put the 'tooth fairy thing' on hold?" Her gaze met his at last, coldly furious. Not a good sign. "Just give up my career goals and personal dreams indefinitely, to pursue a 'doomed' romance?"

He shifted his weight from one foot to the other. Yes, yes it *was* possible to decimate a conversation beyond all hope of actual communication. Outstanding.

He shook his head. "I didn't say that."

"But you meant it." She cradled the where-frog to her chest.

"It's not even *possible*. Your laws don't allow it. Even if you could live on Earth, you're a tooth fairy. That's your career and your choice. But magic wands and fairy wings and where-frogs are a no-go around here. You'd have to be... something else."

"Something else?" She laughed hollowly. "I can't imagine myself in a human career of any kind. The skills I do have are only relevant in Nether-Netherland, and I would die before living somewhere I'd be even *more* useless. Back home, I have a chance. I have friends. I have family. I have the opportunity to make something of myself. But it sounds like you're saying, if the laws were lifted, you'd want me to give up everything I hold dear in order to join you here in your world."

"I would *never* ask you to give up anything you cherish. Just like you wouldn't ask it of me." He grabbed her shoulders, determined to make her understand. "I love... being with you. But your life is there, and my life is here. My house, my career, my family, everything *I* hold dear. I'm a paleo-anthropologist. I'm an interdepartmental summer baseball coach. I can't live in your world, and you can't live in mine. It has nothing to do with either of us giving up our dreams, and everything to do with the fact that humans and magic just don't mix. No matter how much we might wish otherwise." His arms fell back to his sides. "That's what I meant by 'doomed romance.'"

"No romance here." She lifted Bubbles close to her face. "Just a bunch of doom."

With a tiny pop and an accompanying flurry of pixie dust, he found himself alone in his empty living room once again. This time, with no where-frog to feed, no half-angel to snuggle, and no one to blame but himself.

Daisy materialized in the middle of the Neurophysics Compound, more determined than ever to make a wand that worked. Luckily, they had not yet found someone to replace her. After growling half-hearted hellos at the ex-coworkers who dared to greet her, she stalked directly into her old laboratory and slammed the door.

Not that she was upset over anything Trevor had said. Or not said. It's not like she was in love, or anything. Not by a long shot. He was nothing. Cute, that's all. A distraction, really. A six-foot-three-inch, dark-eyed, dimpled distraction. At least she hadn't humiliated herself by clinging on him or begging him to reconsider or bursting into tears.

Shoulders back and chin high, she configured her lab for a new round of wand experimentation. She tried to think about something, anything, except a certain jerktastic anthropologist.

If she'd gotten all—all infatuated with him, well, that was her own fault and she'd just have to get over it. Get over *him*.

Daisy twirled the color dial of her latest wand manufacturing machine to lime green and pressed the Start button. Two hours later, she had a new wand. She didn't need Trevor's.

Figuratively speaking.

She shoved open the exit doors and stepped outside just as her mother coasted onto the Neurophysics Compound's front lawn, Dad right on her heels.

So much for having a moment alone to collect her thoughts in private. She shoved her untested wand into her handbag. "How'd you know I was here?"

"One of your old coworkers ran into us at the bi-monthly bazaar and said you—" Mama gasped, clamping a palm over her mouth to stifle the sound. "Why are your eyes bloodshot and your face so splotchy?"

Daisy forced herself not to test her new wand on her mother.

"Did you deliver the teeth?" Dad asked, tiny lines creasing his forehead.

"Yes. Not to be rude, but could you guys go somewhere else? I was about to test a new experiment and it's not safe for civilians."

"Oh, sweetie, that's so great." Mama beamed at her. "I knew you'd give up that silly toothfairying and return to science. There's no shame in being unmagical. Well, very little shame. Between us. Your father and I don't care what they say about you."

"I didn't 'give up' toothfairying," Daisy ground out. Achilles help her, she *did* care what "they" said about her. And how it affected her parents. "Why does everyone want me to give up toothfairying?"

"You're not?" Mama frowned. "Then what are you doing here?"

Her father's wings unfurled. "You're not making another mechanical wand, are you?"

Daisy spun to face him. "And why not? Is there some reason I shouldn't?"

He stared back, eyebrow raised. "It's illegal."

"Well... besides that."

"Because science and magic don't mix." Mama patted Daisy's shoulder and laughed lightly. "Oil and water, sweetie."

"But I'm a scientist. I'll *invent* a way to be magical."

"Do your experiments, then, if they make you happy. A.J, don't you give me that look. She deserves a break. No sense dashing off to the High Court the very moment you return. You do remember that you have to give the Elders a post-delivery progress report, right?"

"I remember." She slipped a hand inside her handbag and ran her fingertips along the smooth wand hidden inside. *Please* let this one work. "And if I promise to head over first thing in the morning and fill out as many reports as they can conjure, will you let me have tonight to myself?"

Her father frowned, no doubt dyspeptic over bending the rules. "She *should* go today..."

Mama thumped him on the chest. "She did everything they asked, sweetie. There's no harm done in waiting until morning."

"I guess." With a last doubtful look at Daisy, he looped his arm around Mama's shoulders. "After all, all she had to do was drop off the teeth and erase his memory."

With a strangled, sucking sound, Daisy jerked backward, a thousand daggers slicing into her heart. The ForgetMe orb. How could she have forgotten the stupid ForgetMe orb? And no way could she report in to the Elders without fully completing the mission. Not when she'd forgotten to make Trevor forget. What if they made her testify under the influence of a truth spell? She couldn't take that risk.

She struggled to keep her growing horror from showing on her face.

If she hadn't been so preoccupied, she wouldn't have to go back tonight and finish it once and for all. Well, she'd be smarter this time. No sticking around for tree sex and a broken heart. Hello, forget me, goodbye. Easy. Her throat convulsed.

He'd never know what hit him. Literally.

Trevor tore through his briefcase in growing disbelief. Although Daisy had painstakingly translated 12th century documents from Scots Gaelic to modern English, he was no closer to definitive proof after all. The text turned out to be some boring shipping inventory, not a convenient mini-biography conclusively tying Angus to Trevor's dig.

If only Daisy were still here to bounce ideas off of. The best magic she performed took place right between her ears. Him, on the other hand... He was great digging up ancient history in the field and unearthing clues in his lab, but embarrassingly inept when it came to dealing with real live people.

He'd tried calling the Museum of Tokyo. Daisy was right; the archivists did speak English as fluently as Japanese. Nonetheless, they'd already divulged everything they knew. So he'd tried the Costa Rican museums, and then the banks and businesses local to Nuevo Arenal, where bits and pieces of artifacts graced glass-covered lobby shelves. He'd muddled through with his toddler-level Spanish before giving up and heading to Starbucks for caffeinated comfort.

Facility with languages. Now, there was a real skill. Something practical. Something to be proud of. Wings, on the other hand...

Wings were like eyebrow piercings. Something interesting to look at, but otherwise useless. And as lovely as she was to look at—with or without wings—her true worth was a lot more than that. He already missed her more than he would have ever dreamed.

But he was a big boy. He'd get over her. Any minute now.

CHAPTER 19

*W*ith a final ratio of 4:5 (four successful non-pumpkin spells to every five failures), Daisy took a break from wand manufacturing and decided to deal with her troubles.

She wasn't procrastinating a re-visit with Trevor. Not at all. She was simply honoring the Elders' rule regarding tooth fairy teleportation without cover of night. A quarter 'til ten in the middle of the morning hardly counted as night. Technically, the injunction only applied to on-duty travel, but hey. Better safe than sorry. Besides, she had a bone to pick with Vivian Valdemeer.

Bicuspid, to be exact.

Daisy was tired of playing the naïve, trusting ingénue—or rather, being played as such by her glamorous mentor. Was the Angus age discrepancy nothing more than a typo? Maybe. Was the Himalayan Lust Charm really the result of mixed-up charm bags? Maybe. How about sending a novice apprentice out to fetch a cold dead tooth from a live, adult anthropologist? Maybe, as in, maybe Vivian wasn't as benevolent as she pretended.

Maybe she was out to get her.

Okay, maybe Daisy was edging toward paranoid, but Vivian

certainly wasn't offering the caliber of conscientious support one might expect from the highest ranking tooth fairy in Nether-Netherland.

Daisy brought Bubbles from her shoulder to her lips. "My office."

They materialized inside the dark and deserted Tooth Fairy Regional Headquarters, a few feet from the swirling reflective surface of the Mortal Locator.

"Location Request Logs," she commanded the swirling surface. And then, "View Request History."

A list of Costa Rican addresses scrolled down the screen, many sans street addresses in true *campo* style: 2 km east of the gymnasio central, 1 km north of the post office, 100 meters west of the bank. But wait—what was that one? She doubted Nuevo Arenal had a 555 Briarwood Ct. According to the logs, that particular address had been viewed twice. Once during the infamous debacle when she'd set off the alarm on the Tooth Fairy Transporter. And another view request... yesterday.

At that time, Daisy had been with Trevor—er, *with*-with Trevor, as a matter of fact—so there was no way she could be responsible for the location request. And only one other person worked in this particular regional office: Vivian. Had her mentor been spying while she and Trevor were...

Ew. Creepy.

"Bubbles," Daisy said, her anger rising. "Let's go see Vivian."

"Yikes," her mentor choked out when they materialized in front of her magical workbench. "Your hair looks terrible."

"How kind of you to point it out. Unfortunately, I didn't come here to discuss my issues with humidity."

"No?" Vivian slid a mystery pouch into her pocket and then used both hands to stir her cauldron. "Maybe you should've. I assume you're ready to go back to work?"

Daisy's nostrils flared. "I wouldn't assume anything. I've got some questions first."

"Oh?" Vivian arched a perfectly-tweezed eyebrow. "Does that mean you no longer wish to pursue earning your wings?"

"Of course not. You know as well as I do that I—" Daisy swallowed, the full impact of the subtle threat catching her off-guard.

The only person facilitating her one shot at making tooth fairy was the over-tweezed, big-haired diva who might or might not be sabotaging her protégé.

If she spouted off a litany of unproven accusations, Daisy would never, ever see the day when beautiful gossamer wings graced her back. Even if she managed to determine Vivian absolutely had it out for her, so what? Nobody but Daisy would even care. And there weren't any other apprenticeship opportunities on the horizon.

On the other hand, if she allowed herself to be thrown off-track, she wouldn't earn her wings anyway. Or keep her self-respect.

"What about 'little Angus'?" she made herself ask. "He's *dead*."

Bored, Vivian turned back to the cauldron. "Did you kill him?"

"Of course not!" Daisy stumbled backward as sudden steam fogged up her glasses. "He was dead when I got there."

"Well, thank Osiris for that. A tooth fairy's liability on that sort of workplace accident is horrendous."

Daisy's fingers clenched. "He died nine hundred odd years ago. As an *adult*."

Vivian licked the edge of the big wooden ladle. "And?"

"And, the dossier you gave me clearly said 'Age 8'. Not twenty-eight or thirty-eight or forty-eight. Just plain old eight. Or rather, plain young eight."

"Well, there you have it. I must've missed one of the keys when typing it in." Vivian looked Daisy straight in the eye, one eyebrow still arched and both corners of her lips bent slightly upward.

If Daisy didn't know better, she'd suspect that not only was Vivian lying, but also that Vivian knew Daisy knew Vivian was lying and that Vivian further knew that Daisy couldn't do a single thing about it.

Not if she wanted her wings.

Stuck at his desk while eighty students bubbled in answers on Scantron sheets, Trevor clicked through his dig photos for quite possibly the millionth time. So far, the only thing linking the partial skeleton to the legendary explorer was the word of the most unreliable source in the history of paleo-anthropological research papers: a half-magic, no-longer-on-this-planet, pixie-powered dentition spectrometer.

What did he plan on publishing, an article called, "The Tooth Fairy Told Me So?"

Damn it. There *had* to be a way. If one assumed that the captain in question was Angus the Explorer who did in fact sail off for parts unknown, never to be heard from again, then the scanned documents suggested he didn't sail off empty-handed.

He searched his briefcase for the translated vendor shipping list. Three entire pages of stoneware for barter.

Stoneware. Pottery.

Beautiful pieces, the seller's document claimed, gorgeous designs, hand-fired with the company crest, exquisite to behold, perfect for every household. *Inherent beauty, stunning glazes,* and *utter perfection* were examples of obsequious marketing claptrap, but *company crest...* company crest was visible. Tangible. Factual.

Proof.

If even one of the shards his team unearthed contained a matching pattern after all these years... A shiver raced up his spine. Holy shit— it could be true! But how could he get ahold of an antique Scottish company crest?

As soon as class was over, he pushed back from his desk and made his way to Dr. Papadopoulos's office. It would be foolish to make promises he wasn't yet sure would pan out, but it would be equally foolish to let her think he wasn't working as hard as possible to keep his position at the university.

Luckily, she was at her desk and motioned him in. "Good afternoon, Dr. Masterson. I'm glad you stopped by."

His excitement ebbed at the ominous tone in her voice. "Always happy to be of service. What's up?"

She handed him a stack of papers. "I have begun to receive the usual barrage of letters requesting your return as head coach for the interdepartmental summer baseball league. The math department apparently started a petition, and got the entire College of Arts & Sciences to sign."

Flipping through the pile, Trevor grinned as he recognized the names of some of his favorite players. "I would love to continue coaching. I hope my upcoming paper on the results of the recent dig will be received as favorably."

He also hoped he'd be able to come up with enough material to actually write it.

"I certainly hope so. Joshua Berrymellow has presented me with several recent articles on subjects he researches. Will you be presenting us with tear sheets before the end of the semester?"

He fake-coughed into the back of his hand. "Maybe not a tear sheet per se, but if all goes well I will have something to submit. My current project is very worthy, and very exciting."

"Something to submit," Dr. Papadopoulos repeated. "Here's the problem, Professor. This university does not award tenure to individuals with... strange flights of fancy. We reward brains and progress."

Somehow, he managed to keep from throwing himself upon a sword. "I like to think of myself as a very rational individual, and certainly understand your position. For that reason, I would not wish to rush inconclusive research to publication. Facts must trump fancy. And I do believe I have a significant find at my fingertips. I think you will be very pleased."

Before Dr. Papadopoulos could respond, the ringing of her desk phone shattered the silence. She glanced at the Caller ID, gave an apologetic moue, and lifted the receiver.

Trevor slipped out into the hall, closing the door behind him. Now that he'd all but promised results, he absolutely had to deliver. He headed straight to his laboratory. With the grad students off studying for their own final exams, Trevor found himself alone in the lab. Good. He needed to concentrate. He needed to find proof of greatness.

He focused on the pieces of pottery. He hadn't reexamined more than a dozen shards of stoneware before a staccato knock rang out against the metal doorjamb and the lab door flung inward. He sighed. At last, his chance to brain Berrymellow with a femur had arrived.

"I'm busy."

Berrymellow's red head peeked into the lab. "Busy what? Turning people into frogs?"

"Hilarious." Trevor gestured around the empty room. "Do you see any frogs in here? Or people? Then get lost."

Berrymellow straightened his bolo tie. "*I'm* a person."

"And I would turn you into a frog if I could. Are we done here?"

"Not quite." Berrymellow plucked a wrinkled manila file folder from his briefcase and slapped it onto the counter, displacing a cloud of pottery dust.

Trevor's stomach sank. "What's that?"

His only response was Berrymellow's high-pitched titter before the ridiculous prat pirouetted on the ball of one foot and dashed out the door.

Dreading what he might find, Trevor forced himself to open the envelope and pull out the sheaf of papers sequestered within. Another periodical clipping. Of course.

This treatise was entitled, "Destructive Behaviors Caused by Career Envy in the Workplace: Paleo-Anthropologists in Search of Self."

"Goddammit, Berrymellow."

He chucked the papers across the room. They floated down like oversized ashes from a burning building. The embers of his career.

The subtle aroma of vanilla musk wafted into the room, accompanied by a soft, familiar voice. "Am I interrupting?"

He whirled to face her. "Daisy! I thought you'd left me."

Suave, Masterson. He shoved his hands into his pockets so he wouldn't run across the room and hug her to his chest. If he allowed himself to hold her for even a second, he might never let go. It had been hard enough the first time. Besides, he needed to focus on his career, not his love life. And he was never going to be able to do that if he let himself be distracted by how good she smelled, or how much he wished things might have been different.

A faint blush tinged the apples of her cheeks. She looked even more gorgeous than usual. "I thought you didn't want me here."

"I have never stopped wanting you. But even so, you can't pop in and out at the drop of a hat." He stepped closer, wishing she hadn't caught him hurling printouts into the air. "I'm already walking that fine line between professor and panhandler. My competition just published again, this time with a thinly disguised treatise discussing my many faults, and my boss is afraid I suffer 'strange flights of fancy.'" He took a deep breath of Daisy-scented air and hoped she couldn't tell how much her appearance affected him. Or that he wished there was some way she could stay. "None of that has anything to do with you, of course. Between Vivian and the Pearly States, you've got plenty of trouble of your own."

"I know. The problem is you remembering that."

"What do you—oh." His stomachache returned full force. "You forgot to make me forget you."

"I remember now." She opened her handbag.

"Great."

It wasn't great. It was much less than great. He'd forgotten he wasn't supposed to remember, and he was no longer sure he wanted to forget. No, he *knew* he didn't want to forget. If he couldn't have her, at least she could leave him with his memories.

In seconds, he would no longer remember the warmth of her skin, the taste of her kisses, the scent of her hair. He would no longer remember their trip to the tooth fountain, the simple joy of sharing morning coffee, the way she breathed when she fell asleep on his chest. He would no longer remember his new appreciation for the trees behind his house, the way she nibbled her pen while translating documents, or how empty his house seemed without her.

"You'll move on as if I never existed. And when my mother performs the same spell on me, so will I."

He *so* did not want her moving on. A deadly mix of anger and jealousy combusted in his veins, rocketing Trevor from his stance lounging against the counter to a position a mere millimeter from her face, his feet on either side of hers and his hands buried in her hair.

"You can't forget me," said a hoarse, desperate voice that sounded suspiciously like his own. "I won't let you."

And then his mouth was on hers and the world disappeared. The only things that existed were him and Daisy, Daisy and him. Her lips, his tongue. His hands, her hair. His pulse. Her scent. Her taste. His ragged breath. Her soft whimper.

"What if it wasn't illegal?" he found himself asking her between kisses. "What if there was some way we could be together without you getting into any trouble? Would you come back?"

He crushed her to him for another kiss, but she pushed him away with a simple broken, "No." The word was almost too soft to hear, and yet drained his heart of blood and his brain of sanity.

"Why?" he asked, hating how his voice cracked like a teenager's. "If your Elders said you could, couldn't you give up fairying just for a little while, and stay here with me? We've got—" He broke off before he said something stupid. What did they have? Something "special"? A "connection"? Luuuv? "—chemistry," he finished, grimacing at how lame he sounded.

"True," she said, her voice low and her eyes downcast as if she could no longer bear to see him. "But chemistry won't earn wings."

"Who *cares* about wings?"

"I care. They mean success. They mean acceptance. They mean respect." Her eyes flew open. "I don't expect you to understand."

"I understand the importance of respect. I'm killing myself here, trying to earn tenure."

"Exactly. And it's exactly why this can't work. A paleo-anthropologist, trying to earn tenure. An apprentice tooth fairy, trying to earn wings. Two different worlds." She gazed up at him, her eyes sad. "If the Elders said you could, would you give up all this and move to Nether-Netherland? Just for a little while?"

He tried to stifle his instinctive *hell, no* expression, but it was too late.

"So you do understand." She tugged her hand from the pouch. "It's better this way. For both of us."

"No." He reached for her again, but she already had a round black mass of god-knew-what shoved in front of his face.

She hadn't given him a chance to respond. To defend himself. To fight for her. She didn't *want* him to have a chance. For anything.

"Forget," she intoned, the words a low, seductive chant. "Forget, forget, forget. Forget Nether-Netherland. And forget... me. Forget everything about me." Her voice broke. "Please."

Through his clenched jaw, Trevor sucked in a deep breath...

And remembered everything.

CHAPTER 20

*T*here. She did it.

Daisy indulged herself in one last glance at the dark-eyed professor who'd stolen her heart.

He'd never remember the orchid-spiced breeze cooling their shoulders as he kissed her in Costa Rica. He'd never remember sweeping the contents of his desk to the floor in his impatience to make love to her. He'd never remember coming this close to, well, *coming*, beneath the velvet canopy inside the Human Containment Center.

And he'd certainly never remember their weekend of pseudo-dating bliss, starting with libraries, trains, and tooth fountains and culminating in the best sex of her life.

Why? Because he'd be too busy tromping through the mud on his digs, or sleeping on dead people's teeth, or writing papers about the shipping habits of Scottish skeletons, or coaching intra-mural baseball.

She ought to be pleased. He could finally be happy.

Actually, peering closer, he looked more like he was in shock. Strange. Katrina had seemed more vacant. Entranced. Well, no matter. The ten-second window wouldn't last forever. She couldn't waste time standing around staring at him until he snapped out of his ForgetMe haze and started asking who she was and what in Hades she was doing in his laboratory.

With a reluctant nod, she lifted her hand to her collarbone and whispered for Bubbles. The second the where-frog's little green feet settled onto her palm, she heard a soft, hesitant, "Daisy?"

She froze. Unless she'd accidentally conjured a name badge when she'd changed into her tooth fairy outfit, there might be a slight problem here.

Flashing Trevor a brittle, panicked smile, she placed Bubbles back on her shoulder, snatched the ForgetMe orb from her purse, and shoved it within inches of his nose.

"Forget. Forget. Forget." Her voice coming out high-pitched and desperate. Almost as desperate as her heart. "Forget Nether-Netherland. Forget Nether-Netherland's inhabitants. In the name of Mnemosyne, forget *me*."

A tiny muscle twitched at his temple. "You have got to be kidding me."

Her breath caught. He was exhibiting a distinct lack of susceptibility to the ForgetMe orb. She didn't know whether to laugh or cry. She brought the orb up to her own face. Maybe she could be the one to forget. "The same thing worked on Katrina. Why isn't it working on you?"

The muscle under his temple pulsed faster. "You're asking *me*?"

She dropped the ForgetMe orb back into her purse and lifted her face heavenward. Once the Elders caught wind of this latest blunder, she was guaranteed a stint in Purgatory. She was still on probation from the initial snafu. She stared sightlessly at the endless counters. "What am I going to do?"

"You can't make me forget?"

Was there something in his voice that—no, don't be silly. He was just angry. Frustrated at the unexpected setback. Wasn't he?

"No," she admitted, forcing herself to make eye contact.

He gazed right back, expression inscrutable. He still had the longest eyelashes she'd ever seen on a man. And the best smile. Not that he was smiling now. He looked miserable.

His Adam's apple bobbed. "But you're going to go away anyway?"

"I have to."

She did have to. Like it or not.

She'd made a major breakthrough with her newest wand and was positive she was close to perfecting the design. As soon as she could do magic on her own, she could tell Vivian to take a hike. And then Daisy could apply for apprenticeship elsewhere. Maybe even become a fairy godmother like Mama.

Of course, all of that hinged on the success of future mechanical wands, which hinged on her returning to her lab for more experiments, which hinged on the judge not banishing her anywhere, which hinged on her being able to tell the court she'd followed instructions to the letter and put everything back to normal.

Considering yet another spell had screwed up, her life seemed normal.

Trevor shoved his hands in his pockets. "Now what? We pretend to go on?"

She ignored the nausea in her belly. And the hope.

On the one hand, she might've been secretly pleased to be unforgettable if he weren't so callous about remembering. On the other hand, there was clearly nothing wrong with the spell. After all, Mama had made them both at the same time and Katrina forgot right away. She'd never heard of a ForgetMe orb expiring from disuse.

So why hadn't it worked?

"The Elders will lock me away for good." She tried not to hyperventilate.

"How will they know?"

She arched a brow. "Truth spell, anyone?"

"Why would they bother? They didn't before. That was all Vivian." He knelt and gathered his fallen documents. "Besides, I won't be there. Your secret's safe with me."

Daisy sat on her heels to help pick up papers. "You would do that for me?"

"Why not? I'll never see you again."

Daisy handed him the papers she'd collected and stood. So did he, their toes touching, their gazes locked together.

"I see your point," she said. And she did.

She saw that she had no business even fantasizing about him being part of her life. The best thing she could do, for her career and for her heart, would be to take his offer and leave.

This time, for good.

She reached up for her where-frog—really she did—but her traitorous hand caressed the side of his face instead. Her fingers curved around the edge of his jaw, the familiar stubble scraping against her palm.

He didn't move. He didn't lean forward into her touch, nor did he jerk away in disgust. He just stared at her from under those long lashes, his dark gaze unwavering and unreadable.

She removed her hand from his face, bringing her fingertips to her lips and breathing in his scent.

She let her arm fall back to her side. "Thank you."

He flinched, but said nothing.

Daisy stalled for a long, awkward moment before retrieving Bubbles from her shoulder. If he wanted to stop her, this was the time. But he made no such move, and she couldn't stay.

She couldn't have him. She shouldn't even want him. She should go home, make her court appearance, and live a peaceful, humanless life in Nether-Netherland. She might not have love, but at least she'd have wings. Ignoring the sense of loss deep in her belly, she dipped her head to whisper to her where-frog.

Trevor's lips parted. "Daisy—"

But she'd already spoken to Bubbles, and the rest of Trevor's words were lost.

Daisy lifted a brand new lemon yellow mechanical shaft from the Create-A-Wand assemblage press, and tossed the lime green wand in the lab's recycle bin. After affixing a new star atop the sun-colored stick, she headed out behind the Neurophysics Compound for another round of testing with a smile on her face. True tooth fairies missed out on all the fun of engineering experiments.

As planned, Maeve met her at the exit door this time. After a quick hug, they walked in companionable silence. Daisy had already confided a much-abridged version of the story to her best friend when she'd first returned to Nether-Netherland, and totally didn't want to keep rehashing the same information.

She was doing a fine job of dwelling on Trevor all by herself.

They picked their way along the dewy trail, snaking from the compound to the woods. Mud squished between Daisy's bare toes with each footfall on the spongy dirt. Maybe she should've arranged for galoshes to go with her lab coat. No matter. Perhaps this was the day she would finally prove herself magical enough to earn real wings. If this worked, she wouldn't need clothes powder anymore. She would be able to conjure her own galoshes.

Deep inside the woods, she aimed her wand and began the first few practice spells. After a couple false starts—and some hysterical snort-giggles from her best friend—the wand began to follow orders. Maeve whinnied in surprise. Daisy could've done the same.

Thank Isis, she must be close to conquering the secret to engineering a reliable mechanical wand. She tried a few more simple spells. Some worked. Some didn't.

She kept on trying, until a sudden thought hit her. If she *did* perfect the mechanical wand, would she be ethically obligated to return to Earth with a supercharged ForgetMe orb? Or would the ethical path be to leave Trevor in peace?

She lowered her wand. "Can you think of any reason why magic wouldn't work on someone?"

"Sure," Maeve said with a swish of her violet tail. "Lots of reasons. Poor quality wand, anti-magic invisible resistance shields, obstruction of True Love, incompetent spell-casting, interference by—wait." Her impressive nostrils flared. "What magic are you referring to? Something to do with Mr. Eyelashes?"

"Nothing. Forget it."

If there was one thing Daisy was even better at than neurophysics, it was incompetent spell-casting. She'd left out all the illegal parts of her story, just in case D.A. Sangre dragged her on the witness stand again. She couldn't risk having Maeve put two and two together and figure out Trevor was down on Earth remembering things he wasn't supposed to, and why.

Today, however, her ratio had bumped up to five successes for every two failures. Well beyond statistical probability. She was so close to being magical she could almost feel wings protruding from her back.

"Great work." Maeve nudged Daisy's shoulder and nickered. "It's taken a while to get this far, but I have to admit. Your engineering skills are starting to impress me."

"Thanks. Neurophysics was easy, but artificial magic is a lot of work. The entire afternoon passed by in a blink of an—"

"Oh, crap!" Maeve's ears flattened as she glanced up at the darkening sky. "*Work.* Gotta go. If I'm late again, they'll saddle me."

She took off, soaring up over the trees before Daisy had a chance to respond.

After a bit more practice, she headed back to the Neurophysics Compound, washed and reclothed herself, and slid into the overstuffed chair behind her old desk. Bubbles perched atop her encephalopathic endo-periscope, eyes closed as though napping.

While her where-frog might be indifferent to the newest mechanical wand, the artificial magic experiments were progressing fabulously. Even Maeve had complimented her! So why wasn't Daisy feeling celebratory? Was it because she couldn't get a certain dark-eyed anthropologist out of her mind? Well, maybe she should think like a scientist, not like a moonstruck would-be fairy. She should approach the problem logically.

Daisy rummaged through her desk drawer for a pen and a piece of paper. Across the top, she wrote, "Why I Don't Want Trevor Masterson," and waited for rational inspiration.

Nothing came to mind. Except the sound of his chuckle, the warmth of his arms, the passion for his work, the encouragement he gave his students, the thoughtfulness that had gone into the visit to the baby tooth fountain...

She banged her forehead to her desk and sighed. This was going to be a very short list if all she could think of were his positive qualities.

"Fine," she muttered. "I'll do Pros on one side and Cons on the other."

Her where-frog opened one eye and promptly closed it again.

She drew a vertical line down the center of the sheet, labeling each side. She began with Pros.

"He's smart. Respected. Respectful. Thoughtful." The pen slid across the paper, making row after row of neatly printed words. "Sexy. Fun. Friendly. Charming." She paused. Better stop with the pros before she needed a new sheet of paper. "Now for the cons." She nibbled the end of the pen for a long moment.

"Anti-wings," she wrote after a long moment, followed by "Illegal" and then, "Human."

There. Trevor Masterson, summed up in two tidy columns. Slowly, purposefully, she crumpled the paper in her fist.

Gone.

Was that symbolic enough to let her stupid heart move on? Daisy unfolded her fingers and stared at the mangled ball. As if he thought she was baring her palm for him, Bubbles leapt right on top. He ribbited sharply, as if shocked to discover a strange object in her hand. Wide-eyed, he perched atop the wadded paper like a trained bear at the circus.

"Don't be silly," Daisy admonished him.

He stared up at her resentfully. After all, it wasn't his fault she was holding a crumpled ball of paper in her hand. But she couldn't do anything with it with a where-frog sitting on top.

"I'm serious, Bubbles." She wiggled her hand in an attempt to dislodge him. "Get lost."

With a tiny pop, both he and the paper disappeared.

CHAPTER 21

*D*aisy leapt to her feet. What in Hades had just happened?

She stared at her empty hands and empty desk and empty floor. Granted, Bubbles had been in her palm as though waiting for a teleportation request, but he'd somehow left without her.

Impossible.

Skin-to-skin contact was all it took to join him wherever he decided to—oh crap. She collapsed back into her chair. Bubbles hadn't been touching her. He'd been touching an itemized list of reasons why she shouldn't moon over an anti-magic mortal.

Just wonderful. Her where-frog hadn't run away from home in two decades, but Ganesha only knew where the little rascal was now. Daisy wasn't looking forward to hiking all over Nether-Netherland for the second time in a month, but when your where-frog teleports off the job, what can you do?

With a sigh, she pushed back the seat and stood. The Neurophysics Compound hallway filled with commotion. Probably it was a former coworker's birthday. Or an audit. Crap. She sure hoped not.

To protect them from prying eyes, she pulled the curtains on her Create-A-Wand machine and her star topper bins.

She grabbed up her handbag and stepped out into the hall.

An army of burly trolls rushed forward to surround her.

"DAISY LE FEY," boomed the now-familiar voice. "You are hereby summoned to the Elders' High Court for violating the terms of your probation."

One of Daisy's ex-coworkers careened around the corner with several of her ex-interns close behind. From the looks of horror on their faces, they were as thrilled about this surprise visit as Daisy.

Heavy black netting scraped down the hallway, trapping her beneath the thick, scratchy web. She didn't get a chance to ask what she'd done to violate the terms of her probation this time. With her luck, it could be anything. She hugged herself, her fingers ice cold against her bare arms. Judge Banshee was going to love having her back in court again.

Shaking with trepidation, Daisy lifted her hand to her shoulder before she remembered that even her trusty where-frog had abandoned her for parts unknown.

This time, she was all alone.

When Trevor woke up alone, he felt neither rested nor refreshed. For the third day in a row, his bedroom just seemed... lonely.

Sometime during the night, even his blanket had deserted him for the floor. His pillow had shot out from under his head and was now poking out of the white wicker trash bin beside the bed. Only the sheets twisted around his ankles like a 300-threadcount serpent.

He kicked his legs free and stumbled to the bathroom sink. He managed to scowl at his less than charming reflection long enough to get his teeth brushed. Without bothering to shave, he headed straight to the kitchen for his coffee.

The twin pair of no-longer-mint-condition vintage Chicago Cubs coffee mugs were not on his windowsill. They tilted against each other upside down in the dish drainer, probably dinging and scratching one another just to spite him.

To the right, the glass coffee pitcher brimmed with ten cups' worth of hot, steamy tap water. He'd apparently forgotten to fill the filter with fresh grounds the night before.

Great.

With a sigh of defeat, he plopped into the closest chair at the kitchen table and faced a few undeniable facts.

One. He was no longer a morning person.

Each new day brought him a little closer to the tenure vote, and based on the hints Dr. Papadopoulos kept dropping, it wasn't going to be pretty. Plus, it was hard to be cheery when even the coffeemaker was out to get you. Stupid machine probably missed Daisy, too.

Two. He wasn't going to publish in time to save his job.

The markings on the pottery didn't match a single printout. He couldn't prove the damn things were or weren't Costa Rican for God's sake, let alone Scottish. Even if he happened to discover the highway to Atlantis this afternoon between classes, there wouldn't be enough time to draft a decent treatise, publish the research in a respected periodical, and get said periodical in front of the department head's nose before it was too late.

Three. His life was *not* better. He did not feel normal. He felt upside-down and inside-out. Lost. She'd melted his brain with her touch and taste and scent. She'd colored every room of his house with her very presence until his world now seemed a series of empty black lines. He was angry. He was despondent. He was heartsick. And there wasn't much he could do except muddle through and face each day as it came.

He showered, dressed, and stalked into the living room to get his briefcase. A soft scratching sound crinkled from across the room. He glanced left and right to find the source of the noise. He nearly walked into the wall when his gaze landed on a tiny green frog perched on a ball of crumpled paper in the middle of his otherwise empty aquarium.

Bubbles! Delight gave way to confusion. What the hell was Bubbles doing here?

Was this Daisy's idea of a practical joke? Or some sort of pity gift to say, "Sorry I screwed up your life. Here's a get-out-of-jail-free card for when things go south. You can always come to Nether-Netherland and get a janitorial job at the Pearly States."

If Daisy realized she missed him—even a little bit—then she'd show up herself, not send a tiny green emissary to take her place. And if she'd sent her where-frog to tempt Trevor back to Nether-Netherland... well, as much as he'd like to see her, she had to realize how much trouble missing a single day of work was. He couldn't do that again. Not with his job on the line.

"Sorry, Bubbles," he said to the unblinking where-frog. "No can do."

Shoulders back, Trevor walked out the door without a second glance.

~

Daisy rested her sweaty hands on top of the witness stand and did her best to ignore the dozens of familiar faces staring up at her. Maeve, her parents, her neighbors, her ex-coworkers... cripes. Her former neurophysics interns waved sparkly "Free the Fairy" picket signs.

Unmoved and un-amused, D.A. Sangre prowled closer until her blood-spiced breath clogged Daisy's nostrils.

"I have petitioned for a truth spell," the D.A. hissed, her lips curving into her trademark feline snarl. "If you do not answer my questions, I have permission to resort to those measures."

Daisy sneaked a glance up at Judge Banshee, who gave a sharp nod to validate the D.A.'s words. A truth spell authorization. Nothing could have made her more nervous. Or more nauseous. She folded her trembling fingers in her lap and tried to remain calm.

"Yes, I stayed a few days with Trev—with the human. I felt terrible about disrupting his life. Judge Banshee had instructed me to put things to rights. I was there to help him get things back on track."

D.A. Sangre smirked. "By 'back on track', do you mean gallivanting around town playing girlfriend and continuing the unsanctioned physical relationship forbidden by the High Court? Is that what you suppose Judge Banshee meant for you to do?"

Eek. Daisy shifted on the hard wooden seat. She debated how best

238

to phrase her response, terrified of having the wrong word send her straight to imprisonment. The D.A. would love to strip her of her family, her friends, her future. The problem was, Daisy couldn't be sure whether the truth would set her free... or seal her fate. Heart racing, her fingers compulsively clutched the hem of her dress.

D.A. Sangre mouthed "truth spell" and smiled.

"Not precisely," Daisy admitted at last, her hands twisting. "But he's a good guy. I was trying to—"

"The defendant *admits* her *guilt*," D.A. Sangre crowed, facing the audience. She crossed back to her table and sat down with a self-satisfied, "No more questions, Your Honor. The prosecution rests."

"Look," Daisy said, her voice shaking. "I—"

"May not speak unless responding to questions posed by counsel," Judge Banshee interrupted. "Mr. Squatch? Would you like to cross-examine?"

Daisy's lawyer lumbered to his feet. He nodded at the jury and then loped over to Daisy's side.

"Urgh." He leaned in, one furry elbow resting on the edge of the witness stand. "Urrrrrghhhh."

Daisy nodded slowly. Thank Ogma she'd finished the yeti language course on her LinguaLearner. Grammar and sentence structure was as straightforward as neurophysics. Once the different gargling sounds were mastered, the vocabulary just fell into place.

She straightened her spine and tried to project confidence. "Yes. I do care for him. To me, he's Trevor Masterson, a person just like you or me. Not just some insignificant human subject. And I am pleased to have undone as much damage as possible. True, the romantic aspect was unauthorized, but..." She craned her neck to face Judge Banshee. "The High Court makes and breaks the rules at their discretion. Couldn't you rule in favor of allowing a Nether-Netherlandian to pursue a relationship with a human, thus retroactively legalizing all actions undertaken during the course of fulfilling my sentence?"

The judge lifted her gavel.

"Yes."

Daisy gasped. The crowd gasped. Mr. Squatch gurgled.

"You will?" The words squeaked from her suddenly dry throat, her entire body trembling. "Grant me a permit to interact with Trevor on a personal level, I mean?"

The gavel slapped against the desktop.

"No." Judge Banshee glared at Daisy's lawyer. "Next question."

The dampness heating the back of her neck froze into a solid block of ice. A government-sanctioned fairy-human relationship was possible. But not for her.

Never for her.

"Why not?" she asked hollowly.

"Because you did not pursue the exemption through the proper channels, Miss le Fey. Exceptions will not be made."

"Urgh," Mr. Squatch said, his question a low, sympathetic rumble. "Urrrrrghhhh."

Somehow, she forced her mouth to respond. "That's right," she said, the hopeless words sounding flat and dead even to her own ears. "I did follow orders and put things to rights. I put back the teeth, made international phone calls, transcribed documents that listed—"

"Objection!" D.A. Sangre leapt forward. "The defendant wishes her transgressions to be excused simply because she spent her free time playing secretary for a human? Your Honor, she has already admitted her guilt. Any further testimony is a waste of Your Honor's time."

"Sustained," Judge Banshee agreed, hopping onto the corner of her desk. "Miss le Fey. You will be advised that a court order is a court order, and breaking the law necessitates appropriate punishment. Your whims do not outrank those of the High Court."

"Urgh," Mr. Squatch protested, raising a furry fist. "Urrrrrghhhh."

"If you say anything like that again, I'll have you arrested for contempt of court," Judge Banshee snapped. "If you have closing arguments, counsel, now is the time to present them."

Mr. Squatch addressed the jury.

"Urgh." He gestured toward Daisy. "Urrrrrghhhh." The paw swept in D.A. Sangre's direction. "Urrrrrghhhh." His voice lowered for a final, impassioned, "Urrrrrghhhh."

D.A. Sangre rose to her feet, but didn't bother moving closer to the jury.

"Despite Mr. Squatch's creative adulation of Miss le Fey's moral character," she said with a humorless smile, "the defendant has already confessed her guilt. We are not here to examine her charming personality. We are here to mete out justice for crimes committed."

Her fangs flashed before she took her seat.

Daisy's stomach clenched. Her fingers worried at the edge of her dress, slowly shredding the hem. This was it. The next few minutes would decide her fate.

Judge Banshee's small, shiny eyes turned toward Daisy. "Miss le Fey, I warned you the last time, if you violated your probation for any reason—any reason at all—I would instruct the jury to consider the maximum sentence." She pointed a finger toward the jury box. "Ladies and gentlemen, pixies and trolls. This defendant has shown an utter disregard of both my rulings and the essential laws of Nether-Netherland itself." Her finger aimed at Daisy. "I therefore recommend you sentence her to nothing less than Purgatory. We will reconvene here as soon as your deliberation has concluded."

At the disheartening sight of Mr. Squatch's defeated shrug, Daisy let out a little sob and buried her clammy face in her hands.

The banging gavel echoed through the courtroom like gunshots.

Normally, finals meant Trevor was one week closer to getting on the baseball diamond. This time, each exam brought him one step closer to getting a pink slip.

As soon as the morning exam ended, he picked up his cellphone and started on the monstrous list of esteemed historians, anthropologists, and archaeologists with any background at all in Scottish history and lore. He begged the ones who spoke English to mail, email, or fax him any scrap of information they could find on Angus the Explorer, the Scottish trading company, or period stoneware.

The ones who didn't speak English were treated to a humiliatingly butchered website-generated translation of his basic query, followed by muttered cursing when he couldn't understand the response. He couldn't ask any university colleagues for help if he wanted a prayer of confidentiality. In other words, he was completely hosed.

If Daisy were here, he'd be glad to hand her the phone and let her determine any useful information. Screw that. If Daisy were here, he'd snatch her up in a massive hug and beg her to stay. One long weekend hadn't been enough. He wasn't sure a week, a month, a year would've been enough.

His forehead dropped to his desktop.

"Stop thinking about her," he muttered. "You'll make yourself crazy."

"What was that?" came a smarmy voice from the doorway.

Choking back a strangled curse, Trevor jerked his head up in time to see Dr. Papadopoulos frowning at him from the hallway, flanked by Berrymellow.

Nice. His mortal enemy and the department head had caught him talking to himself. Or rather, speaking to his desktop. Even better.

"Nothing." He rubbed the back of his hand across his forehead. "You, ah... caught me in a power nap."

"Sleeping on the job, Professor?" Berrymellow raised his eyebrows at Dr. Papadopoulos. "Told you he was lazy."

"I work twice as many hours as you do," Trevor snapped, then cursed inwardly when he realized he'd been goaded into responding down at Berrymellow's level. "I actually just got off the phone with some international collaborators."

"Hmm." Although Dr. Papadopoulos didn't voice an opinion, her eyes were as sharp and quick as ever. "How *is* the research going?"

"Definitely moving in a positive direction," he answered confidently. Confident that the outlook was positively bleak, that is. If he didn't have something real very soon, his career was going to be over.

Outside the courtroom doors, Daisy stood sandwiched between her parents and Maeve. If it weren't for their support—both emotionally and physically—she doubted she'd have managed to stay upright. Every minute of the jury's endless deliberation chopped at her confidence in the legal system until hope for her future was nothing more than a foolish dream.

"Sentencing," came a shout from inside the courtroom.

Two trolls stepped forward and grabbed Daisy by the arms. They led her back to the defense's table, where Mr. Squatch waited. Due to a combination of his height and his furry face, she couldn't gauge how worried he was about the outcome of the case.

Daisy was utterly terrified. By the looks of their faces, so were her friends and family.

"All rise," the court gnome hollered from his perch beside the bench.

Judge Banshee scrabbled up the side of the desk and onto her perch. "Has the jury reached a verdict?"

A faun stepped forward, clutching a slip of paper. "We have, Your Honor."

"Well, how do you find?" shrilled the judge.

The faun slunk Daisy an apologetic look.

Her breath came in short, ragged bursts. *No.* It couldn't be! She clutched at her attorney's shaggy pelt.

"We find the defendant," he said, and took a deep breath. "Guilty as charged."

Daisy staggered as if each word had drawn blood.

Judge Banshee hopped across her desk. "I see no need to put off sentencing when the defendant has already been warned she would receive the maximum sentence if I found her back in my courtroom." Her gavel sliced through the air, banging against her desk like a gong tolling for the dead. "Mandatory clerical detention stint. Five years. Purgatory. No visitors."

Five. Years.

Daisy wilted against Mr. Squatch's warm, matted side. Soon even he would be ripped from her. Everything she knew, everyone she cherished, gone.

"No!" Mama screamed from a few rows behind. "There's the law, and then there's common sense. These charges are ridiculous. She may have violated the terms of her probation, but she had good intentions at heart. I won't stand for such a severe—"

"You'll stand in lockdown," Judge Banshee shrieked, "unless you sit down and shut up. I'll have order in my court or I'll have you removed!"

Daisy twisted around in time to see the horrified expressions on her parents' faces. Dad reached out his hand with a strangled, "Daisy..." before the trolls were upon her, wrenching her forward with their iron grip.

~

Vivian Valdemeer sat in the back of the courtroom, thrilled with how well her plan was unfolding.

Daisy'd been carried away, bound with anti-magic chains to keep her from kicking the trolls. The judge was not in the best of moods. Getting Arabella out of the picture would be easy—the picture-perfect loudmouth was engineering her own downfall.

Poor A.J., stuck with that mouthy harridan. Even his gorgeous wings drooped below his shoulders. His new future with Vivian would be a welcome respite for the poor man. She couldn't wait to have the big sexy guardian angel to herself, as well as all the power and perks that came with being his lifemate. All of which should've been hers in the first place.

How delicious to finally have the opportunity to steal her ex-boyfriend back!

"Reverse these charges," Arabella yelled up at the increasingly annoyed judge. "If you would've just granted an inter-dimensional relationship permit, these trumped-up charges would be moot!"

"But I didn't, and they're not." Judge Banshee leapt on top of her desk and hopped around on all fours. "Submit an appeal if you disagree."

Arabella ran down the aisle and up to the desk, shaking a dainty fist at the enraged judge. If she kept up the attitude, Ms. Fairy Godmother could earn a trip to Purgatory, too.

Shaking her head in secret glee, Vivian sidled up to A.J. and ever so gently laid a palm on his bicep.

"It's so terrible about our Daisy." She debated whether or not she dared to give him a hug. She could play it off as compassionate commiseration, but... she didn't want him to think of her as friendly, sisterly. She wanted him to think of her as sexy. Indispensable. Superior to Arabella, who was blathering incoherently and two seconds away from getting kicked out of the courtroom.

If Vivian played her cards right, maybe she could get Miss Perfect kicked out of Nether-Netherland forever.

"You know..." Vivian allowed her tone to subtly rise in volume. "I'm surprised Arabella didn't try to prevent this when she went down to Earth to visit Daisy. Seems like that might've been a good time to remind the girl to stay out of the human's bedroom."

"When she *what*?" A.J. growled, his white-feathered wings blooming behind him.

Arabella slowly turned away from the judge's desk, her painted mouth slack and gaping.

"Didn't she tell you?" Vivian lifted one shoulder in a sultry shrug and decided to embellish the truth for dramatic effect. "She popped into a busy university right in front of the human's companions and started firing off her wand. One of them ended up immobilized in stone." She gave a practiced little laugh and patted his arm. "I'm sure it was all a silly mistake."

Abandoning her tirade at the judge, Arabella whirled toward Viv. "You were spying on me? You jealous, conniving—"

"Daisy told me," Vivian interrupted, loving how the lie drained the blood from Arabella's pretty face. "We're very close. She's like a daughter to me."

"You mean it's true?" A.J. advanced toward Arabella, palms facing upward. "You knew Daisy was having illegal contact with the human and didn't tell me? You snuck down to Earth behind my back?"

"You're an angel," Arabella protested, her face and tone beseeching. "You get all bent out of shape when I fudge the rules. Besides, if Vivian had done better fact-checking in the first place, Daisy would never have been sent to a grown man for a fossilized tooth."

Judge Banshee banged the gavel. "Quiet!"

"An honest mistake," Vivian quickly assured A.J. with a winning smile. "A simple typo. Hardly the same ballpark as materializing in front of unsuspecting humans and using unauthorized magic to encase one in rock." No harm in neglecting to mention that the human statue had snapped out of it after a few moments, no worse for the wear. "Besides," she purred, looking up at A.J. through carefully curled eyelashes, "at least I don't lie to you. I admit my mistakes."

"A.J., sweetie," Arabella choked out. "You're not buying this garbage, are you? Whose 'mistake' got our daughter into this mess?"

"'Mistake'," A.J. repeated. "You teleported to Earth in front of witnesses, used magic on a human, and lied to me about your involvement."

"Some of which," Vivian pointed out with a wink in Arabella's direction, "is illegal. Oh dear, did you just confess in the middle of a courtroom?"

"Trollop," Arabella spat. "By all that's holy, that's the last time you—"

"Silence! Arabella le Fey, you can cool your anger in a holding facility." Judge Banshee threw her hands heavenward. "If you try my patience, you'll get worse than that."

"You're an idiot!" Arabella threw her hands in the air and glared at the judge. "I'm not the problem. My daughter's not the problem. The problem is your inability to recognize that woman's blatant manipulation of everything and everyone!"

"I've had it," Judge Banshee shrilled. "Guards! Take her away!"

Vivian kept her palm on A.J.'s arm as the beleaguered trolls dragged Arabella from the courtroom. Vivian peered up at him, softening her gaze as though she gave a damn what happened to his flighty lifemate. Rather, ex-lifemate.

She smiled. Everything was finally back on track. No more daughter, no more mother, no more problems.

CHAPTER 22

$\mathcal{N}$othing like starting your morning with a five-year trip down Purgatory Lane.

Daisy lifted her arms over her head and suffered through the search process at the anti-magic checkpoint. They were wasting their time. Even if she'd somehow managed to bring a wand with her, the only person she was a danger to was herself. She'd manufactured a newer wand, but it still botched spells one time out of every ten. If she'd just had a little more time... but no. There was no more time, and no escape.

A pair of massive iron doors swung open, revealing—nothing. Darkness. Shadows. Emptiness.

Tendrils of icy air snaked out through the doorway and curled up her bare legs. She shivered at the intrusion of murky nothingness.

"Are you sure this is Purgatory?" she asked doubtfully. "I don't want to take a wrong turn into Hades."

"Hades is hot," said the thin guard, enshrouded in a full-body robe the burnt orange shade of rotting leaves. He nudged her forward. "Go."

After a quick over-the-shoulder glance to verify the position of the armed guards flanking the passageway back to Nether-Netherland, she straightened her shoulders, lifted her chin, and marched forward.

The big iron doors closed behind her, enveloping her in blackness. The only sounds were her uneven breaths and racing heart. Where were the guards? The other prisoners?

She froze, waiting for someone to come get her, to tell her where to go, what to do.

Nobody came.

The chill swirled around her neck and arms, just cold enough to be uncomfortable but not quite frigid enough for hypothermia. She hugged herself, shivering uncontrollably. The least they could've done was loan her enough clothes powder to change out of her tooth fairy uniform. Or turned on a light.

She sniffed the dank air and sneezed. Musty. Mildewy. As if she were the first live thing to cross this border in decades. She took a cautious step forward. The icy cobbled stone floor scraped against the bottom of her bare feet. A faint noise sounded in the distance.

Plink.

Daisy cocked her head.

Plink.

There it was again. A soft, wet plop like a drop of water falling from a leaky roof to splatter onto the cold floor.

Plink. Plink. Plink.

She fought a sneeze, covering her mouth with the inside of her elbow. The air was oppressive, dingy and stale with dust and mold and neglect. When she opened her eyes, she caught the faint wisps of light coming from what looked like the cracks around a door off in the distance. She moved closer, sliding her feet forward over the freezing, uneven ground so she wouldn't trip over some unknown object lurking in the darkness.

Plink.

The drops fell with no regular pattern. Sometimes several in a row, sometimes none for long minutes. Her shoulders tensed as she anticipated the next wet splatter. Nothing... nothing...

Plink.

She flinched at the sound. Purgatory, it seemed, was annoying.

Not painful, or horrifying, or tortuous, as she imagined Hell, but certainly not the sunny, happy, choirs-of-singing-cherubs bliss of Heaven.

She finally reached the source of the faint light. A door. With something on the other side. Was it better to know or to not know? Could anything be worse than that dark emptiness? She wrenched open the door and blinked to discover herself in a room full of bustling corporate mayhem.

Dingy fluorescent lights hung overhead. Rutted linoleum covered the floor. Shoulder-high cubicles divided the interior space into five-foot by five-foot sections. A cacophony of monotone voices muffled the intermittent plink of the drippy ceiling.

And gray. Everything, *everything*, was gray.

A long wall dotted with glass dividers separated the apparent office space from what looked like a waiting room the size of Indiana, filled with a winding queue of unhappy people. They shuffled forward, taking their turns at the speakers embedded in the glass dividers before shuffling off to stand in another line.

Daisy rubbed her eyes. "What is this place?"

"Purgatory, of course," came a bored voice.

She whirled to find a sharp-horned minotaur with a large clipboard hovering behind her. Even without the head of a bull, his over-muscled arms and legs would give any prisoner pause.

"Daisy le Fey, I presume?" His tone indicated he didn't care if she were the Queen of Nether-Netherland. When she nodded, he gestured with his clipboard. "Says here you've been sentenced to the Recently Departed section of Purgatory."

"Recently Departed?" Daisy repeated blankly.

He pointed at a queue of hovering bodies lined up on the other side of the wall. "Those are incoming human souls who need to be checked in. You'll be provided with a list of interview questions. All you have to do is take down the information, log their details and duration of stay into the Scales of Justice, and move on to the next person."

"So, I'm not sentenced *to* Purgatory, per se." Slow understanding rekindled her sense of hope. "I'm sentenced to help *run* Purgatory?"

"Trust me," the minotaur said. "This is worse."

She took another look at the queue of incoming souls. "Is Purgatory only for humans?"

"Catholic humans," he corrected. "Come, I'll show you to your cubicle, where you'll spend the next five years."

A cubicle. Purgatory might be Hell after all. "Are there breaks?"

"You get fifteen minutes every four hours during your twelve-hour shift. The break room is on the other side of that wall of filing cabinets. The soda machine is out of everything but Tab."

"How often do they refill it?"

He laughed humorlessly. "That's just how it is. In Hell, prisoners get nothing. In Heaven, sodas come from fountains. We get a self-serve machine that only stocks Tab." He motioned her into a seat in front of a divider window. "Here's your copy of the Interview for Incoming Residents. The login password is 'mediocre,' no caps. See you on break."

And with that, he loped out of sight.

She eased into the lumpy swivel chair. Two of the wheels didn't turn. The back of the chair cantered sideways and fell off when she tried to fix it. This was worse than grad school. There *had* to be a way out.

Except there wasn't.

Five years. Five long, long years. Of no friends, no family, no wings... and no Trevor. Five years of only her memories to keep her company, and nothing at all she could do about it.

Morning melted into afternoon while she interviewed incoming residents with growing horror and sympathy. Wives who murdered abusive husbands, fathers who stole to provide for their families, children who prostituted themselves to survive on the streets. No way could she last five days at this window, much less five years. Her heart was bleeding.

She racked her brain for an escape plan. Preferably something legal.

Mr. Squatch had murmured something about trying to appeal, but with Judge Banshee imposing a no visitors ruling, was that still possible? Daisy assumed her lawyer didn't count as a mere visitor. Matter of fact, she hoped he hurried his furry butt on down as fast as his big feet could take him.

"Busy day," said a gum-popping pixie the next cube over, jerking her head toward the back door. "Here comes another newbie."

Daisy craned her neck to see the minotaur interviewing a familiar winged blonde woman in a flowing powder blue gown.

Mama? Here? She leapt to her feet in horror. Visions of her mother's impassioned outbursts on her behalf replayed through her mind.

Wonderful. She'd not only screwed up her own life, she'd managed to bring her mother down with her. Daisy flipped the sign on her window from "OPEN" to "Back in 15 Minutes." She sprinted over to the wall of filing cabinets in order to eavesdrop on the conversation with the minotaur.

"Let me get this straight." Her mother's words were slow, uncertain. "I'm supposed to straighten the supply closet? That's all?"

The minotaur sighed, his voice inflectionless and tired as though he'd given this speech more times than he cared to count. "Jobs in Purgatory aren't difficult. Nor are they fun. Nothing in Purgatory is all bad and nothing in Purgatory is all good. It's Purgatory."

Mama nodded slowly.

As happy as she was to see a familiar face, Daisy couldn't help the guilt congealing in her stomach. She doubted her glamorous mother would be straightening supply closets if her daughter hadn't been an unmagical screw-up.

When the shuffle of footsteps grew closer, Daisy flattened herself as close to the wall as possible. She bit back a gasp as the minotaur's dark-furred hand pointed past the opening between the cabinets, his thick yellow fingernails mere inches from her nose.

"There's the break room," he said, the tips of his horns a mere stack of manila folders away. "The supply closet is on the opposite side."

A flurry of blue silk fluttered past the opening as Mama floated off toward the supply closet. Daisy didn't move until she was sure the minotaur had returned to his post to wait on the next new recruit.

She slid out between the cabinets, keeping her back flush with the cold metal drawers. When nobody tackled her to the ground, she sucked in a quick breath and dashed around the corner to the hallway.

On her right was a small, dingy room with a big gray table, a marinara-splattered microwave, and a big, whirring soda machine. An orange "Sold Out" light glowed above all the drink selections except Tab.

Daisy hated Tab.

To her left was a cracked wooden door, just enough ajar that both a cool draft and dusty light swirled from the gap. With a final, furtive glance over her shoulder, she slipped inside and squeezed her incredulous mother in a big bear hug.

"Sweetie," Mama said into Daisy's hair, her voice choked with unshed tears. "It is so good to see you. I didn't think I'd find you again... ever."

Daisy pulled away so she could see her mother's face. "I didn't think you'd follow in my footsteps. Why in the world are you down here?"

Mama's cheeks flushed red. "My outbursts in court paled next to the turning-humans-into-stone incident."

"Oh no," Daisy gasped. "How in Hades did D.A. Sangre even find out?"

"She didn't. Vivian Valdemeer said *you* told her." Mama's tone was even, but her eyes were moist and wounded.

"Why would I? She's out to get me. I have no idea how—" Daisy slapped her forehead with the palm of one hand. The stupid Mortal Locator. She should've password-protected the damn thing when she'd altered the log locations, even if it would've caused more trouble. "As much as I needed her help if I was ever going to earn wings, I never did trust her. That woman is toxic."

"What do you mean, 'needed' her help, past tense?" Mama's hands fisted on her hips. "What else did she do?"

"She knows I'm on to her, but she can't get rid of me if I don't come out and say so." Daisy rested her elbow against the jutting metal shelves. "But I refuse to work for someone who'd get my mother tossed in Purgatory, even if it means I'll never be a tooth fairy."

"Oh, sweetie. I'm pleased to hear that, although a little surprised. I didn't think anything short of a cataclysmic apocalypse could interfere with your quest for wings."

"Probably not," Daisy admitted. "I'll never give up. But I don't need Vivian's help at this price. She may be the most visible, high-ranking tooth fairy in Nether-Netherland, but she's not the *only* fairy."

"What are you going to do?" Mama reached out to touch her hair. "If you had your magic wand license, I could put in a good word for you at the Fairy Godmother Association. I've tried several times before, but they just won't accept anyone who can't—"

"I know, I know. But I'm getting there. I've almost worked the bugs out of my mechanical wand."

"Sweetie, you know they won't hire someone who uses false magic."

"I won't mention that part. Besides, I've got five years to work on my résumé." Daisy rested her cheek against her mother's shoulder. "As soon as I'm free, I'll send out as many apprenticeship applications as it takes until I find someone willing to take a chance on me. Without sacrificing my mother. Which brings me to my next question... How long are you here? As much as I'd enjoy your company, please don't tell me five years. I'll start crying." She swiped at her cheek. "Oh crap, I'm already crying."

Mama kissed her forehead. "Thanks to Vivian's big mouth, they sent me down to 'cool off for the night' for contempt of court. I think it's the outraged-mother equivalent of a drunk tank."

"Maybe that's why you got assigned to supply closet duty. Makes sense for one night." Daisy glanced around the cramped, windowless area. "Sure wouldn't be much to do for five years."

The closet wasn't much wider than the door leading to the hall-way, with the added depth of maybe five or six feet. Metal shelves lined all three non-door walls, leaving a two foot by three-foot square of stained carpet free for Daisy to stand on and her mother to hover over.

Most of the shelves were stacked with legal pads, blank name badges, used binders, and boxes of black pens with erasable ink. Any visible areas of wall were covered with brightly lettered signs, ranging from "Wash Hands after Using the Restroom" to "Stay Safe: Always Wear Safety Goggles."

Daisy grimaced.

"Thank Jupiter you're not claustrophobic, or this place would suck even worse." She slumped against one of the cluttered shelves. "I can't believe I got you into this."

"You didn't get me into anything." Mama's soft fingers brushed Daisy's cheek. "By yelling at the judge, I dug my own hole—and Vivian nailed the coffin shut."

"But that's what I mean. It all comes back to Vivian, with special thanks to me. If I hadn't wanted to earn my wings so bad, I would've punched her in the face right after she slipped me that Himalayan Lust Charm."

Mama goggled at her. "Slipped you a what?"

"That's how Trevor and I got together in the first place. Not that we weren't already knee deep in heated glances," she admitted, "but I wouldn't have *slept* with him that first time if we weren't both under the influence of a wicked potent spell."

"As your mother, I'm going to ignore 'that first time' for a second to say, why in the name of all that's holy didn't you tell me earlier?"

"Are you kidding? Who discusses their sex life with their mother?"

A sharp, insistent pain pounded in the back of Daisy's head. Why *hadn't* she complained earlier? Because she was so focused on making fairy above all else, that's why. Maybe she really was the fool that Vivian had played her for. Or maybe she had deceived herself. She'd suspected Vivian's motives weren't one hundred percent altruistic from the moment the dentition spectrometer proved Angus was an adult. She just didn't want to believe it. To lose her one chance of making fairy.

Thanks to tunnel vision, she'd slipped down the rabbit hole into Purgatory... and dragged her mother with her.

On autopilot since leaving the university for the day, Trevor didn't realize he'd missed the turnoff for his subdivision until he found himself driving past the tooth fountain he'd taken Daisy to.

Damn it. Some way, somehow, he had to get that woman out of his brain. It was a gimme that he would've pursued a relationship with her if they'd met under different circumstances. What he hadn't expected was regret for not pursuing her even under *these* circumstances.

The fading sunlight dipped below the rooftops cluttering up the horizon. Before long, he arrived home. Scratch that: to an empty house.

What had Daisy said when they'd first met? She only traveled under cover of night? Well, now it was night. If she wanted him, if she missed him, she would be here. And she wasn't.

He couldn't even look at a tree without wishing he had Daisy up against it. And not just in a sexual way. Sure, he'd enjoyed every second of their lovemaking. But he'd also enjoyed taking her to see the fountain, and cuddling on the couch while they pored over the Angus research.

If she'd happened to be human, she'd be damn near perfect. What kind of twisted cosmic fate caused him to fall for the one woman he couldn't have?

He trudged up the walkway to his front porch. He swung open his front door, turned off the alarm, and stepped inside. No Daisy.

"Stop thinking about her," he muttered to himself. "It's over."

Exhaling deeply, he tumbled backward onto the couch, his sightless eyes staring through the ceiling.

If he could just talk to her again, do over that last conversation. Maybe there was some way she could give him another chance. Sure, ordinary old Earth didn't have fairy wings and pixie dust, but Daisy didn't need any of that crap anyway. She was smart, she was fun, she was perfect just the way she was. Except for the part about her being gone.

A soft ribbit croaked from the aquarium in the corner. Trevor bolted upright. Bubbles. How could he have forgotten Bubbles?

He sprinted across the room to the aquarium. The where-frog sat in one corner, the crumpled paper in another.

Good Lord, he'd forgotten the paper, too. At first he'd just assumed it was a Dear John, and forced it from his mind. But what if it wasn't?

Maybe Daisy was sitting somewhere in Nether-Netherland missing him just as much as he was missing her. Maybe she'd written him a *love* letter, asking him to come for her like a white knight off to capture his fair damsel. And him, moping around for no reason!

Fingers trembling, he reached inside the aquarium for the scratchy ball of paper. Excitement coursed through his veins. He'd explain that he wasn't ignoring her—he'd been too busy wallowing in his misery to realize she needed him right back.

He should probably write her a love letter of his own just to prove it. Maybe even some poetry. What rhymed with Daisy? Hazy. Lazy. Crazy. Maybe he should rhyme "fairy" instead. Was that better? Very. Berry. Marry.

With hope in his heart for the first time since Daisy had disappeared for good, Trevor flattened out the wrinkled paper and froze.

Six little words screamed at him from the top of the page in Daisy's unmistakable handwriting. Heavy capital letters that sliced through his silly hopes and proved once and for all what a ridiculous dreamer he really was.

"WHY I DON'T WANT TREVOR MASTERSON."

A vertical line separated the page into two columns. The longer of the two lists read, "Smart. Respected. Respectful. Thoughtful. Sexy. Fun. Friendly. Charming."

Presumably, those were his good qualities, given they fell under the heading "PRO". Based on the header, though, they weren't good enough.

The "CONS" side of the paper bore only three words. The first was "Anti-wings." He supposed that was true enough, although he could hardly be blamed for it, what with wings being a bit unusual for people on Earth. The second was "Illegal." True, but... he had to believe there was some way around that. The third was simply, "Human."

Human.

He couldn't do anything about that, now could he?

Nausea gripped his stomach. Nausea at his own foolishness. His muscles shook. Her disregard of him didn't stem from how he treated her, or how he felt about her, or whether or not he was a good person at heart. No, she dismissed him for the one thing that no matter what he did, he couldn't change.

He wadded the paper in his fist and hurled the mangled ball into the cold fireplace. He strode to the wall switch and slapped on the gas, desperate to see his list of faults burst into flame and disintegrate into ashes.

What was the point in sending him this garbage? Just to prove she didn't miss him? Didn't need him? Didn't want him?

His heart clenched as he stared into the crackling fire.

Not because his feelings were hurt. No, not at all. If she didn't want him, he didn't want her. He wasn't hurt. Not the tiniest bit. He was angry. Super-angry. Utterly and completely pissed off. And he wasn't going to stand there and take it, either.

He was going to make her stupid where-frog reunite them just so he could tell her off. To her face. Not because he missed her. How could he miss someone who disliked him just because he was human? Hadn't he been willing to overlook her fake wings and scientific magic?

He switched off the fireplace, reset the house alarm, and scooped the tiny where-frog into his palms.

Was he really ready for this? He took a deep, shaky breath, his heart beating a thousand times a second, pumping out more blood per minute than a fire hose on full blast. Would he really be able to say all the things he needed to say in order to exorcise her from his mind?

"Look alive, Bubbles." Trevor did his best to ignore what the desperate crack in his voice might mean. "Take us to Daisy."

A tiny pop whistled in his ears.

Before he could take his next breath, Trevor found himself squished between two warm bodies and a row of hard metal shelves protruding from a cluttered wall.

Daisy! And her mother.

They stared at him in shock, eyes huge and mouths gaping. He tried to back up and couldn't. Damn it. He hadn't counted on Arabella being around when he launched into his big "You can't hurt me because I'm so over you" speech. And he definitely hadn't planned on playing Sardines at the same time.

"Uh, hi." He cleared his throat. "So... Where are we?"

Still speechless, Daisy pointed at something high above his head.

He craned his neck to see a jumble of mismatched signs. "'No Smoking on the Tarmac,'" he read aloud. "'Objects in Mirror Are Closer Than They Appear.'"

Arabella's cool palms flattened against his ears, turning his face a little more to the left. There, in big block letters, was a black and white sign that read:

PURGATORY SUPPLY CLOSET
EMPLOYEES ONLY.

CHAPTER 23

"*P*urgatory?" Trevor stammered. "As in, purgatory-purgatory?"

Daisy nodded.

"Holy shit," he breathed. "I'm not Catholic. I would've never guessed that Purgatory was a supply closet."

"Purgatory isn't a supply closet." Arabella lowered her voice. "And I don't recommend exploring the rest of the grounds uninvited."

He had no intention of going anywhere. He had come in search of exactly one person.

Daisy stared up at him, long lashes framing her eyes. "How are you here? *Why* are you here? Is something wrong with the Angus project?"

He tried not to notice how the mere sound of her voice calmed the tense nerves spasming between his shoulders. He wasn't here to start falling for her again. He was here to take her to task for leaving him a Dear John bulleted list.

"I came," he said slowly, trying to remember the eloquent way he'd phrased the litany of wrongs in his head before dashing between dimensions and landing somewhere between heaven and hell, "because I got your note."

"My what?" Those big hazel eyes blinked a few times before her face erupted in a blush rivaling the intensity of Mount Vesuvius.

"I see you remember."

She slunk a sidelong glance toward her mother, who looked like she'd rather crawl onto a shelf and plug her ears rather than eavesdrop on what would no doubt be a train wreck of a reunion.

He tried to cross his arms over his chest but couldn't un-wedge them from between his sides and the metal shelves. "I can't believe you of all people would be so selfish and close-minded that you have no problem judging me for things outside my control. You can't even collect teeth."

She sucked in a breath and staggered a couple inches backward, acting as though she'd crumple to the ground if there was physically enough space for her to do so.

Trevor wasn't buying it for a second. The kind of person who loved 'em and left 'em just because they were human was the kind of person who didn't give a good goddamn about anybody but herself. Sadly, his roiling gut indicated he'd still go home and pine for Daisy for a few more years.

But hey. At least they'd have a clean break. She wouldn't suspect his heart was clogging up his convulsing throat and that all he really wanted to do was grab her to him and never let go. She didn't want him. Well, her mom could whip him up a new ForgetMe spell—one that worked this time—and then Daisy could concentrate on fairy wings and pixie dust without worrying that she was breaking a human heart in the process.

A soft, quick movement reminded Trevor that Bubbles the where-frog still nestled in his palm, out of sight. Maybe this would be a good time to make a dramatic exit.

"Well, let me tell *you* a little something," said the object of his unrequited affection, rising from her slump against the overstuffed shelving.

Her chin lifted, her shoulders straightened, and Trevor got the distinct impression that if there was enough space for her to do so, she'd jab her finger at his chest until she poked a hole in his ribs.

"You, Professor, lack a fundamental understanding about the

concept of teamwork." Her voice rose. "You're the big bad paleo-anthropologist, not me. I'm just the silly little tooth fairy, the one you don't want around your office unless I'm playing interpreter or stretched across your desk."

Arabella choked on her fist and squeezed her eyes shut tight.

Oblivious, Daisy leaned forward. Her breath steamed against his cheek, hot and moist and angry. Never before had the faint scent of peppermint ever smelled so much like rage. "If you asked me, I'd say you're awful full of yourself, considering most if not all of your recent advances were both created and augmented by my direct involvement."

"I didn't ask you," he muttered, wishing like hell he had a better comeback than that. Somehow he'd visualized this scene unfolding much differently.

"No, you didn't." She jerked her head away, her lip curling above the whiteness of her teeth. "You didn't ask me anything. You just expected me to do whatever you wanted, whenever you wanted, so long as it was convenient for your life. Is that about right?"

"Uh…" He faltered, sliding a glance toward Arabella, whose eyes were now wide open and staring straight at him with avid interest. "No?"

"Well, guess what," Daisy continued, her face flushed and eyes narrowed. "This isn't a good time for me. I happen to be here in Purgatory serving an all-expenses-paid five-year sentence for helping *you*, you big jerk. Where were you when *I* could've used some assistance? When *I* was being paraded in front of the jury as the Promiscuous Apprentice Who Could? When my mother was dragged away just for sticking up for me?"

"You're in jail?" He stared at her in disbelief and horror. "Both of you?"

A sudden knock rapped against the supply room door.

"Hey!" growled a deep, guttural voice. "What's going on in there?"

"Just a second," Daisy hollered, hoping the minotaur on the other side of the door wouldn't burst in and gore them all with his pointed horns. "We're... sorting the erasable pens by size and color."

She held her breath and waited.

After a few grunts and snorts, he bellowed back, "I'll be waiting for you when you come out."

Right. Fabulous. A figuratively bullheaded human on the inside of the door and a literally bullheaded minotaur on the outside.

Mama slanted Trevor a calculating glance. "So," she said in that I'm-about-to-embarrass-the-crap-out-of-my-daughter voice, "what exactly are your intentions toward Daisy?"

"My intentions?" He backed against the metal shelves as if he thought he could flee through solid objects if he tried hard enough.

"Drop it," Daisy whispered, and kicked her mother in the ankle. "His intentions are perfectly clear. He came here to let me know how far I fall below his exalted standards."

During her speech, Trevor's lips pursed, his eyes squinted, and his nose wrinkled. Either he was reacting strongly to her assessment of his motives, or there was about to be a very bad smell in the supply closet.

"I'm not so sure that's what he said." Mama's head tilted to one side. "Purgatory seems a bit out of the way for someone who just wants to be snarky."

"He didn't know we'd be in Purgatory." She stared at him. "He probably thought we were in Nether-Netherland."

Mama shrugged. "Is that any closer to Indiana?" When Daisy had no ready response, Mama turned back to Trevor.

Whatever she was going to say next was drowned out by a renewed round of frenzied knocking.

"How long can it take to organize pens?" yelled the minotaur. "Break's over. Thirty more seconds and I'm ramming the door down."

"It doesn't matter why I came," Trevor said suddenly, his dark eyes focused on Daisy. "I'm here."

Too little too late. She circled a finger in the air. "Yay. Now it's a party."

"Now, sweetie," Mama chastised her. "If you always have such a bad attitude toward men, it's no wonder you can't keep a boyfriend."

Daisy's fingers clenched in outrage. Couldn't keep a boyfriend? How about, wasn't *allowed* to keep this one.

"Can you *try* being on my side? You're my mother!"

A sly smile stretched across her mother's face. "And a fairy godmother."

Warning bells clanged in Daisy's mind. "Don't even think about—"

Something big and heavy and strong hurled itself at the supply closet door with enough force to knock binders and placards from their shelves.

"Look," Trevor said, eyes wary. "Sounds like we should get out of here. Touch me."

Daisy's lungs tangled in her throat. "What? Here?"

"Touch me," he repeated, jerking his head to one side. "Hurry."

She gulped. "I can't, Trevor. The punishment for escape is—"

The minotaur threw himself at the door until it began to splinter.

"No punishment is worth him killing you! Touch me right now, both of you. And hold on!"

Mama locked onto his arm. Daisy still hesitated.

Just as the minotaur's horns crashed through the door, Trevor grabbed her hand and shouted, "Bubbles—Nether-Netherland. Please!"

With a familiar pop, the supply closet walls disintegrated and the stained carpet floor morphed into the white fluffy clouds of her parents' front lawn.

"So that's how—" Daisy said, reaching out to snatch her blinking where-frog from his new best friend. "Bubbles, you little traitor."

She looked up at Trevor through tremulous lashes. She was still afraid—breaking out scared her even more than going in—but she couldn't deny the warm rush of pleasure at just seeing him.

His hair was tousled as always, grazing the tops of his ears as though he hadn't had time for a haircut. His lashes were long, thick. His lips, parted. His cheeks, unshaven. The tanned skin beneath his eyes was lined and puffy, as though he hadn't been sleeping well. Tiny lines creased his forehead as if whatever worried him was still on his mind even now, as if things weren't getting better for him, but worse. His gaze was dark, intense, unwavering. Unreadable.

Bubbles ribbited.

"Here." Trevor's voice was low and husky. "He's yours."

His free hand slid underneath hers, his skin moist, electric. She couldn't have pulled away if she'd wanted to. The hand holding Bubbles nestled atop her palm, trapping her hands between his.

Slowly, gently, he tilted his hand until Bubbles was forced to hop onto the relative safety of her palm. Trevor's hands fell back to his sides. Hers were left chilled, even though Bubbles still rested between her life line and her heart line.

"Thanks."

His lips hinted at what might have passed for a smile, but his eyes were serious.

"Anytime."

"Don't say that." Mama shook a warning finger. "Once was enough. We'll have to talk to Mr. Squatch before anyone figures out you're not where you're supposed to be. Quick, let's get inside." She hurried up the walk.

Daisy glanced back at Trevor. He was watching her, his eyes clear and focused. She wasn't sure whether the brief tremor that flickered across his lower lip meant he was thinking about saying something or kissing her, but she forced herself to follow her mother to the porch without waiting to find out. First they would fix the present. Then they would decide on the future.

She hurried to catch up to her mother. He followed right behind.

Mama swung open the door, her face bright and alive. She called out, "Honey, I'm—" and gagged on the rest of the words.

From Daisy's position on the porch step, she couldn't see what stopped her mother in her tracks, but the strangled pause only lasted for a moment.

With a half-screamed, half-snarled, "You lying, two-faced slut," Mama dashed to the bucket of pixie dust beside the couch, yanked out a wand, and let fly with a shimmering stream of furious magic.

When the big maple door slammed shut behind the two women, Trevor's first reaction was relief. He'd never heard Daisy's mother raise her voice, much less scream and curse. He wasn't really sure he wanted to know what caused her to wave her wand like some psychotic winged she-Anakin.

With a fair dose of trepidation, he stepped onto the welcome mat and opened the door.

Daisy's father stood in front of the swinging doors between the living room and the kitchen, jaw clenched, wings tucked behind him. A.J. didn't look happy, but the two women squaring off on opposite sides of the room looked vicious.

Vivian Valdemeer stood before A.J. in a red sequined, spaghetti strapped, tube sock of a dress. She balanced on the balls of her feet with her hands overhead, knees shoulder-width apart, as if about to catch a pop fly. Her fingers gripped the handle of a steaming silver wand.

Arabella was on the other side of the coffee table, knees bent, legs wide, back hunched, as though about to hit it out of the park. Instead of a bat, she held a large, sparking wand. Not sparkling—*sparking*.

As in, bits of flame fizzed and spat from the shiny star tip.

The wall behind Vivian crumbled to ash. The framed pictures above her head clattered to the floor and dispersed as scattered embers. The stairway behind Arabella was a mushy mess of soggy carpet and what looked like bubbling lava. What was left of the spiral carpet runner had melted into little pools of singed plastic.

Daisy stood behind the overstuffed couch, one hand clutching her wand and the other hand cradling her where-frog, as though she was trying to decide which one she was better off using.

"Arabella," A.J. said, his voice deep with warning. "I am not having an affair. You're completely misconstruing the situation."

Her back to A.J., Vivian arched a skinny eyebrow. Her glossy crimson lips tweaked up at the corners as if to say, "Yet."

Trevor took a step backward.

"Oh, I'm sure she dropped by for milk and cookies." Arabella jabbed her wand toward Vivian's midsection. "In her hurry, she must've forgotten her bra."

Daisy staggered against the big picture window and looked like she might be sick. "Please don't tell me the Himalayan Lust Charm you slipped me was for Dad. If you tell me he's some sort of fairy heartthrob, I might hurl."

"You were going to trick him into having sex with you?" Arabella shrieked, her flapping wings lifting her higher off the ground.

"I don't have to trick anyone into having sex with me." Vivian touched her scarlet fingernails to her lips and then ran the palm of her hand from her neck down to her hip, one of her black-lined eyes lowering into a wink when her fingers slid over her breast.

"You will now!" Arabella's wand fired off a blinding stream of high-voltage power, barely missing Vivian, who threw herself backward to avoid the blast.

Realizing the stiletto-heeled tooth fairy was about to bowl into him like a fallen redwood, A.J.'s hands flew out to brace for impact.

"Don't you touch her!" Arabella charged across the living room, wand outstretched.

A.J. jerked his arms back so fast they probably broke the sound barrier.

Unable to correct her balance in time, Vivian tumbled to the ground. Hard. She recovered with a somersault, then sprung to her feet with her wand upraised, firing on Arabella even before completely upright.

Arabella feinted behind a paisley-upholstered recliner, firing off shots from one side, then the other.

Lava and fireballs decimated both sides of the room.

Trevor inched behind the couch next to Daisy, hoping that if she did decide to take off with Bubbles, she'd at least let him hitch a ride.

"In case you're wondering," she said under her breath, "you're not catching my family on their best day."

"No worries." He wished he could hold her hand. "At least I'm not the one destroying the house this time."

A.J. jerked his head up at Trevor's voice. "What's he doing here?"

"He rescued Daisy from Purgatory," Arabella called out as she scrambled up and over the coffee table like a cat. "And me, too."

266

"Yeah?" A.J.'s eyes narrowed, momentarily distracted from the utter destruction of his home. "How come?"

"He was mad," Daisy said at the same time Arabella answered, "He likes her," and managed to singe the edge of Vivian's gown.

"What are your intentions toward my daughter?" A.J. demanded, his wings unfurling like a hawk's.

"We've already been through that today," Daisy said. "Can we skip it for now?"

Arabella ducked behind the couch as Vivian's wand liquefied the cushions. "Yeah, I asked him earlier."

A.J. frowned. "Well, what did he say?"

"Nothing. Daisy wouldn't let him talk." Arabella army-crawled between the wall and Daisy and Trevor's feet, hauling ass to the other side of the couch. She latched onto Vivian's ankle and gave a hard tug, knocking the skeezy tooth fairy off-balance yet again.

This time when Vivian fell, she lost her grip on her wand as well as a heavy silk pouch that fell to the floor with a thunk.

"Ha! You did bring a Himalayan Lust Charm. You bitch!" Arabella leapt on top of her, one side of the pale blue gown ripping as her knees pinned Vivian's flailing arms to the ground.

"I did not!" Vivian's legs kicked up in the air. Her skimpy dress slid to her thighs, giving Trevor a direct view up her skirt at neon yellow panties. He shuddered.

"I think I might step outside while you two work things out," he said, grabbing hold of Daisy's elbow and dragging her toward the door before the damn thing melted off its hinges. He burned the tips of his fingers on the searing hot metal handle and swore under his breath.

"Go ahead and kick it down if you want," Daisy said with a sigh. "We'll have to re-conjure the whole thing anyway."

Trevor hesitated, not certain he wanted to compound his negative impression in A.J.'s eyes.

Before he had a chance to make up his mind, the door caved inward, splintering into several jagged planks. Trevor threw his arms around Daisy's waist and tumbled her to safety behind the couch as a no-nonsense army of trolls marched through what used to be the doorway.

A.J. stepped over the writhing women and cleared his throat. "May I help you?"

The trolls exchanged glances at the wreckage.

The spiral staircase dipped and sagged in a Gaudí-esque lump of rippling lava. What few walls remained popped and crackled with bits of fire and smoking embers. Arabella still knelt on the floor in her ragged gown, the scantily clad Vivian flailing beneath her like an overturned crab.

"Neighbors filed a noise complaint," one of the trolls said finally, keeping his gaze on struggling duo on the floor. "'Fraid we're going to have to ask you to come down for questioning."

Trevor was beginning to think of himself as a High Court regular. He glanced at Daisy, and immediately pulled her to him. Her face was pale, her skin clammy. She swayed as if she could faint at any moment.

"They're going to double my stint in Purgatory," she whispered, eyes dull with horror. "They'll lock the door and magic away the key."

He held her tight, wishing to Heaven he had words of encouragement.

One of the trolls stepped forward. "Come along, ladies. Fight's over."

"I'm not going anywhere." Vivian clawed at Arabella, who responded by slapping her across the face.

"In that case," said the troll, "I'm afraid we're going to have to haul you in ourselves."

He motioned over one shoulder. Thick black netting seemed to fall from the ceiling, trapping them all in its scratchy web.

❧

A dour-faced troll released them from their holding cell first thing Saturday morning. If the Elders thought an unsolicited overnight at the Nether-Netherland Regional Headquarters Containment Center would ease the friction between Vivian and Daisy's family, they were dead wrong.

She followed her parents, her duplicitous mentor, and her could've-been boyfriend past the vacant courtroom benches. Her pleasure at seeing Vivian finally get a dose of karma paled at the thought that this might be the last time she ever saw any of them again.

Mr. Squatch broke away from a heated conversation with Judge Banshee and loped to her side.

"Urgh," he said, his gurgling voice brimming with chastisement. "Urrrrghhhh."

"Well, it wasn't my idea." She doubted her lame excuse made much difference. "Besides, you never came to see me. I didn't know what to do."

Trevor leaned forward and stage-whispered, "What's Chewbacca saying?"

"Urgh," the big yeti grumbled, shaking a sheaf of papers in front of her face. "Urrrrghhhh."

"Oh." She faced the questioning expressions of her family. "Mr. Squatch fought the charges and prepared an appeal. He says they were on their way to retrieve me from Purgatory for further testimony. But then I had to go and break out, which really is a punishable offense. So I might be going right back." Daisy sighed, and turned back to her attorney. "Where's D.A. Sangre?"

"Urgh," he said, motioning the entire group up to the judge's bench. "Urrrrghhhh."

"We're not under arrest," she translated over her shoulder as they trooped down the aisle to the bench. "Just brought in for questioning regarding the noise complaint. The only one of us in any danger of actual punishment is me." The back of her head throbbed against her skull. "As usual."

Without making eye contact, Trevor touched her shoulder. Slowly, his fingers massaged the tense muscles until she relaxed into him.

His palm slid backward, down the curve of her spine and over the swell of her hip to brush against her hand. Still facing forward, he laced his fingers with hers. Loosely. Tentatively. As if he half-expected her to jerk her hand from his grip and slap him.

She did no such thing.

In fact, her head stopped pounding. She curled her fingers tighter around his, cursing herself for taking solace in his mere presence.

He slanted her an unfathomable look and squeezed back.

"Arabella le Fey," Judge Banshee began, giving the ripped hem of Mama's dress a skeptical glance. "How do you explain the recent activity at your homestead?"

"It was nothing," Vivian broke in. "A slight misunderstanding."

"Nothing?" Mama repeated, her eyes glittering dangerously. "I suppose you 'misunderstood' that A.J. belongs to—"

"All righty," Dad interrupted, stepping between the snarling women before the Elders' High Court could turn into Lava Pit Part II. "I think we're all clear on the situation. We're very sorry to have caused a disturbance, Judge. It won't happen again."

"No, it won't," Mama agreed, "because Vivian will never be returning to my home. Isn't that right, Vivian?"

Vivian's gaze slid from Dad to Judge Banshee and then back to Mama. "Unless I'm invited."

Daisy gagged at the mental image.

Her mother's face went pink. "You're not going to be invited, you back-stabbing piece of—"

"Relevant as that may be," Judge Banshee shrilled, "I can't help but notice the unauthorized return to Nether-Netherland of a certain human being. I don't suppose any of you care to explain that?"

Daisy gulped.

Trevor's fingers tightening around hers. "Believe it or not, I came on my own. And it's my fault Daisy and Arabella escaped from Purgatory. I did it without asking."

"You're right," Judge Banshee said with a snort. "I don't believe you. And didn't I specifically say you were to be returned to your normal life? Somehow I doubt 'normal' human life consists of magical catfights and side trips through Purgatory."

Trevor opened his mouth, but no words escaped. He was probably remembering how much better he liked the human world over Daisy's.

And she couldn't blame him.

"Actually..." Mama stepped closer to the bench, surreptitiously elbowing Vivian's ribs in the process. "I believe you said there was a way that Daisy and Trevor could be together."

His face jerked up. "What?"

Her blood pulsed faster through her veins. If Judge Banshee would grant the inter-dimensional relationship permit, perhaps there could be such a thing as Happy Ever After for unmagical wingless neurophysicists like herself!

"What I said was 'no,'" Judge Banshee shrieked. "However, I'm willing to hear your argument. The provision states that under extraordinary circumstances, Nether-Netherlandians may choose to live on Earth, as long as they maintain the honor, respect, and secrecy of our world and its inhabitants. This means forgoing magical acts and visible accoutrements. Becoming, for all intents and purposes, human."

Daisy frowned. That sure didn't sound like Happy Ever After. "I'd have to give up magical acts and visible accoutrements like what?"

"Does it matter?" Trevor whispered, his eyes warm and shining.

"Living on Earth means," Judge Banshee said with a shake of her gavel, "no pixie dust. No magic. No wings."

CHAPTER 24

"*N*o wings? Ever?" Daisy choked, staring up at the judge in horror. Fairy wings were *the* symbol of magical accomplishment. She'd never garner respect without them. Even for herself. "What's my other choice?"

"The other option is to return the human to Earth for good this time, which is a task I no longer trust you with. In fact, young lady, don't think for a second that you're getting off scot-free. Your five years in Purgatory may have been reversed, but your initial sentence to probation has not. If I see you before this court again, you'll wish you'd stayed in Purgatory after all. Understand?"

She understood, all right. And wasn't thrilled with either choice.

Judge Banshee hopped on top of the desk and jabbed a finger at Mama. "You."

"Me?" Mama staggered backward a few inches, running into Dad's chest. "Me what?"

"You will return the human to his home. You will perform any spells necessary to erase all dangerous memories from his mind. You will not allow your daughter to accompany you or interfere in any way."

Vivian gaped at the judge. "You've got to be kidding. You don't trust Daisy, but you trust Arabella? She's powerful enough to do what you ask, but she's sneaky enough to ignore you completely."

Mama shot her a dirty look.

"Fair enough. A.J. will go with Arabella to ensure she complies with orders." Judge Banshee arched an eyebrow in Vivian's direction. "I assume we can trust an angel of the Lord?"

A faint blush tinted Vivian's cheeks. She snapped her mouth closed with a click and held up both palms.

"By the way," Daisy added while she had plenty of witnesses. "I quit."

"Please." Vivian laughed lightly. "What are *you* going to do, strike out on your own? Without me, you're still as hopelessly unmagical at twenty-seven as you were at seven."

She turned back to the judge, dismissing Daisy altogether.

Daisy glared at the back of Vivian's head in all its highlighted, over-teased glory. All she needed was one more day in the lab and she'd prove it.

Trevor's fingers tightened on her hand. "Daisy can do anything she puts her mind to."

Vivian trilled with laughter. "As long as she puts her mind to science, you mean. She can't do anything useful. Judge Banshee has to send her parents to take you home."

"Wait," said Trevor, tugging Daisy close. "I thought you were coming home with me. What happened to that plan?"

Daisy's insides churned.

Judge Banshee raised her gavel. "Miss le Fey?"

Trevor stared at her, watching, waiting, his eyes dark and uncertain. She smiled uncertainly. He was a good man. Smart. Sexy. Thoughtful. And she wanted him. She truly did. But at what cost?

Leaving everything she knew, everything she was, everyone she loved? She'd had plenty of boyfriends, but she'd never had respect. Some things were worth sacrifice. Her mechanical wands were getting more reliable by the day. Success, nine of out ten times! How could she give up after getting this close?

Mama speared her with a sharp gaze. "Think carefully, sweetie," she said, her voice low, intense. "You won't be able to change your mind."

Daisy wavered, for a moment tempted to give up her lifelong dream of being important in her community and respected by her family, friends, and peers in exchange for a little more time with a maddening human.

Once she had the respect and the power, *then* she could find a way to be with Trevor. Making the hard choice now was the only way to have both. Wings were permanent. Once she had them, no one could ever take them away. She'd dedicated her life to this chance, and couldn't walk away now. Not when she was this close.

"I can't." Daisy's gaze snapped from the judge to Trevor. "I'm sorry."

"What?" He dropped her hand, his eyes and tone dull and expressionless. "Why?"

"Nether-Netherland's my home." Daisy shivered, cold without his touch. "My family. My friends. My future. Earth is too far, too strange, too… unmagical."

He drew a ragged breath through clenched teeth. "So you're rejecting me for being human all over again. What's so great about being magical?"

"Magic makes everything better."

He laughed humorlessly. "Magic makes everything worse."

She tried and failed to imagine a world without magic. "Maybe for you. You live on Earth, where it doesn't matter."

"You were just given the choice to live there too."

"Without friends, without family, without everything I've ever worked toward achieving. I'm sorry, but I don't like the terms."

"Those are the terms you get," Judge Banshee reminded her. "Take it or leave him."

Daisy stared at her bare toes instead of Trevor's stricken face, wishing like crazy there were some way to have it all.

"If you have nothing else to say," he said quietly, "I'm ready to go."

When she didn't respond—*couldn't* respond—he turned his back to her and approached the bench, eyes downcast.

The judge motioned to Daisy's parents. "Go on, then. Take him back to Earth."

No one moved.

Daisy's mind raced, refusing to accept the judge's decree or Trevor's words. Her uneven breathing filled the frozen courtroom. She couldn't give up her goals, her dreams, her entire life. That was too much to ask from anyone. She wanted him. She wanted to *keep* him. But she wanted him here, in her world, on her terms. And that just wasn't possible.

Her parents reached forward, their fingertips grazing the sides of Trevor's arms. He jerked, then allowed them to take his hands.

His leaving signified her life returning to normal. If she put things to rights, she wouldn't have to go to Purgatory. Within hours, she could be back in her lab, well on her way to following her mother's fairy godmother footsteps. So, why did her heart feel like it was shattering in her chest?

She should do something, she should say something, let him know what agony this was before it was too late and she never saw him again. She should tell him that she—

Judge Banshee's gavel rang out amid the deafening silence.

"Now!" she shrieked at Daisy's parents.

And then they were gone, leaving Daisy standing by herself, with an onslaught of could-have-beens racing through her mind.

She didn't want him. *She didn't want him.*

Trevor stood in front of his now-empty aquarium and exchanged awkward glances with his unexpected houseguests. How depressing was it that Daisy's parents visited his house for the first time after their daughter refused to join him there?

Arabella kept sending him sympathetic looks, which could only mean Trevor was doing a shit job of acting like he didn't care. The first thing he needed was that damn ForgetMe spell. The last thing he needed was pity.

"Go ahead," he said to Daisy's father, since Arabella was busy frowning and shaking her head. "Make me forget."

"Can't," A.J. said. "Guardian angels do miracles, not magic. I'm here as enforcement. Arabella, would you please quit stalling?"

"We don't have to do this, you know." She turned to Trevor, silver wand in hand, face drawn. "I could let you keep your memories... if you want."

His stomach twisted. Whether at the thought of keeping his memories or losing them, he didn't know.

"Yes, you do have to do this, and no, you can't let him keep his memories," A.J. growled. "See? This is exactly why Judge Banshee sent me along. Vivian was right."

"Don't you speak her name." Arabella jabbed him in the chest with the pointed star. "As soon as we get home, you and I are going to have a little chat about what it really means to love all God's children."

A.J. grabbed her hands. He pointed her wand toward Trevor, and backed up.

"I'm ready." Trevor's nerve endings twitched in revolt. He wasn't ready. He might never be ready.

Arabella's hands wavered, as if waiting for confirmation from Trevor before acting. "You're sure you want to forget my daughter?"

A.J. didn't interrupt this time, leveling his own fathomless gaze on Trevor.

What was the right response in this circumstance? *Yes, I want to forget your daughter, because she trampled my heart beneath her red painted toes?* Or, maybe, *no, I don't want to forget your daughter, because as it happens, I derive intense masochistic pleasure from torturing myself with her memory.*

"I'm sure," he lied. He didn't want to give up his memories. He didn't even want to give up Daisy. But she'd made the choice without him. He'd laid his heart before her and she'd sent him on his way. "Just... get it over with."

Arabella's lips parted as though she wanted to say something else, but A.J. shot her an impatient enough look that she snapped her mouth shut and aimed the wand.

"Okay," she said with a little sigh. "Bye, son."

A blast of light burst forth from the silver star, smashing Trevor on the chest with enough force to knock him backward. The aquarium toppled to the hardwood floor and shattered on impact.

"Holy crap," he gasped, when he recovered his breath. "Couldn't you have just used a ForgetMe orb?"

"He remembers," A.J. hissed, glaring at Arabella. "All you did was knock him over!"

"I have eyes." She let fly with another jolt of shimmering power.

This time, Trevor flew up and over, smacking his back against the side of the brick fireplace and crumpling to the ground.

"Let me guess," he managed, rubbing his bruised muscles. "You'll make me forget by killing me. If I promise to throw myself in front of a train, will you leave me alone?"

"What's going on?" A.J. demanded. "Why isn't this working?"

"I don't know." She frowned at him. "He shouldn't have been able to *feel* the magic. He should've just... forgotten."

"How 'bout I act like I forget?" He struggled to his feet. "That worked well enough before."

A.J. whirled to face Arabella. "What's wrong with your wand?"

"Nothing," she insisted, glaring back. After a moment, Arabella gasped, eyes wide. "Unless—oh, Heavens, sweetie, he's her One Tr—"

"Impossible," A.J. roared, his wings expanding to fill the air. "He's *human*. Make him forget!"

"I can't." She looked at him in wonder. "Nobody can. Not at this point."

"At what point?" Trevor asked, his worried gaze bouncing from one to the other. "What's impossible? And why?"

"It's out of our hands," Arabella said, her tone bordering on... delight? "If *my* magic doesn't work, the only explanation is True—"

"Sh," A.J. admonished her, his expression oddly shell-shocked. "Don't compound the problem by *telling* him."

Arabella gripped A.J.'s arm. "Be reasonable. Maybe if he understands the situation, there won't be a problem."

"What situation?" Trevor hoped they weren't planning to pop him back in that detention cell. "What problem?"

"The problem isn't whether he understands. The problem is our daughter's decision."

"Here," Arabella said, turning to face him with a strange quirk to her lips. "I'll give you a—a memento." A spray of pixie dust sprinkled the room when she gave a quick snap of the wand. Her fingers uncurled to reveal a small, silver band.

"I don't want a memento." Trevor backed away from her. "Especially not a ring. Mementos are for remembering. I thought I was supposed to forget."

"That had better not be Daisy's tooth fairy homing ring." A.J.'s voice was laced with warning. "The last thing we need is for him to pop into Vivian's office unannounced."

"God, no." Trevor shuddered. "Especially if she's toting around Himalayan Lust Charms."

"Don't worry." Arabella's fist closed around the ring. "I'll deactivate the current settings." She murmured a few unintelligible words into her fingers and then held out her hand, palm side up, ring glittering.

He stared at it through narrowed eyes, empathizing with Frodo more than he ever had in his life. Somehow, he doubted the ring could ever be completely harmless. Whatever the new settings were, the ring could only bring trouble. "I don't want it."

"Good man." A.J. laid his arm across Arabella's shoulders. "I understand what you're trying to do, but I can't allow it. Rules are rules. Even under these... surprising circumstances. It's bad enough we have to leave him with his memories. Let's not complicate things further."

"Fine. No ring." Arabella tossed the silver band into the air, where it exploded into a cloud of shimmering pixie dust.

And then they were gone.

CHAPTER 25

A familiar winged horse was grazing near the edge of the woods when Daisy headed out behind the Neurophysics Compound to test a new turquoise wand. When Maeve didn't look up from the grass, Daisy worried her best friend wasn't speaking to her.

"Hey," she said tentatively. "You came."

"And you didn't go." Clumps of grass fell from Maeve's thick teeth. "Let me get this straight. You chose your contraband Create-A-Wand machine over Trevor?"

"Don't start with me. Bubbles is mad enough for both of you."

"I don't blame him." Maeve's tail flicked to one side. "While I agree Vivian deserved to lose you, doesn't that mean you've given up your chance for wings *and* your chance for love?"

"What?" Daisy's fingers gripped her new wand. "No."

"Then explain it to me again. The part where you get your wings from toothfairying, now that you're no longer a tooth fairy."

"I don't have to be." Daisy took a deep breath and made her decision. If she got caught, the stakes were high. But it was the only way left to earn her wings. "As soon as I can do magic, I can apply at the Fairy Godmother Association."

"I thought they only hired people who do real magic," Maeve said. "Isn't that why your Create-A-Wand contraption is top secret?"

"Now you sound like my mother." Daisy brushed past her to head deeper into the woods.

"Good. She's smart," Maeve said and clomped past her. "I just hope you made a decision you'll be happy with."

"Of course I'll be happy. I'm happy now." At Maeve's dubious over-the-shoulder glance, Daisy added, "Okay, well, I will be happy once I earn my wings and make my parents proud."

"Wings, shmings." Maeve flicked her tail. "It's a Pyrrhic victory. Things change."

"Things do change," Daisy agreed. "Like me. I'm not unmagical anymore. Look."

Before Maeve had a chance to respond, Daisy took aim at the nearest pine tree and muttered, "Circus."

A giant carnival tent ballooned in the small clearing. Fleeing squirrels became loud, fast-talking carnies.

"Fool the guesser," one called toward Daisy, holding up an array of gaudy stuffed animals. "Two dollars! Guess your age, guess your weight, guess your I.Q."

An elephant lumbered out of the open tent flaps, trumpeting at top volume. His trunk curled into the air. A fuzzy brown bear balanced on a red-and-white ball followed close behind.

"No way," Maeve managed with a snorting gasp. "You conjured a freaking circus!"

"I told you. I've been spending every spare moment at the lab working on new wands." She aimed again, and at her soft murmur, the carnies became squirrels again and the tent deflated back into a tree.

"Wow." Maeve stared at her. "This is scientific magic? It's seriously incredible. I'm going to write a letter of recommendation myself."

"I couldn't stop when I was so close." Daisy belatedly realized Maeve had complimented her, not criticized her. So why did she feel so defensive?

She dropped her new wand into her handbag, no longer excited about experimenting.

"I guess I understand." Maeve tossed her mane from her eyes.

"Despite all odds, you did end up both intellectual and magical. You've got almost everything you always wanted."

"Almost everything," Daisy echoed, nudging the grass with one toe.

At nine o'clock the next morning, Daisy stood in the center of a marble-floored lobby, staring at the glittering opulence of the Palace of Fairy Godmothers. Both her parents had needed to pull every magical string they could, but she was finally here. With her latest wand in one hand and her Junior-Level Training Voucher in the other, Daisy approached the front desk.

"May I help you?" asked a young fairy from behind the front desk.

"Ah, yes. I'm here for the Future Fairy Godmother orientation."

"Voucher?"

"Right here." Daisy handed the ticket to the fairy.

"Just need you to sign a couple papers. This one certifies you have a strong belief in True Love and hereby vow fervent pursuit of all clients' Happily Ever After. Which is, of course, any fairy godmother's primary goal."

Daisy tensed. She'd be out bestowing Happily Ever Afters to humans. Too bad humans couldn't bestow a Happily Ever After on her. What if she ran into—no. He wouldn't even know who she was. All that was over.

She dipped a feather in glittery ink and scratched her name across the bottom of the form.

"Great. The other form pertains to your ability to coordinate the client's connection with their One True Love. Your signature certifies your confidence and competence in your magical ability."

Daisy's fingers clutched the quill. Her magic came more from complex nano-circuitry and fractal patterns of curved lightwaves as opposed to natural-born talent, but nowhere did the page outright specify "no engineered 'magic' allowed."

Holding her breath, she signed her name.

"Very well." After filing the signed paperwork, the fairy motioned toward an elderly woman with diaphanous wings and a fluttery gown. "Beatrice will take you from here."

Daisy followed Beatrice into a large auditorium filled with wingless women of all ages and took a seat near the back. A plump redhead she recognized as Ines Hada, the Vice President of Fairy Operations and Treasurer of the Fairy Godmother Committee, stood on center stage, banging the podium with both hands.

"Who are we sent to help?" she bellowed.

"Women in need of magical intervention," chorused the crowd of women.

"Yes!" Ms. Hada's fists slammed onto the podium. "Whom do we capture?"

"Their One True Love," the audience called back.

"Yes!" Ms. Hada snatched the microphone from its stand. "How do we help them live?"

"Happily Ever After!"

"Yes!" Ms. Hada pumped a fist in the air. "This is not a job for the weak of will. This is not a job for the weak of wand. This is not a job for the weak of heart. This is a job for those of you who would be fairy godmothers! Those of you who would make fairy! Earn wings! And spend the rest of your days helping girls to live Happily Ever After on the arm of their One True Love!"

"What... *is* this?" Daisy whispered to Beatrice.

"Pre-fairy Pep Rally," Beatrice whispered back. "You'll get your chance to prove your stuff once this is over."

"'Prove my stuff' how? You mean the first assignment?"

"Maybe your only assignment," Beatrice hissed, and gestured back toward the stage. "Don't count on second chances."

"Fairy Godmothering is a demanding position," Ms. Hada declared, pacing up and down the edge of the stage. "It's the most coveted career for a reason. We are the few. We are the elite. Fairy Godmothers do not make mistakes. You hear me out there? How many mistakes do we make?" She aimed the microphone toward the crowd.

"None," they screamed happily.

"That's right. Zero." Ms. Hada continued pacing. "Ninety percent of you won't make it past your first assignment. Ninety percent of you are too weak of will, too weak of wand, too weak of heart. Of the ten percent of you who remain, very few will make it through your first week. Why is that, ladies? How many chances do you get to succeed?"

"One!" the audience shouted.

"Seriously?" Daisy momentarily forgot to whisper. "Isn't that kind of harsh?"

Beatrice shrugged. "Competitive industry."

"One," Ms Hada confirmed from her position onstage. "The Association of Fairy Godmothers will not tolerate failure. Even if you've been with us twenty years, the first time you screw up a client's chance for Happily Ever After, you're out. Are we clear?"

A few heads nodded uncertainly.

"I said, are we clear?" Ms. Hada roared.

"Yes!" came the crowd's automatic response.

Ms. Hada glanced at her watch. "All right," she said. "We've got seven minutes. Are there any questions?"

Hands shot up all over the room.

"You in the yellow." Ms. Hada pointed. "Ask."

"Um, what about our wings? Do we earn them after three successful assignments, just like any other fairy career?"

"Wings," Ms. Hada intoned, "are forever. Your position here is not. The fraction of you with three consecutive successes will qualify, yes. Provided there are two patrons, both being established and magical Nether-Netherlandians, willing to sponsor you during the ceremony."

"I don't have a sponsor." A young woman near the front stood up. "How do I earn my wings?"

"You don't," snapped Ms. Hada. "Sponsorship is your responsibility, not mine. Other questions?"

"What if we screw up after we've already earned our wings?" called someone else.

"Whether you've earned your wings or not, if you shame this organization with your activities, you will permanently part ways with the Fairy Godmother Association." Ms. Hada's eyes glittered. "Depending on the infraction, we may seek legal action. You may lose your wings. You *will* lose your job. But make no mistake." Her lips curled into an expression more reminiscent of a snarl than a smile. "That's the least we can do."

"You know what?" Daisy whispered to Beatrice. "She's kind of scary."

"That's why they have her speak at the rallies," Beatrice whispered back. "Half the girls here will quit without trying. And like Ms. Hada said, most won't be able to complete their first assignment. How many people would you say are here? Two hundred?"

Daisy glanced around the auditorium. "One hundred eighty-seven, not counting Ms. Hada."

"Of a crowd this size, half will drop out. Ninety percent of the rest will lack either the skills or the stamina to complete the first assignment. Of the remaining half-dozen or so, most will struggle to find sponsorship, and those that do will be lucky not to screw up before the wing ceremony. If there is a wing ceremony. Only one or two ever make it that far."

"Per group?"

Beatrice shook her head. "Per year. Once you're out, you're out. The official policy is No Re-hire, No Remorse."

"No pressure." Daisy gripped her new wand even tighter.

"Time's up!" Ms. Hada announced, returning the microphone to its stand. "Follow your trainers to your cloak closet and prepare to make dreams come true." She disappeared through the folds of the heavy curtain without so much as a "good luck."

Daisy rose to her feet and kept within inches of Beatrice's side, determined not to screw up this early in the game. In fact, she was determined not to screw up at all. She'd dreamt of an opportunity like this too long to let something as cold and irrelevant as statistics stop her.

Beatrice opened a door labeled Cloak Closet 17.

Unsurprisingly, the room overflowed with various types of cloaks, all billowing from golden hooks protruding from every inch of wall space.

"Moss or lavender?" Beatrice asked, holding up two floor-length pools of color. Both bore hoods with color-coordinated faux-fur lining and braided drawstring necks with puff-balls on the ends of the ties.

"Lavender." Daisy reached for the purple silk. The moss-colored cloak was just as beautiful, but she'd had enough green during her short-lived tooth fairy career.

Beatrice smoothed the material over Daisy's shoulders and slipped the hood over her head.

"Your assignment is Lindsay Huffman of Cedar Falls, Iowa. As long as you wear this cloak, she'll be the only one who can see you. Remember, your objective is to make true love flourish. Do whatever it takes." Beatrice cupped a hand over Daisy's ear and added, "The board monitors all new recruits' first assignments. If you make a mistake—they'll know."

"Got it." Daisy swallowed. Love them Mortal Locators.

Beatrice stepped back from Daisy, slapping the ends of her fists together with the thumbs pointed outward. "You're good to go."

"Hear that, Bubbles?" Daisy whispered to her where-frog. "Let's go to Iowa."

They materialized in front of a whirring stationary bike, causing the ponytailed rider to shriek, clap her hands to her chest, and tumble flailing to the ground.

"Holy shit," she gasped, madly trying to untangle her hair from the spinning bike pedal. "You almost gave me an asthma attack."

"How did I do that?" snapped a perfectly-coiffed woman to her left. "You're such a klutz, Huffman. Maybe you should ride a stationary *trike*."

"Sorry," Daisy whispered. "Is there... somewhere else we can go?"

"Don't apologize to me," said the woman on the neighboring bike, glaring down her nose at Lindsay. "I'm not going anywhere."

Daisy stifled a nervous giggle when she recalled she could be heard but not seen. She followed Lindsay into a deserted corner past the door marked Locker Room.

"Who are you?" Lindsay demanded, eyes wide and shining.

"Your fairy godmother?" Daisy responded, deciding to leave "in training" off of her title.

"Get out," Lindsay breathed. "That's awesome. I about fell over when you popped up right in front of me."

"You did fall over."

"Oh. Right. But if I'm the only one who can see you, how come Naomi could hear you?"

"I think it's the cloak." Daisy pushed back her hood. "It hides my body, not my voice."

Lindsay blinked at the sight of Daisy's face, then reached out to touch the fake fur lining. "That would be wicked cool to have on hand for haunted houses. Scare the crap right out of people."

"I'm here to help you find your One True Love." Daisy trailed off. She didn't realize until she'd spoken the words aloud just how stupid and dorky they sounded. Could there even be such a thing as a love that transcends time, that forestalls Fate, that lasts forever?

"That would be Garrett." Lindsay plopped down onto a wooden bench. "At first I thought he was just Mr. Right Now, if you know what I mean, but after our one night stand stretched into months, I realized he really was Mr. Right. I can't imagine life without him."

"How do you know he's the one?"

"Well," Lindsay began, her eyes unfocusing and her dimples showing. "He's incredibly sweet. Every week, he sends flowers to the retirement home where I work as a CNA."

"Isn't that a lot of flowers?"

Lindsay shook her head, eyes glistening. "He doesn't send them to me—he sends them to my ladies. They've been widows for decades, and many don't have family any more. Garrett signs all his cards, 'Love, Your Secret Admirer.' You should hear them giggle like school girls."

Daisy had to admit—Garrett didn't sound like a bad guy. Which was good, since her mechanical wand couldn't conjure True Love. Nobody could. She was just supposed to help him realize he already had it. Fate would take it from there. Once True Love had been established, there was no magic powerful enough to interfere.

She glanced down at her mechanical wand. Hopefully Lindsay just needed something basic, like glass slippers or your garden variety pumpkin carriage. Maybe a circus tent or two.

"How's your relationship?" she ventured. "Do the two of you get along?"

"Like vanilla ice cream and hot apple pie." Lindsay drew her knees up under her chin and hugged her shins. "We always have. I love him and he loves me. I love his family and they love me."

Maybe she wouldn't even need a wand. So far, this was sounding like the easiest assignment ever. "Then what's the problem?"

"*My* family. I'm an only child, and they're convinced no one will ever be good enough for their little girl. That might not be so bad except that Daddy actually came right out and said to Garrett that he hoped I'd find somebody better to marry."

Daisy sat on the other side of the bench to mull the situation. "Did Garrett propose?"

Lindsay shook her head. "He doesn't want to drive a wedge between me and my family. He won't even consider a future until my father gives his approval. Hell will freeze over before that happens, and I don't want to wait that long." A blush crept up her neck. "I can't wait to wear an engagement ring and show Garrett how proud I'll be to be his wife."

"So, you don't need me to conjure any ball gowns or magical coaches or pots of gold," Daisy said slowly.

"Nope," Lindsay agreed. "Garrett likes me just the way I am. All I need is for Daddy to give him a chance. Just because he drives a truck for Meals on Wheels doesn't mean we'll be miserable. We don't need money. We've got love."

Ignoring the pangs in her belly, Daisy reached under her cloak for her wand. She didn't envy this girl. Not in the least. Lindsay fell off exercise bikes, had a controlling father, a boyfriend who sent too many flowers, and she was desperate enough to rely on a fairy godmother to solve her problems.

Why, she was to be pitied, poor girl. Daisy certainly wasn't jealous.

"Okay," she said, rising to her feet. "I'll try."

"Oh, thank you." Lindsay's dimples dipped on both sides of a sunny grin, her cheek pressed against her bent knee. "My life will be perfect once I can share it with Garrett."

Perfect. Humph.

So what if nobody ever sent flowers to Daisy. She lived above a field. If she wanted some flowers, she'd go pick them herself. Besides, she was far too busy for romantic drivel like roses and boxes of chocolate. Matter of fact, she was too busy to worry about men in the first place. Especially a human named Trevor who no longer remembered her. All that was in the past. She had a promising new career to concentrate on.

"Here goes nothing." She tapped her wand against the top of Lindsay's head.

Shimmering pixie dust filled the air. A spark from the pointed star shot sideways and singed a strand of Lindsay's hair. And then there was silence.

"Is that it?" Lindsay asked after a moment, fingering her burnt hair. "Did you do it?"

"I don't know," Daisy answered honestly. "Can you check?"

"Like how? Call Daddy up and ask him?" She fumbled at her waist for a rectangular cellphone, made swirly gestures on the glass, and held the receiver to her ear. "Yeah, hi, Daddy, it's Linds. Yes, still at the gym. Hey, listen, I was just wondering…" She swallowed hard and then made eye-contact with Daisy, who forced an encouraging smile. "Yeah, I was just wondering if you happened to change your mind about Garrett. You'll never change your mind?" Lindsay's initial expression of abject despair was quickly replaced by joy. "You can't wait for him to be your son-in-law and don't know why I've waited this long? No, I'm not repeating everything you say. I gotta go. Love you. Bye." The phone fell from her hands. She knocked Daisy into the adjacent lockers with the force of her sudden bear hug. "Thank you, thank you, thank you."

"Sure," Daisy said, reminding herself to be pleased she'd facilitated someone else's Happy Ever After. "Any time. Tell your friends."

If only it were that easy to solve her own problems.

CHAPTER 26

*D*aisy materialized in Maeve's barn later that morning to find the interior filled wall-to-wall with people and balloons. Colorful bubble letters reading, "Congratulations, Daisy!" draped around a chocolate fountain. Soft gypsy music played in the background.

"Hey, everybody," Maeve yelled when she caught sight of Daisy. "Look who's here!"

Dozens of voices spoke at once as Daisy found herself surrounded by friends, family, former coworkers, old neighbors and schoolmates —even Mr. Squatch was there, tipping back a glass of something green and sludgy.

Maeve cantered over and nudged Daisy's shoulder with her muzzle.

Daisy threw her arms around her best friend's neck. "What's this all about?"

"A show of support!" Maeve whinnied excitedly. "We're all so proud of you. Your mom said most of the fairy godmother trainees went home in tears. Not you, superstar! You came home with your first notch on your wand. We're all fighting over who gets to stand up as your sponsor during the wing ceremony."

Daisy smiled shyly. "I've got two more missions to go, so don't put the chariot before the horse." She patted Maeve's neck. "But if I get that far, I want you, of course. And Mama."

Maeve nickered happily. "Tell me all about fairy godmothering. Any—" She glanced around as if to make sure nobody spied on them through the balloons—"wand issues?"

"After five short years of spending every free moment experimenting in my private lab, I finally worked out all the kinks. I helped a client unite with her One True Love." Daisy grinned. "It was awesome."

"You facilitated your first Happily Ever After." Maeve's ears wiggled. "How cool is that? I imagine you're bursting at the seams with joy."

"Bursting. I can barely believe it."

Across the barn, her mother stood in conversation with some of Daisy's old schoolmates, some of whom had teased her mercilessly for her fake wings and unmagical nature. Mama was no doubt making them eat their words.

Dad was walking toward a tray of brownies when Mr. Squatch lumbered into him. Dad's wings instinctively unfurled. The punch bowl tipped. Feathers covered the brownies.

Mr. Squatch ate them anyway.

Wand in hand, Daisy started over to help put things to rights—imagine! For once she'd be cleaning a mess, rather than making it—when Maeve moved to stop her progress.

"Forgive me for saying so," she said, her voice hesitant. "But a few days ago, you were bursting with more angst than joy. I hoped that would change, but you still seem... incomplete. Are you sure you made the right decision?"

Daisy pretended not to understand. "Are you kidding? Being a fairy godmother trainee is so much better than being an apprentice tooth fairy. I hope Vivian falls into her own moat."

"Not that decision." Maeve paused, tail flicking. "I meant, are you sure you made the right relationship decision? I'm just not sure picking magic over love is... you."

The familiar emptiness threatened to spread from Daisy's stomach, but she squashed the feeling down.

"Nobody said anything about love. Besides, it's too late for that. For all I know, Trevor has a new girlfriend already." Daisy gripped her wand even tighter as a cold shiver slid down the back of her neck. Just the thought of Trevor making love to some human... "Besides, achieving a magical status has always been my first priority. I wore fake wings for two decades because I wanted them so bad."

"I thought it meant you had bad fashion sense," Maeve said as she flicked her tail at a passing balloon. "I didn't think it meant you were stupid."

Daisy crossed her arms, hurt. "Why are you throwing me a party if you think I'm so stupid?"

"I'm throwing you a party because you're my best friend. I'm throwing you a party because you walked away from Vivian Valdemeer, you worked your tail off in that lab, and you're two missions away from earning wings. I'm throwing a party because according to you, you're about to have everything you ever wanted."

Daisy fought the pricking in her eyes. "I have to be proud of me first, before I can expect anyone else to be. I have to prove myself. Earn my own respect. Be someone on my own before giving that up to be part of someone else. I thought you understood."

Maeve gazed at her for a long moment. "Look, you're not stupid. I'm sorry I said that. You're a brilliant neurophysicist and you'll no doubt be a brilliant fairy godmother, too. Everyone here is proud of you. Some of them are surprised, but not me, and not your parents. I've known you long enough to know you can do anything you set your mind to. I'm just not sure you've set your mind to the right thing."

With a click of her hooves, Maeve turned and lumbered to the other side of the barn, apparently through with their conversation.

Daisy stood alone, hanging out by herself in the middle of her own party.

Fine. She didn't need Maeve to have a good time. Nor did she need Trevor. She just... missed him.

She laid awake every night, replaying every moment of their time together, reliving the feel of his lips against hers, the taste of his kisses, the scent of his cologne. But so what? He might be the man of her dreams, but dreams weren't real.

The wand in her hand was real, something she'd made, something she could touch, something she could keep. Fairy Godmothering was real, an amazing opportunity to unite hearts and change lives. This party was real, a taste of the celebration to come when she finally earned her wings.

A floating green balloon popped near Daisy's head, startling her. She pointed her wand at the floating scraps, righting them instantly. She nudged the reformed balloon with one hand, and it coasted away. She stared at her mechanical wand. See? She had magic.

She just hadn't expected it to feel so empty.

Back in the office, Trevor was drowning in grainy faxes and a few hundred megabytes of email attachments. Thank God for leads, because the tenure meeting was one day away.

He shoved the half-graded pile of final exams to one side of his desk in order to pull his monitor closer. He forgot to breathe when he caught sight of something small and shiny over by the window. Small and shiny and silver and round and suspiciously familiar.

The ring.

The last time he'd seen the silver band, it had been in his living room. It now sat in the center of his windowsill. How did it get here? Maybe it wasn't even the same ring. Theoretically, someone could've misplaced their jewelry. A student, the janitorial staff, a colleague.

Maybe... but Trevor wasn't that lucky.

Despite his best efforts to do otherwise, his gaze continued to slide in the direction of the early morning light slanting through his window.

The ring was still there.

He forced himself to face his monitor, not the window. Although his eyes should've been focusing on the messages overflowing his Inbox, they snuck a quick peek toward the otherwise bare windowsill.

The ring was still there.

Damn it. How was he going to get any work done today with that stupid ring sitting there, mocking him?

With a Herculean amount of effort, he dragged his gaze back to the computer screen.

When images of the items alleged to be aboard Angus's ship hadn't panned out, he'd turned his focus to the trading company, and requested every historian on the planet to send him examples of items shipped via that company.

Even if the photographs in no way resembled the pottery he and his team had uncovered, well then, at least he'd know. He wouldn't know about Angus, but he'd sure know he wasn't getting tenure.

He glanced up from the flat screen and jumped when his window came back into view. The ring was still there. Haunting him. Taunting him. Making him apeshit crazy.

He swiveled his seat so he wouldn't be distracted by the silver band on the windowsill. He'd had enough distractions to last him a lifetime.

Not that his relationship with a certain blonde distraction was in any danger of lasting a lifetime. They'd barely lasted a few weeks before she'd decided—twice!—that she'd rather erase his memory than spend another moment with him. When fairies broke up with humans, they were pretty hardcore about it.

With a muttered curse, Trevor gave up on forgetting. Even with his back to that stupid ring, Daisy was still the only thing on his mind.

He began scrolling through PDF after PDF of photographs and scanned images. Stoneware, yes. His, no. Next. This pottery couldn't look any less like the shards he'd uncovered. Next. Nuh-uh. Next. Dammit. Next. No go. Next. Neat stuff, but nothing like his. Next.

This was stupid.

He was stupid.

Of course he hadn't found Angus the Explorer. He was fooling himself because he'd wanted it so badly. To keep his job. To make tenure. To beat Berrymellow.

Doggedly, he kept paging through each attachment. Nope. Next. Still no. Next. Not even close. He opened the second-to-last email, almost ready to chuck the whole project into the trash. Instead, he glanced at the next image.

And stared.

A strange half-cry, half-wheeze burst from his throat. He stared some more, rotating the photograph and zooming in for a closer view.

The pottery itself didn't look like his. Not even close. But the design stamped onto the undersides—the intricate crest stained into the ancient stoneware—was a dead match for one of the pieces in his lab.

Holy mother of God.

Excitement skittered through his veins. He couldn't wait to see Daisy's face when he told her they'd actually—

No. Those days were gone.

His career had always been his life, and that didn't look like it would change any time soon. In fact, he could finally publish. Not in time for tomorrow's tenure meeting, but that didn't mean he couldn't share the good news with Dr. Papadopoulos. She was only one vote toward his tenure, but she held his inter-departmental coaching position in her hands.

Trevor's gaze turned to the small glittering ring. Instead of making him nostalgic, the reminder of his loss grated on raw nerves. Ignoring the pull of the silver band, he headed out the door to find his boss.

Time to move forward with his life.

Half an hour later, Trevor tried to slip into his office alone, despite Berrymellow buzzing around him like a redheaded gnat in a bolo tie.

"Where were you?" Berrymellow demanded. "What were you doing in Dr. Papadopoulos's office?"

"If you knew where I was, why bother asking?" Trevor pointed out.

"I don't trust you." Berrymellow ran pale fingers through his thinning hair. "You're up to something. What did you say to her?"

"Nothing." Trevor gave up on preventing him from entering the office. He crossed over to his desk to sit down. "She wasn't there."

"Ha." Berrymellow's eyes widened. "You *are* up to something. I knew it."

"Goody for you. Why don't you go write a paper about it?"

"You don't have any idea what makes for good research," Berrymellow said with a sniff. "I don't think you—what's this?"

"What's what?" Trevor asked, turning to follow Berrymellow's line of sight. "Don't touch it!" He almost killed himself leaping to the window and blocking the sill before the nosy schmuck had a chance to inspect the item still sitting on it.

"Why do you have a ring on your window ledge?" Berrymellow asked, leaning toward the right.

"No reason." Trevor shifted to block his view.

Berrymellow leaned to the left. "Is it a wedding band?"

Trevor's arms snaked across his chest. "No."

Berrymellow's lip curled. "You're not proposing to your professor girlfriend with that thing, are you?"

"No!"

"It doesn't even have a diamond."

"It is not an engagement ring," Trevor said through gritted teeth.

Berrymellow's eyes narrowed. "Who's it for?"

"Nobody."

"Then why are you so defensive about it?"

"I'm not." Trevor uncrossed his arms and forced them to his sides, trying to effect an indifferent pose.

Berrymellow smirked. "Let me see it, then."

"No." Trevor curved his hands around Berrymellow's shoulders and pivoted him toward the hallway.

"Don't be like that. Let me see it."

"Goodbye." Trevor steered him through the door.

"Know what I think? I think you're planning a proposal."

"Think it somewhere else." Trevor shoehorned him into the hall. "This is my office."

Berrymellow's penny-loafered foot slithered next to the doorjamb, blocking the path of the closing door. "She's going to say no. There's no diamond."

"I swear to God, if you say that one more time, I'll—"

"Gentlemen? Am I interrupting?"

Trevor cringed at the censorious tone to Dr. Papadopoulos's voice. "No. Berrymellow was just leaving. Weren't you?"

"*Doctor* Berrymellow." He scooted his foot back to let Dr. Papadopoulos pass.

Ignoring him, Trevor turned to his boss. "Thanks for stopping by. Please sit down wherever you like. Not you," he hissed at Berrymellow when the unctuous jerk tried to weasel back in through the semi-closed door. "Out. Out!"

Trevor locked the door before taking his seat, just to make sure Berrymellow stayed on the outside. Two twin objects blocked the thin band of fluorescent light between the edge of the carpet and the bottom of the door.

Berrymellow's feet.

The little bastard was going to stand right there and blatantly eavesdrop on the whole freaking conversation. Unbelievable. Too bad Dr. Papadopoulos's chair faced his desk instead of the doorway, or she'd see what a nut job that guy was.

"So," she said, apparently unconcerned about being locked in Trevor's office. Probably Berrymellow pulled that kind of shit on her all the time. "My assistant says you were looking for me?"

"Yes." He tried to think of some way to phrase his discovery so that she would understand and Berrymellow—that ridiculous snooping jerk—would still have no idea.

Nothing presented itself.

"Yes," he said again, forcing himself not to care whether or not Berrymellow eavesdropped. "I have some news."

"Oh?" she said with a polite smile.

Trevor took a deep breath. "There's an old legend about a mysterious Scottish adventurer named Angus the Explorer."

Dr. Papadopoulos nodded. "I'm familiar with the tale."

"You are?" He lifted his brows, impressed. If he'd found the bones pre-Daisy, he wouldn't have had the first clue what they meant. "Do you know where he went?"

She frowned. "I thought no one knew where he went. Wasn't that the whole mystery?"

"It was… but now we do know. Whether he intended to or not, I can prove he successfully sailed to the Americas. Specifically, Costa Rica."

Dr. Papadopoulos leaned forward, her typically unemotional face showing the first signs of true interest. "As in, Guanacaste, Costa Rica? Where you took the students on the senior Anthropology trip?"

He nodded. "His last stop was Nuevo Arenal. Walking distance from our campsite."

Soft choking sounds came from the other side of Trevor's door. Dr. Papadopoulos didn't seem to notice.

Her eyes focused on his. "What would Angus the Explorer have been doing so far inland?"

"Trading," Trevor answered. "Possibly to finance his return voyage."

"Are you sure you can prove his identity?" she asked. "Publishing-sure?"

"I just got confirmation this morning."

The choking sounds on the other side of Trevor's door deteriorated into desperate gagging noises, as though Berrymellow was coughing up a hairball the size of a rat.

"What kind of confirmation?"

Trevor opened his desk drawer and handed her one of the shards of pottery. "See the markings on the inner curve?"

She nodded. "I remember seeing something similar on the other pieces you found."

"Then you'll be delighted to see this." He turned his laptop screen in her direction.

"Branding, that many centuries ago?" Dr. Papadopoulos's eyebrows arched at the laptop screen. "I wasn't wrong about you after all."

Trevor's breath tangled in his throat. As in, she still thought he was a shovel-wielding maniac with an Anthropology degree?

"It—it's not a flight of fancy," he managed to get out. "It's really real. I've spent countless hours calling and emailing and faxing every historian and archivist and curator alive, begging for copies of extant samples, scraps to prove—"

"I believe you." She tossed him a "don't be ridiculous" look. "It's not you I have to worry about."

He blinked. "Who do you worry about?"

Her eyes fluttered skyward. "Joshua Berrymellow, of course."

"Berrymellow?"

His door thunked as if something large and redheaded had crumpled against it.

"I think he might be on the edge of a psychotic break. He's been having increasingly far-fetched paranoid delusions. First, that you'd somehow harmed Katrina, when she was safe and sound in Costa Rica the whole time."

"Yep," Trevor agreed quickly. "Safe and sound the whole time."

"Next, that you'd killed that visiting professor in some bizarre murder-suicide. What was her name? Professor Fey? He swore you'd both entered the office and that neither of you came out. That there had been grunting and screaming and then silence."

"Grunting and screaming," Trevor repeated. "Me and Daisy."

"Poor Joshua was beside himself. We had to break down your door just to shut him up."

Trevor choked back a shout of laughter. "That's why my door was off the hinges?"

"I do apologize for that. Maintenance fixed it as soon as they could." She gave him a what-can-you-do shrug. "The third strike came last week, when Joshua said your friend couldn't possibly be a professor because she was the tooth fairy. The tooth fairy! And that her mother had beamed down into the hallway right before his eyes, like Captain Kirk exploring an uncharted planet."

"Wow," was all Trevor could think to say. "Sounds… crazy."

"Doesn't it? In my opinion, there's no way we can award tenure to someone that delusional. It'll just be up to the rest of the board." Dr. Papadopoulos rose to her feet and headed to the door. "See you at the meeting."

At the sound of the bolt retracting from the lock, the heavy shadow fled from the other side of the door.

The moment Dr. Papadopoulos stepped into the hallway, Trevor grabbed a manila envelope and the stapler from the top of his desk and dashed for the windowsill. He pushed the shiny silver band into the envelope with the edge of the stapler, just in case touching it was enough to snatch him from this dimension. No way was he taking chances, not when he was so close to keeping his coaching position *and* his job.

He licked the flap closed, stapled it five times, and threw everything into the trash. No more ring. No more Daisy.

No more temptation.

CHAPTER 27

*T*uesday morning. *Tenure* morning. Two hours left to go.

With his fingers curled in a death-grip around the strap of his laptop case, Trevor pushed through the entrance to the Anthropology building and strode down the door-lined hallway.

His eyelid twitched. He had to settle down. His muscles tensed and jerked as though he'd been up all night drinking double shots of espresso. *Relax. Think calm thoughts. Don't get ahead of yourself.*

He'd been waiting for this day a long, long time. What was another two hours? After all, Dr. Papadopoulos hadn't said he was guaranteed tenure. She implied she wouldn't be voting for Berrymellow's crazy ass, but that was only one supporter in his corner. He needed more.

Trevor rounded the corner and stopped short of his office. "Well, well," he said with a smile. "If it isn't the socio-eavesdropper."

Berrymellow leaned against the doorframe and glared at him.

Trevor reached around him and twisted the knob. "You want to sob on my shoulder about your impending loss of tenure?"

"Ha." Berrymellow made no move to follow Trevor into his office. "I've got an ace up my sleeve."

"Yeah?" Trevor set his laptop onto his desk, sank into his swivel chair and pressed the power button on his computer. "Cheaters never win."

Berrymellow's eyebrows rose. "Exactly what I'm counting on, joker."

"If you just swung by to drop oblique hints and poker playing analogies, consider your job here done."

"Yours is," Berrymellow said, still lounging against the doorframe. "And I guess you decided not to propose to your girlfriend."

Trevor jerked his gaze up from his laptop. "What does that have to do with anything?"

"I figured you wouldn't." Berrymellow smirked. "No, I *knew* you wouldn't."

"Spare me the dime store psychology."

"Socio-anthropology," Berrymellow corrected. "I study people. Here's what I know. I want tenure just as much as you. And don't worry—I'll be the one to get it. But unlike a door-buster like you, I don't come in until eight. Maybe nine, if my first class isn't until ten. And I'll leave by five. Maybe four, if my last class gets out early. I'm not here from dawn to midnight, soaking up the fluorescent rays and getting chummy with the janitorial staff."

"So, your point is that I'm a dedicated professional and you're a pathetic slacker?"

"My point is that there's no room in your life for a girlfriend. That's why I was shocked to see—" Berrymellow paused, an odd grin curling under his moustache.

Trevor's jaw set. Hopefully that crazy bastard wasn't wearing a wire, hoping to trap Trevor into admitting his unrequited love for the tooth fairy. He didn't even like admitting it to himself.

"To see what?" he asked when the sanctimonious socio-anthropologist just stood there, squinting at him with that weird little smile.

"To see you make a mistake," Berrymellow said at last. "I never thought you'd give me an in, but you did. A small one, yes. But that's all I need."

"Again, I say," Trevor said with an exaggerated yawn. "I have no freaking idea what the hell you're talking about."

"Good." Berrymellow picked up his briefcase and turned toward the hall. "Then it'll come as a surprise."

Trevor stared at the bulletin board across the hall until Berrymellow's footsteps no longer echoed down the concrete block corridor.

What a weird, weird cat.

Unlike Berrymellow, Trevor was dedicated. Hard-working. Conscientious. Once he decided what he wanted to achieve, he concentrated his efforts on the task at hand and persevered until he succeeded.

Most people slogged through life half-ass, not knowing what they wanted to have or be, where they wanted to go, what they wanted to do. In fact, the only person he could think of with similar strengths was—

Daisy.

Trevor frowned. He had to admit she went after what she wanted with a vengeance. And she had plenty of ambition. Being a neurophysicist wasn't enough when she could be a *fairy* neurophysicist. How many people aspired to that? He guessed not many.

She was dedicated enough to put up with that skank Vivian. Trevor broke out in hives just thinking about that woman. Daisy was the poster child for determination. When she set her mind on helping him, she'd thrown herself into the project one hundred percent. Even though it was his project, not hers. If he asked her to do something, she did. Even when he was surly about it.

She wanted Nether-Netherlandian respect more than anything else. More than a relationship with him, he'd thought, and maybe that was true, but… didn't he want to stay at the university more than anything else in the world? Wasn't making tenure just as important to him as making fairy was to her? It's not like he would've traded baseball and anthropology for a job flipping magicburgers.

"God, I'm an idiot." He dragged his fingers through his hair so hard a few strands tugged loose from his scalp.

When she couldn't come to him, why hadn't he gone to her? The school year didn't last forever. He could've offered to spend some quality time on her turf. She'd never asked him to give up tenure for her. She understood it meant his job, his career, his future. Respect.

So why had he expected her to give up wings for him? Didn't he understand they signified *her* job, *her* career, what *she* wanted in her future: the respect she'd been seeking since before he'd even met her?

He'd asked her to choose between him and the one thing she'd never stop wanting. No wonder she'd said no. Who in their right mind would choose a selfish person over their own self-respect?

She couldn't have agreed to that and stayed true to herself. Besides, her beauty *and* intelligence had attracted him to her in the first place. If he'd somehow forced her to stay on Earth with him, away from her friends and family and all hope of ever earning wings, she would've resented him for the rest of her life.

And nothing, *nothing,* was worth that.

After all, he hadn't fallen in love with who he thought she was going to be. He'd fallen in love with who she already was: Daisy, extraordinary ex-scientist and soon-to-be fairy.

His gaze slid to his trashcan, where he'd tossed the manila envelope last night.

There was no doubt in his mind that the ring Arabella conjured would take him straight to Nether-Netherland. Where in Nether-Netherland was another story. Maybe it would take him to Daisy. Or maybe it would take him back to Purgatory. Arabella hadn't exactly been happy with him when she'd conjured it. If so, Trevor couldn't blame her. Lord knew, living without Daisy had been a purgatory of its own.

Maybe the ring was a trap and maybe it wasn't. Either way, Daisy was worth the risk.

He leaned forward in his swivel chair and scooted closer to the trash can. He should go right now and tell Daisy he'd realized what a moron he was for having waited this long. Beg her to let him prove how much she meant to him. Tell her how much he—

Wait. He was an anthropologist, wasn't he?

His entire field of study proved how much louder actions spoke than words. He should do something to *show* her how he felt. Something visible. Something symbolic. A gift, maybe. But what did you give a woman who had anything she wanted at the wave of a wand?

Everything... except wings, of course.

Trevor leapt to his feet, knocking over his chair in the process. That was it!

She'd spent time and effort hand-making fake wings, hadn't she? And what had he done? Destroyed them within moments of meeting her, that's what. Grabbed her to him with complete disregard for her lamé creation, crumpling them to nothingness like some horny Neanderthal. No wonder she'd stopped wearing them.

He should make her some new ones.

They would suck of course, because he lacked the artistic ability of the average four-year-old, but surely then she'd see he really meant the things he said. Not the old, shitty ultimatums he'd given, but the new, eye-opening truths he'd finally realized.

The Creative Arts department was just around the corner, maybe a five-minute hike. He glanced at his watch. An hour and a half until the tenure meeting. Plenty of time to pull together a symbol of eternal love.

He raced across the campus to the Creative Arts complex and grabbed the first art student he saw.

"Where do I go to make something arts-and-craftsy? Is there some kind of supply room with—with—construction paper or something?"

The student stared at him as though he had an extra limb growing from his forehead. "This is college, not kindergarten. You've got to buy your own materials."

"*Please.*"

Her head tilted to one side. "Well, there is the Scrap Closet. That's where everybody leaves their leftover bits. You know, reduce, reuse, recycle."

"Thank you." He took another quick glance at the time. "Can you show me? I'm sort of in a hurry."

"In a hurry for the Scrap Closet. That's a first." She led him down the hall and into a small room brimming with color and texture before sprinting off down the hallway.

He stood and stared.

Discarded paint tubes. Used poster board. Chunks of paper of all shades and sizes. Bins filled with rhinestones and beads. Buckets loaded with buttons and tiny mosaic tiles. Rubber cement. Markers. Glue guns. Half-filled box of crayons.

Now that he was here, he didn't know what to do. He'd never actually made wings before, lamé or otherwise.

He yanked two pieces of poster board from the pile. One bore the life history of Abraham Lincoln, and the other depicted the infant development cycle of marsupials. Nothing said "Please Forgive Me" quite like a wallaby in embryonic diapause.

He snatched a pair of scissors from an overstuffed coffee can and set to work cutting out two large B-shaped "wings". Once he had the base ready, he lined the edges with the aid of a glue gun and covered the perimeter with random, colorful buttons.

He choked when he saw the time. How had half an hour gone by already?

With sweeping, hurried strokes, he covered the interior of the wings with pungent rubber cement before upending a plastic container of jewelry beads and rhinestones over the sticky surface.

Beautiful.

Okay, not beautiful. Tacky. He was never going to have an exhibition in the Louvre. But he didn't need the Louvre. He needed Daisy. He put them beneath a fan to dry. As soon as they were ready, he stapled two swatches of discarded fabric to the undersides for arm straps.

He slid them over his hands to test and grimaced when they wouldn't slide up past his wrists. He'd made the strips too short. Great. Now the would-be wings looked more like Roman shields for a flamingly gay foot soldier. With an aggravated sigh, he burst out of the Scrap Closet and raced back to his office, earning well-deserved stares from the few students milling about between the buildings.

After setting the gaudy wings on his desk for safekeeping, he knelt in front of his trashcan to fish for the manila enveloped ring.

Empty.

Empty?

How could the trashcan be empty? Trevor chucked the plastic bin across the room and slapped his hands to his forehead. He'd lost the ring because he'd left it in a freaking trashcan for the overnight janitorial staff to empty.

How could he have been so stupid? Trevor slumped against the closest wall and slid to the floor. The edge of the windowsill dug into the back of his head. He felt like puking, and he deserved it. After all, he hadn't just lost a ring.

He'd lost Daisy.

The moment she'd been waiting for had almost arrived. Thanks to acing the final two assignments, Daisy's wing granting ceremony was scheduled to take place within the hour. Her best friend and her mother had both agreed to be her sponsors. Maeve was busy conjuring an even wilder party atmosphere in her barn.

Daisy walked across their shared lawn, returning the sea of accidental pumpkins to their original state and putting everything back in its place.

Fairy godmothering was beyond fabulous, and "excited" didn't even begin to describe the elation she felt to be one of only two trainees who qualified for fairy. Everybody she knew would be at the ceremony, watching her earn wings.

Everybody but Trevor.

Her smile faded. No matter how much fun she'd had helping women in love find their Happily Ever Afters, she couldn't get him out of her mind; couldn't help wishing she could turn her wand toward herself and bring about her own Happily Ever After.

And those thoughts were dangerous. Those thoughts implied she'd found her One True Love. And if she had—what had she done with him? Left him. Repeatedly. Then had his memory erased. By now he was back at his university, blithely attending to his career goals, never once suspecting he'd ever interacted with a former apprentice tooth fairy.

Of course, if he didn't remember her, then there was no reason why she couldn't drop by just to peek at him, right? See how he was doing. So long as she kept herself hidden, no one would be the wiser. And maybe she could finally put this lovelorn foolishness to rest.

Unable to resist the temptation, Daisy conjured her lavender fairy godmother cloak and tied it around her neck. She slid the hood over her head and whispered for Bubbles to take them to Trevor. With a pop, they materialized in the gray, cement block hallway outside of his closed office door.

She turned the knob one millimeter at a time and inched the door open a crack. He was on the phone, his back to her. The very sight of him made her ache.

She'd really given him up? This dark-eyed tempter with the low voice, long lashes, and intoxicating kisses? This professor, who enjoyed teaching and studied artifacts and coached a human game? This man, who taught her the Internet and took her to tooth fountains and slept with his body curved around hers?

Had she lost her freaking mind?

She pulled the cloak tighter around her shoulders and nudged the door open a few more inches. He was yelling into a telephone. He looked angry, upset, frustrated. She wanted to put her arms around him, but she didn't dare. She wanted to take back what she'd said to the judge, beg on her knees for the chance at an inter-dimensional relationship permit.

But it was too late. She was too late. Trevor didn't even remember her.

"I just want to know what they do with the trash," he shouted into the receiver. "What's not to understand? I need that envelope. Can I have Jeb's home number? Maybe he knows. No, I don't care what the policy is on divulging personal information. If you would just point me in the direction of the right dumpster, I'd be glad to—"

Daisy stifled a yelp when a loud knock pushed the door open the rest of the way.

"Fifteen minutes to show time," came Berrymellow's voice from behind Daisy's shoulder. She edged further into the room. "May the best man win." He chuckled as he skipped on down the hallway.

Since she was invisible, she ought to go trip him... but she couldn't bear to leave Trevor. Not yet. She couldn't keep returning to Elkhart to torture herself with might-have-beens and should-have-dones. This might very well be the last time she saw him. He was moving forward with his life. She needed to move forward with hers.

Somehow.

Even though Berrymellow had gone, Trevor continued to stare at the open doorway, head cocked to one side. His eyes unfocused. His breathing slowed. His brow furrowed. His nostrils flared. The forgotten phone tumbled from his hand as he took a halting step forward.

"Daisy?" he said, his voice soft, cautious.

She froze.

He remembered her. *He remembered her.*

How was that even possible? Mama had been ordered to erase his memory and Dad had been sent along to make sure she did. There was no way Dad would've let her slide on the judge's orders, which meant Mama had done as she was told. The only possible explanation for magic as powerful as Mama's not to work was—

True Love.

There was nothing Daisy wanted to do more than to throw herself into Trevor's arms. Venus help her, she couldn't live another moment without him. But this time, she had to do it by the book. She loved him too much to risk losing him permanently.

She had Bubbles transport her back to her lawn, only to have both forearms seized by her mother.

"There you are!" Mama gave her a little shake, dislodging Bubbles in the process. "We've looked all over for you. Come now, or you'll be late."

Before Daisy had a chance to protest, Mama doused them with pixie dust and they materialized high above a crowd of thousands. Three white marble pedestals rose from the crowd, each seven feet in diameter.

Maeve stood atop the one to the left. Mama deposited Daisy atop the one in the center. After flinging a handful of clothes powder at her daughter, Mama flitted off to the pedestal on the right. Daisy stared sightlessly at the long silky gown she was suddenly wearing.

The wing ceremony. How had she forgotten the wing ceremony?

Daisy lifted one hand to her shoulder. She frowned when her palm remained empty until she remembered Bubbles tumbling to the grass when her mother shook her.

Okay. She squared her shoulders. Now that she was here, she'd get her wings. She'd never stopped wanting them, so there was no reason to spite herself. And then the second the ceremony ended, she'd head straight to the Elders' High Court to plead her case for a government sanctioned inter-dimensional relationship.

Surely the Elders wouldn't rule against True Love.

Daisy hugged herself as she stared down at all the upturned faces. The crowd roared. She couldn't wait to see Trevor again, to show him her wings, to tell him the good news once the Elders lifted their injunction against them. If only he could be here now, to share this moment with her, the moment would be perfect.

"Now," boomed a deep voice. "Who shall be the first to stand before this assembly and sponsor Daisy le Fey?"

Mama cleared her throat. "I, Arabella le Fey, hereby sponsor Daisy le Fey in this wing-granting ceremony. I vouch for her compassion, her dexterity, and her heart."

Dexterity? Had Mama seriously vouched for her dexterity in front of two thousand people? Daisy cringed. To be fair, Mama couldn't very well mention magical ability, since it was the wand and not Daisy doing all the good work.

"Now," boomed the deep voice. "Who shall be the second to stand before this assembly and sponsor Daisy le Fey?"

"Me." With a whinny, Maeve tossed her forelock from her eyes and grinned at Daisy. "I, Maeve Helicon, hereby sponsor Daisy le Fey in this wing-granting ceremony. I vouch for her wisdom, her determination, and her tenacity."

Tenacity. Daisy fought a smile. That was Maeve's way of saying "stubborn streak."

"In witness whereof," called out the deep voice. "These two sponsors have stepped forward of their own free will and vouched for the worthiness of the woman on the pedestal to be made fairy this very day. Wands up!"

A rustle ripped through the crowd as every fairy present took careful aim at Daisy. She shuffled in a half-circle to present the crowd with her bare back.

"And now," the voice bellowed, "by the powers vested in me by the sovereignty of Nether-Netherland High Court, I now pronounce you: Daisy le Fey, *fairy!*"

Her body tensed and jerked forward. Her feet lifted from the cold marble with the force of so many wands focused on her at once.

The skin covering her shoulder blades began to itch. The skin covering her shoulder blades began to burn. The skin covering her shoulder blades began to break and tear and burst and blossom and... flap?

She jerked her head sideways to gaze at the beautiful scalloped edges of her brand new gossamer wings.

Yes! This, this was what she'd been waiting for, what she'd been wanting, what she'd *needed*. This was the culmination of all her hard work. This was the proof that all her experiments and late nights and sacrifices had been worth every moment.

She faced forward and the crowd cheered.

Wings are forever, Ms. Hada had said. And she was right. Daisy smiled to herself. Trevor was forever, too. Well, if he could find it in his heart to forgive her for everything she'd put him through.

"Stop," shrieked a familiar female voice. "I cannot let this farce continue!"

Loud murmurs crackled through the crowd as someone elbowed her way to the front row. Daisy's mouth dropped open. Her former mentor stood below, smoothing her hands down a slinky red dress.

"I, Vivian Valdemeer," she shouted, "hereby declare Daisy le Fey a fake and a fraud."

Daisy closed her eyes. So much for earning respect. If she even made it to her own after-party, all her peers would be abuzz with Vivian's grand entrance, not Daisy's crowning achievement. Figured. She peeked back at the melee below.

"Daisy le Fey," Vivian yelled, one finger pointed at the center pedestal, "is not, nor has ever been, magical. She uses false magic from a mechanical wand!"

The crowd gasped.

With a flourish, she tossed a pile of Daisy's discarded wands to the ground. Daisy groaned. What had Vivian done, stolen them from the laboratory recycling unit?

"Kill me now." She tilted her face heavenward.

The sun heated her skin, but not quite enough to cause spontaneous combustion.

"Seize her," boomed the same deep voice that had granted her wings.

The breath whooshed out of Daisy's lungs as what felt like an army of trolls tackled her from the pedestal. Her arms and legs flailed against the too-familiar black web as she free-fell through the air to the ground below.

"Oh, sweetie," came her mother's horrified voice from far above.

Daisy struggled against the ever-tightening web. "What now?"

"Now," said the owner of the booming voice. She'd fallen before one of the Elders! "You will have plenty of time to think about your crimes."

Blood drained from Daisy's face. "What do you mean? What's the punishment for—for falsifying magic?"

Vivian's pink-lacquered fingernails dipped in a goodbye wave.

"Banishment," came the Elder's booming reply. "To the Edge of Nothing."

CHAPTER 28

*T*revor bounded out of his office. The cold gray hallway was as empty as his plastic trashcan. Daisy wasn't here. Of course she wasn't here. He swore under his breath and stalked back to his office and replaced the dangling phone on its base.

Whatever he'd sensed, it wasn't Daisy.

He was going crazy. That was the only explanation. His Daisy-starved mind had hallucinated her scent, had filled the room with soft vanilla musk and saturated his tingling skin with hope. False hope.

Was he going to go crazy for the rest of his life, every time he thought he smelled vanilla? His heart was still stuttering in his chest, his breath shaky from the horrible, soul-crushing disappointment.

He'd never see her again.

He had to remember that. And get a hold of himself. Soon.

Trevor glanced at the clock above the doorway. Five minutes and counting. No Daisy, no silver ring. So much for popping into Nether-Netherland to present his visible support of her lifestyle and her need for magic.

That ship had sailed. He might as well attend the tenure meeting as planned.

He kicked at his empty trashcan.

Job security was the thing he'd always wanted, if not the thing he recently discovered he needed. Even though he'd rather have Daisy, he no longer had that choice.

He stared at the hideous homemade wings flopped across his desktop. What was he supposed to do with the stupid things now? Smash them? Set fire to them? Leave them in a corner to mulch?

No. He should drop them off at the Scrap Closet after the tenure meeting. Somebody somewhere might get some use out of them.

Too bad it wasn't him.

He tucked the wings under one arm and opened his office door toward the hallway. Berrymellow stood immediately outside, tapping the toe of his penny loafer and clutching his briefcase to his chest. Smirking.

Yippy-ki-ay.

Trevor glanced at the clock, his whole body suddenly exhausted. "To what do I owe today's stalking session?"

"It's not stalking if I'm going to the same meeting."

"It's *not* the same meeting, genius. Your appointment is thirty minutes after mine. No matter which of us makes tenure and which does not, they'll give us the news privately."

"They needn't bother when it's obvious which of us is superior." Berrymellow caressed his briefcase. "I'm going to steal this promotion right out from under your nose."

"It's not stealing out from under my nose if you stand around monologuing about it," Trevor pointed out. "Besides, I know you eavesdropped on Dr. Papadopoulos and me. She thinks you're crazy."

"So?" A slow smirk curled out from underneath his red moustache. "I know something better. Your reaction alone proved to me the worth of what I'd found. As soon as the Board sees you freak out over that stupid ring, they'll give me tenure so fast your—"

"What stupid ring?" Trevor asked, debating whether or not to bash Berrymellow in the face with a pair of fake wings. "Not your engagement theory again. That ring's long gone."

Berrymellow's eyes narrowed as they suddenly focused on the multicolored creations in Trevor's arms. "What are those?" he demanded. "Fairy wings?"

"Flights of fancy." Trevor slipped one onto each wrist and gave them a little flap.

"You look like a gay gladiator." Berrymellow nearly crowed in delight. "If you plan on walking in there wearing rhinestone shields, you're pretty much handing me my next article to publish."

Trevor rolled his eyes toward the ceiling and tossed the wings atop his desk. "You'll have plenty of time to publish once you're out of a job."

Berrymellow's smile was irritatingly confident. "I have your poison pen right here in my briefcase."

"I'm pretty sure you're mixing your metaphors, but don't worry. You can work on that next year in all your free time." Trevor pushed past him.

He set out for the conference room on the other side of the building, Berrymellow nipping at his heels the whole way. To Trevor's surprise, Berrymellow was wise enough not to barge into the conference room and demand to be present for the entirety of Trevor's appointment. Unsurprisingly, Berrymellow's idea of professional privacy meant he clearly planned to park himself three inches from the conference room door until it was his turn.

Trevor stepped inside the conference room, determined not to think about Berrymellow's arrogant claims. The board had already made their choice. The purpose of the meetings was to impart their decision to the candidates.

The board rose to their feet to greet him. Trevor exchanged smiles with each one as he shook hands across the conference table. Just as he took his seat, he noticed the conference room door was ajar. Berrymellow, of course. And absolutely the last straw.

Trevor opened his mouth to point out the inappropriateness of his colleague blatantly eavesdropping on a private meeting, when his gaze locked with Berrymellow's through the three-inch crack and the sanctimonious prig had the nerve to grin. He wasn't trying to hide, Trevor realized, with a sick flutter in his gut. Berrymellow *wanted* to catch Trevor's eye. He *wanted* Trevor to see him reaching ever so slowly into his briefcase. And he definitely wanted Trevor to see him pull out the manila envelope containing Daisy's missing ring.

His blood pumping at dangerous levels, Trevor's fingers locked onto the edge of his seat, as if trying to keep himself from flying across the conference table, tackling Berrymellow to the floor, and snatching the envelope from his pale little hands.

With a wiggle of his eyebrows, Berrymellow reached forward and shut the door.

Trevor's heart and mind racing, he tried to think what to do. He *wanted* to go after the ring before Berrymellow hid it or destroyed it or, worse, decided to put it on. But that was also what *Berrymellow* wanted. He was counting on Trevor ruining his own career by looking like a complete loon right in front of the tenure board. He could *not* let him win. As it was, the board members had been speaking for a solid five minutes, and Trevor hadn't heard a single word.

He forced himself to make eye contact, to nod and smile appropriately, to listen to their voices instead of the blood rushing in his ears. They were saying… they were saying…

"—which is why we are pleased to extend you a permanent place in this institution. We look forward to many more years of your pioneering fieldwork in anthropology, your leadership in fostering interdepartmental camaraderie, and the pleasure of your continued presence as part of our close knit family here at Michiana University."

He blinked three times before the words sank in. "What?"

Dr. Papadopoulos held out her hand. "Congratulations, Dr. Masterson. We are thrilled to have you permanently aboard."

Dazed, he found himself the recipient of more hand-shaking and back-slapping than he'd dared to dream. He'd won. *He'd won!*

"We have one more meeting scheduled," Dr. Papadopoulos was saying now, "and then we're all headed to Dunlap Draughts for end-of-semester happy hour. We'd love to have you join us."

"Of course," Trevor said automatically, as her words echoed in his brain. *One more meeting.* Berrymellow would not be happy with the news. And Berrymellow had Daisy's ring.

When Dr. Papadopoulos opened the conference room door to signify the end of Trevor's scheduled meeting, he stepped into the corridor half expecting Berrymellow to pounce from the shadows.

Nothing happened.

Unsettled, Trevor glanced over his shoulder at the empty hallway. Something had to be up. First, there was no way Berrymellow would be late to an appointment with the board. Second, what were the chances that the creepiest creeper who ever creeped would choose this, of all moments, to give up his stalking habit?

Trevor tried to shake off his case of nerves. He'd won, and he was damn well going to celebrate. He'd grab his briefcase and his laptop and head on over to Dunlap Draughts to wait for the others.

Once inside his office, his gaze fell on the handmade wings he'd created for Daisy, and his gut twisted. He lifted them to his chest and sighed. If only she were here to celebrate with him. If only he hadn't thrown away the ring! If only Berrymellow hadn't—

"I suppose you think you're pretty special." Berrymellow!

Trevor whipped toward his open doorway. His erstwhile nemesis stood framed in the doorway, a battered manila envelope in his hands.

Berrymellow ripped a strip off one side, peered into the gap, and smiled.

Trevor held out his hand. "Hand it over right now, Berrymellow. Trust me when I say that you do *not* know what you are dealing with."

Berrymellow shook his head. "I have nothing left to lose. Trust *me* when I say you'll never see your little fairy ever again." He began to reach inside the envelope for the ring. "Don't worry, Masterson. I'll kiss her goodbye for you."

With a strangled cry, Trevor lunged forward. Pain slammed his knuckles as his fist made contact with a concrete block instead of Berrymellow's head.

"I knew it was magic," Berrymellow crowed, his fingers locked in a death grip around the rumpled envelope. "I scavenged it from your office last night. Just wait until I tell the board members who it belongs to and why." His eyes glittered with triumph. "*Told* you you'd be going down. There's no way they'll let a fairy-lover keep tenure."

Trevor massaged his knuckles and glared at Berrymellow's triumphant expression. The rest of the world seemed to fade into black and white except for the dull tan of the manila envelope. That ring meant Daisy. And Berrymellow held the envelope in the palms of his hands.

Trevor's fingers flexed around rhinestone-studded cardboard wings as he took a deep breath. He'd wished for a do-over, and here it was.

He could join his colleagues for end-of-semester happy hour, remain professional and impassive during Berrymellow's decreasingly wild accusations—after all, Trevor *was* a fairy lover—and smile placidly as his colleague was carted out in a straitjacket.

Or he could slug Berrymellow in the face, seize the ring, and go get the girl.

No contest.

Trevor's hands whipped out and snatched the open envelope. Berrymellow clawed at Trevor's arms and grappled for the crumpled manila. Trevor slapped him across the face with one piece of button-studded poster board, knocking his head against the conference room door with a thud. Before Berrymellow had a chance to struggle to his feet, Trevor reached inside the envelope and slipped on the ring.

Everything went black.

Had Berrymellow somehow managed to knock him out?

No. As Trevor's eyes adjusted to the murky darkness, uneven shapes loomed into focus. To his right dropped a sheer cliff, its bottomless depth mere inches from his feet. Even as he stood frozen in place, clutching his cardboard wings, pebbles clattered down the precipitous side and disappeared into the shadows below.

"Daisy?" he called, jumping when a piercing echo screamed back from the cliff and faded into the impenetrable murk.

An inky fog obscured the view to his left, its undulating darkness too thick to see through. An odd, sinister chill curled out from the pulsing blackness, rustling the loose rocks toward the edge of the cliff and sending goosebumps skittering down his spine.

Directly in front of him was a shoulder-high slab of jagged rock, crowned by a dark, scraggy cave. Nothing moved but the creepy texture of black wind scraping across his hair, throbbing cool and humid against the back of his neck.

"Trevor?" came a disbelieving voice from overhead.

His name ricocheted off the rocks and disappeared into the humid bank of shadows. Several more pebbles skated down from the overhang below the cave, bouncing on his feet and tumbling over the edge of the cliff. He rolled back his shoulders, determined to lay eyes on her if it was the last thing he ever did. And by the looks of this place, seeing her might very well *be* the last thing he ever did.

He tugged up the wrist straps as high as they would go and held out his arms in what he hoped was a wing-like position. And then he called her name.

If she rejected him now, after seeing him here, wherever *here* was… If she rejected him now, after seeing him wearing homemade wings of his own, he'd know the chase was over, the chance lost, their love a dream he could never have.

If she didn't take one look at the naked anguish lining his face and run straight into his arms, his heart would crumble into ash and disappear into the icy blackness of the wind.

He waited for what felt like forever. He waited until his fingertips grew cold and his arms ached from holding them straight out at his sides. He waited until he saw her.

Daisy's face, wide-eyed and pale, rose above the overhang.

He held out his arms as far as they would reach, displaying both glittering sets of handmade wings. He sucked in a breath and waited some more.

Her gaze took in his eyes, his face, his wings, and she said…

Nothing.

The ice crystals pelting his cheeks from the wind were nothing compared to the chill seeping from his chest. His grand apology was too little, too late. *He* was too late. Too little. Not enough. Unwanted.

The wings flopped downward, Trevor's arms lying dead and heavy at his sides.

Slowly, Daisy stepped to the edge of the overhang. She turned her back to him. At first, Trevor thought she was rejecting him with symbolism of her own—but then he realized it was much, much worse than that.

She had wings of her own. *Real* wings.

She didn't need his. She didn't need him. Not when she already had everything she ever wanted. She'd achieved her goals on her own. Without him. She could care less about his ridiculous apology or the monstrous rhinestone-and-rubber-cement poster board wings falling from his limp fingers to be lost forever to the cliffs below.

Daisy stared into the mouth of the cave, afraid that when she turned back around to look over the edge, she'd discover the vision of Trevor only existed in her mind.

"I'm sorry," he shouted up at her, the wind snatching away his words as soon as they touched her ears. "But I can't take no for an answer!"

She froze, suddenly unable to move. He was really there. He was really *here*. With her.

"Listen," he yelled. "I don't mind you out toothfairying or magic wand manufacturing or whatever career path you want to pursue. It's a big part of your life. I get that. But I want to be a big part of your life, too."

Her eyes increased their rapid blinking. The stupid man didn't yet realize she'd rather have him than an entire mountain of magic wands.

"You can work full time as a fairy," he called out, "or a part-time neurophysicist, or you can be a stay-at-home—uh, whatever. It's totally up to you. Your mom says there's no marriage in Nether-Netherland. I get that, too. We do have weddings on Earth, though, so if one day you think you might want to participate in a human cere-mony, my parents would totally love to—God, listen to me. I'm babbling, and it's all coming out ass backward. Here's what I really want to say."

For a moment all she could hear was her own breathing and the blustering of the wind. And then his voice enveloped her once again.

"You don't have to give up your world, your family, your friends. It's cool if you need your nights to collect teeth, as long as you spend your days with me. And maybe weekends. And holidays." He let out a strangled sound, half cough, half laugh. "Stay as long as you want. A month, a year, forever. Your parents can visit anytime. I've got a futon. Hell, Maeve can come, too. She can hang out in the front yard. Screw the neighbors. I'll let her eat their grass."

She whirled around to face him, unable to bear the hopeless desperation in his voice when he had just lifted the despair from her heart. She dropped to her knees, scraping them on the hard ground. Her fingers curled over the edge of the jagged rock.

"Why do you want me so bad?" she called down to him, sure he could hear the joy in her tone. "All I ever did was screw things up for you in my quest to be magical."

"Are you kidding?" He stared up at her, his dark gaze earnest and intense. "You're one of the smartest, most competent people I've ever known. I'm not sure you realize how much you *don't* rely on magic. You didn't use it when you were helping with my research. You talk to people in their native language, no matter what language that might be. You built that dentition spectrometer thing yourself, which took serious brains. You've got logic, creativity, and perseverance. It's the stuff between your ears that makes you successful, not your wand. You're magical all on your own."

She stared at him, her gossamer wings suddenly awkward and heavy.

He didn't care about her wand engineering because it made her magical, he cared because *she* cared. He was even willing to spend forever after with an apprentice tooth fairy as long as it made her happy. He had no idea what she'd gone through to get here, and as it turns out, it didn't matter. He loved her anyway.

Her heart accelerated against her ribs, sending a pulse of warmth throughout her entire body. No wonder he had displayed a perplexing immunity to ForgetMe orbs from the start. He hadn't *become* her One True Love. He'd been her One True Love all along.

No magic in the universe could alter a force as powerful as that.

"You're pretty magical yourself," she called down to the keeper of her heart, her voice imbued with delight. "I tried to list all the reasons we shouldn't be together, but I couldn't think of anything strong enough to keep us apart."

"Yeah? In that case..." He dropped to one knee, glanced at his hand,

and swore. "Shit. Not only doesn't it have a diamond, it was your ring in the first place."

She tilted her ear toward him. "What?"

"Nothing, never mind, there's time for that later. I think." He got back on both feet and brushed off his knees. "Where are we? And will you please come down from there so we can stop shouting?"

"I can't," she admitted. "I'm afraid of falling over the edge of the cliff. Or worse."

"Or worse? What's worse than falling off a cliff?"

"Tumbling into the Edge of Nothing."

"The what?" He cast a nervous look over his shoulder.

"The Edge of Nothing," she repeated. "Pick up a stick and poke at the black fog and you'll see what I mean. But be careful not to let the Nothing get you."

"How can 'nothing' get me?" Frowning, he knelt for a stick.

She covered her eyes with her hands. When she heard nothing more, she forced her fingers to spread just enough to let her peek between them.

He held a long, knobby stick like a knight with a jousting rod. He gave a quick stab into the darkness. When he pulled the stick back out, only half of it remained. The part that had dipped into the swirling blackness was just... nothing.

"Holy shit!" Dropping the stick from his hands, he jumped back from the Nothing and toppled over the sheer cliff on the other side, arms thrashing against the rocks as he fell.

CHAPTER 29

*D*aisy screamed.

She squeezed her eyes shut so she wouldn't have to watch her one true love flailing to his death. She waited, tense, muscles twitching, but the only sound she heard was her own hitching breaths.

Pebbles fell from her perch to the rocks below.

Then she heard it. The syncopated rhythm of someone panting for air. Her eyes flew open in time to see Trevor swing one leg up over the side of the cliff, both arms grappling for purchase, his fingertips perilously close to the Nothing.

He managed to scramble up the side and crawl back onto the three-foot-wide stretch of rock between Nothingness and the bottomless canyon below.

Daisy reeled, convinced her heart would implode if it didn't stop its thunderous beating.

"Don't move," he shouted as he made his way to the jagged incline below the mouth of the cave. "I'm coming up there. If my legs stop shaking long enough to let me."

"If you fall over a cliff again," she yelled down, "I'll never forgive you."

He hauled himself up the uneven rock face bit by bit until at last he flopped next to her, his hands and arms and legs scratched and bleeding under his ripped and dirty clothes.

She threw her arms around him and cried.

He brushed the hair from her face with his soft, warm fingers and pressed his lips to the top of her head. They lay there for a moment, holding each other, sharing warmth and breathing in each other's scent.

"I missed you," he said, his mouth hot against her hair.

"Me too. I wish I had a wand." She sat up, tearing off strips of her ceremonial gown to clean his wounds. "I'd patch you up in no time."

"You came to a place like this without a wand?" he asked doubtfully. "Let's go get one. Where's Bubbles?"

"He's not here. And it wouldn't matter anyway. Magic doesn't work on the Edge of Nothing."

"Sure, it does." He tugged a silver band off his pinky finger. "I came here using magic."

"Anybody can come here. Nobody can leave. That's why it's such an effective place to be banished." She flung a pebble off the side of the overhang and watched it disappear into the murky shadows. "Allegedly, there's a labyrinthine trail between the two worlds, with the cliff on one side and the Edge of Nothing on the other. The Elders know the secret pathway, but nobody who's been banished here has ever escaped alive."

Startled, he pulled himself into a sitting position to stare at her. "You got banished from Nether-Netherland?"

She nodded miserably. "For being a neurophysicist capable of engineering false magic. And now you're stuck here with me."

He lifted her hand with his and laced their fingers together. "If I had to get banished anywhere, at least it's with the woman I love." He kissed her forehead, then peered over her shoulder into the darkness of the cave. "Don't suppose there's anything to eat?"

She stared at him. "It's the Edge of Nothing, not the Edge of Refrigerator."

He cradled her face in his hands and dipped his head down for a kiss. "I know how we can pass the time," he said, his voice low and sultry. "Let's pretend it's just you and me, alone on a deserted island, with nothing else to do but make love."

Her lips parted. Before she could reply in kind, growing noise shattered the eerie silence. Footfalls and hoofbeats echoed through the swirling wind, accompanied by a murmuring crescendo of voices.

His mouth lifted from hers. He glanced up over his shoulder and muttered, "So much for alone time."

Were the Elders on a banishing rampage today, sending trolls to drop off yet another convicted scientist? Daisy struggled to sit up so she could see, too.

Her jaw dropped open. Not trolls. Jackalopes.

What in Hades were jackalopes doing there?

"DAISY LE FEY," shouted a loud baritone voice.

She poked her head up above the side of the overhang. "Yes?"

"On behalf of the Pearly States, your presence is hereby requested as a material witness in the trial of one"—he paused to check his clipboard—"Vivian Valdemeer. Come with me, please."

Daisy shot a horrified glance toward Trevor. No way was she going anywhere unless the man she loved was coming, too.

He struggled to his feet and reached down to help pull her up. "What about me?" he called back. "I don't suppose you'd let me hitch a ride back into town, too?"

"What's your name?" asked the jackalope, one floppy ear obscuring his expression.

"Trevor Masterson."

Daisy gripped his hand a little tighter as the herd crowded the base of the overhang.

The jackalope shuffled his papers. "Trevor Masterson previously of Nuevo Arenal, Costa Rica?"

His eyebrows lifted. "I pitched a tent there once."

The jackalope consulted his clipboard. "You are also on the subpoena list. I'm afraid you'll have to come with us."

"Thank God." Trevor handed Daisy down to a waiting jackalope. "Playing 'deserted island' wouldn't be as much fun by myself."

"So," Daisy said as she and Trevor were bundled in the back of a narrow wooden cart. She wasn't sure if the jackalopes chose such a conveyance because even the Elders' magic didn't work out here, or because they just didn't trust her with a where-frog. Maybe both. "What did you say Vivian was indicted for?"

"Criminal Negligence of Proper Tooth Request Verification Procedures." The jackalope gave a sharp nod to the rest of his army and they headed down the winding trail. "It's been all over the news. The authorities were tipped off by a comment written on a complaint form."

"Wow," Trevor said, impressed. "That's lucky."

Daisy burst out laughing as the pieces clicked together. "That's not luck. That's me spending two hours filling out comment cards down at the Pearly States local headquarters."

"Good one!"

She shook her head. "I dreamed of bringing Vivian down with the power of my pen, but I doubt a charge like that even carries a fine."

He cast her a commiserative look and held her closer.

She snuggled against his shoulder. She rested her face against his chest and listened to the soft, steady beating of his heart. He leaned his cheek against the top of her head and held her close for several hours, both of them napping on and off.

Eventually, the jackalopes came to a stop in front of the Elders' High Court. Daisy and Trevor stepped out of the cart, gingerly stretching their cramped muscles.

A waiting troll motioned toward the big front doors. "You're expected in Salon C."

Daisy leaned closer to Trevor and whispered, "It's weird going into a courtroom as something other than the defendant."

The defendant, in this case, was seated next to her lawyer when they walked into the overflowing courtroom. The sullen, no-longer-practicing tooth fairy glared at Daisy.

The stands bustled and swarmed like an inter-dimensional soccer championship.

Her parents and Maeve were along one side, a little too far away for anything more than blown kisses and joyful waves. Everybody Daisy knew and many she didn't packed the aisles.

D.A. Livinia Sangre faced the audience and announced, "I call the human Trevor Masterson to the stand."

He squeezed Daisy's hand before heading to the witness stand to be sworn in.

"Human," D.A. Sangre began. "When Daisy le Fey first entered your tent in Costa Rica, did she mention why she was there?"

Trevor cleared his throat. "To fetch a tooth," he answered, "belonging to Angus, age 8."

"And were you Angus, age 8?"

"Um, no. I'm Trevor, age 33. Five years younger than Angus the Explorer when he died over 800 years ago."

The D.A. whirled to face the jury. "The *witness* was *not Angus*," she cried, one pointy nail jabbing the air to emphasize her words. "*Angus was already dead.*" With that proclamation, she took her seat. "Your witness, Ms. Phoque."

Vivian's attorney, a sultry blonde selkie, made her way to the stand.

"Mr. Masterson," she said, her voice a low purr. "Isn't it possible the defendant sent her apprentice to you purely on accident?"

"Are you kidding?" He laughed in disbelief. "Kind of like she pawned off a Himalayan Lust Charm on us totally 'on accident'?"

Daisy grinned. Note to self: Plant a massive kiss on Trevor's mouth.

"Lies," Vivian burst out from the witness stand. "Never trust a human!"

"Control your client," Judge Banshee shrieked, hopping across her desk toward Ms. Phoque.

Trevor glared at Vivian. "If I'm lying, why don't you put me under a Truth Spell like the one you gave me right before Daisy's trial?"

"Ha," Maeve called out from the back row. "I told you he was under a Truth Spell!"

"What?" Daisy's father thundered. "Unauthorized Truth Spells are against the law."

Maeve flicked her tail. "That's what makes them 'unauthorized'."

"Daisy can't be punished for someone else's crime," Mama called out. "None of this was ever her fault!"

"Order," screamed Judge Banshee. "Nobody tells me how to run my courtroom. Ms. Phoque, do you have more questions for this witness?"

"No, Your Honor."

D.A. Sangre leapt to her feet with catlike grace. "Then I call my next witness, Miss Daisy le Fey, to the stand."

Daisy stood. Trevor's knuckles brushed against the back of her hand as they passed each other in the aisle, giving her strength. She slid onto the hard bench to be sworn in.

"The defendant," D.A. Sangre began, "says we should never trust a human. Miss le Fey, do you trust the human sitting right there?"

"Yes." She smiled at him. "With my life."

D.A. Sangre leaned forward. "Did Ms. Valdemeer send you to the wrong tent?"

Daisy considered. "If Vivian hadn't falsified the collection request, I would've never met Trevor. But yes. She knowingly sent me on an impossible mission. I was set up to fail from the start."

"Did she exhibit any other unmentorlike behavior?"

"Well," Daisy said slowly. "When the courts mandated I erase his memories with a ForgetMe orb, she gave me a Himalayan Lust Charm instead. As mentioned, she snuck into Trevor's cell to give him that Truth Spell. Oh, and she attacked my mom in our living room when we caught her trying to spring a different lust charm on my dad. She repeatedly misappropriated the Mortal Locator to spy on me, on my mom, on everything going on down on Earth. She—"

"Lies," Vivian interrupted, her expression desperate. "She's a convicted scientist!"

Judge Banshee's gavel sliced through the air. "Ms. Phoque, if you don't silence your client, you'll both be in contempt of court. Ms. Valdemeer, you are not presiding over this courtroom. Based on the testimony, I reverse the ruling sentencing Daisy le Fey to the Edge of Nothing. I believe she's suffered enough. Livinia, do you have additional questions for this witness?"

D.A. Sangre shook her head. "No, Your Honor."

"Well, I do." Ms. Phoque sashayed up to the witness stand. "Miss le

Fey. Those are some shocking claims against Ms. Valdemeer. Isn't it true you have no way to prove any of your wild accusations?"

Daisy's gaze slid from Ms. Phoque to the rest of the people in the crowd. Everyone stared back at her, eager to hear her next words. Daisy knew Vivian had done those things purposefully. She *knew* it. But how could anyone ever prove someone else's motivation? Especially when it was all so easily explained away.

Vivian could claim the falsified collection request form was a typo. She could claim the Himalayan Lust Charm was a silly mistake. Twice. She could claim she thought the Truth Spell had been announced quite properly and she was horrified to learn that it hadn't. She could even claim she had no idea life on Earth was falling apart for poor Trevor, because she was safely tucked away in her office, painting her nails and putting on—

Wait. No she couldn't!

"Yes." Daisy's voice rang out strong and clear. "I can prove it."

Ms. Phoque blinked. "What? How?"

"The wall-mounted Mortal Locator in Vivian's office keeps detailed records of Location Request Logs. I know, because I got busted for looking up Trevor's address when I was still searching for the Angus tooth."

"But how do you know Vivian used it for any reason other than to verify incoming collection requests from qualified children?"

"Because I altered the settings through the control panel. Instead of the logs being sent to Vivian, they're now stored locally in the mirror. When I returned home after the accidental lust charm interlude, I saw Trevor's address on there. Twice. Once when I looked him up, and once when I was there. Er, *with* him. Vivian watched the whole thing."

The courtroom overflowed with a cacophony of startled exclamations.

Despite the inherent embarrassment, Daisy's shoulders straightened. "She spied several times after that, too. On me, on Trevor, on my dad. Go check it. You'll see."

"You *spied* on me?" came her father's incredulous voice.

Vivian sank lower in her chair behind the defense's table. "Does this mean I lose my rights to mentor aspiring tooth fairies?"

"Honey," D.A. Sangre said through her four-fanged smile, "this means you lose your right to be a Nether-Netherlandian."

"Closing argument, Livinia?" Judge Banshee asked.

D.A. Sangre shook her narrow head. "Daisy just provided mine."

"Ms. Phoque?"

Vivian's attorney rose to her feet. "Ladies and gentlemen of the jury. My client should be dealt with lightly. There were many mitigating circumstances, not the least of which is her continued affection for Mr. A.J.—"

"You've got to be joking," Daisy's father interrupted, his wings unfurled. "Vivian lost me thirty years ago."

"Thirty years ago," Daisy's mother added with a peck on his cheek, "you met me."

"You said you'd come back when I was the best fairy." Vivian shouldered forward. "I'm the best fairy!"

"When I said I wanted the best, I was referring to Arabella." He kissed her forehead. "I don't care about fairy pageants. Arabella is the best for *me.*"

Vivian's face went from pixie-pink to vampire-pale. "You lying, cheating, double-dealing—"

"Jury!" Judge Banshee shrieked. "In light of these recent developments, I encourage you to consider the maximum sentence. Banishment for life."

"Purgatory?" Vivian choked out, clearly horrified.

Judge Banshee shook her head. "The Edge of Nothing!"

Vivian's limbs lashed out in all directions as several burly trolls hauled her screaming out the side door. Chaos erupted in the courtroom with people swarming everywhere.

Daisy broke through the throng to approach the big golden desk next to the witness stand. "Your Honor. In light of what you've heard here, would you please consider bestowing me a boon?"

Judge Banshee's eyebrows rose. "I'm listening."

"If you would be so kind as to grant us an inter-dimensional relationship permit, I'd—I'd—" Daisy stuttered to a stop. Her eyes met Trevor's and suddenly she knew exactly how much she was willing to sacrifice for true love. "I'd live out the rest of my life on Earth, without wings or contact with Nether-Netherland, following the letter of the law."

A shocked gasp rippled through the courtroom.

"Wait!" Trevor burst through the crowd to Daisy's side. "Are you sure? I mean, I want you more than anything in the universe, but I don't want you to regret your decision and resent me for your loss. And it would be a loss. I know how much being a fairy means to you. But more than that, I know how much you love your friends and family. And how much they love you."

She pressed the palm of her hand against the side of his face. "But do you know how much *you* mean to me? True love only comes along once." She peered up at him through lowered lashes. "I choose you."

He pulled her into his arms and slanted his mouth across hers for a hot, urgent kiss.

This time, the courtroom filled with catcalls and whistles.

Maeve whinnied. "Hey," she called out. "Look at these lovebirds. Can't the court beat that old offer? As I recall, Judge, you said there were options for extenuating circumstances when True Love crosses two dimensions."

Judge Banshee rapped her gavel for order in the court. "First," she said. "The wing obfuscation procedure."

A group of cloaked fairies strode forward, arms outstretched, wands pointing straight at Daisy. She flinched as beams of sparkling light shot at her from all angles. When the cloaked fairies stepped back into the shadows, she glanced over one shoulder with a hollow feeling in the pit of her stomach.

Her wings were still there.

"Whaaah?" she managed, casting Judge Banshee a questioning look.

"Wing obfuscation," the judge repeated. "From this moment forward, they will only be visible while you are on Nether-Netherland soil. On Earth, you will appear human."

Trevor's arm tightened around Daisy's waist. "Does that mean…"

"It means no one can rule against True Love. The court hereby grants an inter-dimensional relationship permit to Trevor Masterson and Daisy le Fey, provided that their primary residence be on Earth, and that both individuals abstain from magic while on said planet." The gavel crashed down. "Next case!"

"We won!" Delirious with joy, Daisy leapt into Trevor's arms. She clung to him as he claimed her mouth with a kiss.

He held her tight, laughing and grinning between jubilant kisses. "You know, I suspect we're going to have one magical Happily Ever After."

And they did.

THE END

~

THANK YOU FOR READING

Don't forget your free book!

Sign up at http://ridley.vip for members-only exclusives, including advance notice of pre-orders, as well as contests, giveaways, freebies, and 99¢ deals!

Check out the official website for sneak peeks and more:
www.EricaRidley.com/books

In order, the *Magic & Mayhem* books are:
Kissed by Magic
Must Love Magic
Smitten by Magic

In order, the *Gothic Love Stories* are:
Too Wicked to Kiss
Too Sinful to Deny
Too Tempting to Resist
Too Wanton to Wed

In order, the *12 Dukes of Christmas*:
Once Upon a Duke
Kiss of a Duke
Wish Upon a Duke
Never Say Duke
Dukes, Actually
The Duke's Bride
The Duke's Embrace
The Duke's Desire
Dawn With a Duke
One Night With a Duke
Ten Days With a Duke
Forever Your Duke

In order, the *Rogues to Riches* books are:
Lord of Chance
Lord of Pleasure
Lord of Night
Lord of Temptation
Lord of Secrets
Lord of Vice

In order, the *Dukes of War* books are:

The Viscount's Tempting Minx (FREE!)
The Earl's Defiant Wallflower
The Captain's Bluestocking Mistress
The Major's Faux Fiancée
The Brigadier's Runaway Bride
The Pirate's Tempting Stowaway
The Duke's Accidental Wife

ACKNOWLEDGMENTS

As always, I could not have written this book without the invaluable support of my literary agent and my critique partners. Huge thanks go out to Lauren Abramo, Courtney Milan, Janice Goodfellow, Darcy Burke, Emma Locke, and Erica Monroe. You are the best!

Lastly, I want to thank my *Historical Romance Book Club* and my fabulous street team. Your enthusiasm makes the romance happen.

Thank you so much!

ABOUT THE AUTHOR

Erica Ridley is a *New York Times* and *USA Today* best-selling author of paranormal romantic comedies and historical romance novels.

In the *12 Dukes of Christmas* series, enjoy witty, heartwarming Regency romps nestled in a picturesque snow-covered village. After all, nothing heats up a winter night quite like finding oneself in the arms of a duke!

Her two most popular series, the *Dukes of War* and *Rogues to Riches*, feature roguish peers and dashing war heroes who find love amongst the splendor and madness of Regency England.

When not reading or writing romances, Erica can be found riding camels in Africa, zip-lining through rainforests in Central America, or getting hopelessly lost in the middle of Budapest.

Let's be friends! Find Erica on:
www.EricaRidley.com

Printed in Great Britain
by Amazon

22785615R00199